D0042051

GLITCH

GLITCH

HEATHER ANASTASIU

ST. MARTIN'S GRIFFIN

NEW YORK

GLITCH. Copyright 2012 by Heather Anastasiu. All rights reserved. Printed in the United States of America. For information, address St. Martin's Press, 175 Fifth Avenue, New York, N.Y. 10010.

www.stmartins.com

Library of Congress Cataloging-in-Publication Data

Anastasiu, Heather.
   Glitch / Heather Anastasiu. — 1st ed.
      p. cm.
   ISBN 978-1-250-00299-0 (pbk.)
   ISBN 978-1-250-00911-1 (e-book)
   [1. Individuality—Fiction.   2. Emotions—Fiction.   3. Thought and thinking—Fiction.   4. Psychic ability—Fiction.   5. Government, Resistance to—Fiction.
6. Science fiction.]   I. Title.
   PZ7.A51852Gli 2012
   [Fic]—dc23

                                                        2012008986

5043 7135 2/13

First Edition: August 2012

10 9 8 7 6 5 4 3 2 1

For Cherie Haggard, my fourth grade teacher. You read some of my first scribbled novel and, even though I was just eleven, said I could be a published writer one day. You helped me believe it, and all these years later, here it is. This one's for you.

Acknowledgments

Thank you to Charlie Olsen, my amazing agent. I still remember where I was sitting when I got your email saying you'd read the first hundred pages of my novel and wanted to set up a phone call. You changed my life and I cannot thank you enough for your support, guidance, and all-around awesomeness since that day.

To Terra Layton, my kick-butt editor, thank you, thank you, thank you! Your editorial instincts have always been spot-on, your enthusiasm for the book and characters has been a constant encouragement and spur, and I feel so lucky to have landed with you. Thank you also to the whole team at St. Martin's and to Ervin Serrano for the gorgeous jacket design.

Thank you to the amazing Lyndsey Blessing. Your endless efforts gave *Glitch* an international stage, which still gives me chills every time I think about it.

Thank you to my Texas writer's group, who were with me from the beginning when I first started seriously writing five years ago: Paula Armstrong, Kelly King, Rose Knotts, Rachel Sanborn, and Katherine Toivonen. You ladies were the perfect mix of punch and patience. And Katherine, words are pretty paltry to express my gratitude for the support and advice you've given me both in writing and in life.

Thank you to my first readers: Anthonee Alvarez, who read every single manuscript I ever wrote, even the really bad early ones. Thank you to Bouquet Boulter, Emily Shroeder, Amy

Shatila, Abby Dimmick, Erin P., Eric Pendley, Danielle Ducrest, and Eve Marie Mont.

Thank you to the Apocalypsies! It's been an honor to get to know and support you all as we went through this crazy publication process together.

The San Marcos Public Library deserves a special shout-out, especially the young adult book buyer who unknowingly helped me as a poor grad student keep up-to-date on the newest YA releases.

Mom and Dad, you provided me with the best childhood. I love you guys and can't thank you enough. You are a big part of the reason I had the confidence to envision something so ridiculous as writing a novel in the first place, and then finding the tenacity not to give up in the face of rejection.

To my ladies at Classic Tattoo, Morgan and Andrea, thank you for providing me amazing body art. I wear your work proudly!

And last but not least, Dragoş, we both know I would never have gotten here without your continual help, encouragement, and love. *Încetu cu încetu.* Love you.

GLITCH

Secrets were strictly forbidden in the Community. Of course, it had never been a problem before, because we weren't supposed to be capable of secrets. It was secrets that started the wars and almost destroyed the planet. Secrets and lies and destructive passions. But we were saved from all that. We were logical. Orderly.

Secrets were wrong. Keeping one was wrong. But I had more than one now, dangerous secrets, piling up like the lies I had to tell to keep them hidden.

Chapter 1

I FELT IT COMING THIS TIME. I shoved my drawings into the hidden slit I'd made in the back of my mattress, then grabbed the metal bed frame to steady myself as my brain suddenly jolted back into connection with the Link.

The retina display flickered into view and scrolled a chatter of data at the edges of my field of vision. Auditory inputs clicked back online too, a slight hum in the background. One by one, each of my senses dimmed, replacing my connection to the physical world with the connection to the Link. In a blink, the small bit of color in my room seeped away to a monotone gray. I inhaled deeply and tried to hold on to the smell of my small concrete quarters—antiseptic and dust—but they, too, were lost by my next breath.

Panic gripped my chest as I drowned in the Link's rising tide, but I concealed it behind my perfectly still mask. I was lucky it happened while I was alone here in my quarters, where I was safe. I could use the practice. I focused, carefully relaxing each of my facial muscles into perfect, expressionless stillness, betraying nothing of the turmoil inside.

I'd glitched for a little over an hour. Precious silence in my head. Sometimes I could fight the creeping dullness of the Link, but I didn't have any time to waste this morning. The glitching woke me an hour before my internal Link alarm, but if I didn't get moving, I'd be late.

Still, I allowed myself to pause at the door to my quarters and smile defiantly for one last, fleeting moment before the Link made me forget what smiling was. I reached back to make sure my hair was secure, and my fingers brushed against the input port at the base of my neck. My smile dimmed. It was the same port we all had implanted at birth: slim, less than half an inch long, and only millimeters wide. I knew from looking at other people's ports that thin subcutaneous wires with tiny lighted microfilaments swirled out in rectangular patterns on both sides, glowing visibly through the skin. The port connected straight into the V-chip at the base of the brain, enabling the Link connection.

I ran my fingers over the port, tracing the ridges nervously. What if there was something different about it? There was no way for me to get a good look at it, since we had no need of mirrors in the Community. Maybe the light filaments surrounding my neck port had stopped glowing, or changed color, or the port itself was noticeably damaged somehow. Something had to explain why I was different, why the glitches were happening to me. I hurriedly tugged on my long loose curls, arranging them carefully down the back of my neck and over the port, just in case.

I opened my door mechanically and walked five paces down the hallway to the largest room in our unit. The retina display readouts bounced at the edges of my vision, unnecessarily showing the schematics for the room: ten-by-ten-foot area, concrete walls, a simple table and four chairs, room enough to prepare food, eat, and at night pull down the wall equipment to exercise. *A healthy body means a healthy Community.* The phrase from the Community Creed sounded over the Link and seemed to ping around my skull.

Father was in the room, his back to me as he prepared breakfast. I lifted a hand to tuck a loose wisp of black hair behind my ear. Orderly.

"Greetings, Father."

"Greetings, Zoel. Materials Allotment duty this morning, correct?" He didn't look up from the protein patties he was taking out of the thermal unit. He dished the patties and equal portions of hard bread onto four white plates.

"Correct, Father." I picked up the plates and set them equidistant on our tiny square table, perfectly aligned in front of the four chairs. Markan, my sibling, was already sitting down, staring blankly at the wall, no doubt zoning out to the video and audio feed of the Link News playing in the million silent theaters of everyone's heads.

I glanced cautiously at him. He was thirteen, four years younger than me. He'd already set out silverware and napkins folded into neat, orderly triangles. Order first, order always. I studied his face, looking for a trace of the smile I'd been secretly drawing in my room this morning. We didn't look alike, but I could see bits and pieces of our parents' features in his face, features carefully selected and manufactured at the laboratory from the blend of perfect gene partners. He favored our father, with a wide nose and thin lips, but his round cheeks betrayed his youth.

His expression was blank. Detached. No trace of a smile or any emotion. Watching him felt like looking at an empty room—the walls and furniture were all perfectly in place, but it had no life.

Did I look like that when I was lost in the Link? The question was my own, a wisp of smoke snaking through the foggy cloud of the Link. After glitching, reconnecting with the Link was like a sliding door closing over my mind, severing my connection to my own thoughts. But if I focused intensely on a few specific details, it was possible to let just a sliver of myself slip through the crack. Sometimes it worked and sometimes it didn't, but with enough practice I planned to eventually find a balance between myself and the Link. With that tiny inch of control, maybe one day I'd be able to control when I glitched. I could keep the glitches to myself, safe from witnesses. Safe from possible deactivation. This morning was my most successful practice yet. It had been ten minutes since I'd stopped glitching, and I could still hear the occasional whisper of my passing thoughts amid the constant din of the Link News.

My gaze settled back on my brother. My emotions were still almost completely dulled by the Link now, but I felt my stomach twist ever so slightly as I watched him. It was a strange mixture of feelings I couldn't sort out—sadness and pain and happiness all at the same time, blinking into sharp focus one moment and then slipping away into Link numbness the next.

The feelings had started only after I started glitching. The word *sibling* had begun to feel like more than just a word. I imagined looking at Markan and taking his hand, protecting him from harm. It was impossible, I knew. Just one more of the many things I couldn't change. But deep inside I clung to the hope that one day I might see his face light up with the same warmth, the same life, that I had drawn on his face this morning.

Market Corridor. The hub of our underground city. The subway train had stopped with a hiss of brakes, exchanging passengers promptly every quarter hour. I breathed in and looked around me. It was overcrowded as always, but subjects entered and exited the train in evenly spaced, perfect lines. Order first, order always. Light green schematics and readouts laced the edges of my vision, analyzing measurements and quantities. I exited the subway, turned eighty degrees, and moved twenty paces toward the Bread Supplement Dispensary line.

The Corridor was an expansive tunnel with high, rounded gray ceilings that echoed with the methodical sound of shoes on pavement and the high trills of machinery. There was a muffled hum as subjects carried on short, efficient conversations and waved their wrists over ID scanners. Dispensaries lined both sides of the Corridor, providing everything a healthy subject could ever need—clothing, toiletries, protein supplements, hard bread, beans, rice, occasional allotments of fresh fruits and vegetables.

I'd let myself fade to gray for the ride here. Individual thoughts had grown hazy around the edges. Unique sights and smells were overcome by a block of unisensory experience. The sliding door of the Link had closed completely. It always did, eventually.

I proceeded to the stack of lightweight collapsible carts and unfolded one, catching a glimpse of dull blue out of the corner of my eye. Several Regulators were stationed against the far wall of the platform. Their hulking forms kept silent watch wherever large numbers of subjects congregated, impossible to miss with their blue coveralls and intimidating bionic additions. For all regular subjects the inserted hardware was discreet, but the Regulators had large, glinting metal plating over their necks and arms for protection. Protection from what, I couldn't say.

I'd never given the Regulators much thought before, but now whenever I glitched I found them terrifying. Maybe it's because they were looking for anomalies, for things out of order. Things like me.

I looked away, my face as blank as those surrounding me. The Regulators scanned the crowd, their heads turning in methodical, measured movements. Their eyes did not follow me when I passed by.

Three rising tones sounded in my head, signaling the start of the Link News. For a few seconds, all subjects froze in place. People stopped midstep, the allotments workers paused with their arms outstretched, holding boxes of food and supplies. Total, hushed silence. The only movement was a fallen bean spinning at a man's feet.

Then, right after the three long tones ended, the movement began again as if it had never stopped. The Link News feed reeled out in mechanic monotone: *Flu 216 vaccinations available next week in local Sector Six dispensary. Continuing water shortages in Sector Three. Chancellor Supreme of Sector Five visits to discuss trade agreements. Beware anomalies: an anomaly observed is an anomaly reported. Order first, order always.*

Anomalies. They were talking about me. Glitching meant something was broken inside me. I'd remembered seeing other subjects behave anomalously before. One time at the Academy a girl had started screaming uncontrollably, leaking water from her eyes. The Regulators spotted her and dragged her away and she came back the next week in complete working order. Better than new. If I reported myself, they would just fix the anomaly. I should report myself and get fixed. I needed to be fixed.

But then again—another memory floated to the surface—there was the other boy, the one who'd been taken away several times for anomalous behavior. I could still see his face, see him screaming and running. The Regulators had chased him down, tackled him to the ground. They'd broken his nose and there was so much blood . . .

The memory came with a jolt of fear, bursting temporarily through the solid Link barrier that kept my emotions silenced. I almost gasped, only barely managing to suppress it at the last moment. This had never happened before. Normally once the Link had taken complete control, I felt and thought nothing until I glitched again days or weeks later.

Inside I flailed in panic, trying desperately to keep every muscle twitch, every shift of my eyes completely under control as the fear pulsed through me. I didn't dare turn my head, but I looked around as discreetly as possible at the people near me in line. The small aluminum circle under the skin of my chest, my heart and vitals monitor, vibrated slightly in response to my increased heart rate.

The subjects nearby hadn't noticed the buzzing—they were too zoned out to the Link—but I knew that if I didn't get my panic under control immediately, the monitor would start a loud beeping alarm, alerting the huge crowds of Market Corridor that I was anomalous, possibly defective. The Regulators I had passed moments before would drag me away. Would I be like the girl, and come back all fixed and never glitch again? Or would I be like the boy, and never come back at all? The questions only made the panic rise higher.

The Link News had ended and another three rising tones sounded to initiate the Community Creed. I took a deep breath and mentally repeated along with it: *The Community Link is peace. We are Humanity Sublime because we live in Community and favor above all else order, logic, and peace. Community first, Community always.*

I repeated the creed over and over again in my mind to lose myself in the soothing dullness of repetition. I blinked slowly and tried to slow my heartbeat to match. I'd practiced this. I could do this. My face remained still, though a bead of sweat started to slide down the side of my face.

If I triggered the monitor, it would be recorded at Central Systems. Individual anomalies were not usually cause for an immediate removal, since heart-monitor alarms were more often caused by pain than malfunctioning hardware. Pain was one thing we were still able to feel, because it was necessary to safety; otherwise alloy workers would burn their fingers off by touching a hot kiln and not feeling it. But repeated malfunctions, or a single clearly anomalous event, would have any subject taken away. A malfunction in such a public arena, where I was clearly not in pain, would definitely count as a single clearly anomalous event.

I repeated the mantra over and over, holding my breath and focusing on relaxing my facial muscles as carefully as I could without drawing attention. It seemed to take hours, but eventually I felt the vibration of my heart monitor slow, and then go still. Fear was replaced by relief. I didn't know how close I had gotten to setting off the alarm, and I didn't want to know. The sudden small crack that had opened in my mind with the rush of fear began to close, slowly shutting off sensation and returning me to the safe embrace of the Link.

"Subject," said a voice gently behind me, "move forward."

I looked up. The line had moved ahead but I'd stayed still, focusing on the Community Creed. I hurried forward, giving a glance backward at the boy who had spoken.

He seemed about my age, tall and lanky with skin the color of warm brown bread crust, but as the Link continued to dim my last slivers of sensation, it was his eyes that caught me with a jolt. They were a translucent aquamarine green and they looked vibrant and alive. Even with the mounting grayness of the Link, I could still *see*—see the uniqueness of the color flickering at the edges of his pupils. The next second, he looked away, gazing straight ahead like everyone else.

I turned around and faced forward, alarmed by the strange flush that was creeping up my neck. I wondered if the boy behind me could see it. I wondered what it meant.

I was hopeless at understanding and controlling all of these new emotions. I'd looked them up in the history text archive and was working slowly to build a catalog. Most of the history texts described how each dangerous emotion had led to the nuclear destruction of the Surface, the Old World. So far, some of the emotions hadn't seemed as terrible as the texts described. Except maybe fear.

Fear was the first feeling I recognized, and eventually I could differentiate fear and not-fear, good feelings from bad ones. I also started dreaming. Almost every night I dreamt of that boy who kept glitching—his screams, the look on his face, the way his body crumpled to the ground; he haunted my nights. Sometimes in the dreams, he was screaming my name. He never came back to the Academy. He was deactivated. It wasn't meant to be scary, or a punishment. Subjects weren't supposed to be able to feel fear or guilt. It was just a fact. When something was too broken to fix, or too defective to contribute to the Community, deactivation was the only logical solution.

My six-month hardware checkup was coming up in two weeks and they would run diagnostics on all my hardware and check my memory chip. All of my training and practice was leading up to that moment, and I needed to be able to control myself and not glitch during a diagnostic exam. Part of me knew they would most likely discover my malfunctions anyway. It was only a matter of time before they scanned my memory chip and found the evidence of my glitching, the drawings, and the . . . *other* thing, the secret that was far too big, far too terrible, to hide.

"Greetings," said the man behind the Bread Dispensary counter. I looked up, realizing I'd reached the front of the line.

"Greetings," I said. "Bimonthly allotment."

He nodded, pulling a box from the top of the stack behind him. He gestured at the small instrument at the side of the window. I lifted my hand and waved my wrist in front of it, hearing the small *beep* that meant I'd registered and the allotment would be subtracted from my family's account in Central

Records. I slid the three boxes over the counter and stacked them neatly in my cart.

I moved away, careful to keep my face blank. Later, when I glitched again, I would remember the paper they wrapped around the bread. It was perfect for drawing. Three boxes of bread meant twelve pages. It was too risky drawing on my digi-tablet—every mark I made would be stored in memory. But the paper could be hidden. Paper could be secret. Like the stack tucked away in my mattress.

I pulled my cart behind me and headed over to the next line, the Protein Dispensary. I gazed at the rich dark brown of the protein patties. Color. The first time I'd glitched was at the Academy when I noticed another student's bright orange-red hair. I'd frozen in place as the shocking color first broke through the interminable gray, bobbing brightly through the crowd of gray heads marching down the corridor. It had only lasted for a moment, thirty seconds at most, but it stirred something in me. Something new.

Then the glitches started happening more often and lasting longer. I'd notice the deep green of a spinach leaf, the smooth browns and creams of people's differing skin tones, hair, eyes . . . I inadvertently glanced backward in the direction I'd last seen the green-eyed boy, but he was gone. That was a completely new color to add to my short list.

Emotions were the next thing that came with the glitches, and they still made no sense to me. Like how, after an especially bad nightmare, I'd walk through the darkened housing unit and slide my brother's door open gently and watch him sleep, his face relaxed, his arm slung over his head. Watching him made this stinging sensation come from behind my eyes and my chest would tighten until I could barely breathe. It wasn't happiness and it wasn't sadness. I still didn't know what to call it. It made me feel like I needed to make sure he was safe.

But safe from what? The Community was the safest place that ever existed. The only danger in this world was *me*. The guilt of glitching was like a shadow, following me everywhere.

I stepped forward in line as the subject ahead of me moved. The barbaric Old World was once full of people like me. There was a whole race of humanity full of all the emotions and desires that I felt, people who almost destroyed the Earth with greed and anger and hate and indifference. They warred until the clouds rained toxic ash, the chemicals making people's eyes boil in their sockets and their skin peel off like cooked potato skins. So much toxic material that we could never go back to the surface. Our history texts showed detailed pictures of the process, a detailed reminder of the horrors of the Old World.

Those who had foreseen had begun the tunneling down, the orderly planning of humanity's future. Only a small percentage survived. We were a logical, orderly race—the descendants of survivors who had seen the worst of human emotion and destruction. We had learned the lessons of the past and finally scrubbed out the animal in man. We protected ourselves, blotted out the things that made us dangerous, and rebuilt. The First Chancellor called us Humanity Sublime. We lived by order and logic alone. We lived in Community.

And here I was, a traitor tucked secretly within the safe walls of the Community. A single person cultivating the same emotions that destroyed the Surface forever. I was like a ticking bomb, and it was just a matter of time before the evilness of human emotion took control. How much would I destroy before they caught and stopped me? I should go report myself.

Right now.

Right this instant.

I looked around. The Regulators were only ten paces away, rotating slowly and efficiently as they patrolled the crowds in their thick metal boots. Just a few words and I'd be free of all the secrets and lies.

It would be easy. It was the right thing to do. I'd be free from these weighty secrets. I could become a functioning member of the Community again.

My hands dropped from the cart handle. My legs took a few steps toward the closest Regulator, mechanically, almost as if they had been waiting for this moment to finally arrive.

But, wait. I couldn't.

There was a reason I didn't want to. A very important reason. I blinked several times until I remembered. There was *the thing*—the one thing they couldn't find out about, or else they would destroy me, deactivate me.

But the Community always comes first. . . .

I was an anomaly, a danger to the Community. I needed to be repaired. I turned again toward the Regulators, waiting to catch their attention and report myself. There was a murmur of dissent in the back of my mind, but it was too quiet compared to the strong clear stream of information flowing through the Link.

A Regulator had reached the end of a dispensary line and was turning slowly back to head in my direction. In a few paces, his head would sweep in my direction. I would calmly catch his attention and report myself for diagnostics. Just a few paces more.

But suddenly the quiet voice inside my mind was screaming. And then, like being underwater and then breaking to the surface, I was suddenly glitching.

The retina display flickered and disappeared from view, and the sound echoing through my mind stopped, midstream, and I was left in silence. I could breathe again. I felt myself expand in the same moment, color and sound and sense flooding back in, overwhelming me with a rush of smells and sounds.

Beside me, I heard a loud crash.

I turned in surprise and saw that two full carts nearby had toppled over sideways, knocking into an aisle of stacked boxes. A stack tipped over, the boxes breaking open and spilling rice all over a nearby subject's shoes. He looked down for a moment before moving out of the way dispassionately.

No one else registered surprise. They weren't capable of it. But I was, and I felt every inch of surprise and dread and terror. Emotions flooded in. It was all too fast and I couldn't tell if I was masking one emotion before the next rose up.

One thing was sure—I was malfunctioning way too much for such a public place. Someone was bound to notice and report me. I had to get out of here. *Now.* I didn't care that I hadn't gotten all of our allotments. I felt too frantic to stay crowded in this flood of gray-suited bodies, watching them placidly kneel down to clean up the spill while I was choking inside. I tightened my grip on my cart to hide the tremor of fear in my hands.

The Regulator had made his way over to investigate the spill. He scanned the crowd, but most of the subjects had already moved away, stepping around the spilled rice and moving on to the next line. I cautiously followed suit, tugging my cart out of line and heading toward the subway. It was only then that I realized that I had glitched right as the carts were knocked over.

Electromagnetic carts malfunctioned all the time. Not all the time but surely they did sometimes. I mean, there was no reason to think the spill had anything to do with me.

The sleek black subway train arrived at the platform just as I pulled my cart close. I stepped on, glad for the distraction, and moved to an empty space along the far wall. The communication panel under the skin of my forearm lit up as I touched it, and I quickly messaged my parents that I wasn't feeling well and hadn't been able to pick up all the allotments. I knew it meant I would have to undergo a health screening when I got home, but I would explain that I'd simply forgotten to take my daily vitamins with me. I took my daily vitamins out of my pocket and tossed them discreetly into a waste dispenser.

I envisioned the way the lie would fall so easily from my lips. I was getting better and better at it. It had been such a strange thing at first, to say the opposite of what was true. To defy and disobey clear orders in the Community Code, even by my silence. *An anomaly observed is an anomaly reported.*

I swallowed hard, looking around me in the unusual silence, the Link absent from my mind. Everything was so much sharper without the Link fogging me—sights, sounds, smells. It was exhilarating and shocking and terrifying. I knew my emotions had grown too strong. They were dangerous to the Community. They were dangerous to me.

But still, I wanted color. I wanted to soar with happiness even if it meant dealing with the weight of fear and guilt, too. I wanted to live. And that meant that I couldn't give the glitching up. At least not yet. Just a little bit longer, I'd told myself each day in the beginning. Maybe I'd report myself tomorrow. But then each tomorrow had become another *not today*, and now after two months, I still hadn't reported myself. As much as I might not like it, lies and secrets were my way of life now.

Chapter 2

I WAS FULLY LINKED the next morning as I walked down the corridors of my housing-unit grid. My wrist lifted and waved in front of the sensor to open the front gate. After a blip of recognition, the door slid sideways into the wall with a slight hiss as sealed air was released. Air quality was carefully regulated everywhere in our underground city, in all of the buildings that were dug down deep into the earth and all the tunnels connecting them.

I stepped two even paces into the small portal room. One door sealed behind me and the next opened to the tunnel system. My hand secured the strap of my school-tablet case over my shoulder. Three rising tones noted the coming Link News—but I didn't freeze in place. Instead, the now-familiar rush of sensation swept over me. No more Link readout on the periphery of my vision. No more voices in my head.

I was glitching.

I smiled, breathed a sigh of relief, and stretched my neck. Even though I knew it meant I'd have to be extra careful until the Link clicked back in, I was glad to have my head to myself again. I felt a tinge of unease at the sudden frequency of my glitches, but I couldn't worry about it right now. I never knew how long a glitch would last or how far apart the glitches would be, and I didn't want to waste the glitch time with constant fear and worry.

I stepped into the narrow whitewashed concrete tunnel and

looked around. I was alone, so I let myself linger and look. The walls around me were concrete and aluminum, but I could suddenly see the slight differences in the colors and textures. I breathed in the dry smell of old paint and dust. I listened to the noise of my shoes and slight swish of my pants, echoing down the three-foot-wide tunnel. I looked left and right, but still there was no one else coming, so I trailed my fingertips along the rough walls of the tunnel, lingering on the cool aluminum of each housing-complex door as I passed.

I stayed for another moment, but eventually I dropped my arms and squared my shoulders, posture-perfect, and passed through a small archway into the much wider subway access tunnel. Our housing grid was on Sublevel 2, almost level with the subway hub. Gray-suited subjects entered from other similar tributary tunnels and fell silently into line walking down the low-ceilinged tunnel.

The *clack* of black-heeled shoes echoed off the concrete floor and walls of the tunnel, reminding me of the storm I'd seen almost two months ago. A pipe had burst and flooded the lower levels at my school and they'd moved us into one of the few Sublevel 0 rooms. We were at the top level just below the Surface in a room with low ceilings. Sheets of toxic rain crashed against the building. The Surface had only been an abstract idea before, but suddenly it felt far too real.

Then came the thunder. It was my first experience of terror—it was so much worse than fear. I'd backed away from the sound and massaged my seizing chest. My heart monitor went off for the first time in public. I'd forced myself to calm down fast enough to avoid an immediate diagnostic, but only by hiding from the sound of the rain. I'd never wondered about the Surface again. It must be a terrifying place.

I tried to dismiss the memory of the storm by losing myself in the back-and-forth robotic pace of walking. I studied the back of the heads in front of me, trying to memorize every texture and color. It kept me busy for the half-mile of walking. I only realized we'd arrived at the subway when the people in front of me slowed down.

I looked around the wide platform and the high concrete ceiling arching above the track. The openness of the subway tunnels always made me uncomfortable—the air always seemed a little thinner here, and I wondered just how closely the air quality was regulated in such a large chamber. The walls and ceiling arched over our heads about thirty feet up.

People stood like statues as they waited for the train to take them to school or work—all except for one blond little girl who tugged on her mother's hand. My eyes flickered uneasily to the Regulators standing near the back columns. The girl hopped around with exaggerated motions, giggling whenever her feet hit the concrete. Her actions looked completely out of sync with her tiny starched gray suit. The sound of her feet and laugh echoed throughout the tunnel. I tried to memorize her features to draw later. She was so beautiful, so *alive*. Watching her made me feel light inside.

The learning texts referred to the Old World emotions as childish. Glitching happened from time to time with children because the V-chip hardware couldn't always keep up with their rapid development. It was difficult to accomplish complete control. Too much V-chip control and the brain wouldn't develop into adulthood correctly. Simply downloading information had turned subjects into vegetables—they'd been forced to deactivate them. The human neurons needed to stay active or the brain deteriorated. That was why we still had to go to the Academy until we were ready for labor at eighteen. Then we got our final, adult V-chip, the chip that would control us and protect us from glitches for the rest of our adult lives.

The rumble of the train in the distance made everyone stand up straighter, more alert. I glanced at the clock on the wall and tried to move unobtrusively toward the front of the crowd. I'd be late to school if I didn't catch this train. I couldn't risk any anomalous behavior, anything to bring more attention to me. I accidentally bumped a man in the shoulder and he looked at me with too much interest. I slowed and made my face blank—nothing anomalous here, just a normal subject waiting for a train. He paused, hesitating, then looked away.

Out of the corner of my eye, I saw the little blond girl still bouncing around as the train neared. Her mother motioned with her hand for the girl to come. When she didn't respond, the woman called her name.

I couldn't hear the mother's voice over the roar of the approaching train, and apparently, the girl couldn't either. She kept dancing. She was very close to the edge of the platform. Too close. I risked another glance at the nearby Regulators, but they hadn't moved. They weren't programmed to prevent accidents, and glitching children did not pose immediate grounds for removal. I looked back at the girl, a frantic feeling growing in my chest. She twirled closer to the ledge, arms out and eyes closed.

The train came around the corner. The mother reached out and almost managed to grasp the girl's little jacket. But the girl hopped just out of reach and landed with one foot off the platform.

She toppled backward toward the tracks below, no fear on her face, still that clueless little smile.

"No!" I screamed, reaching my hand out involuntarily. Her mother reacted as well, but too slowly. The train noise was deafening, drowning out my scream.

And that's when I did it—the thing I swore I'd never do again, the secret I kept trying so desperately to deny existed.

I mean, it simply wasn't possible. It was illogical. But I did it now, without thinking or acknowledging that I fully expected it to work.

I reached out to the girl with my mind. I searched out the shape of her in the milliseconds as she fell. I felt the unique high-pitched ringing sound in my ears and concentrated on the lines and planes of her face, the geometrical cut of her suit, the tiny curves of her feet. I surrounded every part of her with the invisible force of my will. And then *I yanked.*

The girl's momentum changed in midfall and she vaulted back onto the platform a mere second before the train flew past, brakes screeching as it slowed. Her mother caught her and calmly smoothed down the wrinkles of the girl's coat as if nothing had just happened.

Relief poured over me. I did it. I saved her. She was safe.

But there were eyes on me now. Several subjects were looking directly at me, and as the train came to a complete stop, the loud beeping of my heart monitor rang out in the silence. I looked down at the ground, trying to still the fear tearing through me. I shuffled into line as if nothing was wrong, as if my heartbeat wasn't still beeping with an inordinately loud noise over the quiet subjects' orderly movements to board the train. I focused on my training. Slow, measured breaths, repeat the Community Creed, concentrate on the still lines of my face.

A few people tapped on their subcutaneous forearm panels. They must be reporting me. Reporting my anomalous behavior: the screaming and what had surely been a look of panic on my face as I'd reached uselessly for the girl. I looked around me, searching for any Regulators heading my way.

Then I saw one. In the crowd of moving gray bodies, he was standing perfectly still, eyes locked on me. He was watching me with a look that wasn't completely uninterested. He started to move in my direction. There was nowhere to run, but I couldn't help trying. I hurriedly stepped on the train and moved as far away from the door as I could without attracting more attention. I tried to glance back at the Regulator, but in the flood of people entering the train, I couldn't find him again.

I worked to appear calm and disinterested, blending in with the crowd. The Regulator had no reason to capture me. My heart monitor beeped only briefly, and no one would make the connection between my yelling and the girl flying back up onto the platform. Surely they wouldn't. I barely believed it myself. Logically, it was impossible. That's why I'd denied it, even though it had happened a few times now—like my hair-brush that flew across the room into my hand when I'd merely thought about it; the glass cup falling off the kitchen table that I'd unconsciously caught with my mind before it shattered on the floor; the shopping cart at the Market.

The doors sealed closed and the air-filtration system hummed as the train started smoothly forward. I stole a glance around, trying to look blank and completely disinterested. If the Regulator was on this train, there would be no escape.

No sign of the Regulator. Everyone's faces seemed to have settled back into indifference as they all stood evenly spaced apart, holding the floor-to-ceiling poles studded throughout the train car. The incident with the girl was completely forgotten. I was safe.

I took a deep breath to soothe my jarred nerves. But then amid the empty faces in the crowded space, my eyes latched on to a pair of bright blue-green eyes. I realized with a jolt that it was the same boy from the day before in the Market Corridor. And he was looking right at me.

He was tall and thin, with hair so dark it looked black and those eyes that stared at me with an intensity that seemed to sizzle through my skin. What had he seen? Why did he keep looking when the others' faces had gone empty?

I stood still, clutching a pole for balance and staring at the rounded corner of the dark subway window. I hoped my eyes looked glazed over, because inside, my emotions were roiling.

Could he possibly know about the . . . thing I could do? Would he report it? And what would happen if he did? Would they deactivate me so they could dissect my brain to understand how it worked? Or simply deactivate me and dispose of my defective hardware? There were just too many questions I couldn't answer.

I clenched my eyes shut to stop the dizzying tumble of fears, then realized that might appear anomalous. I went back to staring at the window's edge, jittery with nervous tension for the rest of the ride to the Academy. I wanted to get off this train and forget about what had happened on the platform and the boy with the piercing eyes. As the train slowed at the station, though, I saw the boy move toward the doors. My eyes widened in spite of myself. Was he following me?

I tried to think back, to remember if I'd seen him around at the Academy or on the train before now. I didn't know. I spent so much time making sure I acted normally, I was sometimes oblivious to the subjects around me. I stepped off the train and entered the flow of kids my age heading toward the Academy entrance tunnel. Then, with a flood of relief, I felt the familiar tingling sensation at the corners of my mind, marking the return of the Link connection. I embraced it, letting my fear drift away into nothingness.

It was lunchtime when I glitched again. I blinked a few times, then stared down at my plate until I was adjusted. I'd let myself go numb all morning while I was Linked, not even trying to fight that last inch of complete control. But now that I was all to myself again, the fear I'd successfully subdued all morning came rushing right back.

I was sitting alone in the Academy cafeteria, one of the largest open spaces in our sector. It was a wide, low-ceilinged room with columns placed every fifteen feet throughout for support. It was bare, utilitarian, and gray, like everything else. There was light chatter in the dim cafeteria, students discussing classwork mostly.

Several luminescent 3-D projection cubes were set up on some tables with varying figures rotating inside them as students worked on assignments. One group of students was studying the internal mechanics of bionic data nanodes. Another group examined the image of a rotating human head. As I watched, one student clicked on the translucent skull. The model zoomed in to reveal lobes of the brain. Another click revealed the complex bustles of nerves, tissue, and thin Link hardware threaded all throughout. Training and studying all day for the time we'd reach adulthood, receive our final V-chip, and join the Community workforce alongside our parents. Everything was normal.

But inside, I was still recovering from the morning's close call. Clearly I needed to find a better method of controlling my glitches. There were no guarantees that there would be a well-timed train to rescue me next time. And I was starting to suspect that the boy on the train, the one with the bright blue-green eyes, was a sign of an even greater danger. A sign that I had likely already been reported a few times as anomalous.

When a report of an anomaly was logged in the Community records, a Monitor would be sent to discreetly observe and report whether the subject was malfunctioning enough to warrant repairs before their biannual diagnostic checkup. That was the Monitor's job: to locate and identify anomalous glitchers. And they were experts at it—more observant and keen than the average subject, and more aware of the minor symptoms of glitching than the brute Regulators. They had no distinguishing hardware or features. They were like ghosts, hidden within the ranks, anywhere and nowhere all at once.

Maybe someone had noticed the way I faltered when I glitched at the Academy. Or what if my parents or Markan had found my sketches? Would they have reported me if they had? I swallowed again. Of course they would. There was no such concept as loyalty to the family unit, only loyalty to Community. Even then, it wasn't an emotion, only clear, cold logic. *An anomaly observed is an anomaly reported.*

I glanced at the four Regulators stationed at each corner of the room. The Regulators at the Academy were younger than the ones I'd see patrolling the Markets and at the subway; they were Regulators-in-training. My chest jumped at the sight of them, but I soothed myself with the knowledge that there was no need to worry. If someone had reported me to Central Systems for what happened on the train platform this morning, I would have been taken away by now. Still, I glanced back and forth between the crowd and my salad, lingering at every opportunity on the Regulators, and wondering where the green-eyed boy, the Monitor, could be.

I chewed my salad silently, counting to five with each bite. Slow. Methodical. A tomato crunched in my mouth and the juice exploded between my teeth. I wanted to close my eyes and enjoy the wild taste of it—slightly sweet and yet not quite. I knew they grew all this produce in underground hothouses but it still seemed wonderfully impossible to create from a tiny seed something so beautiful and complex. I speared a piece of broccoli with my fork and chewed on it thoughtfully, enjoying the texture on my tongue and the crunch that echoed in my ears with each bite. I wished I could draw this feeling so I could hold it in my hands.

"Zoel," said a voice to my right, almost making me jump. "I request your assistance on the homework we were assigned today."

I looked over at Maximin and had to stop myself from smiling. He'd tested through to the biotech track just like I had three years ago, and as adults we were both destined to become V-chip technicians. But he was hopeless at memorization. He'd asked for tutoring two months ago, but now study lunches with him were part of my daily routine. I kept telling him he should ask for memory-enhancement programs, but he insisted that with practice and study he could learn it on his own. If we were capable of it, I might have thought he was stubborn.

Stubborn was another word I had learned from the old archive texts at the central library database. Along with *happy, sad, guilty, lonely, angry, afraid*. The green-eyed boy's face flashed in my memory. What had the expression on his face meant? Angry? Afraid? No, none of those things. I was just so desperate to see something, anything, on someone else's face that I imagined it.

"Assistance willingly rendered, Maximin," I said. "Let me retrieve my tablet."

I reached down to unclick my case and pulled out the thin tablet. As I tapped the screen to load the neurochem text, I kept thinking about the green-eyed boy from the subway. Maybe it was just his eyes. He had probably zoned out to the Link and happened to be looking at me, not watching me carefully and reporting on my anomalous behavior. I needed to stop thinking about him.

"Shall we begin?" Maximin asked.

"Yes," I said, careful to keep my voice placid and even. I

looked over at Maximin, whose shock of blond hair and pale skin looked bright in the cafeteria light, his athletic build filling out the entire left side of my vision.

I touched my subcutaneous forearm panel. The two-by-six-inch panel lit up underneath my skin and I tapped on it to get to my notes.

"Read through the text again," I said. "Then we can look over my notes."

Maximin nodded and took the tablet to read. I watched him for a moment, then looked at my lit-up arm keyboard to get my mind off my larger worries. The smooth subcutaneous panels were implanted at age five, then upgraded at ages ten and fifteen. The skin was smooth over the top. We only needed a 2-D image to see my notes, so I took out one tiny black pyramid projector from my tablet case and set it on the table. I tapped my forearm keyboard to connect it. An eight-by-twelve screen appeared flat on the table, and with another click my meticulous notes filled the illuminated space.

Maximin put down my tablet, then leaned over to look at my projected notes.

"I could sync my notes to your tablet if you want," I said.

"No, I just need to observe them for a moment." He compared the diagrams I'd drawn with ones in the tablet text. "The auxiliary nerve tension between synapse quadrant one and two. Can you sketch it in my notes?" He held out his forearm panel to me.

"Where's your tablet?" I asked.

"I always remember better when I see you draw it out piece by piece rather than looking at the finished whole. My projector's acting up too. You can just trace directly on my arm panel." He switched it from keyboard to draw mode.

I nodded and leaned over closer to him. A curly strand of hair fell out of my clip, but I was too focused on explaining as

I sketched to care. I used my finger to sketch the first quadrant on his forearm and then looked up to see if he was following me.

I almost bumped into his nose because he was leaning in so close. There was this look on his face. Like he wasn't thinking about synapse quadrants at all. His eyes were on my neck. He reached up and rubbed the escaped strand of my hair between two fingers.

"So soft," he breathed out.

"Maximin," I said. He dropped the hair and went back to the sketch, and I quickly pushed the stray strand behind my ear. My arms were frozen and tense.

What just happened? That was certainly anomalous behavior. Could it be some sort of Monitor's test to see if I would report an observed anomaly? Was I being watched from here? Or could it be . . . ?

Hope bloomed inside my chest. What if I wasn't the only one who glitched?

But when I looked again, Maximin's face was completely blank, without a trace of the energy and alertness I'd seen a moment before. Of course. Once again, I'd been so focused on my own emotions that I was starting to see them everywhere.

I struggled to keep my shoulders from sagging. Maximin wasn't a glitcher like me. He was part of the Community, part of a greater whole where each person was a small but necessary node, Linked in thought with all the other nodes. Humanity Sublime. It's what I missed the most when I glitched, that feeling of wholeness and connection, of belonging to something bigger than myself. Now it was just me. What good was it to have color and happiness when I couldn't share it with anyone?

Community first. Community always. Hot guilt swept over me again, that constant heavy sense that I was *bad*. Wrong. Broken. After all the lessons I'd been taught about how individuality and selfishness were destructive, here I was not only refusing to report myself, but looking for a companion. Actually wanting Maximin to be broken, too. What was wrong with me? I was beginning to understand the dangers of the barbarian human traits that caused the destruction of the world.

Lunch ended and Maximin's body bumped against my side as we walked down the dimly lit hallway to my last class of the day. I looked over at him curiously. The four-foot-wide hallway was crowded as always and, true, it was a narrow fit, but not *that* narrow. His face was blank though. I stopped in front of my last class, Algorithm Design. Maximin continued on down the hallway, turning to take a long glance back at me. Then he was lost in the mass of subjects.

I turned in to my classroom and only barely managed not to stumble in surprise. The tall green-eyed boy was there, sitting in the seat next to mine.

Everyone else sat down methodically, calmly pulling out their tablets and typing on their arm panels to check the day's lesson. I sat down, conscious of the boy's long gangly limbs stretching underneath the table into the row in front of us. Extraneous space was an unnecessary luxury in sublevel buildings, so all classrooms were small. The room-length metal tables and chairs were lined up tightly to fit as many students as possible, five rows to a room.

I tried to breathe normally. There was no reason to panic.

I just needed to cut out all other thoughts and concentrate on the lesson about algorithm development. But I couldn't help discreetly sneaking glances at the boy. He was typing calmly on his forearm. At least for once he wasn't watching me, and even though his limbs were long, he wasn't touching me. Almost as if he was being careful *not* to touch me.

Suddenly, the professor stopped talking. All the students tilted their heads up expectantly. Must be a Link announcement,

I thought. I hoped it wasn't too important. I tried to make my face mimic the others in the room, as if I were concentrating on the Link info. But then all eyes in the class turned to look at me.

"Zoel," the professor said, "are you not paying attention to the Link feed? You are to report to Room A117 immediately."

My heart monitor started vibrating loudly in the silent room.

Chapter 3

I FUMBLED putting my tablet into its case. The loud scraping of my chair on the concrete floor echoed in the small space. No one was watching me; their attention was back on the lesson in spite of my beeping monitor. I got out of the room as quickly as possible and recited the Community Creed as I walked down the hallways to the south elevator.

What I wouldn't give to click back into the Link again right now. After a few more recitations, the heart monitor finally stilled. But then, how many times had the monitor gone off today alone? I must have triggered an alert at Central Systems. I wanted to kick myself. How could I be so stupid? So careless?

My finger paused before I put it to the small touch panel to call the elevator. I was still glitching. I wasn't going to be able to hide my secrets any longer. I would be caught and repaired, or I could run away right now. I could get on the subway, take the connecting line, and try to get lost somewhere in the Central City. Disappear.

My hand started shaking and a high-pitched hum echoed through my mind. Desperate, hopeless thoughts. I straightened my body, calming the fear and panic soaring through my limbs. I couldn't stay hidden forever. Everything in the city required either wrist-chip or fingerprint access. I'd be found instantly.

But then the secrets and the hiding would be over. The loneliness and the nightmares would go away. I wouldn't be broken anymore. I would be just like everyone else, whole again, part of something. This was something that had to happen.

I touched my finger to the panel to call the elevator before I could talk myself out of it, and heard the responding whir of the elevator coming down the shaft. There was no choice, not really. I stepped into the circular white elevator tube and watched the door slide shut behind me.

"Sublevel One." My voice shook. The elevator moved but I could barely feel it. This was the right thing, I reminded myself. I was doing the right thing. I couldn't think about my drawings and the beauty and the happiness and all the things I'd lose. When the door slid silently open, I stepped out and followed the numbers on the wall to Room A117.

The door was open and light from inside spilled out into the hallway.

"Greetings?" I called. "Subject Zoel Q-24 reporting."

"Come in," said a deep male voice.

I took one last deep breath and stepped over the threshold into the room. But then I looked around me in surprise. It wasn't an exam room. It was a bedroom. There was a bed, desk, even ambient-light lamps instead of the ceiling light cells. I remembered now that the school had a wing of residential rooms for people of importance traveling through. Then I saw the computer and mobile diagnostic equipment in one corner. Had they called in a specialist to deal with me? How much did they know?

My brow must have furrowed, registering my confusion, because the short, round man standing in the corner said, "Come in. We just need to run a quick check on your systems."

He was middle-aged with thinning brown hair and a sheen

of sweat on his forehead. He wasn't wearing the regulation gray but instead the black uniform and red insignia of officials. High-ranking officials—Class 1 and 2. This wasn't just an ordinary diagnostic appointment.

"Have a seat." He motioned to a chair beside the equipment.

I swallowed, trying not to let my fear show. An official here for an impromptu diagnostic check. Something was seriously wrong. That moment on the train platform, the boy with the aqua eyes—someone must have seen what I had done and ordered an instant deactivation. That had to be it. They probably wouldn't even try to fix me. It was all over. I forced my feet toward the gray chair and sat down.

"They said you were pretty." He smiled at me and dabbed at his forehead with a cloth as he came toward my chair. He took a small metal instrument off the equipment table.

"Excuse me, sir?" I didn't understand his words and I didn't understand the look on his face. "Sir?"

"Sir." He smoothed down his sweat-slicked hair and organized the tools prepped and aligned on the desk. "So respectful."

Involuntarily, I frowned. For some reason I couldn't pin down, he made me feel uneasy. His behavior seemed anomalous too, but then, I'd never met an official before. Obedience to officials was a Community duty. Officials couldn't be anomalous . . . could they?

I had the strangest desire to get out of the chair and run back down the hallway to get away from him, no matter the consequences.

"You aren't in trouble. This is all quite routine."

I tried to breathe normally so I wouldn't set off my heart monitor. Something felt wrong. Whatever he said, this was definitely not routine. The urge to run welled up again, but I forced myself to sit still. He was an official. I had to obey.

But the uneasy feeling only worsened as he moved behind

me and lifted my curly ponytail. I knew what he was looking for—the access port at the back of my neck. My chest constricted, cutting off my air. If there was anything wrong with my port, he was going to be able to see it. And if not, he would run the diagnostic and the scans would tell him everything.

This must be what happens right before a subject gets deactivated. I glanced back at him and saw him take a tiny data drive off the table.

"I just need to run a quick program, girlie-girl. You won't remember a thing."

I didn't like the way he said *girlie-girl.* I didn't like the tone of his voice or the look on his wide, red face. In fact, nothing about this felt right. Suddenly, obedience and duty were forgotten—I knew I had to get out of here. *Now.* But just as I moved to get up from the chair and pull away from him, the man grabbed my ponytail roughly and inserted the drive into my neck port. "Voice-activate program 181," the man said in a breathy voice, coming back around to face me.

I tried to reach around to yank the drive out of my neck but I couldn't move. I was completely immobile. I could still feel everything—I could feel my arms and legs but I *couldn't move them.*

He reached out and put a sweaty hand on my face, then moved it slowly down to my neck. What was going on? I tried to pull back or yell but my lips didn't move and no sound came out. He started laughing, A chill ran down my still spine.

No, I tried to yell. I knew he could deactivate me in an instant, and I could do nothing to stop him. He could upload anything through that drive and break my programming and hurt me in so many different ways—ways I couldn't even imagine. I could only sit in mute horror, and my eyes stung in the strange way they did when I was scared or sad. I was suddenly sure that even though I didn't know exactly what was going on, something very bad was about to happen. And I was powerless to stop it.

My heart was hammering in my chest but the monitor was silent—another result of whatever horrible hardware he'd invaded me with. Out of all the things I'd feared, this, whatever *this* was, hadn't even been on my list.

My eyes were the only part of me that wasn't completely paralyzed, and I looked frantically around the room. There had to be something I could do, but all I could see was myself, alone and frozen in the room with a stranger who had absolute control. A stranger who was getting close to me, wielding tools I had never seen before.

I heard the high-pitched hum in my head—the same as when I'd seen the girl falling from the platform. I paused. *Of course.* He might have my body trapped, but what about my mind?

My panic bubbled up and I embraced it, reaching out with my screaming thoughts to surround every contour of the side-table lamp with my mind's humming energy. But I couldn't control it. I could never control it. The lamp exploded, and my heart pounded in panic and dread. The man looked up, surprised at the noise. Terror made the buzzing in my brain explode.

As the official let out a surprised gasp, the door crashed open and a lanky boy burst in. With a burst of fear, I immediately recognized the green-eyed boy. He scanned the room before finding a blanket, yanking it off the bed, and throwing it over the official, his arm wrapping around the man's neck in a tight V and squeezing. The man's arms fluttered uselessly and then he crumpled forward and stopped moving.

In my mind I was screaming, but I still couldn't move, couldn't even make a sound. The boy glanced my way and saw the terror shining in my eyes.

"I'm so sorry I didn't get here sooner," he said in a rush. "I didn't see until too late."

See what? I wanted to ask, but my vocal cords were still paralyzed.

The boy glanced back to see if I'd heard him and his face went red. He ran over to me. "Oh crackin' hell, I'm sorry. Deactivate program 181. Authorization code 5789345."

I was released. My hands flew to my face as I scrambled onto the floor. I quickly reached behind me to yank the foreign hardware out of my neck.

"No, *don't*!" He half-turned around to me, holding out one hand. He stopped just short of touching me. "Don't pull out the drive, or we're both cracked."

My hand paused on my neck. How had he known about the drive? My sense of relief was immediately replaced by fear. "Why shouldn't I? How did you know that code? Are you working with him?"

"No, of course not!" he said. "Hurry, we don't have much time."

I didn't need to be told twice. Whatever the boy's motivations, at least he'd freed me from the paralyzing control of the program.

"Who are you?" I asked. "What are you doing here?"

"I'm Adrien. And I can't tell you more than that right now."

I adjusted my hair, careful not to dislodge the hardware in my neck. "Are you from Central Systems?"

"No shuntin' way," he said vehemently. "I only want to help you."

I pulled my arms tight against my chest, hugging myself and looking over at the misshapen lump on the bed. "D-d-did you . . . deactivate him?" I whispered, the terror of all that had just happened truly starting to sink in.

"No," Adrien said, "I'm tempted to, but an official's death would get more investigation. This way it just looks like he passed out. Speaking of." Adrien reached down and pulled something out of his bag. It was a small metal cylinder, a little bigger than a tablet stylus. He pulled off the cap and I could see two tiny needles sticking out at the tip. He rolled the big man over and jammed the tip of the cylinder into his backside.

I looked away and rubbed my neck, a shiver running down my back when I touched the foreign hardware again. "So why can't I pull the drive out?"

Adrien looked back at me, carefully capping the needle and putting it back into his small black bag. "With it in, you're disconnected from the Link and everything is being recorded separately on the drive. None of your vitals are registering but the moment you pull it out, your skyrocketing adrenaline and heart rate will get reported right to the doctors in Central Systems and we'll get caught instantly. At the very least, they'll turn the godlam'd cameras in this wing back on." He pointed to black circular disks on the ceiling.

"Those are cameras?" My stomach dropped. All the ceilings and hallways had those black dots. The underground tunnels. The subway cars. My parents' dining room.

He nodded and held out his hand. "Come on, let's get out of here."

"And go where?" I asked, still shocked by the idea that I could be watched all the time, even when I was alone. Of course, it was obvious now that I thought about it. Fingerprint systems weren't enough to track subject movement. They would want more comprehensive control. Whoever *they* were.

I made the mistake of looking over at the man on the bed one last time. My hands were trembling. "Was he about to deactivate me?"

I felt something moist on my face. I looked up instinctively to see if the ceiling was leaking somehow. Then I touched my face and realized the water was coming from my eyes. I pulled my hand back and stared at it in bewilderment. I couldn't handle another malfunction. Not today.

"Come on, Zoe," Adrien said, his voice gentle. "We gotta get the crackin' hell out of here. I'll explain everything later. I promise."

Panic seized my chest again. How did he know my name? Not just my name, but the shortened name I used in my private thoughts? I'd chosen it for myself when I was looking through the old texts and found out it meant *life*. But he couldn't know that.

"Why did you just call me that?"

He smiled distantly. "It's a better fit."

He held out his hand. I hesitated, looking first at the strong hand he held out to me and then at the sincere expression on his face. And then, with a jolt of surprise, I realized that he must be able to feel emotions. That was what I was seeing on his face. I wasn't imagining things this time. He was different from any person I'd ever met—his easy confidence, the life in his voice, the strange words he used. He was awake, alive.

I didn't know him, didn't trust him, but I knew with all of these anomalies and what had just happened with the official, I'd be deactivated for sure if I stayed. My lungs squeezed at the thought. I didn't want that. The gray of being Linked was bad enough, but what was beyond the gray? What was death like? I closed my eyes, trying to shut out the terror of the thought.

"Zoe." His voice was quiet, but I thought I could hear fear behind it.

I opened my eyes and grabbed his hand firmly.

"Okay."

———

Adrien shut the door quietly behind us. He looked both ways down the dim hallways, then pulled me hard to the right, away from the elevator. I kept watch over my shoulder, as if any second someone would burst out into the hallway and catch us.

And then what would happen? Every moment it sank in more deeply that I had no clue how the world really worked. I was in too deep now and the only thing that gave me the courage to keep moving forward was the slight pressure of Adrien's hand pulling mine. His touch was intentional and, somehow, it made me feel safe.

We came to a dimly lit dead end. We'd passed several closed doors as we went down the hallway—doors that could open any minute, and we'd be spotted immediately as anomalous. Still holding one of my hands, Adrien reached down into the crevice in the corner between two concrete slab walls. His fingers seemed to find something in the darkness, a button or catch of some kind. Then he whispered, "Open Sublevel One, manual override verification code 999452385." I held my breath, having no idea what to expect now.

I almost jumped at the sudden grating noise behind us. A jolt of energy rushed down my arm, tingling in my hands. My head was still buzzing with fear.

"What was that?"

He slowly turned us around.

"Our way out." In the dim light, I could see a small smile on his face. He nodded toward the wall. My eyes followed his and I saw with amazement there wasn't a wall there anymore. I stepped forward to examine it and could see that the wall had slid back on a track and then rolled to one side.

It was pitch black in the tunnel beyond. My trembling started up again but I kept going anyway. I kept a firm grip on Adrien's hand as he paused to close the panel behind us. The darkness was so dense and complete, it made the air feel heavy—I could feel it pressing down on me. It smelled strange too, kind of damp and sour, like spoiled milk. Nothing like the antiseptic clean of the Academy hallways.

I touched my forearm panel and it lit up a small sphere in the darkness. I could barely make out two narrow walls leading forward into the black.

"Good idea." Adrien touched his arm panel as well. "Come on." There was only room for one person at a time, so Adrien led the way. I was used to small spaces, but squeezing through the two-foot-wide tunnel was unnerving, even for me. I lifted my arm panel for light but could only see the outline of Adrien's back. I noted with a sense of dread that there would be no easy escape if we were found in this narrow space.

"How far do we go?" I whispered.

"I memorized the blueprints of this place. We'll walk about a hundred paces before we get to the next panel."

"How do you—?"

"Later. I'll answer any question you have later but now I need to focus on counting our footsteps so we don't miss the panel."

I nodded, even though he couldn't see it. We started forward and without thinking, I silently counted our steps too. In my nervousness, I lost count somewhere in the sixties. Adrien kept steadily leading me along, so I hoped he knew where we were going. If we were found, it would be impossible to explain logically. Adrien stopped suddenly.

"Now what?"

"Now, I find the sensor switch." He searched up and down the wall with the light from his arm panel. I held mine up, too, for more light.

"Here we are," Adrien finally said. He sounded relieved and I realized he wasn't as certain as he'd seemed. He quickly whispered another activation code. I heard the scraping of rock again like we'd heard before.

"Won't opening these doors set off an alert somewhere?" I asked, suddenly worried. What if we went through all this only to find a squad of Regulators waiting on the other side?

"We got this set up when I came on assignment here. This was always my emergency way out. Of course," he said, more to himself, "I didn't expect to be using it already."

I bit my lip before asking who *we* was. I imagined that was one of those many questions to be answered later.

"Okay," Adrien said, "It's open. Come on."

The light from our arms didn't penetrate very far into the open doorway. I took a step while Adrien closed the door behind us. I stumbled but caught myself before I fell.

"Cracking hell," he said. "You okay?"

"Fine." I winced. "Just stubbed my toe."

"Sorry, I should have warned you. This isn't a hallway. It's a staircase." The door finished closing behind us.

"A staircase . . ." I raised my arm and saw the steep concrete stairwell.

"Yeah, I guess you're used to elevators." He seemed to sense my anxiety and went in front of me. "There's no railing, so just keep a hand on the wall and follow close behind me."

After we'd climbed more than fifteen steps, I wondered just how much farther there was to go and where exactly we were going. I tried not to think about the steep drop behind me, one that would surely kill me if I fell backward. I lifted my other arm to hold the walls with both hands for support.

"How much farther?" I finally asked. I wasn't strained for breath—everyone in the Community did a long cardio workout every night; healthy bodies meant a healthy Community, after all—but my thigh muscles were cramping up. I was used to running on a treadmill, not stair climbing.

"Not much," he said. He didn't sound out of breath at all.

Again I was struck by the mystery of this boy. Who was he? How did he know so much? Why was he helping me?

Before I could continue through the long list of questions racing through my mind, we reached a small four-by-four-foot plateau at the top of the staircase. Adrien found the switch easily this time and spoke the authorization code. And then, as the last door swung open and my eyes were stung by blinding light, I learned the answer to at least one of my questions.

Adrien wasn't trying to help me at all.

He was trying to kill me.

Chapter 4

I FLINCHED AND COVERED my face even though I knew it wouldn't help. Exposure to the outside air was deadly. And if it didn't kill you right away, the radiation would lead to tumors soon enough.

I turned to race back down the stairs but Adrien grabbed my upper arm.

"Let go of me!" I shrieked and wrenched away. "Do you have a death wish?"

Images from our textbooks flashed in my mind as I struggled to hurry down the stairs. Boiling skin. Slow, painful deaths. It was probably already too late.

"Zoe!" Adrien grabbed both my arms now, holding me back from the stairs. "Zoe, be quiet or someone will notice!"

I kept pulling away, viciously scratching him with my other hand, anything to get away from that rectangular doorway of toxic Surface air. He growled in pain as I dug my nails in deep. He suddenly twisted me around, holding both of my arms across my chest, encasing me like a straitjacket with his body behind mine. He had me trapped, but I continued to struggle, holding my breath for as long as I could. Icy cold fear raced up and down my spine. He faced me toward the door and the toxic air beyond.

"Calm down!" he said. "Crackin' hell, I should have just told you before, but I knew you'd never come if I told you we were going to the Surface. Listen to me, it's not toxic out there!"

My body stopped struggling for a moment in shock at what he said. His voice was an intense whisper, blowing the hair by my ear.

"Walking around without gear won't kill you. It's harmless, in fact. The bastards lied, Zoe. They lied about the whole history of the Old World."

"But the nuclear bombs—"

"Only a few bombs were released on D-day. Just enough to make it convincing. And Community Corp did it themselves. They did it intentionally. Don't you see? The Community didn't save you—they caged and enslaved you."

"You're lying," I snapped. "The Community protects us. Everyone knows that."

I tried to break away from him. I closed my eyes, begging to hear the hum in my head, to summon the ability to close the door with my mind. Nothing.

"Just hear me out," he hissed in my ear, tightening his arm around me. "Community Corp *created* D-day. And then they made everyone believe they were the only ones who could save us from total nuclear destruction. The only ones who could save us from *ourselves*. After a few generations, no one remembered the truth anymore—only what they'd been told. It's almost all lies. Zoe, most Community government buildings are above the godlam'd ground."

I twisted around as much as I could to look back at him.

"You're . . . you're broken. Anomalous. You don't know what you're saying." I glanced at the rectangle of light. It didn't hurt my eyes so much to look at it anymore. How long had we been standing here exposed?

"I'm not cracked, Zoe," he said. "The Surface is completely harmless."

He loosened his tight grip on me a little and I pulled away a step. He held me by the hands, turning me around to face him.

"You guys from underground sectors always have the hardest time dealing with this part. People like your parents are mindless midtier quality-control reps, but in other parts of the sector, there are subjects working aboveground as drone planters and harvesters."

He took a breath, watching my face closely. "Think, Zoe. You know they've lied about what the Link does. You know the hardware does more than connect people together. It doesn't protect them, it controls them. But they can't control you anymore now that you're glitching. You *are* dangerous, but not to the other subjects. You're dangerous to the officials and Uppers who run the Community. You are their worst fear."

My pulse started to race. He'd been watching me, he knew a lot about me. But why was he taking me to the Surface? To die? He could have just left me in that horrible Room A117.

I shook my head and took one step back down the stairs. Even though he was still holding my hands, he didn't try to stop me.

"Going with you was completely illogical. We need to go back and see a diagnostic specialist."

He shook his head. "How can you say that? How could you go back and let them rewire you until you're no longer *you*?"

I looked down. How many times had I asked myself that same question? All the strange thoughts that drifted through my mind made entirely from the soft matter of my imagination instead of cold hard fact. The colors. The light. All the wild emotions. There was a reason I hadn't turned myself in, and Adrien understood. It was impossible, but this stranger understood me.

"And that's not even to mention your ability," he said. "Moving things with your mind. Telekinesis. We haven't met one quite like you before."

I felt my eyes widen. He couldn't know. It was impossible.

What I'd thought just a second before was some deep connection between us now seemed calculated. He must be a Monitor. I looked around frantically. This was a trap.

"I don't know what you're talking about," I stalled.

Panic bubbled up inside me. My head filled again with a growing hum, and I tried to latch on to it, to use whatever ability I might have to reach out behind Adrien and close that door. But I was too shaken.

I looked up and saw him studying my face. Then something he'd said earlier struck me.

"Who is *we*?"

He smiled. "You're not the only one with gifts, Zoe. There are others."

I started. *Others.* Others like me. That meant . . . I wasn't alone?

Adrien sighed, raising his hands in surrender.

"Please. I'd like to take you to meet them, but I can't drag you kicking and screaming. Number one, we'd get caught, and number two, I'd never do that to you. You're away from the control of the Link now. You have your own mind, and you can make your own decisions. I'm giving you what the Community never will—a choice." And with that, he stepped back.

I immediately fled down a few more stairs to get away from the open door, but then, in spite of my terror, the warring thoughts in my head made me pause. I looked back up at Adrien, trying to work through the jumble of chaotic new ideas.

Others like me. It sounded too good to be true. My thoughts raced too quickly to finish one before another swallowed it up. Could I trust him?

He took a deep breath.

"Come with me. There are other Gifted people here, living

on the Surface, free and real and *alive*. I'm one of them. That's how I know about the pictures you draw. You draw the world as you wish it was. I know about the one you drew yesterday, a boy's face—it was your brother, right?"

"How did you know—?"

His words poured out in a rush. "I know that you drew him in the picture like you wish you could see him in real life. The way he looked at you from the picture, it was love, wasn't it? That's what you drew in his face?"

I felt my mouth drop open. "How could you know that?"

"It's my Gift. I can see glimpses of the future."

I blinked rapidly, letting the ramifications of that statement sink in. Everything he was saying was impossible. Everything that had happened today was impossible. This person standing before me, anomalous just like me? The Surface, safe? And a boy who could see the future? It was crazy. But then again, I could move objects with my mind—that was just as impossible. And he was right about the picture I'd drawn. How could he have known so much about my deepest secrets if he wasn't telling the truth?

"If you can see the future, then what will happen if I don't go with you?" My voice trembled, and I held onto the concrete wall behind me to steady myself.

"I don't cracking know." He breathed out and rubbed his eyes, looking unsure for the first time. "I'm still learning the limits of my Gift. I haven't seen what happens next but I hope you'll choose to come with me anyway. The Resistance will keep you safe."

I looked up at his face, the thick brown hair that was cropped regulation length but still stuck up anyway, unruly and rebellious. I looked back and forth between the intensity of his green eyes and the open door. Everything I'd ever learned told me that the Surface was dangerous and that the things he said were impossible. But I could feel he was right about one thing—the Community was lying to us about the Link and V-chip.

What other lies did they tell us? And what would they do if they found out I knew?

"Zoe, you know what they'll do if you go back," he said quietly, as if he'd read my mind. "They'll run the diagnostic on you and find out you've been glitching. They'll find out about your telekinesis. I've seen a few people after they get done experimenting on them. It's shuntin' horrid."

His voice cracked; then he shook his head and looked at his arm readout.

"*Shunt*, we're running out of time." His face turned pleading again. A faint rumble sounded in the distance, somewhere on the Surface.

"Please, Zoe, let's get out of here. Come with me."

He stood back and held a hand out to me, for the second time that day. An invitation. One I could refuse if I wanted. I stared at it, the hand of this broken boy who said crazy things. I was trapped. I knew what awaited me if I went back. A diagnostic, my secrets all laid bare, deactivation, or, worse, repairs.

I thought again of the boy who'd tried to run, the boy who haunted my dreams—I remembered the crunching noise of the bones in his nose breaking as they slammed him down. I took one glance back down at the dark stairway that was dimly lit now by the doorway.

These were my options. I could go back to the Community, face deactivation and the certainty of never glitching again. Or I could venture out onto the Surface, either dying quickly in the toxic air or, just maybe, having a chance at escape.

Behind Adrien's frame, I caught a glimpse of the Surface. It was so bright, all I could see at first was the light, but then in the distance my eye caught on the edge of something man-made—a building that looked tall and strong and not at all destroyed.

Before I could change my mind, I grabbed Adrien's hand and said, "Let's go."

Chapter 5

ADRIEN SWUNG HIS GRAY PACK around and rummaged through the bag.

"What are you doing? I thought we were going." I was going to lose my nerve if we didn't get out of here now.

"One last thing. I'll do it to myself first so you can see what I'm doing." He was all business again, looking sure of himself and the situation. He took out a small metal device, about the size of a stylus, but different from the one with the needles.

Something thudded from the darkness of the stairs below. We stood there, eyes locked, breathing evenly for several moments. The door to the surface was still open a crack. If someone was coming, they'd see the light and know there was something anomalous. I was glad my heart monitor was disabled, and from the look on Adrien's face, it was clear his monitor must have been deactivated somehow, too.

I let out a gasp of surprise. Adrien slammed a hand over my mouth, his eyes wide with fear as he looked around us.

"Shhh." He waited another moment before dropping his hand. He stayed close to me, and I could feel his chest as he slowed his breath.

A few moments passed, and he seemed to accept that the sound was not a person approaching. He took the device in his hand and jammed the tip into his forearm right above the subcutaneous panel.

"What are you doing?" A small trickle of blood seeped from

where the device had bitten into his skin. He clicked a release switch and a tiny metal chip *tinked* as it hit the ground.

"Disabling the godlam'd tracker," he whispered back. "Now we need to do yours. Give me your arm."

I glanced at the doorway. Well, if I was going to trust him enough to chance going out into the open air, I might as well trust him with this, too. I held out my arm and squeezed my eyes shut. I bit down hard on my lips to keep from crying out, but after a short second of pain, it was gone.

"All done. You okay?" He kept a hand on my arm.

"I'm fine," I said, trying to keep the panic in my voice down to a minimum. Before I could say anything else, much less reconsider, he pulled my arm and we went out the door into the open air.

The light was shockingly, painfully bright. For the first few steps, I closed my eyes entirely and stumbled along after Adrien.

"Here, put these on." He handed me a pair of glasses, like the ones we wore in chem lab, except these were tinted dark. I took them gratefully and put them on. When I opened my eyes again, I could see without pain. Adrien was already pulling me forward. It was only after a few more moments of trying to orient myself to the light that I was finally able to look around.

It was so open. There was so much *space*.

Huge, horrible open space, interrupted only by giant steel buildings jutting upward.

Concrete buildings and open air were all I could see. The air was warm and moist. It felt thick when I breathed it in. It smelled wrong, though I didn't have the right words to describe it. It was too much to take in at once. We passed a huge plaza in the middle of a complex of buildings and I couldn't stop staring. It was empty of people, but it was not the destroyed and deadly ruins I'd seen in my history texts.

I'd lived my entire life going from room to room, tunnel to

tunnel. Sure there were bigger spaces, like the subway platform rooms or the cafeteria, but it was nothing compared to this. I could always reach out a hand to find a wall, ceiling, or another subject. Here I reached out and I touched nothing. We ran close to the outside walls of the buildings, then Adrien took us down a narrow space, finally something similar to the tunnels I was used to.

Until I looked up. I stopped cold, letting go of Adrien's hand.

Sky.

My breath started coming in strained gasps. What had I done? The sky was right above me. It was beautiful and horrible all at the same time. It was just like in my nightmares, making me dizzy like I could fly one second and then feeling like it was pressing down and compressing my lungs the next. Or was that just the toxic chemicals I was surely breathing in? I put a hand to my chest, wheezing heavily. I barely noticed Adrien calling my name.

"Zoe. Zoe! What's wrong?"

"Can't breathe!" I collapsed against the cool, reassuring wall of a building. Underground. I needed to get back underground. I gripped my throat, clawing for air.

Adrien knelt down beside me, putting his hands on my shoulders and leaning his forehead into mine. "Zoe, you're hyperventilating. But we can't stop here. Try to calm down and take deep breaths. Come on, I've seen you do this before, whenever your heart monitor is about to go off. You're a pro at this. Just breathe and calm down. We're almost to the transport."

He breathed slowly with me, our eyes locked. Slowly, my lungs stopped burning. I allowed him to pull me to my feet and I stumbled forward. I kept trying to breathe but the air was so warm and moist. It felt *wrong*. I could just imagine the invisible poisonous particles I was breathing in and how they would worm their way through my internal organs.

I tried to keep my eyes focused on the dirty concrete under my feet. I counted my footfalls, letting my stride fall into step with Adrien's. I breathed in on every third step and out again on every sixth. Left, right, left, right, left, right, left, right, left.

"You're doing great, Zoe. Almost there. Keep it up. I see the transport."

I looked up and saw him pull open the door of a sleek white transport vehicle. I'd seen these on the Link News before, but of course never in real life. And usually they were entered in sealed tunnels or manned by people in biosuits. Adrien pushed me onto the hard gray seat and shut the door behind me. He ran around the front of the vehicle and got in the other seat beside me. I felt a little less tense about toxic exposure once we were inside the vehicle. It appeared well sealed. I hoped it had a good air-filtration system. Adrien tapped on a key panel beside the wheel; then he looked over at me.

"Ready?"

I managed a small nod, feeling anything but ready.

"Oh, your seat belt," he said, reaching across me for something. I didn't know what he was doing. His chest was close to me right as I breathed in and he smelled so . . . good. Not good-food-smell good, but good in a different way. I swallowed as tingles drifted down my body. He pulled the belt across me and clicked it in. Then he was settled back in his seat and we were in motion.

I watched in stunned fascination, trying to take in everything at once. I'd ridden the subway my whole life but it was nothing like this. The motion of this vehicle with its rapid acceleration and deceleration made me queasy—and that was without considering all the wild things I saw out the windows.

The Surface world was full of geometric shapes, square and rectangular buildings, some with triangle roofs reaching up into the sky. I averted my eyes from the sky. Looking at it made me feel nauseated from anxiety, so instead I focused on the straight streets and the buildings at eye level. Everything was concrete, gray as my underground world, except for the occasional shock of green—weeds coming up through the concrete, trees and overgrown brush on the sides of the road. Overall, though, it was clean. The paved street we drove on was smooth. The buildings looked well kept. Operational, just like Adrien had said.

Still, it was all eerily deserted. In my sublevel world, people were always crowded together—orderly, but crowded. The only place of solitude was in our tiny efficient housing units, and even there, I could only be truly alone in the few square feet of my personal quarters. I simply couldn't fathom the space and emptiness of the Surface. The tall buildings looked like monstrous uneven teeth jutting up. It was a nightmare-scape, cruel and uninviting.

Occasionally we passed other vehicles on the road, but the glass of each car was so darkly tinted I couldn't see the people inside. Adrien's knuckles whitened on the wheel every time one went by. I finally stopped looking out the windows and focused on him. I couldn't tell how long we'd been driving in silence—twenty, maybe thirty minutes? His face was taut, almost blank. For a second, he looked like he was connected to the Link, but then I noticed him chewing his bottom lip.

He was tense. He'd seemed so confident ever since he'd burst into the official's room, it was strange seeing him looking anxious.

Maybe I shouldn't have come. Maybe he didn't really know what he was doing. How much did I even know about him?

"Are you in acceptable condition?" I finally asked, my voice sounding overly loud in the small space of the car.

"What?" He looked over at me as if he'd forgotten I was

there. "Yeah, I'm fine. Sorry, I'm just on edge. I don't like being out in the open like this."

"I don't like it, either," I said. "There's so much space." I dared a glance upward out the window, then pulled back quickly. "It's too big."

He laughed. "No, I love *that* kind of openness. I've felt so claustrophobic the past few weeks. I hate being underground and not being able to see the sun. It's so godlam'd cold down there too. I don't know how you guys do it."

"But you said—"

"I just don't like driving on roads I know are monitored. Makes me feel exposed. I think we made a clean escape and this vehicle looks regulation from the outside, it should pass their satellite cams without a problem. The Rez." He looked at me and smiled. "Sorry, I should be explaining more as I go. Rez is short for Resistance. Anyway, we just usually avoid the cities, you know, so it feels kind of cracked to just be cruising down these streets out in the open." He glanced over at me. "But it's nothing to worry about. I've run ops in the city before."

I stared at him openmouthed for a second, then shook my head. "You do realize that nothing you are saying makes any sense."

He laughed again. His laugh was completely different from how the official's had been. It sounded nice. In spite of all the feelings and new sensations swirling around right now, the sound of it made me feel warm inside.

"I've never met anyone like you. . . ." I paused, trying to find the word. "Someone else who's . . ."

He reached over and squeezed my hand, his eyes still facing forward. "You aren't the only one, Zoe. You're not alone anymore."

He removed his hand and put it back on the wheel, but his touch left behind a lingering warmth. I ran my finger over that part of my hand in wonder.

"Can you talk and navigate at the same time?" I asked. "Because I would like to hear some of those answers you promised earlier."

"Soon," he said. "We're almost at the checkpoint. Besides . . ." He glanced over at me. "My mom can explain it all better than I can."

"Your mother! You mean, she's not . . ."

"Nope, not a Link drone."

I was stunned. I hadn't even imagined the possibility of parents who were free of the Link. I looked out the window, upset and confused about what I was feeling. This was an emotion I didn't have a name for. My eyes stung and when I reached up under my glasses to rub them, my fingers came away wet. Everything was happening too fast. I couldn't sort out one confusing thing before another came up.

"What about your father?" I asked. I knew there were more pressing questions, but I was still stunned by the thought of parents who weren't Linked. After adulthood and the final V-chip installation, subjects never glitched. They only worked at their Community jobs all day and night until their bodies become unproductive and they were deactivated. Glitching parents were an impossibility.

"He died when I was small," Adrien said. "It's just been Mom and me for as long as I can remember. She's kind of a hard-ass."

He glanced over and must have seen my confusion at the term. "She's really protective of me. My dad died doing work for the Rez, so she shuntin' hated it when I started working for them a few years ago." He gave a short laugh.

"Why do you do it, then?"

"We've been on the run our whole lives. I don't know any-thing different."

He looked over at me, his eyes intense. "I have to crackin' believe the world can be different. That we could be safe and . . . *free*."

I nodded slowly. *Free.* The concept was foreign, but . . . yes, it felt so right. It felt like the perfect word to encapsulate exactly what I'd been longing for.

Suddenly, he sat up straighter.

"What?" I asked.

"We're at the city gate."

I looked up and saw a huge gray concrete wall ahead of us. The road led straight into a tunnel through the wall, but as we slowed down to a stop, I saw armed Guards in front of the huge sliding steel gate.

Adrien laughed once, nervous. "Now we'll see if Mom was able to contact the Rez in time. Otherwise, this is going to be one short godlam'd trip."

Chapter 6

"SORRY," ADRIEN SAID, looking over at me. My terror must have been clear on my face.

"I'm sure she got the message to her guys. They always come through, okay? Nothing to worry about. I'm going to open the window now so just keep your glasses on and stay still while I talk to them."

I reached up a trembling hand to make sure my shades were still on straight. I closed my eyes but popped them open again when I heard a light *ping, ping, ping* on the windshield. Rain. My chest seized as I thought of the rainstorm that terrorized me when I was first glitching. What if Adrien was wrong about it not being toxic? There were too many things to be completely terrified about right now for me to even see straight. I didn't realize I was gripping my seat so tightly that my knuckles were white until Adrien reached over to squeeze my hand.

"Hey," he said. "It's gonna be fine. Don't worry. The Rez does stuff like this all the time."

He let go of my hand and pushed a button that retracted the window.

A man in a gray uniform approached. The Guards weren't full Regulators but I could see some bionic modifications, like the metal eyepiece that covered the upper left portion of his face as he scrutinized us. He was wearing thick outer gear and a helmet but not a biosuit or even a respirator.

I looked away as he leaned over. My heart jumped with every

drop of rain. It suddenly seemed impossible we wouldn't get caught and deactivated. In the rhythm of the drops I seemed to hear the word repeating in my head like a ticking gear "*deactivate, deactivate.*"

"What is your business?" the Guard asked, leaning into the window.

"Alpha Six Gamma Fifteen Approach and Release," Adrien said, enunciating each word precisely.

The Guard suddenly stood up straight, his face completely blank. He made a motion with his arm and the gate opened smoothly. Adrien pushed the button to raise the window. We drove slowly through the gate, entering the tunnel.

"What did you do to him?" I whispered after we passed. "Why did he let us through?"

"Auditory trigger to a sleeper subroutine the Resistance implanted. I wasn't sure if they'd get my message in time to hack today's Guard, but it looks like they came through."

"But won't he realize something's wrong? Or one of the other Guards when they see him?"

"Nope, it's a stopgap memory installation. It'll self-erase in two minutes and it'll erase the video taken from his eyepiece recorder stored on his memory chip, too. All he'll know is he doesn't remember those two minutes very clearly."

I shivered. It sounded a little too much like what the official had done to me. I glanced over at Adrien.

"But how could they, what did you call it, *hack* them? Did they use some kind of hardware?"

He was concentrating on the road as we entered the tunnel. "No, the Rez has a way to do wireless memory hacks. It's one of our big one-ups lately. Central Systems thinks they've killed all outside wireless access to the Link network, but we've developed tech that can get around it, at least for Regulators and Guards."

"Why only Regulators and Guards?"

The light from outside only penetrated about twenty feet into the tunnel and then it was darkness. Adrien switched on the vehicle's lights.

"They already have subroutines installed in their architecture for memory erasure. Because of some of the terrible things they make Regulators do—it was affecting them emotionally."

"Emotionally?"

"Yeah. The V-chip can only strip away so much humanity. Some things are just, you know," he shook his head, "so shuntin' horrifying, that the emotions are too intense for the V-chip to stamp them out entirely. It was triggering glitches, and trust me, you don't want to see a glitching Regulator. So they have a remote memory-erasure feature to delete memories right after they happen. And that's how we can get in with the hacks."

I nodded in the darkness and didn't ask any more questions. I didn't want to think about what kinds of things Regulators did that would be horrific enough to cause the kind of glitching Adrien was talking about.

The tunnel we drove through was longer than I'd expected, not that I'd exactly been able to gauge the distance well as we approached. I was so nervous, every second felt like an eternity. After we'd gone about three hundred feet into the black tunnel, the only light coming from the car's headlights, Adrien slowed to a stop.

"What are you doing?" I asked, glancing back nervously for Guards. "Is something wrong?"

"This is where we get out." He clicked the release on my seat belt, then reached across me and popped my door open.

"Why are we getting *out*?" I whispered.

He got out and hurried around to my door. He pulled it farther open and held out a hand. "Come on, we gotta hurry."

I heard the driver's-side door open, and a strange man stepped in. Fear flushed me, but I managed to squelch the yelp of surprise in my throat. Adrien reached in and grabbed my hand, quickly pulling me farther into the dark.

"It's okay. That's Brandon. He's going to keep driving the car so it looks like a routine maintenance vehicle continuing on to its destination. If anyone checks satellite images, it won't seem out of place."

"What about cameras? You said they were everywhere." I walked as quickly as I could behind him in the dim tunnel, feeling exposed even in the darkness. The air felt thick in my throat, like I was breathing through a suffocating blanket. The hallways and tunnels back home were always dry—too dry even, people got nosebleeds sometimes—but it was necessary for the intense air-filtration systems. Or so I'd been told.

"Don't worry so much." He laughed. "Didn't I tell you we do this all the time? They've disabled the cameras, too."

He stopped and the metal door scraped as he opened it. A single light panel shone inside, illuminating a dirty stairwell. I went through the door willingly, glad to go anywhere that led underground and out of the reach of atmospheric particulates and the unnerving rain.

Adrien led me down the stairs and opened a circular service hatch on the floor at the bottom. A ladder led down into shadows.

"You go first. I'll follow right behind to secure the hatch. Make sure to get a good hold. It's a long godlam'd way down, and the ladder can be slippery."

I nodded, not trusting myself to speak. I dropped my legs into the dark space and got a foothold on the ladder. I descended carefully in the dark, tapping my arm panel for light. I could still only see the ladder and a small area around me. I glanced down but the ladder disappeared after a few feet into the thick darkness.

I moved down rung by rung, trying not to think about the long drop into the empty space below. It was cooler down here, but it smelled horrible. The ladder was slick with what felt like slime. I tried not to think about the potential of radio-active sludge. Adrien's footsteps sounded on the ladder above me. I glanced up just as the crescent of light disappeared when he locked the hatch behind us.

"It should be about forty more feet down or so." He called down quietly, his voice echoing. "Once I get down, I'll grab a flashlight from a stash we keep there."

I nodded, even though I knew he couldn't see me. I concentrated on getting a good grip on each slick rung. My feet splashed into something wet when I stepped off the ladder.

"What's on the floor?" I asked nervously. I waved my arm panel around to try to see better but the ground just looked black. Adrien dropped down the last couple feet beside me. I heard a metallic click and light flooded the space.

"Oh!" I gasped.

We were in a huge cathedral-like space, complete with massive concrete supporting arches leading up to the ceiling. But it was the sludgy water I'd landed in that concerned me more. I could feel it soaking through my socks. Huge rats scurried away from the light and I shrieked and jumped back up on the first rung of the ladder.

"I was going to warn you but I wasn't sure if you'd come."

I glared at him in the dim light.

"You seem to be doing that a lot!" I whispered. "Next time, just warn me!"

He held up his hands. "Okay, okay, will do. It's a little gnangy down here and I'm not denyin' that there's a . . . bit of a rodent population. But it's not dangerous."

He handed me some thick rubber knee-high boots. "Here, put these on. We keep 'em stored here along with flashlights."

I shook my foot to try to get the excess water out of my shoe, slipped one leg into the boot, then the other. Adrien held out a hand and I dared to step back into the ankle-high water. It was black and oily, with a thick scum covering the surface. And it smelled horrible, like rotten eggs and rancid butter mixed together.

"Here's a flashlight." He handed me a heavy black flashlight. I wiped my hands on my pants and took it. The chamber we were in was huge and rectangular, with arched concrete struts that led to the ceiling, which was so high I could only barely make it out. As we made our way down the chamber, I realized that what had looked like black circles on the wall were actually other tunnels leading out.

"What is this place?" I asked softly. "Are you sure it's safe? No cameras?"

"Nope, not down here. This is an old combined sewage and storm-drain tunnel. It used to be called the Deep Tunnel. It goes for hundreds of miles all throughout the city."

"Then how have I not heard of it? I mean, I *live* underground."

He nodded. "Downtown, most of these old tunnels were demolished or rebuilt as part of the infrastructure of the underground city. These ones were too prone to flooding, so they left them alone."

He motioned me forward and I followed him, keeping my flashlight beam in front of my feet so I'd know where I was stepping.

I put one arm over my nose at the smell. "I think I might vomit."

"Sorry," Adrien said. "Just try not to think about it. It'll get better once we get out of the central chamber."

I nodded and followed him, trying to move my feet through the water smoothly rather than taking big splashing steps. As we came to the end of the chamber, I peered down the circular entrances that opened in the walls like giant gaping mouths. The light from the flashlights only cut through the first ten feet of darkness down each tunnel.

Adrien stopped. "Third tunnel on the right. Here we are."

He pointed his flashlight toward a tunnel at least thirty feet in diameter. He stepped up, his boots splashing up the foul water as he went. I followed, trying to lift each foot slowly to keep the splash to a minimum. I swept my flashlight ahead but could see only the endless tunnel until it curved out of sight to the left.

"How far are we going?"

"Far," Adrien said. "A mile down, we'll branch off again to a narrower tunnel that leads to my mom's place."

"You really know your way around here."

"I grew up haunting these tunnels." He walked smoothly, sure-footed even in the sludge. "We spent a lot of time here when I was small, running ops into the city. Sometimes a cell would get cracked and my mom'd have to stow me away somewhere safe, like these tunnels. Always with a map to memorize and a backpack full of provos in case she didn't come back." His voice quieted at the end.

"Adrien . . ." I felt so sad for him suddenly—imagining him as a small child, cowering in the dark all alone—but I didn't know the right words to express it. I thought about earlier, how he'd squeezed my hand when I was afraid and how it had made me feel better. I reached over and took his hand.

He seemed caught off-guard by my touch.

"Thanks. It's okay." His voice was a little rough. "Long time ago, you know. Anyway. You said you had a bunch of questions. We have some time, so ask away."

"Okay," I said slowly, thinking. All the little bits of information he'd haphazardly given here and there jumbled to-gether in my mind. "You said D-day never really happened. But how is it possible that the Community could deceive everyone so completely?"

He shook his head. "History isn't all fact—it's just the story the victors tell to keep themselves in power. And it's been a slow revision. The more time passes, the easier it becomes to reinvent the past."

"So then what *is* the truth?" I asked in exasperation. "What really happened?"

He stepped around a buildup of mud and sludge that had caked up against one wall. I grimaced, but at least he'd been right: The smell didn't seem quite so bad anymore. I didn't know if I was getting used to or if it wasn't as strong in this side tunnel.

"People in the Old World had been talking about a Global Community for a while," he said. "Some globally spanning corporations were formed and they got more and more power-ful. Especially Community Corp. It was an impressive tech-nology company with military connections. Then there were the major breakthrough advancements with the creation of bionic supersoldiers. That's when they realized the potential of the V-chip for soldiers."

He shook his head. "Some shunting genius realized they could use the V-chip as an artificial amygdala."

"The amygdala," I said, my mind going back to my neuro-tech text. "That's a vestigial part of the brain. It's useless, like the appendix. That's why they put the V-chip there, because it won't interfere with the necessary brain processes."

"Another lie," he said gently.

He led me around another buildup of gunk and garbage. I saw movement in the dark. Rats. I'd never seen rats before today. Really, I'd never seen many animals in my whole life other than flies or gnats or sometimes roaches. We didn't have any meat-processing centers in our sector. I shuddered and moved away, even though it meant I was walking through the deeper water at the center of the tunnel.

"The amygdala's supposed to facilitate emotional response," Adrian continued, oblivious to my reaction to the rats. Either that, or he was trying to distract me. "But the V-chip dampened feeling 'til emotion was done away with completely. Then the Link was expanded for military use so that a unit of soldiers wasn't a group of individuals anymore—they were a single entity, all Linked together to a single commander. I mean, think about it." He waved his hands as he explained. "With a completely obedient army under their command, an army that had no patriotic loyalties, no conscience, no fear, Comm Corp suddenly had a huge amount of power."

He looked over at me. "And that's when they planned D-day. They could finally wrench control away from governments and bring the V-chip to the masses. And the masses agreed to it willingly." He laughed darkly and shook his head. "The ultimate corporate acquisition. Our own minds."

A shiver went down my arms as I realized just how much people had given up, and all for a lie. How *could* they? I couldn't believe that anyone would volunteer their freedom, their mind, without a fight. As a drone, I'd never known what I was missing until now, but for them—they'd experienced freedom. They knew exactly how much they had to lose.

"People will do a lot of things that don't make sense when they're scared," Adrien said. His voice was gentle now; it had lost its dark sardonic edge. "Comm Corp was producing implants that they said could protect people from the aftereffects of the bombs. It's totally cracked, I know. But people will grasp at anything if they believe their survival is at stake, no questions asked. They went to Comm Corp for help, and they all left with V-chips."

A loud splashing from behind brought me out of my thoughts and sharply back to the present. I stopped and spun around, flashing my light. All I could see was the tunnel leading on infinitely into darkness.

"Are we being followed?" Panic spiked through me.

"Don't worry, it's just the rats," he said.

Great, just the rats. I swallowed uncomfortably and turned around. The tunnel went on seemingly forever ahead. I was used to tunnels, but the darkness and noises and foreign smells of this place were getting to me. At least I wasn't alone. I thought of Adrien as a child huddled alone in the tunnels and shuddered again.

"This is crazy," I said. "I've lived my whole life believing we were a new race of survivors, superior because we'd overcome all our destructive instincts. And you expect me to believe this horrible nightmare, just because you say so?" My voice cracked on the last word. The water was coming out of my eyes again.

"Zoe," he said quietly, looking over at me as we walked. His green eyes seemed to glow in the dim luminescence of the flashlight. "You've known something was off for a while now. Ever since you started glitching. You know this is wrong. The officials and Uppers, they're making you all slaves."

"They tell you when and where you live, where you work, when you eat, when you sleep. They pair you with genetic partners and create your children in test tubes and when you're no longer useful and productive for them, they deactivate you." He waved the hand not holding the flashlight to emphasize his words. "You never have a *choice*. You never get to *think*. All you know is work. They work you 'til they wear

67

you out and then you're deactivated and tossed in the incinerator. You're just *tools* to the Community, not human beings."

His voice grew more and more impassioned as he talked. His face lit up with a warmth and fire I'd never seen before. Deep down, something new stirred inside me. The way he talked about it, it did make our lives seem horrible. It *was* unfair. I'd just never thought about it this way. The deep sadness gave way to anger. Cracks were forming, threatening to shatter everything I'd ever believed, everything I'd thought was absolute. I felt my body shaking.

Something again splashed loudly behind us. I looked backward in alarm. "That sounded closer than before." I gripped Adrien's arm.

Adrien flashed his light beam. "Probably just more rats. Don't worry." But in spite of his easy words, his voice sounded strained, and the arm I held was tense and taut.

"Don't worry," he said again, more relaxed this time, and he nudged my shoulder. "'Sides, they can't bite through the thick rubber of your boots." The flashlight glow bounced off his grin.

"That is not comforting!" I said, but I smiled back.

I realized I was still holding Adrien's arm. I let go, surprised that I'd grabbed him so un-self-consciously. I never touched anybody in my normal world, but it had just felt natural with him. I wondered what other things would become natural the longer I was disconnected from the Link. There were entire worlds to be discovered. The thought momentarily awed me: *Maybe it will be worth all this confusion.*

A giant rat scurried past me, bumping into my leg as it went. Several more ran by. I looked up at Adrien, ready to hear his reassuring words about how this was all normal and there was nothing to worry about. But his face was tight with alarm. He flashed the beam behind us and I saw a small army of rats, big fat ones, some a foot long, all coming toward us.

"Cracking hell." Adrien grabbed my arm and ran, pulling me awkwardly along after him until I matched my pace to his. We were both in shape and running fast, splashing water all over ourselves as we went, but the rats quickly caught up with us. The whole ground beneath me was suddenly moving, alive under my feet.

I tripped and went facedown into the water. Horrible rat bodies surrounded me, crawling all over me with their tiny claws catching on my clothes and hair. Putrid water splashed in my nose and mouth. I flailed in desperate panic, trying to get to my feet, anything to get away from the disgusting matted fur and hissing squeals of the rats. I shrieked, a terrified hum raging in my head.

Suddenly all the rats around me were gone. I looked up to see if Adrien had pulled them off but instead saw a wave of twisting rat bodies flying away from me on all sides like I was at the center of an explosion. Adrien had ducked just in time to keep from getting hit in the face. The rats hit the wall with so much force their squirming bodies were ripped apart. I screamed in shock at the bloody sight just as Adrien pulled me forward again. The look on his face told me he was as surprised. Did that mean somehow *I* had done it?

I didn't have any time to think about it. I sputtered the rest of the disgusting liquid out of my mouth and barely managed to get my feet securely underneath me before we were running again.

"Almost there," Adrien yelled. He was gripping my hand tightly now and when I tripped again, he steadied me before I went down. The rats were thick around us, and as much as I hated to look at them, I had to watch the ground to make sure my next step was clear of their squirming bodies.

And that was when I noticed the water level rising. It crept up to my shins and instead of being just stagnant water, now there was a tugging current to it.

"Adrien!" I screamed. "The water!"

Chapter 7

"I KNOW," he yelled back over the cacophony of screeching rats and the flowing water that now approached our knees. "We're almost there, I swear."

But in another moment, running became impossible. We slogged through the water as quickly as we could. Adrien half-dragged me as I slipped and stumbled forward. I dropped my flashlight, plunging us into near darkness, but at least it meant I could hold on to Adrien with both hands. If he dropped his flashlight too, though, we'd be lost in the darkness with the rats.

A rumbling from behind us echoed down the tunnel. Adrien looked back, and in the dim light I could see his eyes widen in terror. I didn't have to look behind us to guess what was coming our way: a wall of rushing water, sweeping through the tunnel to wash away everything in its path, including us if we didn't get out of here *now*.

"Faster!" he yelled. "There!"

He pointed with the flashlight beam. I saw the off-shooting tunnel situated about five feet up the wall. It was clear of the water and too high up for the rats to get to—I knew we'd be safe if we could just manage to get up into it. If we could just make it there.

"Up, up, up!" Adrien shouted, making a foothold with his hands. I grabbed his shoulders, put my foot in his hands, and launched myself up into the tunnel, then reached back to pull Adrien up.

But I was too late. Just as I got ahold of both of his arms, the wave of water hit, knocking his feet out from under him and sweeping him sideways with the current.

I lost my grip on his left hand and screamed as the water yanked at him. I was on my stomach and quickly grabbed his other wrist with both hands, digging my nails to keep hold of him against the forceful current of the water.

I would *not* let him go. I would not lose him. His body was battered against the wall as the water crashed and frothed around him. His weight pulled me inch by inch forward off my perch.

"Let go!" he managed to yell before the water swallowed him up again.

"No!" I screamed back, but my grip was slipping. The rushing river had reached the height of the tunnel's base. With a sinking feeling, I realized we were both going to be swept away.

The water started spilling over into my tunnel, and I pulled with all the strength I had left in my body. In my desperation, I unthinkingly yanked with my mind too. I pulled with every thought, every piece of myself that wanted to survive, every hope and dream and memory that had ever made life worth living.

"Please," I pleaded through gritted teeth, though I didn't know to what or whom I called out. "*Please.*" In the next heartbeat, my whole body became electric with urgency and a racing heat.

Adrien's body suddenly emerged from the water, like a popping cork. He slammed into me, knocking us both backward farther into the tunnel. My arms and legs were weak from the exertion, I felt like I had no strength left, but somehow Adrien was alert enough to pull us both to our feet again and start splashing down the tunnel before the water could really rush in.

The tunnel led steeply upward and water was running down it, but the adrenaline rush from our narrow escape was enough to keep us fast and steady even on the slick surface. When one of us tripped, the other held on and kept them stable, until the tunnel lightened beyond the beam of Adrien's flashlight. We paused and looked at each other, managing weak smiles, then hurried forward until we reached a small concrete platform with a ladder.

"You first," Adrien said, breathing heavily. They were the first words either of us had spoken in a while. I nodded. I was too exhausted to argue. My limbs were numb from overuse. Water was pouring down on my head but I didn't care about toxic rain or cancerous tumors—I would have braved anything to just break free from these death-trap tunnels. Even if it meant returning to the Surface. I climbed up the rungs, looking down every so often to make sure Adrien was coming up safely behind me.

At the top of the ladder, a half-clogged grate was lodged securely between us and freedom.

I pushed to open it, but it didn't budge. I tried again and again, getting more frustrated and exhausted with each attempt.

"Move to one side of the ladder and hang on," Adrien called from below. I did and he climbed up beside me, our feet barely managing to share the narrow rung space. I made the mistake of looking down at the deep abyss below us, then quickly forced my eyes back up.

"Can you get it open?" I asked.

Adrien's face was full of concentration as he felt along the edges of the grate. He reached around to his back. "Cracking hell," he swore. "I dropped my pack. It had the pry bar and wrench in it."

"What are we going to do?" I tried to keep the panic out of

my voice. I couldn't imagine heading back down into the watery darkness and trying to find another way out.

"Zoe, do you think you could use your power to pull the grate away or to yank off the bolts?"

I felt my eyes widen. "I don't know—I mean . . . I've never tried anything like that." I stared at the grate. "I don't know if I'm strong enough."

He laughed. I stared at him incredulously. How could he laugh at a time like this?

"Zoe, you just lifted my entire shunting body out of a torrential current! You have power you don't even know about yet." His voice softened as he rested a hand on my shoulder. A fluttering warmth spread through my stomach. "Believe me. I've seen it in my visions."

His face was close to mine and I studied the smooth, angular planes of his face, the arrowlike tip to his nose, his dark curly hair that was soaked and dripping down his cheeks.

I gulped hard, my heart racing. I didn't know if it was the adrenaline, the idea of what he was suggesting I could do, or that his face was mere inches from mine. I shook my head. What was wrong with me? Some near-deactivation experiences and having my world turned upside down had to have made me half delirious.

"I'll try," I whispered, finally looking away from his gaze. I turned toward the hatch and closed my eyes, trying to concentrate and remember what it felt like when I'd used my power to pull Adrien into the tunnel just moments ago. But how had I done it? It had always just happened on its own. I tried to envision the grate and the bolts. I squeezed my eyes shut hard, reaching my hand out toward the grate. *Pull.*

I pictured the decrepit grate and each bolt, rust streaming over their surfaces.

Pull. Pull. PULL! I gritted my teeth, sweat dripping down the sides of my forehead.

Come on, MOVE! Please!

I opened one eye to peek. Nothing.

"I can't," I said, huffing in frustration. "I don't know how."

"I know you can do this." He looked at me with such an open expression of genuine belief. "Just picture it in your mind."

I clenched my jaw and stared at the rusted bolts holding the grate in place. They were so small. Adrien was right. If I could lift a toddler from the path of a speeding train, I should be able to do this. *Come on, Zoe.* I closed my eyes and tried again. But as soon as I closed my eyes, all I could see were the rats and the terror of all that water. I thought I might collapse from exhaustion. This was hopeless.

"I can't do it!" I finally yelled. I grabbed the grate with my fingers and yanked on it angrily, shouting in frustration.

Adrien put a calming hand on my back. "It's okay. My fault. I shouldn't have pushed."

"But how are we going to get out of here?" I was so upset, I felt like hitting something. The grate was looking like a good target.

"Well . . ." Adrien held up the heavy black flashlight. "Maybe some brute force will work. These bolts are gnangy rusted. Turn your head away—I don't want to hurt you."

I ducked and put an arm over my head. The bang of the metal flashlight on the ancient bolts was loud—its echo bounced down the cavernous tunnel. I hoped whatever was on the other side of the gate couldn't hear all the commotion.

There was a loud *pop* and the sound of something small and metal hitting the ground and rolling away. Adrien let out a whoop. "Got one!"

"Let me try," I said, eager to do something useful. I smashed the flashlight into the bolt with a satisfying thwack.

In the next few minutes, we'd broken all of the bolts off. He lifted the grate up and shifted it over. He climbed up, looked around, then reached a hand down to me with a wide grin on his face.

We were in a concrete culvert choked with leaves. It was the most colorful sight I had ever seen. I paused, my head just out of the grate, and stared. So much green. I realized with a numb, stunned sensation that we were surrounded by trees and bushes.

"Thank God we got to the west-end tunnel," Adrien said. "We're not too far from Mom's house. We just gotta make it to the woods, then we'll be safe from the satellite cams. Home free. Come on."

He seemed to finally notice the frozen, shocked look on my face. "Zoe, are you okay?"

I just nodded, staring dumbly ahead at all the green. I climbed out into the culvert, but couldn't stop staring. There was so much color, and the air itself moved as if it were alive. All the pictures I'd seen of trees seemed dull and faded compared to the real thing. We were still soaked through but I wasn't cold; the air was strangely warm and moist—suffocating almost.

I tried to take a breath, but instead found myself wheezing.

"Zoe?" He sounded worried. I blinked hard, still looking around me and trying to get a full breath. He slanted his head to the side and looked at me hard.

"So much green. Can't breathe," I said in between gasping breaths. Why couldn't I seem to get air in my lungs?

His eyes narrowed with alarm but he just grabbed my arm and pulled me forward. "'Kay, let's get movin'. My mom's place isn't far from here. You're probably just having another panic attack. Try to calm down and breathe."

I blinked and swallowed. My throat felt gritty and my eyes

began to water. I nodded, wiping my eyes clumsily with the back of my hand.

Adrien led us straight into the trees and thick brush. The rain was just a drizzle now but big fat drops of cold water still landed on our heads from the branches. I doubled over, my hands on my knees, trying to fill my lungs with just one good breath. Just one full breath, that was all I needed. It seemed so ludicrous—breathing was so easy. Why couldn't I do it?

"Zo?" Adrien turned around and his face immediately dropped.

Realization dawned on me, and I pulled away from him, stumbling.

"You lied!" I backed away, pointing at him. I tried to swallow, my heart racing. After all this, I was going to die out here in the toxic air, all because I wanted so desperately to believe this boy with the pretty green eyes and his promise that I wouldn't be alone.

Adrien raised his hands, defensive. "The Surface isn't toxic! You just seem to be having some kind of reaction. Maybe it's just panic at being up here. I mean, you always thought going outside meant certain death. . . . So maybe it's just psycho-symptomatic." He didn't sound like he really believed that.

"Or?" I tried to shout, but it came out a whisper.

"I don't know," he said quietly. "Asthma, maybe? Let's just get you to Mom. She'll know what to do."

He grabbed my arm, pulling me to run. The plants and tree limbs smacked me in the face as we went. I could only think about the toxicity hiding beneath the plush greenery. It was as if the limbs of the trees were reaching out to claw at my throat, suffocating me with their soft leaves. My legs were starting to feel rubbery but Adrien didn't slow his pace. I stumbled over a giant moss-covered tree root.

"Whoa, got ya." Adrien caught me. His eyes flashed with

alarm. "You're doing great. Just listen to the sound of my voice okay? We'll get there as quick as we can." I nodded and he pulled me forward again, moving fast even though I could only stumble behind him.

"Almost there." Adrien's voice sounded odd, a little too high, too bright. "My mom's place is like a little outpost in this part of the sector. It's secluded, far enough away from the city that it's out of the patrol zone."

He was trying to distract me, I knew, but all I could think about was that I could no longer see the path. My chest felt like it had been put in a vise, twisting tighter with every step. My breathing became more and more labored. I wanted to stop but couldn't bear the thought of spending any more time gasping in this air. I needed to get to shelter, away from the green.

Adrien led us around the base of a wide tree and changed directions, heading in a diagonal from the path we'd been on. He pulled a thick branch hurriedly out of our way so we could pass.

The trees were dancing and laughing at me now. They swooped dangerously in one direction, then pulled back with a mocking sway.

Adrien turned around and scanned my face. He wasn't bothering to hide his worry anymore. We kept going.

My body felt so heavy. I paused and put a hand on my forehead, then rubbed my eyes. Everything hurt. I accidentally caught a shaft of sunlight straight in the eyes and my head felt like it was going to explode. My tongue was wrong. Clogging my throat.

"Zo, I can see the house!" Adrien's voice sounded far away and hollow, as if we were back in the tunnel.

I looked at him through swollen eyes. The light glowed around him and he looked like he was floating. He was a glowing creature from another world, opening his gossamer wings and beckoning me. I wanted to tumble into his embrace. We'd be able to fly and I wouldn't mind the sunshine or the sky if he could just hold me forever.

But when he looked at me, his face changed from hope to terror. I tried to open my mouth, but my throat was closed up tight and I couldn't choke out a single sound. I reached for the sunlight wings on his back that would fly us far away from here to a place where we could breathe the sweetest air.

But instead, I was flying without him and it was all wrong, because I was dropping down, down, *down*. I was only faintly aware of the crash of my body hitting the ground as everything went dark.

Chapter 8

MY FINGERNAILS were claws at my throat. I was sliding in and out of a dream, images flashing before my eyes. Adrien screaming. The boy from my nightmares running, being chased down. Green everywhere. So much green.

Shh, Zoe. Don't make a sound.

The boy's body crashed into the dirt, leaves in his hair—he turned to look back at the Regulators who'd tackled him. He looked just like my brother Markan. He was screaming my name as the men in blue—artificial musculature coiled with savage strength beneath their reinforced suits—slammed his head into the ground, over and over. Blood poured down his face. The boy with my brother's face looked at me one more time, an indecipherable expression on his face, before his jaw went slack and his eyes rolled into the back of his head.

Markan! I didn't mean to! Run, Markan! Run!

Another face. A woman. Liquid gray spots bubbled around the edges of my vision, then went black. Muffled, urgent conversations. I was floating through the air one moment, then surrounded by warmth the next. A searing bite on my leg. Rats, I was covered with rats, biting me, eating me alive! I tried to open my mouth and scream but I couldn't. Why weren't the voices helping me, the rats were eating me alive! Blood rushed in my ears with a screaming buzz.

Shh, Zoe. Don't make a sound.

The world went black again.

My eyelids felt like they weighed a thousand pounds. My throat burned, but I realized with a rush of relief that I was breathing without any problem. I started to take a long, deep breath, but then I winced. My whole body was so sore. With every breath in, I could feel the contours of both aching lungs and the tenderness between my ribs. It hurt to breathe, but at least I was able to.

Noises filtered in. Voices. I hadn't noticed them at first but they were getting very loud.

"I can't believe you brought her here after everything we talked about. Are you *trying* to get us all killed? What did I tell you over and over? No unnecessary risks!"

"Mom!" I recognized Adrien's voice. "You didn't see what I saw. I *had* to save her. What was I supposed to do? What use is having visions if I can't do anything about them?"

"You need to stay focused on the big picture here, Adrien," the other voice said. It must be his mother. "There are too many lives at risk to act so impulsively. If you compromise your mission, it puts all of us in danger. We can't afford it. There's too much at stake, and you know it."

"How can you say that?" Adrien slammed something loudly, maybe the wall or a counter. "What the crackin' hell have we been fighting for all these years? To stop this kind of thing from ever being able to happen again! To stop the Uppers from treating people like tools or stock animals instead of human beings."

"You could have been caught!" his mother hissed. "Our safe-house location could have been compromised. We have a protocol for a reason. She's just one girl! I thought you understood that, or I never would've let you go."

"As if you could have stopped me. And she's not just some girl. You know she's not."

"Certainly not. She almost tore this place apart in her sleep. She's completely out of control, and bound to be more dangerous than useful. Your visions alone are not enough to justify putting all of the Rez in jeopardy."

Adrien's mother sighed. "Ever since the first vision when you started talking about this girl nonstop, your judgment has been off. Your teenage hormones and overactive imagination have made you obsessed. You're inventing reasons why she should be important! She is not the princess locked away in the fortress and you are not some hero who's going to save her."

"*Stop* it!" Adrien yelled. "I can't believe you're saying this. The Rez believes me about her. I'm not a shuntin' kid anymore, and I know the difference between visions and fantasy. I know what I saw was real."

There was a harsh laugh in response. "Okay, you're not a child? Then stop acting like one. If I hadn't had the epi on hand, she would have died. Do you realize that? Then where would your visions have been?"

I let out a loud groan. Like I'd hoped, they quieted and after the sound of chairs scraping on a wood floor, I felt the cool touch of Adrien's hand on top of mine.

"Zoe, you awake?"

I nodded my head infinitesimally, then cracked my eyes open. I saw the blurry outline of his head. He pushed back some hair that had fallen in my face. His cool hand was soothing. My whole face felt stiff and a little swollen, like I was wearing someone else's skin.

"Wh-wha happen?" I asked, my voice raspy. My lips were too big and my mouth tasted funny.

"Here, drink some water if you can." Adrien lifted a glass to my lips. I sipped slowly.

"You had a severe allergic reaction," he said. "Probably to the pollen or something, we don't know yet." He swallowed hard, his jaw working as he leaned down closer. "I'm so sorry, Zoe."

"You couldn't have known," I managed. My mouth felt a little better after I sipped the water. I lifted a shaky hand and took the glass from him to drink some more.

"Still." He shook his head and looked angry at himself.

I took another sip and was finally able to open my eyes all the way and take in my surroundings. We were in a small room but it didn't feel cramped. It was dark, with stained wooden walls, and there weren't any windows but I was pretty sure we were underground. The air smelled different. Cooler, less moist. I was lying on a worn couch with a faded flower design. A few pillows had been put under my back and head to prop me up.

I was wearing fresh gray clothes too and my hair was clean, but everything else in the room was in complete disarray. Overturned stuffed chairs, pillows tossed about. A table was knocked over in the middle of the floor, a chipped leg pointing straight up. A mug lay next to it, broken and resting in a dark wet puddle. I had never seen anything that wasn't orderly and perfectly organized. This was complete chaos. Then I remembered what I had overheard a moment before.

"Did . . . did I do this?" I asked, pointing around the room.

Adrien smiled, looking almost proud. "It was impressive. I've never seen anything like it. A little like being inside a tornado. Seriously, the other Gifteds are going to be amazed when they meet you." He paused when he noticed the look on my face. "Don't worry about it. Really. Nothing was damaged, and it's all just junk anyway."

Adrien gestured to the woman standing in the shadowed corner. "This is my mother, Sophia. She washed all the allergens off you, so you should be fine here, for now. You're safe."

She stepped forward and I got to see the face of the woman

with the angry voice. She wasn't what I'd expected. She was thin, with long gray-blond hair that had been twisted into a ton of tiny ropes that hung halfway down her back. Her skin was dark but not caramel like Adrien's—hers looked worn and leathery. She was wearing green trousers and a sleeveless undershirt. Her eyes were keen but a little glazed like she was tired. I nodded to her, unsure of what to say and wondering if she knew I'd heard most of their conversation about me.

"Greetings," I said, using the Community salutation without thinking.

She raised one slim eyebrow. "Greetings," she said caustically, then shook her head and left the room through a side door.

"She does not approve of me." I stared after her.

"Ignore her," Adrien said. "She's just . . ." He paused, looking after her with a frustrated look. "Just . . . my mom.

"Anyway." He came closer. "I'm so glad you're awake. You scared the cracking hell out of me. You'd stopped breathing and I was so afraid—" He shook his head like clearing away the memory. "Luckily Mom keeps an epinephrine shot in her med kit. Can you sit up? Or do you need to rest more?"

"I want to sit." I tried to push myself up with my tired arms. I felt more exhausted than I had in my entire life. Adrien sprang up and helped me into a sitting position, arranging the pillows behind my head so I didn't have to hold it up on my own.

"Do you think you can eat?" He handed me a plate with a few pieces of buttered bread. I took it eagerly. I was starving.

"This tastes good," I said, my mouth full of bread. I felt like I hadn't eaten in days.

He smiled and pulled a chair close, sitting quietly while I ate. I chewed slowly. He was so kind, so concerned about me. Someone who understood. I couldn't keep my gaze away from him. The strong line of his jaw, his sharp aquiline nose, thick eyebrows. And then those clear crystalline eyes.

"Zo? Something wrong?" he asked.

"No. I just like looking at you."

"Oh." A flush came into his cheeks and I wondered if I'd said something wrong. But he smiled quickly and leaned closer. "I like looking at you too."

I smiled, and it actually felt natural on my face. I liked the idea of him looking at me that way. And it felt so nice to be able to move my face into so many different expressions without fear of being seen, caught, and deactivated.

"So, do you like our secret hideout?" He laughed. "Actually, it's an old bomb shelter. So far Comm Corp hasn't discovered it yet. Mom and I stumbled across it years ago and come back to it every now and then."

He sat back, stretching his arms up to lace his fingers behind his head as he looked around the room. His shirt was tight on his chest when he did that, showing his lean, sharp muscles moving underneath. He was skinny, but far from emaciated. I could see the outline of his ribs when he took a deep breath, but then my eyes followed the line of his torso up to his wider, wiry-but-still-muscled chest. His lips curled up on the edges, smirking at some thought that had crossed his mind. My breath seemed to leave me again as I watched him.

I looked back at his face, and was startled to meet his eyes. One side of his lips quirked up further into a wide smile.

I turned away quickly, trying to relax my face into something more casual.

"I heard you and your mother talking. About visions of me. What did you mean?"

He fiddled with the edges of a blanket that had fallen off me.

"I'm sorry you had to hear that. She can be crackin' harsh.

I know she means well, but—" He hesitated, studying me, as if he were about to say something else. He shook his head, quickly changing his mind. "Yeah. I had visions of you. Sometimes my visions help us discover and track down new glitchers so we can try to get them out before the Community cracks them. You were my assignment at the Academy, and then I saw you get in trouble, so I did an emergency extraction. There's always a risk, but I don't regret it, not for a second." His gaze was intense before he looked away again. "My mom is . . . well, she's a mom. She worries. And she always gets more nervous than usual when we come back this way. She grew up out here."

"In the Resistance? I mean, the Rez?"

"No." Adrien shook his head. "She grew up like you—under V-chip control, in the Community."

I could feel my eyes widen. "Really? How did she escape?"

"She started glitching. Hers was the first generation we know of that had some who were Gifted. Still, it was rare. My dad . . ." He paused. I couldn't read the expression on his face—it looked like a mixture of pride and sadness at the same time. "They had some Rez informants in the schools. One of them noticed her. Dad got her out and then they just kinda fell in love."

"Fell in love?" I frowned. "Love makes you fall?"

He laughed a little. He paused, looking up toward his brain, something I noticed he did when he was thinking. "It's just a saying. It means that two people start loving each other. I guess because it can feel really sudden and because it's powerful. Like gravity—an unstoppable force."

I was still puzzling out the concept. "It sounds violent."

He laughed and nodded. "But in a good way."

I was amazed. I'd read so many confusing things about

emotions in the history archives, but love was the most confusing of all. A thrill prickled as I realized I was actually talking to someone who'd really experienced all of these confusing
emotions and could help me understand.

"Have you ever fallen? In love, I mean?"

He laughed again but it sounded different, higher pitched
than normal. He shifted in his seat. "I'll get back to you on
that one."

I nodded. I guessed not even someone who was born outside
of the Community could know everything. We were quiet a
few moments, but it was a comfortable quiet. Silence usually
meant I was glitching, which meant I was separate and all
alone, but this was strange—it was a together kind of quiet. I
studied Adrien's profile, his long face and the triangle shadows
underneath his sharp cheekbones.

"Can you tell me more about the Rez?"

He looked at me, a small smile on his face.

"I suppose now that you're here, you'll probably meet some
of them soon. And other Gifteds, like us. Some of us were
born out here, outside of the Community, and others escaped.
There's plenty of people out here in hiding, on the run, out on
deserted land or in abandoned buildings. Not everyone's in
the Rez. Me and Mom, we were on our own for a while. She
didn't want anything to do with the Rez, not that she'll tell
me why. I think she had some vision of it." His smile ebbed as
he looked in the direction she'd left.

"Anyway, I got tired of living on the run instead of fighting
back. When my Gift started coming in, I dunno." He shrugged.
"For me, it's like I knew life was supposed to be bigger—that I
was supposed to be doing something more. With the things I've
seen—the drone labor in the mines, not to mention the farms—"

He shuddered. "I just knew that a Gift like mine meant,

I dunno," he looked up, "it meant that I had a *responsibility* to use it well."

I knew so little about the world he had seen, but his feelings connected with something deep inside me, a sharp pang of recognition.

"Duty," I said, nodding slowly. "Duty is important." It was something we were taught in the Community. A wave of guilt swept through me. Just yesterday I had thought duty meant turning myself in to the Regulators. Now I didn't know what to think.

Adrien seemed to sense my confusion.

"Duty is important when you're working for something worthwhile," he amended.

"But how do you tell the difference?" I frowned. "Good and bad look the same sometimes."

He shrugged. "You just gotta keep asking questions to find out more. And then just follow your intuition. Your conscience."

"Conscience?"

"Oh, right." He sounded surprised, giving a small laugh. "I guess you wouldn't know. It's, uh, knowing the difference between right and wrong, good and bad. Your conscience is the part of you that makes you want to do good and help people."

I looked at him quizzically. "It's part of me? Where?"

He laughed again. It was a warm hearty sound that made my chest curl in happiness. "Sorry, you'd think I'd be better at explaining all of this by now. Usually I have more time to prepare a glitcher for the outside world. And being around you, I just get . . ."

His face colored as he looked away. "Anyway, a conscience isn't like a physical part of you. It's just there, or it *should* be there, in everyone. It's part of what makes us human. Sometimes you can feel it. Right here." He reached out, hesitating just above my heart monitor, pausing. Then he looked into my eyes and dropped his hand.

I frowned. "But what about my Gift? Where does that come from?"

Adrien scooted back in his chair. "The easy answer is evolution. That's how I always start off explaining it anyway. They started shunting around with our brains and inserting all that cracking hardware. They thought they could get total control over people. But they forgot one of the basics of life on Earth—" His eyes sparkled as he leaned in, grinning conspiratorially. "—organisms adapt!"

"Old World scientists called it 'plasticity.' Basically, the brain can rewire itself even if crucial parts are damaged. *Evolution* might be the wrong word—it's not like glitchers are a new species. Just highly adapted. We've started developing abilities that get around their programming, making neural connections to subvert the hardware. Even with all our tech, the brain is something we've never completely understood." His hand movements grew wilder as he got excited. "Maybe it's something that *can't* be completely understood. There's still so much mystery. Not to mention the parts about being human that are simply—" He lifted his hands. "—intangible. Like our souls or spirits, or whatever it is that makes us *us*."

"Souls?" I arched my eyebrows, barely stopping myself from scoffing. "Like in the barbarian Old World religions?"

He smiled and shrugged, some of his energy seeming to wind back down. "I don't know. But you've felt it, haven't you? Those feelings that seem to get so big in your chest, like something is so beautiful it aches?"

My mouth dropped open in surprise. He was right. I had felt exactly that. When I'd seen color for the first time, or when I watched my brother sleeping.

"What *is* that?" he continued. His face had a quieter intensity as he leaned over. His green eyes caught every bit of light in the room and seemed to refract it in a thousand sparkles. "Beauty, happiness, they're things so big they can't capture them with their scientific words. It's like what they used to call magic."

I sat for a moment focusing on what he'd said, never looking away from his eyes. I wasn't able to follow everything—but watching him get so excited, it was unlike anything I had ever seen before. I'd never seen so much emotion on a person's face. It lit me up inside, made my chest feel bright and warm. It was like there was a connection between us, like somehow he *knew* me. Like he could reach right into me, pluck out the things I felt and thought, and put them into words in ways I hadn't learned to express yet.

But I couldn't agree with him completely. I looked at him regretfully.

"But even emotions can be broken down to electrical synapses and chemical reaction. Isn't that what the V-chip proved? Emotion *is* all physical response. No invisible soul to it."

"Yeah, but even under their complete control of synapses and chemicals, your mind managed to break free." Adrien looked at me warmly. "That you exist this way, Zoe, you're the ultimate proof that we can be so much more than just the sum of our parts and knee-jerk impulses. Something about you just could not be controlled, just had to be free."

I couldn't help smiling again at his enthusiasm. "I don't think I can quite agree with your theory, but I like the way you talk about it. It makes life seem—I don't know—more special? More important?"

He grinned, his eyes catching mine again until I felt like there was some kind of electric current passing between us.

"Sorry if I've been rambling. I just never get to talk to anyone about all this. Mom never wants to hear it—she says it doesn't matter *why* things are happening, just that they are. But talking with you just feels so . . . natural."

"Even though I might agree with your mother?"

"No, you're different," he said firmly. "I've watched you discover emotion, discover the world around you. I mean, before having the visions of you, I'd never felt . . . ." He stopped himself abruptly. "Okay, getting ahead of myself. I realize the fact that I've had visions about you might seem kind of gnangy. It's a violation of your privacy. I'm so sorry." He looked down. "It's just that the more time I spend around someone, the more I see in my visions. I'm sorry—I keep trying to control it."

Adrien looked away, biting his lip.

"And you saw me?" I asked. "You came to the Academy for me." Even as I said the words, pleasure bloomed at the thought. I smiled. He'd come because of me. Or he'd come because of my *ability*. I frowned at the thought. That was the logical reason.

"I'm sorry." He cringed, seeming to mistake my frown for something else. "I know, creepy. I first had a vision of you over a year ago. You were here. We were talking, like we are now. Cracking hell!"

He smacked his forehead.

"It was probably this very moment I saw. Isn't that amazing?"

"But that's not why you came to the Academy, not just because you saw us talking." I tried to contain the nervous excitement tingling in my stomach. This was what I had been waiting to talk about ever since I opened my eyes. Without the Link and its constant instruction, I was completely lost. This boy had offered me escape, but I had no idea what came next. He did.

"No." He paused, and my stomach sank. "I had other visions of the future—the farther-off future—at least I think so because you looked different than you do now. I saw that you're going to be an integral part of the Rez. Not just that." He bit his lip again. "I'm sorry, I don't know how to tell you this without cracking you out. I'm not even sure how much of my visions I should tell you—if it will shunt up the future somehow if you know ahead of time. I don't really know how this all works yet."

"Just tell me," I said, the desperation clear in my voice. "Ever since I started glitching I've felt so lost and confused. You've seen what I'm supposed to do, what I'm supposed to be. Please. You *have* to tell me."

He was quiet another moment, looking down so I couldn't read his face as he searched for what to say. I reached over and touched his hand lightly.

He looked up and I realized how close we were, both of us leaning in together. I blinked a few times, suddenly light-headed, but not like before when I'd passed out. Being so close to the smooth dark skin of his face, getting lost in the shifting shades of his green eyes, it felt like my insides were fluttering and melting. Not like when I was nervous or afraid, but in a nice way. In a really wonderful way.

This was what it felt like to be connected to another person without the Link. I couldn't describe the feeling, but I felt the pricking behind my eyes again. This was what it felt like not to be alone. And Adrien was right—I didn't have words to describe this feeling. It was what I'd always wanted before, but didn't even know existed. It was mystery and it was beautiful.

My hand was resting on his wrist, and I trailed my hand up his forearm without thinking about what I was doing. The texture of his shirt was so rough compared to the smoothness of his skin. My fingers traced up his shoulder and then over the soft skin of his neck. I felt his skin warm and his pulse quicken at the touch of my fingertips, responding in a way that was totally different from logic and programmed electrical impulses.

I kept going, awed by the growing sense of connection, the feel of the curly hair at the base of his neck, the way his breath ruffled my eyelashes. The pools of water gathered at the edges of my eyes, brimming over. He suddenly trembled and leaned in closer, eyes open wide in surprise.

We sat there like that for a moment, faces so close and my heartbeat pounding in my chest in a frantic flurry. He stared at me intensely, his jaw clenching and unclenching until, with a sigh of release, he closed his eyes and leaned in. His lips ever so gently touched mine, and suddenly I felt everything stirring inside me grow wings, let loose, and fly.

"Oh Adrien," came his mother's voice loudly from the doorway. Her face was stony, but behind her tight eyes there was resignation, and some sadness. Adrien pulled away from me quickly.

"Just tell her already," she said. "You think she's going to lead the Resistance. You think she's our only hope to deliver the whole human race from slavery."

Chapter 9

I LOOKED BACK AND FORTH between them in confusion. There had to be some kind of mistake. All of the blooming feelings froze in my chest.

"Mom," Adrien said, sounding angry, jumping back from me. His face reddened as his mother strode into the room.

Sophia rolled her eyes. "It doesn't matter what you tell her right now anyway. Or what you *do* with her."

"Mom!" It was a warning.

I touched his hand to try to calm him down.

"It's true," his mother continued. "You forgot she's still got the memory disrupter inserted. She won't remember a thing from the entire time since it was inserted till it's taken out. And frankly, that's a good thing, because she can't stay. She has to go back."

My hand went to the back of my neck. Oh no, she was right. Adrien had said everything was recording separately on the drive, but I'd forgotten all about it. And soon I would forget all of *this*. My hands trembled at the thought.

"Why?" I asked, my voice barely above a whisper.

"She can't go back," Adrien said. "Neither of us can. They'd cracking lobotomize us if we did."

"Don't be so dramatic. Besides, you are not going back. But she has to. She'll die if she stays here on the Surface."

"What?" Adrien and I both asked at the same time.

"I had her blood tested. Her allergy is extreme. Her mast

cells will keep producing histamines and sending her into ana-phylactic shock."

"Then we'll keep her away from mold," Adrien said.

"Adrien." Sophia pinched the bridge of her nose, looking tired. "Sanjan ran the medical tests twice. She is allergic to the most common outdoor molds. Almost all of them. I'm surprised she lasted as long as she did up here. An epi shot is just an emergency fix—it will wear off in twelve hours and then she could go into anaphylaxis again. She'll die if we don't take her back."

"We'll keep her inside, then."

She walked toward Adrien and her tone softened. "Look, honey, I'm sorry. I know how much you wanted this. How much you want to believe your visions and the hope they bring you. But your dreams and the facts just don't add up."

He brushed her hand off when she touched his shoulder. "I know what I saw. I've seen visions of her out in the open, un-der the sun. Your results were wrong."

She tilted her head sideways. "I understand this is hard, but there's nothing we can do for her. No Resistance safe houses have the kind of air-filtration systems she needs to survive. We're already running out of time on the epi, and she'll die if she breathes any air except from where she's from." She paused a moment. "I'm sorry, but the Community is her best chance at survival right now."

Adrien turned to look at me, the fight draining from his face. "No. There has to be another way. Some of the research labs must have the kind of air-filtration systems she'd need. Or we could build—"

"Enough!" his mother said sharply. "We don't have time for this." She looked at Adrien. "Don't get your hopes up, but the Rez has been building a Foundation for glitchers. Maybe they could modify it to be air-safe for her. But it won't be ready for months." Her voice softened again. "You could go back for her then."

"Okay, what about allergy shots? We could—"

"Immunotherapy takes months to work, years sometimes, and with all the different kinds of molds she's allergic to, it would still be a long shot."

I cleared my throat. "If I went back—is there a way for me to pass the diagnostic tests without showing up anomalous?" They both paused to look at me.

"With the memory disrupter in place, nothing that's happened could be recorded or found on your memory chip," his mother said, scrutinizing me as if for the first time.

"No," I said, "but everything else will. The glitching, the drawings and the tele . . . What did you call it again?"

"Telekinesis," Adrien said, turning to me with an ashen face, "but Zoe, you can't go back. It's too dangerous."

I turned back to Sophia. "Can we fool their diagnostic equipment?" I asked stubbornly.

"Yeah. We have subware that can mimic memory info so they aren't tipped off. But Zoe—"

"If someone could get the immunotherapy treatments to me there," I said slowly, "then I could escape again when this Foundation is ready."

I paused, an image flashing in my mind that sealed the decision. Markan. My chest flooded with hope. "And I could get my brother out, too."

"Is he glitching?" Adrien's mother asked.

"No, but he might when he gets older. And I can't leave him there. Not knowing what I do now."

Adrien was quiet. He paced for a little bit, one hand massaging his forehead, before finally stopping and nodding. "It could work, I guess. If we drop you back, they'll know something anomalous happened to you, but with the drive removed, even you won't know exactly what it was."

"And I won't remember . . ." I trailed off, looking down at the ground. "Is there a way to download the info onto an external memory drive so I'll still have it? So I can remember . . . you know, about the immunotherapy stuff and why I need to do it?"

"Too risky," his mother said immediately. "In the wrong hands, that drive would reveal compromising information about Adrien and me and the Rez. I can't let that happen."

"That's why I'll be there at school with you," Adrien said, "and I'll help you remember."

"No you will not!" his mother exploded, grabbing Adrien's arm roughly and yanking him away from me. "This has gone on long enough. I'm fine with getting her a supply of medicine, but *you* are staying here. We've taken far too many risks already."

Adrien yanked his arm back from her, his eyes flat. "Nothing has changed. I probably shouldn't have taken her away from the Academy. I see that now. But even this was meant to happen. The other visions will come true, too, even if I can't see how—"

"Enough!" Sophia's frizzy ropelike hair flew around her as she advanced on him. "She's shunting allergic to the world! Get it through your head! She's not the one you were hoping for."

"I'm sorry, Mom." He took a step toward her. "I'm not trying to hurt you, but I *am* going back."

"But how?" I asked in a whisper. "They'll figure out we were together—that you were the one who took me away."

He shook his head. "Not if I'm sick with Flu 216. I'd be out for a week without suspicion. We'll stop at Sanjan's on our way back, so he can infect me with the samples I know he keeps."

"No," his mom said. "I won't let you. I'll tell him not to give it to you."

"Mom," he said, more gently. "Even if they don't believe she'll become our future leader, they know she's telekinetic. To you, she might just be one girl, but the Rez will see she's too valuable to lose."

His mother took a few steps back, her face shifting. She stared at him for another long moment; then she spun on her heel and left the room, slamming the door behind her.

The silence was heavy after she left. I stood near the wall, stunned by all that had just happened.

"I'm sorry about that," Adrien finally said, breaking the quiet.

"Is what she said true? That you've had visions of me as some sort of leader of the Resistance?"

"Sorry." He walked across the room to me. "I know it's a lot to take in. This whole day must seem like one long nightmare. But you'll wake up. Once we remove the memory disrupter, you won't remember any of it."

"How is that supposed to make me feel better?" My voice rose in pitch. "I only found out today that a Resistance even exists, and you think I'm going to take it over one day?" It was all too much. All I'd wanted was to *feel* things and understand what was happening to me. But he was saying someday everyone was going to be looking to me for answers?

I squeezed his hand. "Maybe your mom is right. I'm nobody. I'm not a leader. I'm not meant for any of this."

"You're not nobody," he said, covering my hand. "And it's not about that. Even if you don't become some great godlam'd leader, I'd still come back with you."

"You would? Why?" My voice trembled. My face suddenly felt hot.

"Because . . ." He pulled back and cleared his throat. "Because I care about you."

"You do?"

"I didn't come to the Academy because I care about the future of the Rez. I mean, yes, it's incredibly important. And that's what I told the local cell leaders, so they'd arrange it for me. I came because I'd seen you, even gotten to know you through the visions. I couldn't *not* know you."

My heart started beating faster at his words. He wanted *me*? Just me, not my Gift?

"Experiencing the world through your eyes, feeling your first emotions with you." He shook his head in wonder. "You were the first beautiful thing I'd seen after a couple of really dark years. You made me realize I'd taken for granted how beautiful life can be. I'd just been working so hard, killing myself with discipline to be a good soldier, deadening anything that made me feel emotion because I thought it made me weak. But then I started having the visions of you and . . ." He gulped hard before looking back up at me. "It changed me—*you* changed me—and it showed me just how much we're fighting for. Not just because I was angry at what they'd done to us. Not just because I wanted revenge for my dad. But because there's goodness and beauty in the world, and that alone is worth fighting for. Maybe even worth dying for. The way you made me feel, even before I ever met you, it's—"

He ran a hand through the hair at the back of his head. "God, here I go again. Giving too much information. Look, I know you just met me and that this is the worst possible timing, and I don't expect you to feel the same way—"

"Wait," I said.

He glanced up at me, his face wide open and full of tentative hope. I grabbed his hand again, so many emotions rising up and tumbling over themselves inside of me, I couldn't begin to sort them out.

"I want to feel that way," I said, my voice oddly high. "I want to feel those things. For you. And—"

I thought about everything that had happened since I'd met him, how I'd instinctually trusted him from the start, how his touch calmed me and made me feel safe, even in the most tense situations. How his face had lit up earlier when he was talking about beauty. How intensely *connected* I felt with him, and how he made everything inside of me twist and turn.

"—and maybe I already do," I finished slowly.

He stood frozen for a second, stunned. Then, those green eyes trapping mine, he put his hand on the side of my face. He pulled me closer until his lips breathed me in, until we were sharing one breath.

My whole body sank forward into his arms. His lips moved against mine, exploring my mouth so gently. I tried to mimic his movements—slowly, uncertainly, until I didn't have to think about it at all. It just felt *right*. He let out a soft moan at my reaction and cupped his hands behind my head, pulling me closer until I couldn't tell where my mouth ended and his began. A liquid sensation swooped throughout my stomach. It was the most amazing thing I'd ever felt and it kept growing, the vibrating heat expanding outward. I was surprised I was still able to stand.

Until Adrien's hand brushed against the memory disrupter in my neck.

I froze. My heart sank back down from its floating heights, and I pulled away. All the happiness I'd just been feeling was suddenly sliced through by a horrible, sour ache. I looked sadly into his face. Circumstance was betraying us, and there was nothing we could do to fight it.

"I won't remember any of this. I won't remember you." The cutting loss of the thought felt almost like a physical pain. I squeezed my eyes shut. I knew I'd only just found it—found him—but being with him felt like the single most significant thing that had ever happened to me. It wouldn't be imprinted on my memory chip, but it seemed too important a thing to be removed so simply, so permanently. Adrian said that our humanity was a precious and unbreakable thing, but how could that be if it could be stolen away with a single piece of hardware? It wasn't fair!

I tried to bury my thoughts so I wouldn't lose this moment here with him. I couldn't think about the future or the past. All I could do was be fully present right now. I reached up a finger to trace his full lips. Tears gathered in my eyes. "You'll just be another subject in the crowd. I won't know you. I won't remember how to do this—" I lifted my lips to his.

He finally pulled away, sounding out of breath. His eyes blazed into mine with an intensity I'd never seen before.

"Listen to me, Zoe," he said, his hands resting firmly on my shoulders. "We will find each other. I will get your medicine to you. And we'll escape that shuntin' place for good this time. I'll teach you how to kiss all over again. I know it."

"Because you've seen it in a vision?" I asked.

He looked down. "No, not exactly," he said. "But there are other kinds of faith than the kind I have in my visions. This is too strong, too real. We'll find it again."

I hugged him hard, nestling underneath his arms, my ear to his chest, wishing we could stay there forever, that I never had to leave. "You promise?"

"I promise," he whispered in my ear, holding me tight against his chest and stroking my hair.

We stood there like that for a long time, until he finally pulled away. "I gotta go make some arrangements for us to get back into the city and get my pretend parents—they're spies for the Rez," he said in answer to my questioning face, "to call the Academy and say I'm sick right when school opens tomorrow.

Hopefully, I'll be able to get back to the apartment before they come to check me out. The sooner we get back, the less suspicion there will be."

"But Flu 216 is so dangerous," I said. "People die sometimes. If you died because of me . . ." Guilt choked me. I thought of those beautiful eyes turned lifeless. The thought made me nauseated. "I couldn't live with myself."

"Stop that." He took my chin and lifted my eyes to his. "No one's going to die. Sanjan will make sure to give me the mildest strain. I'll be fine." He said it with such confidence I could almost believe it.

He led me to the couch. "Try to get some sleep. It's three in the morning and I'm sure it will take me a few hours to arrange everything. I'll just be in the next room if you need anything, 'kay?"

"Okay." I tried to sound strong, confident. Tried not to be weak and pull him onto the couch with me and make him swear to never let me go. But he said we'd be together again. He'd promised. The idea of trust was brand new to me, but I didn't have a choice. I had to trust him.

He smiled and kissed me gently, then went into the other room, turning the light off as he went. I tucked the blankets up around me tight and tried to sleep.

I woke up to Adrien caressing my brow. I sat up, dreamy and smiling, then remembered with a crushing blow that I was going to leave him. But just for a while, I reminded myself. And we wouldn't really be apart. He'd be at school with me. We'd be together, even if I wouldn't know it or remember him.

"It's time," he said. I nodded and rubbed my face as I got to my feet. My eyes still felt swollen and tired. My whole body ached but the sleep had helped.

Adrien led me into the adjoining room that looked like a

combination office and lab. A med table was lodged in one corner and a short middle-aged man stood in front of it.

"Zoe, this is Dr. Chol."

"Greet—I mean, hi, Dr. Chol," I said. I was surprised at his last name—only officials had real last names instead of just work designations.

He smiled and shook my hand. "It's nice to finally meet you. I've heard a lot about you."

I felt my face flush, remembering what Adrien had said about his visions of me as a leader. Did this man Chol think that was true? Did he expect that of me?

"Come on, have a seat," Adrien said. "Chol's our resident head doctor. He'll fix up your hardware so after you pull out the drive, you'll be connected to the Link and the glitching will be masked."

Chol sat down on a chair in front of me. His hair was graying around the edges but his skin was smoother and less worn-looking than Adrien's mother's. "We'll be going in manually, since your access port is already occupied. You've seen these before, right?"

He gestured to a pair of half-tube forceps and a six-inch-long snaking metal probe on the table.

I nodded. I'd had similar procedures done my whole life when new hardware was inserted as I'd grown up, but the probe had never seemed quite so big before.

"I'm going to insert the subware right at one of the back corridors of the already existing hardware, so it shouldn't look anomalous if they run a scan."

He picked up the intimidating instrument and clicked on an ancient video monitor on the table that I guessed he would use to navigate. "Okay. You ready?"

I nodded, hoping he didn't notice my trembling.

He came around to face me, forceps in hand. I tried not to

wince as he inserted the forceps deep into my nose to make a smooth path for the probe. My hands gripped the armrests as the forceps went deeper and deeper. Chol leaned in close, eyes intent on the monitor.

I let out a little whimper before Chol finally said, "There. Got it."

Adrien took my hand. "Just close your eyes and it will be over soon."

I nodded, hearing the clink of metal on metal as the snake probe slid up the shaft provided by the forceps.

"And . . ." Chol said slowly, "we're in. Keep absolutely still."

I swallowed, trying to keep my head still while I did.

Chol was right. This part didn't hurt—much. It was just an incredibly uncomfortable sensation. The occasional tug of the tiny probe felt like bugs squirming under my skull.

Adrien squeezed my hand. "You're doing great. Chol installed all my hardware, which is pretty impressive, since I'd never grown up with any. He's the best." Chol looked over at me and winked. I squeezed Adrien's hand, infinitely glad he was here with me.

After about ten more minutes of trying to sit as still as possible, Chol announced he was done. He slid out the probe, then pulled out the forceps. I jumped off the chair as soon as he was done, rubbing my head to get rid of the sensation. I let the shudder I'd been holding back run through my body, jumping up and down a few times and stretching my neck.

"Your turn," Chol said to Adrien.

I looked at him sympathetically.

He laughed. "Just a routine checkup. No probe for me 'cause my access port is free."

"No probe, huh?" I asked with arched eyebrows. I walked around him and pushed aside his thick bushy hair to look at his input port. I'd never really had the opportunity to look at one up close for very long. I'd seen them everywhere, of course, but it wasn't like I could go up to someone and ask if I could inspect their input port out of curiosity. The tiny lights under the skin lit up along the microfiber wires, and I traced the swirling line gently. The filaments flickered, blues and purples and oranges brightening in reaction to his brain patterns.

I realized with a blush how long my fingers had lingered tangled in Adrien's hair and I dropped my hands. Adrien let out a sigh, and I realized he'd been holding his breath. I smiled shyly, amazed at the completely new experience of sparking emotion in another person.

"Nope, he gets off easy today," Chol said, grinning and pushing Adrien into the chair I'd just vacated. "Let's just plug this in here—" He attached a slim wire cable into the access port in the back of Adrien's neck. "And voilà! Oh. Hang on, this machine is a little temperamental."

Chol banged his hand a few times on a monitor, muttering, "Godlam'd secondhand piece of junk— A-ha! There we go." The screen flickered to life, showing the map of Adrien's internal hardware.

"Now. Let's just make sure he's completely clean and he won't set off their equipment as anomalous when you go back."

I nodded, watching the screen with interest. It looked identical to what we studied in school in my biotech classes. Most of the sliver-thin hardware webbed around the amygdala but tiny branches connected to other nerve receptors all throughout the brain. Chol tapped the screen to zoom in.

"This would work better with a 3-D imaging system," I said, leaning in to look.

Chol smiled. "Yeah, well, we don't exactly have the same resources available to us as the Community. Mostly we get Community discards and junkyard parts. Stuff the Community won't miss. But we manage just fine."

I nodded, watching him check the coding on the tech to make sure it would clear. He was moving too fast for me to really follow all that he was doing. And it wouldn't matter anyway, I thought, pulling back. It's not like I would remember anything I learned here.

If they were able to create an architecture in Adrien's brain that mimicked V-chip hardware, while keeping him protected from Link control, then there had to be a way to do the same thing for everybody else. I wondered what other advances the Rez had made and if that's what they had in mind.

And where did I fit in? Telekinesis was amazing but what good was being able to grab a hairbrush from across the room in the larger scheme of things? I mean, I couldn't even control it.

"We're done." Chol released the cable from Adrien's neck.

"I guess it's time to go back," I whispered.

He nodded. "Mom has a biosuit ready for you."

I stared for a moment into his aquamarine eyes, then hugged him tight. He pulled back. "Shh, it'll be okay. It'll be—"

He didn't finish the sentence. His arms were still pressed around me but his face had gone slack and he was staring beyond me blankly. I looked behind me, terrified at what I might find. But nothing was there.

"Adrien? Adrien!" I tried not to shriek. "What's wrong?"

I shook him but he barely budged. I tried to squirm out of his grip so I could try to get help, but his hands seemed frozen in place around me.

"Adrien!" I said again, feeling near hysterical tears. Was he broken?

He suddenly blinked rapidly and dropped his arms.

"Adrien! Are you okay? Did something go wrong with Chol's programming?" I pushed up the hair at the base of his neck to look at his input port, but his hand stopped mine.

"I just had a vision." His voice came out low and strangled-sounding.

I looked back at his face. His caramel skin was mottled and flushed. There was an intense, unreadable expression on his face.

"What is it?"

His eyes finally focused in again on my face, his features still tense, somewhere between angry and scared. He closed his eyes tightly, tilting his forehead against mine and rubbing his hands up and down my arms gently, as if he was memorizing the feel of my skin. As if he'd never be able to touch me again.

"Oh, Zoe." He cupped my chin gently, tears welling in his bright eyes. "Try not to forget. I know it's impossible, but try not to forget me."

He kissed me again softly, then urgently, twining his fingers in my hair. Whatever he'd just seen had obviously terrified him. I sank against him, overwhelmed at the urgency of his kiss. I kissed him back just as eagerly.

We stood, holding each other's faces, memorizing every last detail. I was desperate with my own need to capture this last, lingering moment, desperate to forget the horrible sink at the pit of my stomach telling me all this would be lost forever once they pulled the chip out. *Please don't let me forget.* I opened my mouth to his and tried to take him in so deep that my soul, if I had one, might remember what my brain forgot.

Chapter 10

"DO YOU REMEMBER anything else from your disappearance?"

"No." I sat in a chair facing a sharp-featured woman with a smooth, oiled bun. It was a seat I had filled every week for the past three weeks. The retina display played out at the edges of my sphere of vision. I didn't need the readouts to provide me with more information on the woman sitting in front of me in a charcoal-gray suit with tightly wound brown hair. Chancellor Bright, the head of the Academy. She'd been appointed the new Chancellor a week after my disappearance. I'd never encountered the previous Chancellor, or many officials at all for that matter, but ever since my disappearance, I was seeing a lot of Chancellor Bright. I didn't know why she kept calling me in—my story was the same every time.

"Do you remember anything that happened while you were on the Surface?"

"No," I repeated. "I still retain only the knowledge of what I reported upon discovery. I was heading to Room A117 and then I was walking down a road. I followed protocol for anomalous events and attempted to locate an official to whom I could report myself. At Entrance Gate C10, I made myself known to the Guards who contacted Central Systems, underwent transport and extensive testing once back at a treatment facility, and was returned to my family quarters by the next evening."

"Yes, I know all that," the woman snapped. She lifted a hand to smooth the side of her hair, collecting herself. She reached over to the table next to her, lifting a teacup and saucer to her lips. She sipped her tea, her eyes studying my face closely.

"Do you know why I've been appointed here?" she asked. She paused as if expecting a response, her eyes again searching before she continued.

"The Uppers requested me specifically for this position because I always produce results. They require an explanation for the assault and subsequent disappearance. I have yet to produce any explanation, and that is unsatisfactory."

She set down her teacup and leaned toward me. "But I don't believe it was your intention to harm anyone. I think someone else was there, perhaps someone who incapacitated you both and then kidnapped you. I'd like to help but you *must* tell me what I want to know." She reached out, touching the top of my hand and piercing me again with her sharp eyes.

"So tell me, Subject Zoel, who else was there? What else did you see outside the city?"

I met her gaze. "I have no details of that time period. I was informed that a memory disrupter was utilized."

Her nostrils flared slightly at my answer. If she were capable of emotion, I would say she seemed frustrated. Her face smoothed, and her eyes looked at me calmly.

"The Uppers will find this highly dissatisfying. These anomalous events are grounds for deactivation, but it is at my command that you remain here at the Academy." Her face shifted suddenly and she seemed about to say something else to me, but she sighed as if she thought better of it. Her eyes flicked to a black circle on the ceiling of her office.

"I trust my command will not have to be overridden due to additional anomalous behavior. You will notify me immediately of any anomalous behavior you observe in your systems."

I stood, a slight tremor passing through my hands. "I will report to you directly if anything does occur. Community first, Community always."

I had turned toward the door when suddenly the Link dropped, knocking me off balance with the sudden rush assaulting my senses: the musty smell of the carpet in the room, the acrid taste in my mouth left over from my daily dietary supplement, a choking rush of fear. It was dizzying, but with all of my strength, I willed myself not to reach out to steady myself. The beeping of my heart monitor filled the room.

I bit my lip, willing myself to stop shaking from wave after wave of clear, vibrant sensation. My head was buzzing in fear, and my hands started to tremble and pulse with heat. I willed myself to be still, to not show the panic that had gripped every part of my body.

"Subject Zoel Q-24," the Chancellor said, crossing the room in a few quick strides.

Oh no, oh no, oh no.

"What is the cause of this disturbance?"

I squeezed my eyes and took a deep breath. There had to be an explanation she'd believe—something that would save me from the deactivation that she'd seemed all too ready to command. I reached a hand down to rub my shin. I took my time, breathing in slowly and thinking of Markan. I had to be still, for Markan. If he ever glitched, he would have to struggle all alone if I didn't survive. By the time I raised my head to look at her, I'd managed to collect myself.

"I miscalculated the distance from that chair." I tried to keep my voice to its previous monotone. "I imagine the pain adrenal response tripped my monitor."

She leaned in closer, tilting her head to the side in a way that made her sharp-featured face seem birdlike. Something about her gaze made my scalp tingle. "Are you certain? Tell me again what just occurred."

I forced myself to return her piercing gaze without looking away. I repeated my previous explanation. She said nothing, only continued her unnerving stare like she could see right through my skin to my glitching V-chip.

"May I leave, Chancellor?" I asked, finally breathing calmly enough that my monitor fell silent.

She pursed her lips tightly, making the tiny lines around her lips multiply and crinkle. She pinched her face and leaned in, putting a hand on my arm. She paused, as if stopping herself, and pulled away, quickly rearranging her features into either a smile or a grimace. I could not tell which.

She held my gaze for another too-long moment before nodding to the door. "You may leave."

I turned on my heel and tried to walk as calmly as I could manage out the door and down to the elevator, pausing to slow my heart rate and quiet my monitor. Glitching like that in front of the Chancellor herself. This was becoming far too dangerous.

What was wrong with me? What I'd told the Chancellor had been the truth—I didn't remember anything before I was discovered walking down a Surface road. But now that I was no longer Linked, reliving the memories of walking down the dusty road in the bright orange suit filled me with terror. I'd been on the Surface! I shuddered, remembering the huge open sky over my head. How did I get there? A chill raced down my spine. And why was I still alive?

Every step I took felt like walking farther and farther into enemy territory. But there was no option for retreat. No safe place, no refuge for me. I was knee-deep and surrounded on all sides.

My lungs tightened in my chest at the thought. Panic bubbled up even as I tried to swallow it back down. But still, my breathing became shallower. I looked around. Even in this empty hallway, my skin crawled with the sense that I was being watched.

I glanced up almost involuntarily at the ceiling and saw the small black circles embedded every ten paces. Something about them tugged at the edges of my mind and made me feel uneasy. I didn't know why. But what if . . . What if it was a memory from my time away? But that was impossible. None of it had been stored on my internal memory chip because of the disrupter.

Panic spiked at the reminder, sending shooting sparks up and down my arms. Before I could control it, several loud pops sounded and thin tendrils of smoke escaped out of the black circle directly above me. I looked up in surprise, then spun around sharply as I heard the sound behind me. One by one, each of the black circles behind me down the hallway let out a pop, hiss, and cloud of smoke.

I swiveled back around and headed away as quickly as I could. I needed to get out of here, *now.*

Stupid, stupid, I chided myself. All I wanted was to avoid drawing any attention to myself and after three weeks without a single glitch, I was suddenly out of control and creating all kinds of anomalies.

I tried to quickly and calmly remove myself from the hallway before I was spotted. I couldn't be connected with what just happened. Just as I was about to round the corner, I heard loud footsteps behind me. It took every ounce of self-discipline I had not to look backward.

It was probably just another Academy student. Nothing to worry about.

Except that the footsteps sounded heavy. Really heavy. Metal-reinforced-feet kind of heavy.

It must be a Regulator. At this point he must be walking right through the smoke spilling from the black circles on the ceiling. He had to have noticed, and as I was the only person around, he would know I must've had something to do with it.

I quickened my footsteps down a narrow gray hallway, hoping to make it to the next cross tunnel at the end before he rounded the corner.

"Halt, subject."

I should have paused and stayed calm. I should have answered his questions and pretended to be a bystander who'd just happened to be walking down the hallway when the ceiling equipment shorted out. I should have, but I didn't.

I ran.

I sprinted down the adjoining hallway, hoping the surprise from my illogical behavior might make the Regulator pause to reassess protocol procedures. Foolish, since in the end it would only mean that they'd have more evidence of anomalies against me.

But I'd already bolted and there was no going back now. I forced myself not to look over my shoulder, even though I heard his heavy footsteps start again behind me. If he was able to do a scan and get facial recognition, I'd be cracked for sure. I had to get out of his range. I ran faster, pouring my panic into my feet. Behind me I could hear the loud clang of the Regulator's boots as his pace sped up to match mine. I turned in to another snaking hallway, knowing it was only a matter of time before he caught up with me or I ran into someone else who would note me as anomalous. But then I realized where I was, and why there were no other subjects around, and an idea sparked.

I turned sharply around another corner and paused for just a moment to pull a hair tie from my pocket before sprinting down the hall. I gathered my fluffy flying hair into a tight bun. I could still hear the hydraulic hiss of the Regulator's boots as he pounded his way into the hallway behind me. I hoped he hadn't seen me too clearly.

I took the left branch into another hall and stopped short. A herd of students filled the width of the hall, filing slowly past me in the direction of the cafeteria. Lunchtime. I forced myself to breathe normally and keep my heart monitor still. I stiffened my back into the ramrod posture of all subjects and eased into the crowd. Over my shoulder I heard the Regulator reach the end of the hall behind me, but I kept walking steadily forward, not daring to look. Students flanked me on all sides, a slow tide of gray bodies sweeping down the hallway.

Inside, my mind was screaming to run, escape, but I forced my limbs to move slowly. I kept my face perfectly still as I passed by the Regulator. He was scanning the crowd along with the rest of the nearby Regulators, but his eyes passed right over me.

For the first time, I was glad for the monotony, glad we all looked exactly the same. Maybe I did have a place to hide after all. In plain sight, camouflaged by looking exactly like every other drone around me.

"Greetings, Zoel," Maximin said when I sat down at my customary place at table 13. I was still glitching, and my nerves were frayed. I was glad to see a familiar face, and when he requested assistance with neurochem, I wanted to hug him for being something normal and reliable. But my mind was still wrapped up in the terrifying events of the morning.

Not to mention I still had no idea what had happened during my disappearance. I'd not only found myself on the deadly Surface, with no explanation, but somehow the diagnostics had *not* discovered anything anomalous in me? Not the glitches, not my ability, *nothing*? Or had they discovered it all and fixed me? In that case, after three weeks of silence, why was I broken again?

"Zoel?" Maximin asked.

I looked back over at him, realizing I hadn't heard a word he'd said.

"Pardon my lapse in concentration." I counted to ten over and over in my head to calm down. I clicked through my text tablet to get to the lesson we were studying, but my mind was racing. Nothing made sense.

I took a long sip of the fruit supplement on my tray. The thick fruity concoction shocked me with its flavor. My eyes widened momentarily, and I barely recovered enough to keep a surprised gasp to myself. I looked at the smooth pink liquid in the stainless-steel cup, trying to identify each individual taste. Peaches. Maybe mango, too. I inspected the liquid closer and saw tiny black seeds. Strawberries. That was the other flavor. Every taste was suddenly and overwhelmingly strong.

"Zoel?"

I chided myself internally. I was completely shaken up today, but I had to go back to basics. Just as I'd practiced for so long, I had to remember that the first rule of glitching was to keep it hidden.

But to make matters worse, the dark-haired boy with aquamarine eyes was back. The same one I'd thought could be a Monitor. It seemed like everyone was watching me more closely since my disappearance, right when my glitches were suddenly the most difficult to keep under control.

I searched my memories. His case of Flu 216 had caused an Academy-wide priority vaccination. Could it be just a coincidence that it happened at the same time as my disappearance? I didn't know what to believe anymore, but I knew I had to stay away from him. I couldn't trust myself to hide my glitches anymore, and even though the boy didn't turn his eyes to me once during the entire class, I had the prickling sensation that he was acutely aware of my every breath.

I was glad when we were released from classes and I was able to make my way to the subway station, away from such constant observation. I longed for the peace and quiet of my personal quarters. I could have sworn that when I'd first started glitching, everything had gone slower. It had been a gradual awakening to feeling and sensation and emotion.

This time I felt like I'd just been dumped in a tub of ice water. I didn't know if it was just because it had come back all at once, or if something had gotten knocked loose in me while I was away. The glitches were sudden, random, and more intense than anything I'd felt before. I had no idea why, which made it all the more terrifying. I couldn't afford to attract any more attention than I already did, but I couldn't even trust my own body not to betray me.

The train ride back to my quarters set my teeth on edge. The screeching as the train rounded each corner made me jolt in surprise. It felt like the train was skidding and sparking on the edge of my jarred nerves. Bodies were all packed in tightly together, swaying in unison to the rhythm of the train. It was suffocating. I wanted to close my eyes and stop up my ears. I needed to escape, to hide. But there was nowhere I could go. Nowhere I was truly safe.

Home.

I was surprised at the overwhelming emotion I felt at the word. Walking in the door, I felt the stinging in my eyes and leaned my head back against the doorframe for a moment, taking in a breath of relief before heading to my quarters.

"Greetings, Zoel," my brother said when I passed by his room.

"Greetings, Markan," I said, stopping at his door. He'd been sitting in the chair at his desk underneath his loft bed, staring blankly at the wall. I recognized the pose. It was the default position for Scheduled Subject Downtime. In the afternoons after Academy, calming Link harmonic sounds played, putting subjects in a kind of trance, a scheduled break to support efficiency and productivity. Looking at him made me swallow hard. He looked peaceful. But at what price?

I barely stopped myself from going into the room and putting my arms around him. The impulse made me pause. I didn't know why I thought that touching a person could bring comfort, but I felt sure of it.

"Are Mother and Father home?" I asked, wanting any excuse to linger and talk to him.

"No. They don't arrive home until ten p.m. You should know that."

I nodded. "Of course." I couldn't stop looking at him. He seemed to have grown in the past month. His shoulders seemed wider. At thirteen, I supposed I could expect his physical appearance to change rapidly as he entered puberty. But no sign of any glitches yet, and no guarantee they would ever come. Each year edged him closer to adulthood, and the impossibility of ever glitching or feeling emotion. And then he'd turn eighteen and be lost forever. The thought pulled at something in my chest.

"Do you require something?" Markan asked.

"No," I said. "I'll let you know when I finish with the treadmill so you can do your evening session before dinner."

He nodded and then moved his attention back to the wall, or rather, the Link. I took one last lingering look, then went into my tiny, compact room and changed.

Before I headed out to the treadmill, I shut the door to my room and reached my fingers into the slit in my mattress.

My drawings were gone.

Panic spiked in my chest. They couldn't be gone! I hadn't been deactivated, or taken away. I reached farther into the mattress. Still nothing. I frantically lifted the mattress to look underneath, all the while my mind racing, each thought worse than the last. If they'd been found—

There they were! My searching fingers grabbed on to the crinkling papers that were piled under the mattress at the foot of the bed. I slumped against the wall in relief, then felt like laughing and crying at the same time.

But my relief was short-lived—it was the wrong spot for my drawings. I was always so careful to hide them *in* the mattress. I strained to remember my last drawing session. I was almost sure I'd put them back in the right place. What if . . . what if someone *had* found them?

I shook my head and banished the thought. That was ridiculous. I wouldn't be here if any of my drawings had been found. There was no way they'd have allowed me to live. I must have been careless somehow. All this fear and pressure and strain was making me crack around the edges.

I took several deep breaths, hoping to stop the panic from setting off my heart monitor, but I couldn't stop the alarm going off in my head. Nothing made sense anymore. The feeling I had when I entered our house unit, the safety and comfortable familiarity, was gone.

I lifted a hand to the wall separating my room from Markan's. I was sure there could be so much more to him than a body staring blankly at a wall, but I wasn't sure if I'd survive long enough to see it.

I swiped at my stinging eyes, hid the drawings, then went to exercise. For as long as I could, I had to at least pretend that nothing was wrong. It felt good to run, to feel the pounding rhythm of my feet hitting the track. It made me feel alive and, at the same time, calm inside. For the first time since I'd glitched this afternoon, I was able to let go, just for a moment, and forget about whatever had happened when I'd arrived at Room A117 three weeks ago.

I woke up in the middle of the night to the beeping of my heart monitor. I must have still been glitching in my sleep. I scrambled out of my blanket. It took me several horrifying moments to realize I was in my room, not drowning in a raging tide of water. I sat up and put my back against the cool wall, gulping in breath after breath. I wiped the sweat off my forehead with my forearm. After another couple of minutes, my heart calmed down and I closed my eyes, trying not to relive the terror of flailing uselessly in water.

Markan had been there too, drowning with me, begging for my help, but I couldn't do anything. I just watched helplessly, trying to keep myself above water while he sank underneath. He never came back to the surface, and it was my fault. Horror and guilt were thick in my throat. I swallowed hard and went to the bathroom to get a glass of water.

Dreams. Nightmares. Darkness. I'd forgotten about those parts of glitching. I didn't miss them. The Link directed REM patterns and sleep cycles and no one ever experienced disrupted sleep.

I rubbed my face in both of my hands once I was back in my room. Ugh, how had I done this before? How had I kept all this to myself and managed to stay sane? Even in my sleep I wasn't safe. Then I frowned, thinking about the dream—there'd been so much water rushing by, more than I'd ever seen in real life. I closed my eyes and tried to envision the scene again but the memory of it was fading.

I climbed back in bed and tried to get back to sleep, but it was impossible. I got out of bed quickly and pulled out a clean paper bag from our bimonthly Materials Allotment and the marker I stowed under the foot of the mattress. The drawings could be dangerous, I saw that now. I'd find a way to destroy it or get rid of it after, but I still had to get the image out of my head and onto paper. I lay down with my head near the tiny night auxiliary light cell in the wall so I could see the paper. I concentrated hard, determined to learn something—anything.

I sketched out the mass of flowing water. A couple of times, I was remembering it so clearly, I felt bowled over by the sensation of being soaked through, shivering in terror. But then I tried to pull back from the scenario, to see from the outside rather than from within. I needed to simply record every detail about the scene. I kept going, trying not to think, only to draw in the dim light. When I finally stopped, I'd covered one entire side of the crumpled bag. I put the marker away and laid it down to try to figure out what the images meant. Mostly the page was covered with the roiling mass of water, edged only by the circular walls.

There was a figure in the water—it was Markan but at the same time, it wasn't quite Markan.

I frowned, looking at the face I'd drawn. Markan looked older in the picture than he was in real life—his cheekbones were sharper, all the baby fat gone. He kept showing up in my dreams—sometimes in this new drowning dream, or in the old dream of the glitching boy being chased down. Always with Markan's face staring straight at me in absolute horror. And why did I wake up feeling like it was all my fault?

"Greetings, Zoel," Maximin said as I sat down at lunch a few days later. I almost smiled at his predictability. I waited patiently for him to request my help with the lesson.

"Greetings, Maximin."

"Would you be amenable to tutoring me after school? I have received authorization for you to come to my housing unit after school hours."

My fork paused midway to my mouth. I kept the surprise off my face. I guess I'd heard of other students doing this. It was just so completely against my mission to stay below the radar, out of suspicion.

But I had no logical reason to say no. "Yes, I would be amenable," I finally managed to say.

"I will meet you after school then at the Central Subway System entrance."

"Okay," I said, still a little stunned. We spent the rest of lunch studying but I was uneasy now that my routine had been disturbed. If abnormal things kept on happening, how could I pretend everything was normal?

We went to a different subway line than the one I usually took. Other than a few voices here and there, the almost fifty people waiting were silent. I didn't know why the silence sounded so loud today—it had been like this my whole life. But then, everything felt new again without the shield of numbness the Link provided. I'd been glitching the entire day. As I looked at the blank faces around me, I thought about the three whole weeks I'd spent as a walking drone, just like all of them. It made me shiver.

"Are you cold?" Maximin asked. He stepped closer.

"Just a draft," I said, pulling back a little bit from his chest. I knew the proximity meant nothing to all the people around me, but I'd noticed lately that touching other people made me feel different emotions. When I brushed up accidentally against my parents or Markan at home, it felt nice, as if somehow their touch could ward off the bad dreams. It was illogical, I knew, and I was sure I was just so eager for any sign that

I was not completely and utterly alone. There could be no real comfort in the closeness of my family unit, but I still felt it all the same.

Maximin leaned in close and I could smell the musky scent of his soap. It made me feel strange inside and I pulled back. It wasn't just the normal strange feeling of being close to someone. There was something else I couldn't quite define—something that made me uneasy. We were a wrong fit, like unmatching puzzle pieces.

After about half an hour, Maximin announced his stop was next. He lived farther from the school than I did, but the tunnel from the subway platform to his housing grid looked exactly the same as mine. Same low-ceilinged space, same gray concrete dirtying around the edges, leading to the same bay of elevators that led up and down to units in the eight-level housing blocks. Monotony was the rule, even in city design.

I glanced over at Maximin and was surprised by his steady gaze. I almost frowned at how long he'd kept his eyes on me before he looked away.

"Here we are." He touched a finger to a small panel beside one of the middle elevators and we waited in silence. I looked around at the others waiting—they were mostly adolescents, our age or younger, returning from the Academy.

The elevator pinged at Maximin's floor and we stepped off. I followed him down the hallway to his apartment and watched him wave his wrist in front of the sensor beside the door, and I realized that Maximin and I would be alone in his home. Adults usually worked eleven or twelve hours a day, especially when they were still young enough to be productive and not tire easily.

In less than a year, I would be just like them. After finishing at the Academy, I'd get my final V-chip and begin working at one of the bioengineering firms, slowly progressing through the ranks as my knowledge base and ability were tested each year. That is, if I didn't get deactivated first. And what if I never got caught, and I became another adult drone, incapable of ever feeling again? I'd be safe, but was that even worth it anymore? Whittling away my life every day, completely empty inside as I worked until I was exhausted, slept, and then woke up the next morning just to do it all over again? And then one day I would be genetically paired with another person, someone who felt nothing, thought nothing, had never known beauty or fear or joy.

That future stretched out before me, a lightless road that was my only reward if I managed to keep my anomalies undetected.

An angry heat rushed to my face. No. I couldn't do it. That wouldn't be my life.

Escape. The word whispered with a red thrumming energy through my mind.

My glitches were more unpredictable than ever. The sensations during glitches were overwhelmingly strong and I couldn't always mask them. At the same time, there were more eyes scrutinizing me than ever before. All this added up to an invisible noose around my neck, squeezing tighter and tighter. It would cinch closed eventually.

I had to stay completely off the radar for as long as it took until I was no longer under constant observation from the Chancellor, the Monitor boy with his aquamarine eyes, and the patrolling Regulators. Then I would need to find somewhere to hide, to disappear, to glitch freely and live undetected for as long as possible until my inevitable capture and deactivation. I wasn't sure any of this was possible, but I suddenly knew I had to try.

I was so wrapped up in my distressing thoughts that I was completely unprepared when Maximin closed the apartment door behind us and spun around quickly to face me. He wrapped his arms around me, pulling me into his chest.

"Zoel, I was so worried when you disappeared," he whispered fiercely. "I'm so happy you're back."

He put his lips to my ear and his lips fluttered down my jawline. "You don't know how long I've waited to do this."

He dropped his lips to my mouth.

Chapter 11

"MAXIMIN!" I PUSHED BACK in surprise before his lips could touch mine. My mind immediately hummed with fear and confusion. "What are you doing?"

He smiled, dimples I never knew he had appearing on both cheeks. My mouth dropped open slightly. "Zoel, I've wanted to tell you for so long, ever since I noticed you'd started glitching too."

My chest cinched up in fear, my mind racing through every possibility. Was this a test? Was I being watched right now? I looked down the narrow walls of his entryway before looking back warily at him. My eye paused on a black circle installed on the hallway ceiling.

The look on Maximin's face made me soften. This was *Maximin*, not some spying Monitor.

Still, I held my features in a calm, blank expression, willfully quieting the energy racing up and down my arms as I gestured robotically to the hall.

"Let's go to your personal quarters," I said.

He nodded and grabbed my hand to pull me down a short hallway. His house was set up like mine, only in reverse—the tiny entryway led to narrow hallways with four small offshooting rooms to the left instead of the right and a bathroom at the end. We turned in to the second sleeping compartment.

He slid the door closed behind him, still smiling. His gray

shirt looked out of place next to his flushed cheeks and bright brown eyes. He looked so animated and alive, I barely recognized him.

"And it's Max, not Maximin," he said, still not letting my hand go.

I felt excitement rise up inside even though I knew I ought to be cautious. But it only made sense—there was no other explanation for the expression on his face. It was impossible, too incredible to be true, but at the same time I wanted to believe him more than anything.

"When did you start glitching?" I asked, still torn between caution and hope.

"Three months ago." He sat on the edge of the desk that was underneath his loft bed. He gestured for me to take the chair. I looked around—his room looked exactly like mine, down to the same shade of gray painted on the wall.

"About a month before you did," he said. "I was so scared at first but then when I saw you get this alert look on your face at school sometimes, I knew I wasn't alone. That's why I asked you to tutor me in the first place, so I could be close to someone else who was glitching."

"Why didn't you say something sooner?" I sat down in the chair, overwhelmed by the implications of what he'd just said. *Not alone.* Wasn't that what I'd been wishing for?

I studied Max's face again, unsure whether I could truly trust what I saw. He had a sharp, aware look on his face—the same expression I'd always hoped to see in my brother.

I squeezed his hand.

"I was going to tell you but I could never find the right moment. And then when you disappeared . . ." He shook his head. "Zoel, you don't know—"

"Zoe," I interrupted. "I want to be called Zoe."

"Zoe. I like it." Max smiled briefly. "Anyway, I was so terrified to lose you when you disappeared. I kept thinking, maybe if I'd told you sooner, maybe it would have made a difference."

"I don't know," I said. "I don't remember anything about what happened to me—where I went, or who I was with—I have no idea."

"And they didn't notice anything out of the ordinary when you came back? When they ran the diagnostics?" He watched my face carefully.

I shook my head. "No. Nothing. When I got back, I wasn't glitching anymore, at least not for a few weeks. So whenever they'd run the tests, everything looked fine. But . . ." I swallowed hard, afraid to voice the fear I'd been working so hard to bury. I cleared my throat. "Now that I *am* glitching again, next time I have a diagnostic, I'll test anomalously."

"I'll help you." Max's narrow lips tightened, making his face look suddenly intense. His hand gripped mine harder. "I won't let them do anything to you."

I smiled sadly. It felt nice to have someone want to protect me, even though I knew it wouldn't do any good.

"Max, if I get caught, there's nothing you can do."

He smiled sideways at me and leaned in close. "Not necessarily."

"What do you mean?"

"Zoe, don't you see?" He laughed; then his eyebrows lowered. When I didn't respond, he looked unsure.

"I thought if you were glitching like me, that meant we had other things in common as well." He paused, swallowing. "The . . . powers?"

"Wait," I said slowly. "Are you saying you can move things with your mind?"

"What?" He seemed confused.

I kept my mouth tightly closed, suddenly afraid I had betrayed too much, too soon. Moments later, a look of amazement crossed Max's face.

"Whoa!" His eyebrows shot up high. "That's not what I meant. Well, I guess it makes sense that we might change in different ways. I have another power."

"What is it?" I was full of relief, and both thrilled and scared to know the answer. Talking about any of this felt dangerous. I wondered if it was foolish that, after being so cautious, I'd suddenly opened up to Max without any hesitation.

"Okay, don't be alarmed. I'm going to show you what I can do." He closed his eyes and sat perfectly still for a moment. Then the air around him seemed to shimmer, reflecting the light.

In the time it took me to blink, Max was gone and the Chancellor was sitting in his place.

I fell backward off the chair, my breath coming out in a strangled gasp. It *had* been a trick. The Chancellor must have had a subprogram installed at my last diagnostic to trick me into talking to Max, revealing my secrets.

I scrambled back against the wall in my panic. If I could just get past her, then I might be able to get out the door and—

I looked back up at the person leaning on the table. Suddenly it was Max again, and he was laughing.

"Stop it—" I said, my voice hysterical. How was she doing this to me? I grabbed the back of my neck to see if there was anything in my port. "Get out of my head!"

"Zoe." The person who looked like Max seemed alarmed. "It's just me, it's just me, okay?" He leaned closer and I flinched, my heart monitor beeping.

"Zoe it's me, it's Max," he said again, his face concerned. He reached out to put a hand on my arm, then thought better of it. "I'm sorry. I didn't mean to scare you. The Chancellor wasn't actually here. I just took her shape. Zoe, it's still me."

I was huddled on the ground with my hands up, but something in the tone of his voice made me stop and look at him. "But—" I searched his face. It looked like him, so real, but I didn't know what to trust anymore. Water streamed down my cheeks.

"Oh no, Zoe," Max said, his eyebrows bunched up high. "I didn't think it would scare you. I didn't think about it. You're safe. I promise."

I got back to my feet and edged closer to Max, still cautious. I kept one eye on the door, ready to dart past him and escape. It did look like him, but still, what he was suggesting . . .

"This is—"

"Impossible?" he said, smiling now, his face relaxing. "I know. But it's true."

I sat down on the chair by Max and reached up tentatively to touch his face, still half afraid. "Do it again," I said, my voice shaky. "But not the Chancellor this time."

He grinned, and a second later a girl was sitting in front of me with pale skin and dark curly hair pulled up into a hair clip. It took me a second for recognition to register.

"It's me!" I finally exclaimed. I watched my face break into a smile. I leaned forward in curiosity. We had little use for mirrors in the Community. My lips were fuller than I'd imagined and my cheeks were rounded. But my nose was bigger too. I frowned, leaning in to examine myself more closely. Max changed back to himself, grinning widely.

I lifted a hand to my cheek and nose without thinking, still lost for a second in the memory of my face. Then I realized the ramifications of what Max said he could do and looked up at him sharply.

"But how?" I asked. "What I can do with my mind, it's improbable, but it still feels like it's within the realm of possibility, at least if you stretch certain theories on the transference of energy. But this." I shook my head and traced the line of his blond eyebrow with my forefinger. "Your body actually changes shape? How is that possible? The amount of energy necessary for the cellular reproduction—"

"I seem to project a mental field that affects anyone around me," Max cut in.

"But it looked exactly like her! How were you able to control such detail?"

"I'm not projecting an image—I'm literally affecting what and who *you* see. I make it so that you expect to see the Chancellor and boom, that's what you see. To myself in the mirror, I look the same. But to everyone else, even the mirror would reflect who I wanted them to see."

"Crackin' hell," I whispered in awe.

"What?" Max asked.

"Nothing." I frowned, not knowing where the strange phrase had come from. I shook my head. There were bigger things to focus on here.

"So," I said slowly, trying to puzzle it out. "You, what, think of the person you want the people in your . . . your projected area to see? And then, it just happens? Do you feel anything?"

He nodded. "Yeah, I guess I kind of hear this high-pitched buzzing noise in my ears. And then I *will* it to happen and it just does. It wasn't as easy at the beginning. I've been practicing."

"I can barely believe this," I whispered, still in shock. "Do you have the dreams, too?"

His eyes widened and he smiled. "Yeah, I do. I mean, at least that's one good part of all this."

"Good part?" I asked, confused. "You think the dreams are *good*?"

He looked uncertain. "Are we talking about two different things again?"

"My dreams are terrifying. Aren't yours?"

He smiled, a slow grin that edged across his face. "I've had a couple of the bad dreams. But for the most part, it's the other kind."

"Other kind?"

"You know," he said. "The good-feeling kind. Pleasurable."

Pleasurable. I'd only heard the word used to talk about the destruction of the world. "I'm not sure I know what you mean. Pleasure is wrong."

"No!" His eyes opened wide. "Pleasure is wonderful. Really. I'm surprised you haven't found it out on your own. I thought for sure anyone glitching would discover it right away like I did. Can I look at your genitalia?"

"What?" My voice hitched up an octave.

"Aren't you curious? I could try to show you what I mean." He moved closer so that our legs were touching. He leaned down and put a hand on my knee. "I've thought about you for so long."

"You have?" I looked down at his hand on my knee in confusion.

"Do you even know how beautiful you are?" he whispered. He moved his hand from my knee to my hair; pushing away a stray strand and then reaching back to undo the clip keeping the rest in place. My hair tumbled around my face and he leaned in and inhaled. His face was so close to mine, it made my breathing erratic.

"Do you ever think about me?" He pulled me close and slid his hands down my back.

I frowned. "Maybe."

I focused on the pressure of his hands. They moved farther down. It felt kind of nice. But it also felt weird. Then he squeezed and I jerked away quickly, scooting out of the chair and over to the wall.

"What's wrong?"

I crossed my arms over my chest. "This is all new to me, and too fast. I don't want to do any more of that right now."

"Oh." He seemed surprised. He sat back.

I was starting to get irritated. "You just told me that you glitch, too, and that you have all these powers. I want to talk about *that*."

"But don't you want to know about the pleasure?"

"Maybe later," I said uncertainly.

He nodded. "Later, then. I guess it can all be kind of confusing at first."

I nodded and let out a small laugh. It sounded strange in the tiny room and I put a hand to my mouth in fearful reflex. Max was grinning at me, though. He understood. I could laugh in front of him. I could finally share all the things I'd been feeling. I grinned back, feeling warm inside.

"So, show me what you can do," he said.

I blinked a few times and frowned. "It always just kind of happens," I said after a moment. "I don't know if I can *make* it happen."

He shrugged. "That's odd. I'm able to control mine."

I frowned deeper. It was always something I'd been so afraid of happening. It was too dangerous, too conspicuous. I'd never thought about trying to do it on purpose.

"Okay," I said slowly. "I'll try."

I looked at the pillow placed neatly at the top of his bunk. It was small and light. It should be easy. I stared at it, willing it to move.

Nothing. Not even a twitch. I reached my arms out, trying to focus my thoughts and energy through the extension of my fingers. Max shifted awkwardly in his seat while I concentrated, gritting my teeth and staring at the pillow for another five minutes. I finally gave up, a sheen of sweat glistening on my brow.

"I've been glitching longer than you," Max said. "I'm sure it will get easier the longer you try."

"Maybe," I said, still frowning at the pillow. I felt frustrated that it hadn't worked. Max had seemed excited about his power, and I was disappointed I couldn't show him mine.

"So what about when you disappeared? What happened? Where'd you go?" He leaned back on the desk so his back was against the wall.

I told him everything I remembered, and it was a relief to tell the story to someone other than the Chancellor.

"Nothing feels different, but I know something must have happened to me, to my body. And why didn't the diagnostics pick up anything anomalous when I returned?"

"I snuck a peek at some of your records after you returned and everything tested normal," Max said. "I've seen other things though. They can do whatever they want and then lie about it."

"How do you know that?"

He smiled and raised an eyebrow. "When you look like the Chancellor or other instructors you'd be surprised at the things you can see and overhear. At what people will tell you straight to your face."

"Max!" I said. "That's so dangerous! What if they caught you?"

He laughed. "I'm careful. I don't really go walking around as the Chancellor. I usually try to be someone inconspicuous. Someone no one notices or bothers to be careful around. Besides, no one knows what I can do. They don't even suspect. No one knows but you."

The thought made me feel warm and cold at the same time. He trusted me with his secret. But at the same time, it was another burden to carry and keep safe. Then again, maybe everyone other than the Link drones had secrets.

"So what have you found out?" I asked. "If they're lying to us, what are they trying to hide?"

"I don't know all of it yet. But it's a lot, Zoe."

Prickles ran up and down my arms. And it wasn't just fear now, there was something else bubbling to a boil inside me— anger. I was so happy to have someone like me to talk to, but what about everybody else? What about all the people who would never get to experience these beautiful senses and emotions? Was the life the Uppers forced us to live as unthinking, unfeeling drones, really all that different a fate from being deactivated altogether?

What if— An idea sparked inside me like a flash of fire. What if, with more information, we could find a way to save others, to let everyone feel the things Max and I were feeling now?

"Max, we have to find out." I grabbed his hand. "Just think about it—all of those kids in the Academy with us, Linked and never knowing anything different." The more I thought about it, the angrier I got. "What they're doing to us all is wrong!"

Max lifted his shoulders with a shrug, but he didn't let go of my hand. "It's not like we can change things. The Community is too big. I've been listening for a while and this thing is global. We don't stand a chance against something so powerful."

"But then why do you risk so much to find out information?" My anger turned to a tingling excitement. I stood up, pulling my hand out of his as I did, and paced in the small space. "It's because you want to know, you *need* to know. Well, I need to know too. Maybe everybody needs to know."

I thought about my brother and the empty look on his face during SSD. Just telling him about the lies wouldn't be enough.

He wouldn't understand, not while he was still under the control of the Link.

"We need more than information," I said with more certainty. "What if we could *do* something about it?" My mind was spinning with the possibilities. I'd thought escape was the only answer, but what if there was another way? A way for everyone to be safe. "Maybe the Uppers and officials work so hard to control information because they know if enough people knew the truth, they'd lose their grip on us."

Max laughed. "All we need to *do*—" He pulled me lightly down beside him again, his thigh side by side with mine. "—is survive and learn how to work the system. I want to help you survive, too. Whatever happened to you on the Surface—it's even more reason not to take risks. But we can still stay safe and find a way to have a happy life. You and me together."

"A happy life?" I asked, incredulous.

"Don't you see? We've been given these gifts and we need to enjoy them. We can't risk losing it. We're special. Different from everybody else."

"But what if other people at the Academy are glitching?" The excitement rose up again. "If enough people started glitching, then we'd be able to unite together and find a way to change things."

"Zoe, you can't—" He stopped suddenly, cocking his head sideways. "Wait. I just heard the front door. One of my parents is home." He pulled me to my feet. "We can talk more later. I arranged another home tutor session in two days."

I held on to his arm, suddenly afraid of leaving him, of having to go back out into a world where I couldn't be myself. Where I had to walk around constantly fearful someone was going to discover my secrets. Where I'd suffer the sick feeling of walking side by side with people who were so abused and used, but didn't even know they were victims.

Max reached out to open the door, then stopped and turned to me, wrapping his arms around me tight. I leaned my head into his chest, surprised by how good it felt to be held. He was right—touching did feel good. It made me feel so overwhelmingly safe.

We stood like that, holding each other tightly until the click of his parent's shoes sounded in the hallway. He let me go and I quickly tucked my mussed hair back into its clip.

"Greetings, Mother. This is Zoel Q-24."

"Greetings, Maximin. Greetings, Zoel," his mother said, her face blank and emotionless. "Was the tutoring session productive?"

"Yes." Max turned to me. "I'll see you in two days for follow-up?"

His mother continued by and he turned back to me and winked. I grabbed my tablet case and headed out the door, my mind spinning. More secrets, piling up on other secrets. I was both thrilled and afraid. But at least now I had someone to help me bear them. The memory of how safe I'd felt in Max's arms made me smile long after I'd turned the lights out that night. I wasn't alone anymore.

The next day at school, I was constantly aware of Max. I couldn't stop sneaking looks at him across the hall or the classroom or at the lunchroom table. He never looked anomalous once. I wondered if he could give me tips. He'd told me he was mostly disconnected from the Link these days, but from what I could see, he hid it perfectly.

At lunch, we went through our normal tutoring ritual—though now I wondered if he'd actually needed the tutoring in the first place. He only seemed to be watching me, not the texts or notes. And then there was the way he would touch me whenever possible. He'd put his hand casually in contact with mine on the table, or he'd press our legs together underneath the table.

"Can I try something?" he said when I went over to his housing unit two afternoons later. He shut his bedroom door, even though his mother and father would not be home for at least another hour.

"What?"

"I want to touch your lips with mine."

"Why?"

"Because I think it will feel really good. For both of us. We can stop if you don't like it."

"Okay . . ."

He pulled me close eagerly and smashed his lips against mine roughly. I felt his tongue moving to open my lips. It felt wet and when I opened my mouth like he seemed to want, our teeth clicked against each other awkwardly.

I stood stiffly with my eyes open, watching his face and trying to measure how I was feeling, trying to understand what pleasure *felt* like. I thought about pulling away, but he'd been so glowing and excited about trying and he'd seemed so sure I would like it, too. He sucked on one of my lips for a second, which mainly just felt strange, but maybe nice. I wasn't sure.

He pulled away, smiling. "Did you feel it?" His lips were wet and his face was flushed.

I didn't want to dampen his excitement. "Um. Maybe."

He broke into a giant grin. It was like his whole face lit up, and I suddenly noticed how well formed he was. His face was square with a wide, strong jaw. He seemed to exude strength. I reached up tentatively and touched his short blond hair at the crown of his forehead. He closed his eyes and sighed, putting his hand over mine and pressing it to his face.

He leaned down, burying his face in my neck. "You're all I can think about. Your lips. Your body. Your legs, your back."

He cupped my hips and pulled me into his, nuzzling his face at the base of my neck.

I laughed and pulled away. "There's so many things I want to talk about and we don't have much time."

He sighed, hands still grasping me around the waist and pulling me tight to the front of his body. He let out a low groan. "But all I want to do is *this*. I finally have you here with me and I don't want to stop. I've dreamed of this for so long."

I took his hand. "Maybe later."

He brightened and ran both his hands through his short blond hair several times, then squeezed his eyes shut.

"Okay," he said. "Slowing down." He moved away from the door where we were standing and walked around the room, jumping up and down a few times and stretching out his muscles. "Slowing down, slowing down."

I laughed. "I'm sorry. I didn't know this would be so hard for you."

He shrugged, finally coming to sit down again. "It's okay. I didn't realize it would all be so new to you. But we can learn together."

"Right." I took his hand, then frowned. "Your pulse seems accelerated. How is your heart monitor not going off?"

"I disabled it." He grinned proudly. "I recorded a small section of normal activity and set it on a loop. I can do yours, too, but I need to borrow some equipment."

"When you say *borrow* . . ." I said. "Won't they know it's missing?"

"I'd take it back the next day. I'll get it tomorrow."

I nodded, knowing it might be dangerous, but still, to have my adrenaline levels and heart rate not constantly monitored would help me escape detection during my more intense glitches. At the same time, I hated the idea of Max putting himself in danger for me.

"I'll think about it. Don't do anything in the meantime." I looked hard into his eyes to make sure he agreed.

He nodded reluctantly. "Well, maybe next week."

"I've been thinking about everything you told me last time," I said, changing the subject. "There have to be others like us. Maybe even in the Academy or riding on the train with us or at the Market. We have to figure out who they are, so we can help them like you helped me. It's made all the difference to know I'm not alone."

"But, Zoe," he said, his expression losing some of its brightness. "I don't need anybody else. It's fine with just you and me. With just us, the secret stays smaller, easier to keep. We can watch out for each other without anyone noticing. The more people you involve, the easier it is for someone to make a mistake, for us to get caught."

"But Max, if there are kids like us, just imagine how scared they are. Being alone is the worst part of glitching. You know that. The fear was so bad that I thought about reporting myself and letting them fix me. . . ." I paused after I said it. That seemed like a lifetime ago. So much had happened. It was hard to imagine I could ever have wanted to destroy my ability to feel, to be *myself*, whatever the risk.

I froze.

"What? What is it?" Max asked.

"I think I remember something," I whispered. Realization slowly dawned. "I think I was caught. They found out." I stopped still and shut my eyes tight, trying to hold on to the wisp of memory. "There was someone there. A boy." I bit my lip trying to concentrate, to make out the features of the shadowy image I could almost remember. I reached and reached with the fingertips of my mind.

"Adrien!" I finally exploded, making out the features. "That new boy, Adrien. He was there!"

Max looked instantly angry. "He must have turned you in."

"I think he was there when I was caught, or maybe he was working with the officials. Or something," I finished lamely. I shut my eyes again, hoping to find out more, to attach the face with some setting, but I couldn't.

"How can you be remembering anything if you had the disrupter plugged in your port?" Max asked.

"I . . . I don't know," I said, looking up at him. "It shouldn't be possible. Unless . . ." I paused.

"Unless?"

"Well," I said slowly, working it out as I went. "What if memory isn't only kept in one place? I mean, our powers can't be the only unusual thing our minds can do. What if memory resonates in other parts of the brain?"

"Whatever it means, you need to stay away from that Adrien guy." Max looked tense, even angry. "If he's connected to all of this, then he's dangerous. These people, the Uppers, are capable of doing some terrifying stuff. They could have been testing on you, removing your memories, even creating false memories. This Adrien kid is probably a Monitor, like you thought. But he could be something worse."

I nodded and pulled away from the embrace. "And let's watch for other glitchers, too—to see if there are any others like us."

"Zoe—"

"Fine, *I'll* keep a watch," I said, feeling frustrated at his reluctance, but then softened my tone. "I know you just want me to be safe. I'll be careful. And you be careful, too. Promise me?"

"I promise," he said. We were quiet a moment. He tilted his head, his gaze intense. "You are so beautiful."

I paused and looked at him, his sandy blond hair tussled and bright brown eyes so earnest. "You are also very well formed."

He pulled me close again. "Maybe once we get your heart

monitor fixed," he said, "then you'll really be able to relax and let yourself feel the way I do."

"Maybe," I laughed as I stood up to go.

A few days later I sat by Max at our customary cafeteria spot at the end of table 13. I had clicked on my projector to go over the day's notes when I noticed Max's face suddenly pale. His mouth dropped open.

"What?" I said, for a split second not bothering to mask my concern. I quickly made my face blank, looking around slowly to see if anyone had seen me.

His eyes swiveled over to mine. "Zoe," he whispered. "They just called for you over the Link. You are to report to the diagnostic center on Sublevel Two immediately."

I felt my eyes widen and my mouth go dry. I'd known in the back of my mind the Chancellor would call me in soon for another checkup, but I thought I'd have more time, or that I'd be connected to the Link when it happened.

But I was glitching all the time now. There wasn't much chance that I'd suddenly reconnect to the Link in the time it took to walk from here to the diagnostic center.

This was it.

This was the day they'd be able to see my anomalous self, lit up like a spotlight in the diagnostic readouts.

I thought I'd have longer. More time. I felt sick to my stomach but stood up calmly and gathered my tablet, swinging the case over my shoulder. I remembered to breathe and tried to stay calm so my heart monitor wouldn't announce my terror to the entire room. I didn't look at Max again. I didn't think I could manage to keep my composure if I did.

I moved out of the room with even strides. Only a few people glanced up as I passed by. I walked mechanically through the exit and into the narrow hallway. It was empty at this hour because everyone was either in the lunch hall or in class. I walked toward the elevator but my hand paused, shaking, as I reached out to swipe my wrist over the sensor to call the elevator.

I felt a sudden overwhelming sadness as I realized I was voluntarily going to what almost assuredly would be my own destruction. I'd been a fool to even think escape was possible. If they didn't deactivate me after this diagnostic, it would at least be the end of the life I had discovered, the person I'd become, my conversations with Max, everything that mattered to me now.

Oh no. *Max.* My stomach lurched. If they read my memory chip, they'd find out about him, too. And it would be all my fault. Just like in the dreams with Markan. I yanked my arm back from the elevator panel like it was about to bite me.

I spun and started walking in the opposite direction, away from the elevator. A plan was loosely forming in my mind as I turned down a side hallway. Maybe I did have a choice in all this, and I chose to run. Even if it meant certain deactivation, I had to at least *try.* I'd get on the subway and go to the city. I didn't know how long I'd make it before they found me, but I couldn't go without a fight this time.

Just as I was about to walk through the doorway to the last hallway leading down to the subway, I heard sudden footsteps directly behind me. Before I could turn around to look, a drive was roughly inserted into the access port at the back of my neck.

"You!" I managed to say before I went numb under the control of the drive.

Chapter 12

"I'M CRACKIN' SORRY to do this to you, but we don't have much time. If you started screaming or your heart monitor went off, they'd catch us both. I couldn't risk it." He spoke in a rush.

I could only stare numbly at Adrien, the last person in the Community I could trust. He dropped his hand after the drive was secure. My mouth, along with the rest of my body, was completely frozen in place.

"Look, I'm uploading a new program that'll reconnect you back into the Link. The program will give you control over when you connect and when you glitch, so you can be connected whenever you want or need to." He was talking so fast, I could barely keep up. "Just whisper the access code—Beta Ten Gamma Link," he said, reaching around and gently lifting my ponytail off the back of my neck. Something sparked in me at his touch.

"Beta Ten Gamma Link, 'kay?" he whispered. "Your voice will be the only one it recognizes—it'll set itself the first time you say it. Then you can go for your diagnostic and the equipment won't find anything anomalous. I promise. Once you're done, just say the code words and you'll disconnect again. They don't usually scan memory chips at these kind of diagnostics, so we'll have to hope for the best."

I had a thousand questions screaming to get out, but my mouth wouldn't open, my vocal cords wouldn't make a sound.

It was a horrible feeling. And then too, there was something about Adrien . . . some memory teasing at the edge of my mind.

Adrien ran his hand through the back of his hair. He looked upset. "I can't imagine what you must be thinking right now but, please—" He leaned in, his intense aquamarine eyes searching my blank face. For a few silent seconds, his face opened and his eyes bored into mine like he expected something from me, some recognition or sign—of what I had no idea.

He stepped back in the next moment, his face hardening back into a blank mask so that he looked just like every other grayed-out Academy student.

"Just go back up to the diagnostic center. Everything will be all right. And be careful of the godlam'd cameras. *Please*, be careful."

He pulled back and reached around to the back of my neck, his fingers a whisper on my skin. Then he yanked out the drive and I stumbled with the sudden use of my limbs and fell into the wall.

"Wait!" I said in a loud whisper, looking around me after I'd gotten my balance back. But he was already gone. I stood still for a moment, turning back and forth between the hallway he'd left through and the doorway leading to the subway platform.

My mind raced. If I tried to escape I knew it was doomed. I would be free and myself until the end, but it would all be over, and soon. Or I could trust Adrien, the boy who might be a Monitor.

"Beta Ten Gamma Link," I whispered and was immediately jolted back into the Link. The familiar three rising tones of the Link sounded. I instinctively paused my step while the three tones finished. The colors immediately seeped out from the hallways around me. *The Community Link is peace. In the time of the Old World*— I took a deep breath and made my way back to the elevator tube.

I passed by Chancellor Bright's office on my way to the diagnostic center.

"Subject Zoel," she said.

I stopped and stepped into her office.

"Yes?"

"Why are you late to your diagnostic appointment? We called for you fifteen minutes ago."

"I required use of the bathroom facilities," I said. I was amazed. I was Linked, but it was like the sliding door remained half open. I still had access to my own thoughts. I could still keep my own secrets. She stared at me through narrowed eyes, but I didn't blink or look away despite the scared tension gathering in my chest. I focused on my breathing to keep my heart from racing.

Embrace the Link, I thought. *Let the gray spread. . . .*

"May I continue?"

"Yes," she said, finally glancing back down at the tablet on her desk.

I turned and tried to let the Link numb me as I kept walking down the hallway. The diagnostic center was at the end on the right.

Gray standing partitions sliced the large room into a maze of smaller cubicles. The Link laid schematics of the room over my vision. The hallway lining the left side of the room was exactly twenty paces long. Doorways led into other rooms— the surgery rooms for student hardware installation and updates.

"Subject Zoel Q-24 reporting."

The small ash-blond woman at a desk near the door looked

up. She glanced back down to her small projected tablet screen, tapping the screen a few times.

"B-11." She sounded blank and disinterested. Just like I would sound again if Adrien had tricked me after all and made me deliver myself to my doom.

I went six paces down the hallway and turned left into the small area marked B-11. I sat down on the intimidating diagnostic table. The table had a padded oval cutout near the top for when subjects lay facedown for neck-port access. All equipment was installed in the concrete walls on huge metal arms that could be pulled over to reach either side of the diagnostic table.

Attached to each arm was a different instrument: a piercing bright light, imaging screen, chest-port plug-in, the hardwired neck-access cable, and other measuring and surgical equipment. The whole thing looked like a giant robotic spider buried in the wall, its spindly legs reaching sinisterly outward to surround the operating table.

I rubbed my neck uncomfortably, thinking about the drive Adrien had put in there only minutes before. I hated the sensation of being immobilized. The thought of the cold metal hardware that lined the walls being forcibly inserted into my body made me squeamish. I needed to go gray again and let the Link take over, but my anxiety was unfortunately keeping me sharp.

I tried logic. I should be used to this. Every test had been run thrice over after my disappearance, not to mention that I'd been subjected to the diagnostic table ever since I was a kid. It was only since glitching that I'd started feeling how *unnatural* it all was. In spite of my efforts to stay calm, my chest stayed tight with anxiety.

The technician entered the cubical and drew the curtain

closed behind him. He was the same technician who usually worked on me.

I automatically lay down on my stomach and fit my face through the oval. The technician pulled some of the equipment arms over my prone body, and then he leaned over me.

"Zoe," he whispered in my ear, "it's me, Max."

I jerked in surprise and turned my head sideways. For a quick second, the technician's face disappeared and was replaced by Max's impish one.

"Here to save the day," he said with a smile before he reverted to the technician's façade. "I'll just pretend to use the equipment, then change it in the computer afterward."

"Shouldn't be necessary, I'm Linked," I whispered in a rush of relief. "I'll explain later." I caught Max's look of consternation just as I fit my face back into the oval.

He clicked the access cable into my neck and then shifted the three imaging panels on three sides surrounding my head. I could see his feet move away as he went to sit at the table with the projected 3-D diagnostic screen.

The curtain swung suddenly open and I lifted up to look, banging my head into one of the imaging panels as I went.

It was Chancellor Bright.

"And how is our subject doing, Dr. Campbell?" She tilted her head sideways in her penetrating, birdlike manner.

"Perfect," Max said, not even missing a beat.

I buried my face in the oval facing the floor so the Chancellor wouldn't see the worried heat flushing my cheeks.

"As you can see," he said, gesturing to the 3-D image of my brain that was rotating in the imaging panel. "Not anomalous."

"Hmph," the Chancellor said. I saw her feet move close to where Max was standing. I tried to keep as still as possible, and after a minute, she stepped back.

"Yes, everything appears normal." She sounded disappointed, confused.

A tool scraped as it was picked up off the instrument tray. "Let's see if her pain-response system is working."

I felt the cold metal touch my neck below my ear. Then with a sharp motion, she jammed it inward and my body lit up with pain. I screamed as my body jolted on the table.

The buzzing blasted in my head at the shocking pain. The crash of instruments hitting the floor coincided with the sound of my beeping heart monitor filling the room. The probe was released and the Chancellor whipped around to look at the tray of instruments I'd accidentally flung against the wall with my power, an unreadable expression on her face. She almost seemed to soften for a moment before turning back to Max.

"Her screaming startled me," Max covered quickly. "I backed into the tray."

There was silence. I imagined the Chancellor turning her penetrating stare on Max. What had I done?

I swallowed my terror down so my heart monitor would stop beeping. I kept my face firmly in the face rest, though a droplet of sweat managed to fall down my cheek. Out of the corner of my eye I could see Max calmly and methodically picking up the fallen tools.

The Chancellor was silent while he finished, her feet completely still. I had no idea what she might be thinking.

"Adequate pain monitor response," she finally said, her voice unreadable. "Make sure to run all the tests. I don't want anything slipping through the cracks with this one."

"Of course, Chancellor," the technician's voice said, each syllable as monotone as the last. I had to remind myself it was Max beside me, he was so convincing. He hadn't even flinched when I'd screamed. I wondered if that was part of his power—

that he was completely believable as whatever person he projected—or if he was just that good a liar.

The Chancellor's footsteps echoed as she left. Max didn't say anything more, just went through with the rest of the tests, making marks on the technician's tablet as he went. I was surprised he knew what he was doing so well. I wondered where he'd learned it. In fact, I was starting to realize there was a lot about Max I didn't know.

He finished quickly and I felt his rough hands on my neck as he removed the cable from my access port.

"Tomorrow night" was all he said but I knew what he meant. I nodded slightly as I sat up. I knew he had questions and I had plenty of my own. I didn't want him putting himself in any more danger. And I had to tell him about Adrien, the enigmatic boy with the blue-green eyes that I still didn't know if I could trust.

I was up all night. Questions about Adrien and the Chancellor kept me restless and awake well into the morning hours. Without Max there to help me, would Adrien's solution have fooled the equipment all on its own? Or was he actually a Monitor after all? But if so, wouldn't he have turned me in, not tried to help me?

It hadn't mattered so much in the end. Max was there. Maybe Adrien had known that, and he just wanted to give the *appearance* of help to gain my trust. I shivered, remembering the feeling of being immobilized after Adrien put the port in my neck. That was reason enough for me to avoid him.

I tried to put it all out of my head and lose myself in the back-and-forth motion of walking, the cadence of all the morning commuters' footsteps ringing like a dull roar around me. Too many questions and no answers was enough to drive a person crazy. I needed to start focusing on solutions. Problem solving. First one thing, then another, then another. Logical. Orderly.

I stepped onto the train and held on to a pole near the dark window. The doors closed with a hiss as the air-filtration system in the subway car kicked in. I looked around me at the dull gray subway car and the clean orderly people all standing at attention with perfect posture, most of them zoned out to the morning Link News.

A few Regulators got on at the next stop, their blue suits jumping out at me from among the clusters of gray. I breathed in and out slowly to make sure my heart monitor didn't go off at the sight of them. I'd gotten lucky before, but that didn't mean I would today. My eyes flickered up at the Regulators one more time before I fixed them on the ground, turning slightly away so they couldn't see my face.

They looked too young to be full Regulators. They were probably just Regulators-in-training heading to the Academy like I was.

After I felt my heart rate normalize, I looked around at every face, trying to make only my eyes move while my face remained blank. Did any of them glitch? Were any of them hiding the same secret Max and I were?

I worked methodically through every face in the car, back to front, pausing occasionally to make sure I appeared to be just as blank as the rest of them. I used the black of the window like a mirror, so I could watch people indirectly. I continued my gaze down the train, not noticing anything unusual about anyone.

I wasn't discouraged—look how long it had taken for Max and me to find each other. It would have to be by chance that we discovered anyone else. Though, if other people were glitching as often as I was, then maybe there was more hope.

Just when I'd given up on the possibility of finding any

glitchers, I caught a glimpe of someone who felt anomalous. I could only see the back of his head and I couldn't exactly put into words why I thought he was a glitcher. His posture looked straight but there was something about it. Something in his body language didn't look quite as blank as the rest of them. There was an alertness to the set of his shoulders. I wondered if, when we got off the train, I could get a better look at his face. Then, as if he could feel my eyes on him, he turned around. My breath caught in my throat.

Adrien. It was as if my body itself reacted to him. My face flushed and I felt hot all over. I swallowed. I didn't understand why I felt this way, or what it was even that I was feeling. His blue-green eyes met mine in the mirrored glass.

The instant our eyes met, he stiffened and I could see his grip tighten on the pole he was holding for balance. His eyes suddenly became vacant, staring beyond me. I glanced behind me in confusion, trying to figure out what he was looking at, but there was nothing there. I turned to look back at him.

After another few tense seconds, he blinked and looked around him like he was trying to reorient himself, his head swaying slightly. I breathed out and forced my eyes down to the floor, wondering if that was what I looked like when I glitched in and out of the Link.

I dared to look back again but his carefully composed posture was different now. His eyes flicked back and forth between me and the group of Regulators-in-training. He took a step toward me, weaving through the crowd of unmoving bodies on the train car. People barely glanced at him as he brushed past, grabbing a pole close to my left for balance just as the train curved around an especially sharp corner.

What was he doing? He was acting anomalously right in front of the Regulators! And worse, he was coming toward me, bringing attention to me, too.

My heart monitor started vibrating. I swallowed, put my head down, and squeezed my eyes shut to get myself under control. I couldn't afford to have it start beeping here, not while I was trapped in an enclosed space with all of these witnesses, not to mention the Regulators.

Just then I heard a disruption at the other end of the train, a loud *clunk* noise that echoed throughout the otherwise silent train car.

I looked up, momentarily distracted by the sound. It was one of the Regulators-in-training. He was grabbing his head and stumbling around. He'd banged his armor-plated forehead into the wall again—that was the sound I'd first heard.

"Regulator Anderson," said one of the other young Regulators, reaching out an arm to steady the unstable Regulator. The one called Anderson knocked the arm away. The loud clang of metal on metal from their steel-alloy bionic arms was so loud and piercing that I winced. Several of the people on the train began tapping their arm panels, no doubt reporting the anomalous incident. I felt a wave of relief, followed by another of shame. I was glad it wasn't me they were reporting, but what about this poor Regulator? What would happen to him?

Anderson let out a sharp yell as the other three Regulators-in-training attempted to subdue him. They surrounded him but that only made him more wild. He thrashed outward with both bionic arms at the Regulators and sent one flying halfway across the train car into the standing crowd. The heavy Regulator knocked over a group of people, his momentum only stopping when he slammed into a metal pole. The pole snapped from the ceiling and hit a woman hard in the torso, knocking her down.

It was all happening so fast, I could barely register what was going on. Out of the corner of my eye I saw the other two Regulators still tussling and trying to get Anderson under control. Then I was forced back against the far wall from them by the crowd, and I didn't have a good view of what was going on anymore. It was only after another quick look that I realized it was Adrien's body in front of mine, blocking me against the safety of the back subway-car wall.

He swiveled his head to the side, whispering urgently, "Stay against the wall. A glitching Regulator is shuntin' deadly."

Anderson let out a feral shriek at the other end of the subway car. The knock of metal on metal and the beeping of at least ten people's heart monitors triggered by pain filled the space. I craned my neck to see over Adrien's shoulder just as two of the Regulators pinned Anderson against the side wall. He thrashed violently under their grip, his face mottled and red. Spit dripped down over the metal that framed his jaw. His blue jumpsuit had ripped, revealing more of the metal alloy that had been grafted into his skin.

"Deactivate, Regulator Anderson," said one of the Regulators who held him. "I repeat, deactivate."

My heart jumped into my throat at the word. They were going to kill him? Did he have some kind of internal hardware that would kill him at the simple command of their words? Over all of the chaos in the train, a high-pitched buzzing blared in my ears.

"Don't!" Adrien whispered just as the arm of one of the Regulators holding Anderson was yanked away by an invisible force. *My force.*

"I didn't mean to," I gasped, my eyes wide. Adrien stared at me in panic.

Anderson had taken the momentary freedom from the Regulator's grip to pull away. The others lunged for him but he twisted away and ran headfirst into the opposite wall. The hydraulics on his legs contracted and then released as he sprang forward with incredible force, taking a subject who'd been standing in his way with him. He was so crazed, he didn't even aim for a window—his body smashed through the wall with a horrible crash and the squeal of twisting metal.

A panel of the wall was ripped outward and the sudden rush of wind from outside the train was deafening. The lights in the cabin flickered off and on and I saw in the brief flash of light before we were swallowed in total darkness that the person who'd been in his way was impaled on a spike of twisted metal. The metal sparked as it contacted the side of the outer tunnel, casting enough light to see that the top half of his bloody body had been severed at the torso.

Anderson hadn't made it all the way through either. One leg was caught in the twist of metal near the floor and the whole train rocked unsteadily on its tracks every time he twisted his heavy body in an attempt to free himself.

People banged against me on all sides in the darkness, losing their footing in the rocking train. I screamed and pushed at the bodies surrounding and suffocating me. They were ripped violently away from me—but it wasn't the chaos of the train that had sent them flying. It had been me, my power accidentally unleashed again.

I tried to look and see if I'd hurt them, but between the howl of the wind, the screech of metal against the outer tunnel, and my own screaming, I couldn't make sense of anything. I couldn't tell if the other Regulators were trying to fix the situation and I couldn't tell where Adrien was either. A large man fell against me when the train rounded another corner, knocking me to the ground. I managed to quiet the buzzing in my mind fast enough to keep from throwing him away from me.

The train car scraped along against an especially tight portion of the outer tunnel and illuminated the interior long enough for me to see the chaos of tossed bodies. A brown-haired woman stumbled toward the ripped-open wall. She tripped on the Regulator's leg and tumbled out through the open space out into darkness.

"No!" I screamed, but it was too late. She was already gone. The wail of my scream was swallowed in the roaring wind.

The buzzing from fear and anger I'd been barely holding in seemed to explode outward from my body as I lost control. I felt the energy pulse out, but couldn't stop it. In the space of a single heartbeat, I saw the other Regulators finally making their way across the train car toward the open space, but it didn't matter—my power had already ripped away the rest of the panel and sent the glitching Regulator plunging into the darkness of the tunnel.

The tenor of my scream changed as I realized what I'd just done. But I didn't have time to feel the full horror of it, because the train car suddenly rocked violently to the left, sending all of us sliding into the opposite wall.

My head banged painfully against a pole as we flew past and then other bodies piled up against mine until I felt suffocated. I managed to push some of them off me, enough to realize that the entire train car was tilted sideways. I could tell from the unnatural angle of the car that one of our rails must not even be touching anymore. The body of the Regulator must have gotten caught underneath the train and derailed us.

Someone grabbed my arm and pulled themselves toward me. "Zoe!" Adrien's voice screamed above the chaos. "We're about to lose traction and jackknife!"

I nodded. My head was a tornado of thoughts and sensations, but I focused in on one thought: I was the one who'd thrown the Regulator's body under the train. I had to fix what I'd done. A high-pitched scream ripped its way out of me, in harmony with the buzzing in my head.

In one painful instant I felt my mind split. I was expanding outward and it was like I could *feel* all nine of the cars in the subway train. We were the second to last in the line but if we kept pulling the rest sideways off the track with our momentum, Adrien was right—we'd fishtail and all the cars would crumple into one another like an accordion. I took another deep breath and pushed with all my might, envisioning a huge counterweight on the train rails that weren't touching, pulling us back down to the track.

Sparks flew as we suddenly made contact again and the cabin righted itself. Another person flew toward the gaping hole in the side of the train, but I caught them just in time, flinging them backward. My head was too cloudy and confused to be delicate about it.

The lights in the cabin flickered back on as the train slowed. Blood was everywhere. Several other people had been crushed by the weight of the heavy Regulators who'd been thrown off balance just like everyone else. At least one person was slumped against the wall, eyes staring forward, unmoving. All the heart monitors around me were sounding, mine included.

I lifted a hand weakly to the painful spot on my forehead as I took in the surreal scene all around me. I leaned over and threw up. When I took my hand away from my head, I saw it was covered in blood. The red was so bright against the gray of my shirtsleeve.

"Beta Ten Gamma Link," I whispered. Then I passed out.

Chapter 13

I WOKE UP in a strange medical center a day later, the Scheduled Subject Downtime program blaring in my brain. *Community first, Community always.* Three long tones sounded, drowning out space for any other thought. The Community Creed repeated. *The Community Link is peace. We are humanity sublime because we live in Community and favor above all else order, logic, and peace. Community first, Community always.*

The harsh tones sounded in my head again, I knew the noises were supposed to be soothing or numbing, but they only exacerbated my headache. I looked around at the small, cold cubicle. I couldn't hear much of anything beyond the horrible Link tones and mind-numbing mechanical voice that repeated the mantra over and over.

A thermal blanket covered my body. I was sure it was keeping my body at the exact correct temperature, but it felt suffocating. Between the invasion of the Link in my head and the sense of being strapped down to the bed by the blanket, I felt trapped. I wanted to scream and drown out the sound of the Link with my voice. I was the only one allowed inside my head!

Then I remembered—I had the passwords to get release. I started to whisper in a hoarse, rasping voice, "Beta Te—"

A doctor stepped through the curtain. I turned to look at him and as I did, I felt the pull of the cable attached to my neck port. My eyes widened.

I was plugged in. I was plugged in, and I'd almost whispered the words to disconnect me from the Link. The anomaly would have been recorded on the equipment.

Stupid! Now was not the time to be so careless. Who knew what else had shown up on the machines while I'd been unconscious.

The doctor wore the dull gray-red uniform of his profession. I wondered morbidly if doctors wore red so the blood of their patients wouldn't stain their clothes. He was tall and lean, with brown hair and a disproportionately long nose. He didn't speak to me, but only picked up the tablet at the base of my bed. He touched the screen. Every second he spent clicking through the information and not speaking seemed like an eternity.

I cleared my throat. "What is your assessment of my condition?"

"Mild concussion, eight deep lacerations, internal contusions." His voice was cold, uninterested. "Internal hardware has not suffered any damage. Cellulo-reproductive acceleration gel has been applied to all lacerations. Healing rate is within normal parameters." He finally looked up from the chart to me. "However, having accessed your historical bioinformation, I find anomalous activity."

Panic started to rise up in my throat like bile, but I choked it down. The last thing I needed now was for the monitor to go off when he was right here. He pulled back the thermal blanket. I felt chill bumps rise all over my arms at the rush of cooler air.

His fingers were cold as he touched the small aluminum circle embedded in my chest. I had to stop myself from cringing. He clicked the top off of the coinlike circle and pulled a rodlike instrument from the belt around his waist.

He touched the tip of the instrument to one of the tiny circuits. I felt a small shock that made an involuntary tremor run through my body. Was that was supposed to happen? Or did it prove I was anomalous?

Whatever it meant, the doctor's face remained unreadable. He reattached the tool to his belt and left the room without another word. I looked down at my heart-monitor flap, still open to the air. I felt horribly exposed, but I didn't want to rearrange the covers over myself and look even more anomalous. Why didn't he say anything else before he left? What had the instrument showed? Could he tell something was wrong with me? The word he'd used echoed in my head, managing to drown out the Link: *anomalous.*

I repeated the Community Creed along with the Link voice in my head to keep myself calm. The doctor finally came back into the cubicle, carrying a tiny box. I was full of questions, but managed to keep my mouth shut. He opened the small case and pulled out a tiny piece of hardware.

Was this the device that would deactivate me? I swallowed hard, trying to take in every feeling and sensation of this moment in case it was my last.

"Commencing monitor battery replacement with neo-alloy battery, part number X89." His voice sounded lifeless. I held my breath as he pulled out the sliver of hardware.

Just a battery replacement! Relief swept over me. The monitor let out a high-pitched squeal, but the doctor was not perturbed. He slid in the new battery and the noise stopped.

"Replacement battery X89 complete." He must be talking to a voice-recording device that kept patient records, because he barely seemed to notice I was even there. "Release scheduled for six p.m. today."

He clicked the top of my heart monitor back closed and left without ever looking into my face. The trembling I'd been holding back the entire time started in earnest. The doctor had treated me like a piece of equipment. If I'd been more broken, if there had been more extensive damage than just a concussion and easily healable lacerations, he would have de-activated me with the same indifference.

He had neglected to cover me again with the blanket. With shaking hands, I pulled it up to my chin. It had seemed suffo-cating before, but now it seemed only a paltry shield against a creeping, horrible cold.

I had the strangest longing for my mother, wishing she were here to push the hair back from my face and tell me everything would be okay. But of course, she wasn't. I was sure my par-ents had been alerted to what had happened but they had work of their own to do. Why would they wait around with me and watch me sleep? It would be unproductive, illogical. Instead, I waited alone in the empty space, repeating the Community Creed to keep my heart monitor quiet, trying to hold my feelings in check, until I was released five hours later.

I had to take the subway home. My heart rate sped up as soon as I stepped into the subway car, in spite of how sluggish and ex-hausted I still was. The inside of the train looked just as nor-mal and benign as the one I'd stepped into two days ago. I blinked and remembered the spattered blood. The crumpled bodies with beeping heart monitors strewn all over the ground.

I forced my eyes back open and worked on breathing nor-mally. My whole body still ached. My hand went numb from gripping the pole tightly the entire way home.

When I got into the apartment, I heard the rhythmic noise of footfalls on the treadmill in the front room. I paused, watching Markan's arms pump calmly while he ran. He didn't look up or acknowledge me. I stood for another few moments, hoping he'd see me, but he just stared blankly at the wall. Zoned out to the Link. My parents weren't home either. I don't know what I'd been expecting, but I guessed I'd ridiculously hoped for some kind of welcome. Something to let me know that they'd been worried about me or missed me, or even that they had noticed my absence.

I'd expected coming home to my family quarters would make me feel better, that I'd feel that sense of safety and belonging that I sometimes did. But home was just a lie I'd made up to make myself feel better. The realization was as chilling as the empty hospital cubicle had been.

I slid the door to my tiny room shut and sank down to the floor, finally crying the exhausted tears that I'd had to hold back while I was at the hospital. I took the pills the doctors had sent me home with and slept through the next day.

I woke to someone shaking my shoulder. I blinked slowly.

"Max!" I sat up quickly and threw my arms around him. The movement sent an ache through my side from the still-healing lacerations, but I didn't care.

"Why are you here?" I finally asked, still not letting go of my grip.

"I came as soon as I could," he said, pulling back. "I tried to see you at the hospital, but I couldn't figure out their security system in time."

"You tried to see me?" I asked in surprise. It was so reckless of him, but then I thought of waiting all alone in that horrible hospital room. Someone had wanted to come, someone cared about me, was thinking about *me*. I wasn't just another drone to be poked and prodded. Not to Max.

I hugged him hard again. "I'm so glad you're here," I said into his chest. His arms around me were like walls—real protection, real connection. *Friend.* I'd read about the word in the archive texts, but now I knew what it meant.

"How are you feeling?" he asked.

I finally pulled away and looked at him. He'd climbed up to the loft bed and was sitting on the edge, legs dangling over the side. I stretched my limbs. I was drowsy, but I could already tell my body hurt less.

"I'm okay. Better."

"What happened on the train?" Even though we weren't hugging anymore, he'd taken my hand in his and was tracing patterns with his thumb. Every touch was a point of connection whispering: *Not alone, not alone, not alone.* "There's been no news on the Link about it and all I can get from my other sources is that there was some malfunction on the train. The camera went out with the lights, so I couldn't get my hands on any recordings."

I wanted to berate him for taking risks again but I knew it wouldn't do any good. I told him about the young Regulator glitching.

"It was like Adrien knew what was going to happen," I said. "We have to contact him."

"No way. I don't trust him," Max said darkly, dropping my hand. "How could he know what was going to happen unless he had a hand in it? Maybe he did it to force you to reveal your powers."

"How can you say that?" I pulled back. "This was the second time he's helped me!"

"You didn't need his help when you were called over the Link for the diagnostic." He clenched his hands into fists. "I had everything taken care of already. You don't even know for sure if what he did would've gone undetected in the scan."

"Max," I shook my head, "I thought you'd be excited. This means there's someone else out there like us. Maybe he has, you know—" I leaned in. "The powers like we do. This was what we wanted, to find more people like us."

"It's what *you* wanted."

I looked at him, confused. "Don't you, too? Now that you see how important it is?"

He shook his head. "With just the two of us, we'd be safer. We could avoid detection more easily."

"But for how long? The train accident was just one example of a hundred ways things could go wrong. We need more people on our side."

"Why? What do you think this is going to turn into, some army or something?" He was upset but I didn't understand why.

"No, of course not!" I felt exasperated. "That's not what I meant. . . . I just . . ." I trailed off.

"You just want to go around recklessly involving other people and endangering us," Max said.

I sat still, breathing hard. Why was he being so difficult? I was suddenly tired again and wetness pricked at my eyes.

"Oh no, Zoe, I shouldn't have said that." He put a hand gently on my arm. "I know you've just gone through something horrible. The thought that I wasn't there to help you . . ." His brown eyes were intense as they searched mine. "You're everything to me, you know that, don't you? You're all that matters, all I think about. Everything I do is to try to keep us safe."

"I would never do anything to put us in danger," I said, wiping my eyes. "I just thought he might be able to help us."

"Us," he said, more gently now. "There's an *us*?"

I blinked, confused. "Yes, of course."

"What I mean is, I want there to be an us. I want us to be together. You know, *together*. You getting hurt again—" He shook his head and swallowed before looking back into my eyes. "It made me realize I never want to live without you. I can't." He took my hand. "When we're old enough, I'm sure I can use my powers to arrange for us to be marital partners."

"Marital partners?" I asked, stunned. "You mean staying here and getting the adult V-chip installed? But we'd never glitch again!"

"Zoe, relax." He waved a hand. "I'll find a way around the hardware and the system."

"Even if we could uncover a way around the chip," I said, slow horror gripping me at the ramifications of staying in the Community forever, "being marital partners would mean they'd create children for us."

I thought of the little girl who'd danced on the platform and imagined her growing colder and less human every time a new V-chip was installed. Just the thought made me feel like throwing up. I thought I'd saved her that day on the train plat-form. But had I? She would still grow up and forget what it had ever felt like to *feel*.

"I don't want to procreate," Max laughed, not seeming to sense my dark mood or thoughts. "I just want you. For my-self." He leaned in and his voice got suddenly low.

"Don't you understand? I want to spend my life with you. I want you to be there when I go to bed at night and when I wake up in the morning."

"Oh." I thought about it. I didn't know how Max thought we could stay in the Community our whole lives and some-how be safe. But then, the way he talked about it—waking up next to someone every morning. Not being alone. Ever again. I slowly smiled.

I still felt a nagging sense of worry about Max's confidence. It seemed too simple, even reckless. On the other hand, it gave me a flush of happiness to be wanted. My own parents didn't even want me. Not really. I was just part of their Commu-nity duty. They didn't miss me when I was gone or care that I'd been hurt. Max *wanted* to be family with me. Being family had to mean even more connection than just being a friend.

"Yes, I'd like that," I finally said. "I'd like to be family with you."

"Good." He grinned and let out a big breath I hadn't noticed he was holding. He pulled me closer, his lips immediately on mine. He held me tight and then swung his legs up onto the bed to lie down beside me.

"I want to be the one to protect you," he said into my ear. His hands moved down from my neck to tuck themselves securely around my waist. "You know I can protect you, right?"

"I never said you couldn't." I separated from him and propped myself up on my elbow. His blond hair was mussed and I smiled and reached over to smooth it down.

He grinned, his dimples catching in the light.

"So do you have notes and homework for me?" I asked, feeling an uncomfortable blush in my cheeks at the way he was looking at me. "Or was that just an excuse to come over?"

"Yes, I brought notes," he laughed. "I already synced my tablet to yours while you were sleeping."

"Well let's do some homework so if anyone walks in we won't look anomalous."

"You shouldn't be studying right now. You need to rest. I just had to see you and let you know I can take care of you." For a moment he stared beyond me at the wall. "I'm making sure of it."

"What?" I sat up in alarm. Something about the way he said it filled me with dread. "What do you mean, Max? How are you making sure of it?"

He smiled and waved a hand, the intense look disappearing from his face. "It's nothing. Don't be afraid. I'm always careful. Everything's going to get better. You'll see."

Chapter 14

I WAS WALKING DOWN the hall when someone stopped suddenly in front of me. I ran right into them, my tablet case clunking to the ground in my surprise at the impact. I bent down, trying not to let my irritation show or betray any other anomalous response, but then I looked up and saw it was Adrien. My eyes widened just a fraction before I made my face blank again. He'd dropped his tablet case too with the impact and he stooped to the ground at the same time, too.

I'd had a twinge in my stomach all day at the thought of seeing Adrien again, but now that he was here in front of me, I didn't know what question to ask first.

"I have a way to get into your house unnoticed," he whispered, turning his head toward mine but keeping it facing the ground. "I'll meet you in your bedroom at eight tomorrow."

I opened my mouth to speak, but he didn't give me the chance.

"I'll answer any questions tomorrow," he whispered quickly, then stood up. I sat another moment watching after him, dumbfounded. His tall, lanky body quickly disappeared around a corner. I finally realized I might attract attention if I kept crouching on the ground like this, so I got up and turned toward the lunchroom.

I had to work hard to hide the excitement and nerves bubbling in my chest. *Finally*, I might get some answers. Adrien knew things. He might be dangerous, and I'd have to be on my guard, but I was desperate for answers. Whether he was a glitcher or not, I wasn't sure, but he definitely was not Linked. And he had access to some advanced tech. I couldn't help but wonder if he'd know a way for us to live undetected or avoid the adult V-chip. It was a hope so precious and fragile I almost didn't dare let myself think it.

"You've been talking about him nonstop since we got here," Max said at our tutoring session that night.

I turned and looked at him. "So?"

"So maybe I'm tired of hearing about him! And he's gonna meet you in your bedroom? Is that even safe? We don't need him, and it's not worth the risk. I told you *I* could protect you."

I waved his words away with a swipe of my hand. "This isn't about protection. It's about figuring out what he knows. He's got to be like us. I want to know what he knows and get him on our side."

"The only people who need to be on our side," Max stood up, his face flushed, "are *us*."

I stopped pacing finally, seeing Max's face and sensing he was quietly fuming.

"What's wrong with you?" I asked.

"What's wrong with me?" he echoed incredulously. "What's wrong with me is that all I can think about all day and all night long is *you*, but you are obviously spending all your time and energy thinking about *him*."

I threw my hands up in the air. "Of course I'm thinking about him! I have this feeling like he knows things that could be useful to us—"

"I don't care!" Max said suddenly, almost shouting. I was taken aback and finally stopped talking. I'd been so caught up in my own thoughts I hadn't realized just how angry he was getting.

"Don't you understand?" he said, pulling me to him. "I want you to be thinking about me." His eyes were burning intensely as he put his hand behind my neck, pulling my mouth to his.

"Kissing," he said, still embracing me tight. "It's called kissing. I've been learning all kinds of things that people used to share with each other in the Old World."

"How have you been learning things?" I said in surprise. "Where?"

"I snuck into a visiting official's room and looked through his stuff. He had data on his text tablets that was nothing like I'd ever seen."

"Max! How could you do that? It's reckless."

"It's not reckless, not with my powers. I made myself look like the official and walked right into the room. Anyway, do you want to hear about what I found out, or not?" He grabbed both of my hands in his tightly.

I pursed my lips in disapproval but nodded reluctantly.

"This," he leaned in immediately, lips on mine, then pulled back, "is called kissing. And I found out what marital partners in the Old World did, and it wasn't just sitting around waiting for the Center to mix their DNA together in a test tube."

"Wait, you mean like the passions?" I said, alarmed. "Like the history archives talk about? The animal flaw that brought down humans in the Old World?"

"Yes, but they aren't like that. I was trying to tell you the other night."

"But why did an official even have any of that on his tablet?" I asked, confused.

"That's the biggest lie of all," Max said. "You won't believe this, but the Uppers, the officials, all the people in charge . . ." He paused. "None of them are even Linked, Zoe. They're all free."

I felt like the wind had been knocked out of my stomach.

"That's not possible," I whispered. "They say being Linked gave us all a better life, a peaceful life. It's in all of our history texts. It's in our Community Creed!" I paused, thoughts swirling. "If it truly is a better life, then they'd be Linked themselves. And if they could *feel*, they wouldn't do this to us. Turn us into drones. They couldn't . . ."

Max eyed me intently. "They could, and they do. They've done it for two hundred years or more now. Keeping all the rest of us as drones while they let themselves do and feel anything they want."

"But if they can feel, they know how much it is to lose! It's—" I choked out, my mind stumbling on each thought as it rose up. "It's inhuman!"

Max suddenly pulled his shirt up over his head. His chest was wide and muscled, with a light tufting of blond hairs. The metal of the circular heart monitor in the center of his chest glinted in the light.

"It's horrible, I know. But forget all that, Zoe. The only thing we can do is try to forget it all and enjoy ourselves as much as we can." He reached for my waist and grabbed the bottom of my shirt.

"Wait, Max, I don't know—"

His voice was low and breathy with excitement. "We deserve this, you and me. We can make up right now for everything they stole from people."

He started a trail of sizzling kisses down my neck. My face flushed. My mind raced even as my body reacted in ways I didn't understand. Everything was happening too fast. He was so intense, holding and kissing me like he wanted to devour me.

Everything with Max was hot and cold. We'd just been arguing a moment ago, and then now he had suddenly changed again. He was reckless and wild, but he was also someone who cared for me so much. Who wanted to be my family. Wasn't that what I wanted, too? I let myself kiss him back in my confusion.

He put his hands on my pants and began unhooking them.

"Stop," I said, yanking away and moving to the far wall. The word was out of my mouth before I knew what I was saying.

"Why? What's wrong?" Max's wide chest heaved as he stared at me in confusion. He started to move toward me but I held up a hand.

"Wait, this is too fast. I don't even understand what's happening!"

"Why not?" Max's voice was suddenly hard. "You don't want *me*. Is that it?"

"That's not what I said. Of course I want you. I don't want to talk about this anymore," I said, feeling the stinging at the back of my eyes. Everything was wrong. Max usually made me feel safe and secure but right now I just wanted to be anywhere but here with him.

"I came here because I thought you were going to help me figure out a plan. Not this."

Max raised his voice too. "The other day, you said you wanted to be together with me. Well this is what togetherness is, what humans are *supposed* to do. Maybe you aren't as free from the Link as you think you are."

His voice kept getting louder and louder. "There's a whole other world out there, and the Uppers, who've never been Linked one day of their lives, know all about it. Because it's what's normal. Because they're not brain-gone freaks."

"Fine," I interrupted him. "I guess I'm not normal then." The moisture in my eyes brimmed over. Broken. He was saying I was broken. I was too broken to stay Linked, and now I was too broken to even glitch properly.

"I guess I don't want to be normal. I don't want to be together with you, either." I yanked his bedroom door open. I walked so fast I was almost running toward the front door.

"Wait, Zoe." He caught up to me and grabbed my arm hard.

"Let go of me!" I wrenched my arm away. I tasted salt between my lips and realized water was streaming copiously from my eyes now.

"Zoe, stop, I feel bad." He sounded like he meant it. "This isn't going how I thought it would. Just wait."

I wiped my eyes with my palms and looked up at him. He seemed sincere but I was still too upset. I couldn't even completely say why. I just wanted to go to my family quarters, where things made sense. Where my parents would be sitting at the square table with their perfectly portioned food. Logical. Orderly.

"I'll see you at school tomorrow, Maximin." I didn't look at him. I left through the door, managing only barely to keep my footsteps calm and even as I walked to the subway.

I avoided Max the next day, staying intentionally Linked so I could ignore him. It wasn't so much that I was angry with him—it was just that all the emotion I'd felt when we'd become so upset with each other was the most intense thing I'd felt in my life, even more than fear. It hurt still to think about his words, which got stuck in my head like a worming virus. *Brain-gone freak.* I didn't know what *freak* meant but I didn't like the sound of it and the way his voice had sounded when he'd said it—so harsh and ugly.

And he was wrong. I wasn't a drone anymore. I just didn't feel the things he'd wanted me to feel, and now I was sure I had lost him. I didn't know where I fit now. Not with the drones, and not with him. I was alone again. I looked around the cafeteria and saw Adrien sitting near the wall. The sight of him calmed me. At least I'd get answers tonight.

Max nudged my foot under the table. He'd been doing it throughout lunch, but this time I finally looked at him.

"Study at your unit tonight?" he asked, his voice soft.

I gave a quick nod and then rose to put my tray away.

I could tell Max was straining to say something the whole ride to my housing unit. He tried to hug me right when we got to my room, but I held him back with one extended hand.

"Zoe, I feel . . ." He squeezed his eyes shut. "I don't have the words for how I feel—wrong, bad, as if I shouldn't have said what I did to you. I want to go backward and not say it, but I can't."

"Shh," I said. "My brother is right next door."

"He's on the treadmill, he won't hear." He took the hand I'd been barring him with and cupped it in his. "This is all new for me, too. I need you." His look was sad, sincere. "I want to be with you, even without the passions. You know that, don't you?"

"Maybe," I said, feeling all of the sudden like crying again. "I don't know what you mean when you say you want to be with me. You *are* with me. I'm with you. You are the person who is"—I looked at the wall, casting around for the right word—"more *significant* to me than anyone. The words aren't right, maybe. But I feel like family with you. It hurts so much sometimes that my real family doesn't seem connected to me at all. It's like we're just bodies that happen to occupy the same housing unit, with nothing else connecting us."

I took Max's hands. "It's just wrong. Family should mean some kind of bond. It should signify that even though no one else in the world cares about you, you're special to someone. And that's what I have with you. You're my only true family."

"Family, like a marital unit?" His hands tightened on mine, his face tense, but hopeful.

"I don't know, Max." I felt helpless. "I'm not even sure what you mean by that. I think you want it to mean something different. Isn't feeling like family enough? Like siblings used to be, back in the Old World, what I wish I could have with my own brother."

"Brother?" Max's voice was hot with disgust. He dropped my hands. "I don't want to be your brother!"

My face must have showed how his words hurt me.

He groaned and his shoulders sagged. "I'm doing it again. Saying bad things. It's just that I want to be more than your brother." He crossed the small space between us. He cupped my face gently and leaned in, putting his lips ever so softly against mine.

For the first time, I really let go and let him kiss me, trying to understand the tingling sensation that was slowly waking up inside me. I raised my hand, about to reach out to his face, when one of the ceiling tiles shifted and a tall form dropped down into the room.

Max recovered from the surprise quicker than I did and launched himself at the figure just as I said, "No, wait!"

Max tackled Adrien, easily taking the thin boy down. He put his knee in Adrien's sternum to keep him down and punched him hard in the face. I jumped forward and grabbed Max's arm just as he revved up for another swing.

"Stop, Max, it's Adrien!" I shouted in a hoarse whisper. "He told me he had a way to get in unnoticed."

Max's face was taut with a look I didn't recognize. It looked like anger but at the same time, it seemed like more. It scared me.

"Get off of him," I hissed, yanking at his arm. Max finally moved off. Adrien lay still for another moment, hand to his nose, before finally sitting up. When he moved his hand, I saw there was blood.

I gasped. "I'll go get some tissue. Stay out of sight," I said to Adrien, suddenly worried that all the noise we'd made had been noticed by my brother. I opened the door and looked out cautiously. The rhythm of pounding feet on the treadmill didn't change and I let out a sigh of relief. Good, Markan hadn't heard.

I got some bathroom tissue and came back to find Max and Adrien standing at opposite sides of the tiny space, each eyeing the other coldly. This wasn't going well at all.

"I feel so bad," I said, handing the tissue to Adrien. "I told him you were coming but we were still surprised."

"It's fine," Adrien said, managing a smile. "I wish I'd had more time to warn you. I'm sorry for startling you." Adrien addressed it to both of us.

"Sorry?" I said in confusion. "I'm not familiar with the word."

"It means I feel bad," Adrien said, taking a moment to think before finishing, "and wished I hadn't hurt you or made you afraid."

Sorry. I nodded, adding it to my mental list of emotive words. It seemed like an important one.

"So how'd you get in?" Max pushed off the wall and came to stand between Adrien and me. "And why are you here?"

"We have members of the Resistance planted in the unit above this one. We cut through the floor over a shared ventilation duct."

"Resistance?" Max asked, narrowing his eyes.

"Let's all sit down," I said nervously. "Adrien, why don't you start from the beginning?'

"Sure."

Max's face was still hard. He pulled me down to sit beside him on the ground. "You can take the chair," he said to Adrien. Max's behavior was confusing me. I didn't understand it and I didn't like it.

"I don't know exactly where to begin," Adrien said.

"Do you have a glitcher power?"

"Max," I chastised sharply.

"It's fine," Adrien said. "Yes, I do have a power, though we refer to it as a Gift."

"Well, what is it?" Max's voice was rough and insistent.

"I get visions of the future." Adrien met Max's angry eyes calmly. He turned to me. "That's how I knew you were in trouble on the train that day."

He explained quickly about our trip to the Surface. All the questions and confusion—the water dreams, my memories of the forest, all of it was explained in the space of ten minutes. It almost seemed too simple. Something tugged at the back of my mind. There was something else he was leaving out, something I'd forgotten. I sat stunned while he went on.

"What is this Resistance movement?" Max interrupted.

"It's basically a sustained rebel faction," Adrien said. "It's been alive in some form since the beginning. Some people escaped being chipped and kept a record of what was really going on after D-day. But they were powerless to actually stop it. We still are, kinda. It's not like the Rez has ever been strong enough to make a stand against Comm Corp or fight them straight out. Mainly, we just try to keep a strong non-chipped presence, an alternative for those who can manage to escape government control."

"So you don't actually *do* anything?" Max said harshly.

"I didn't say that." Adrien looked at Max. "We believe preparation's essential, that a time will come when we have enough people and enough power to make a stand. We get weapons, recruit spies among the Uppers, and make tech to combat Community tech. We're trying to find ways to disable the Link system for good, to give people back their voices—" He looked at me now. "—and when that happens, the Rez will be able to provide the infrastructure and resources to help the people rise up against the bastards who've enslaved them."

"And when is this great revolution going to happen?" Max's voice was caustic.

Adrien looked down, with what I thought looked like sadness or uncertainty. "We haven't found a way to disable the Link permanently in any significant population. Until we do, it's impossible to make a lasting change."

"So what are you doing here at the Academy?" I asked.

"I'm looking for glitchers. I'm a recruiter, kinda. I mean, visions aren't the most reliable way to make sure we've found all the glitchers at an Academy." He looked down self-consciously. "But it's something. My task is to find as many as possible, prepare them for the outside world, then escape with the Rez's help."

Escape. He'd said the word out loud I barely let myself whisper furtively in my head. Did I dare let myself believe it? Was it really possible that there was a place where we could live without the constant, strangling threat of deactivation?

"And Markan," I cut in suddenly. "We have to take Markan too. I don't care if he's not a glitcher." I said it with such certainty I almost sounded angry. I blinked, surprised at myself, but Adrien only nodded.

"Of course. But"—he had that pained expression again on his face—"we can only take Markan because there's a hope he'll be a glitcher like you. We can't take your parents. Even away from the Community and the Link, there's no way we've found to extract the adult V-chip hardware without it killing the subject."

"Why?" I asked. "Surely you have the equipment to take the hardware out."

"It's not that. By the time people reach adulthood and get the invasive final V-chip installed, they can't survive without it regulating their limbic functions. Their brains become completely dependent on the hardware. We can keep them alive on life support, but the damage just gets worse till they're brain-dead."

"It's all so horrible," I whispered, his words sinking in. "How could human beings do this to one another?"

"It'll be okay." Max moved closer and put an arm around my shoulders. "I would never let anyone hurt you."

"But Max," I said, pulling away from him in exasperation, "this isn't just about me. There are so many other people out there being hurt. We have to help them."

His jaw hardened. "You can't just save everyone—"

Adrien cut him off. "Maybe not everyone, but we can help some. I know there's at least one more girl. I had a vision of her a couple days ago. I'd been laying low so they wouldn't notice anything anomalous about me, but I had to contact you after I saw the vision. Her name's Molla—she's a year behind you at the Academy and she's been glitching for a couple weeks now. She's not handling it well. If we don't get to her soon, they'll crack her for sure."

"What are her powers?" Max asked, glaring at Adrien.

Adrien shook his head. "I don't know, that wasn't part of the vision. I'm not even sure they've manifested yet. She's been glitching such a short time, and they don't always show up right away."

"Maybe we should wait until we see if she's worth it," Max said. "There's no point in risking exposure if she isn't powerful enough to be useful to us. It'd just be dead weight."

"Dead weight." My mouth dropped open. "She's a *person*, Max!"

He waved a hand. "You know what I mean."

"No, I really don't," I said, suddenly furious.

Adrien cocked his head sideways, listening. "Your brother's getting off the treadmill. These walls are cracking thin. We can't risk talking anymore."

"Fine." My whole body shook in frustration at Max. "I'll try to talk to Molla tomorrow. Will you point her out to me?" I asked Adrien.

"Yes," Adrien whispered, "but be careful. New glitchers can be unstable, sometimes they struggle with it and turn themselves in. The Chancellor's been watching you very closely ever since you disappeared, so you gotta be crackin' careful with how you approach Molla. If she's skittish, back off, or we could get all cracked."

I nodded. "I'll be careful. Now you guys, go."

Max's jaw set. "Not until after he does."

"Max!" I barely managed to keep my voice under control. Everything that came out of his mouth tonight made me want to punch him.

"It's fine," Adrien said calmly. He looked at me, like he wanted to say something. After a moment he just closed his mouth, shook his head, and climbed up the ladder to my loft bed. He lifted his body up through the square space of the ceiling tile he'd removed.

The door to my room suddenly opened and I felt my heart stop cold. It was Markan.

I clenched my fist tightly behind my back, my fingernails digging into my palm as I stifled a yelp of surprise.

Markan was sweaty from the treadmill, but his eyes were sharp and alert as he scanned the room. He looked back and forth between Max and me, his forehead furrowing. Max and I stood still. I held my breath, wanting to look up and make sure that Adrien was gone, but made myself resist. I forced my eyes to stay on Markan, knowing I'd give something away for sure if I glanced at the ceiling.

"I heard voices," Markan said, his head tilted sideways as he looked at me with an uncanny acuity.

"Maximin and I were discussing an Academy assignment." My voice was a little high in spite of my attempt to control it.

Markan's gaze quickly shifted to Max. "I thought I identified more than two voices."

My neck stiffened, but Max didn't flinch.

"You were incorrect," Max said coolly.

Markan's gaze flicked around the room, but then he exited, sliding the door behind him.

After the door was securely shut I immediately looked up. The tile was only half closed. Markan hadn't seen the tile slightly askew, or else we would all have been reported. Adrien didn't say anything, but Max and I watched in silence while he shifted the tile quietly into place above us.

I looked back at the door Markan had just shut. If he'd walked in just one moment earlier, or if he'd glanced up and seen the tile . . . a terrified chill clutched my chest.

I was about to say something, but Max put a finger on my lips and shook his head. His glance went toward the door and I knew what he was thinking. Markan might still be listening. We were all trained to investigate and report anomalies, after all.

Adrien had just talked about living free in the Rez, apart from the Community, but I suddenly wondered if that wasn't just a dream made of smoke. I felt with a sinking sureness that the day was coming when I wouldn't be so lucky—when the Uppers would find me out for what I was. But what I hadn't fully understood until now was the horrifying realization that it all could end so easily at the hands of the brother I was trying so hard to save.

Chapter 15

I FIRST SAW MOLLA in the crowded cafeteria and tried to memorize her face. At first glance, she looked ordinary, like the rest of us. One problem with all the monotone suits and functional haircuts was that they made it hard to tell us apart. She looked like most of the girls around her, but I did notice a sprinkling of freckles over her nose.

The more I watched her, the more I saw other ways she stood out. Little things, like the way she tapped her toe or fidgeted with her tablet strap. People around her walked in calm, measured movements, but she seemed to radiate nervous energy. I could see why Adrien was worried. At least she had managed to resist reporting herself. That was something.

Still, I felt anxious just watching her. My eyes flicked over to the Regs-in-training, trying to see if any of them were giving any attention to the restless girl. Their faces were impassive. It was impossible to tell what they were thinking. Besides, it was more the job of Monitors to look for more subtle anomalies, and Monitors could be anywhere.

I glanced around the room, trying to be unobtrusive as I did. The last thing I needed while worrying about Molla was to look anomalous myself. But the thought that any of the students I went to the Academy with every day could be a Monitor, secretly working for the officials . . . it sent a shiver of fear through me.

After a few more minutes, in spite of my fear, I stood up

and made my way toward Molla. Just like Adrien had said, this girl didn't have long before she was found out. We had to get to her first. The flood of students exiting blocked my way, though, and by the time I got to the column she'd been standing in front of, she was gone.

The rest of the day was just as disappointing. She wasn't in any of my classes, since she was a year behind me. I caught sight of her once in the hallways but it wasn't as if I could push my way through the stream of students to get to her without attracting notice. I went to each class more frustrated than the last. But then I finally found my moment. Right before my last session of the day, I saw her slip into the bathroom. This was the best opening I was going to get.

I hurried as quickly as I dared across the hallway and into the bathroom after her. I peeked under the stalls. Only one set of feet. I went into the stall beside her and quickly popped the cap off the marker I'd brought from home. I grabbed a wad of toilet paper and scribbled a quick message on it: *You're not alone. We will contact you again soon. Until then, stay calm and stop fidgeting all the time! Flush after reading.* I shoved the paper under the stall and hissed, "Molla!"

I saw her feet hesitate. Then slowly her hand came into view and she took the paper. After another minute, the toilet flushed again and I breathed out. Good. I unlatched the door and walked to the sink. I glanced at her. Her face was pale and she was staring at me, her eyes so wide they looked like they might pop out of her head. Then she turned and bolted from the room.

I started to call after her, but another girl came in. I put my hands under the spout and pretended I'd been washing them. I stood there, my hands under the water longer than necessary to hide their trembling. Max was right. This was a huge risk. I hadn't thought about what I'd do if Molla didn't believe me, or if she was caught and reported me. I hoped she'd flushed the note I'd given her like I'd instructed, but then she'd run away. What if she'd run straight to the Regulators?

I forced my back ramrod straight and walked out to the hallway. I made my face blank through the rest of the day, secretly terrified that I'd jeopardized everything. I wanted to signal to Adrien, to let him know what had happened. I'd wanted so badly to help, to *do* something, but on my first try I might have ruined Adrien's entire mission.

That night at home, I waited impatiently until I saw the ceiling tile shift. I let out the tense breath I'd been holding and whispered the Link release words.

"I tried to talk to Molla," I burst out in a vehement whisper as soon as I saw the shadow of his torso coming down through the hole in the ceiling. I was sitting on my bed waiting for him and I got up on my knees to talk to him as he settled beside me. "But I think I did it wrong. She ran away! What if I made everything worse? What if we're all in danger now?"

"Zoe." Adrien took my chaotically waving hands and shook his head. "You did fine. You made first contact. That's cracking huge. It'll make her more careful and hopefully she'll be less afraid the next time we approach her."

"But—"

"But nothing," he said firmly. "Risks are part of everything we do. But we're fine. We're safe. Besides, with my Gift, I'm sure I'll get a vision if we're about to get cracked. Don't worry about it."

"Do you always?" I asked anxiously. "Get visions before something happens?"

I could see his thick lips curving up in the dim light from the night pod light by my bed. "How do ya think I lasted this long? It's why the Rez sends me in on the long-term missions. I can see danger coming before it shunts things up."

I sat a moment, taking in all he'd said. It was comforting to know we weren't just barreling into a dangerous future completely blind. Still, it seemed too good to be true. "But do the visions always come true?"

"It's too soon to tell for some of them, but I think so." He sat back against the wall and I could see the outline of his silhouetted face. "Most of them have been fulfilled, but others haven't happened—least I don't think they have. I just know things *will* happen, not *when* or even *how*. I'm trying to hone it so I can get a clearer sense of timelines. It's not perfect, but I'm getting better and better at it." He smiled.

I looked at him quizzically. "How can you hone it? My powers just seem to *happen*."

He nodded. "It was like that for me at first too. But I started to practice focusing the visions whenever I have them. Sure it's cracking frustrating 'cause I have to wait for them—I can't *make* them happen. But when they do, I try to slow them down, notice details—anything to get more control over it instead of it just crashing over me. The visions are getting more detailed too since I've been working on it." He moved a little closer on the bed. "It's one of the things I wanted to talk to you about. You should be practicing your telekinesis."

I shuddered, thinking about it. It seemed to take all of my energy *not* to use my power. It was volatile, unpredictable, like a caged monster underneath my skin. It felt like only a matter of time before it hurt someone, or got me caught. So I kept it locked up tight inside, hidden behind my mask with the rest of my emotions.

"Think how much better it would be if you could call on it when you need it, like Max does with his," Adrien said.

"It just always seems so risky when he uses his power."

"It doesn't have to be," Adrien said, and I thought I detected some disapproval in his face. "Max takes a lot of risks, from what I've seen. But if you just practiced here at home where no one can see you, you could get to be in control of your powers. I could help you."

"It only happens when I'm not thinking about it," I said. "Like a reflex. And even then, it doesn't always react the way I intend. Like on the train." I swallowed hard. The pain of that night rose up and almost choked me. "People *died* that day because of my powers."

"No, Zoe, you've got it all wrong," his voice was low, but insistent. "People *survived* that day because of your powers. All the people on the train lived because you were able to set the train back on the cracking tracks. *I* survived that day, and it wasn't even the first time you've saved my life!"

I couldn't decipher the look on his face. It was so frustrating not understanding emotion. His features changed before I could even try to figure it out.

"Do you mind just giving it a try?" he asked. "We'll start small, like with that pillow."

I nodded reluctantly, and he settled in next to me, both of us facing the pillow at the top of my bed.

"Now, it sounds like for some reason your power works best when you're in an emergency. It could be fear, or adrenaline, or some other reaction that allows you to access that power. Maybe with the right trigger, we can channel that so you'll be able to call on it whenever you want."

I nodded, my eyes never straying from the pillow. I stared at it intently, memorizing its shape and willing it to lift off the bed. I squinted my eyes shut, teeth clenched in concentration. I waited for the high-pitched buzzing that usually seemed to accompany my power.

Nothing. I kept pressing, my eyes boring holes in the pillow as I summoned memories of fear and dread and channeled it through my eyes toward the pillow.

Suddenly, Adrien picked up the pillow and tossed it in my direction. I gasped in surprise, then felt the soft thud of the pillow hitting my face.

"Why did you do that?" I asked.

"I thought maybe some element of surprise would help you."

We stared at each other. Adrien looked at me, taking in my tousled hair and confused face, and his face slowly spread to a wide-eyed grin. His shoulders started to shake with silent laughter. Soon I joined him, my laughter muffled into the pillow he had thrown at me.

Adrien wiped at his eyes. "Okay, so that strategy clearly doesn't work. Maybe we have to try something more dangerous next time."

"If you wanted to scare me, a pillow is probably not the best choice."

"Okay, we'll try something else next time," Adrien said, still laughing. "It was a good first practice, though. Just remember, Zoe. Keep trying. Find out whatever it is that gives you that power, and hold on to it."

"But when I use my power, I can never direct it the way I want to." I felt frustrated all over again. "It's unsafe. There's no way I can control it and keep it from hurting anyone."

"That might be a risk you'll just have to take. It's the only way you can get better at it. See if you can access that power first, and then we'll worry about controlling it."

The smile slipped from his face and he became serious once again. "There's something else I need to tell you, too. About when you were away. I didn't want to talk about it in front of Max the other night."

"What?" I immediately frowned. "Is it something bad?"

His brows furrowed. "Sanjan—our crank who specializes in this kind of stuff—he said it shoulda been impossible for you to have an allergic reaction like you did without being exposed to it before. Maybe someone from the outside had some mold gnange on their clothes and you came into contact with them. Though secondhand exposure isn't usually enough to do it." He shrugged.

"Molds." I sat back, frowning in thought.

He nodded slowly. "Yeah, the attacks would get worse every time you're exposed. But!" He brightened, reaching back into the ceiling to pull down an aluminum case. "There's some medicine we can try. It's called immunotherapy. I brought it with me when I came back. It's gonna mean regular injections, though."

"For how long?"

"It could take months. But if we do the injections regularly, we might weaken the allergy enough to be able to get you out of here safely."

I let go of the curl I'd been twirling. "Are you sure it will work?" My eyes flicked back up to him.

"I hope so." He paused a moment before opening the aluminum case and just watched me. "Do you trust me? You did once. I hope you can again." He seemed to see the hesitation in my eyes and ran his hand through his hair. "Look, I don't wanna pressure you but the sooner we get started, the sooner we can see if it's having an effect and start planning the escape."

A thrill rushed through my body at the word *escape*. I nodded.

"Good. Then as soon as your allergy is neutralized, or the Rez can find a safe place for you to live with the allergy, we'll take whatever other glitchers we've found and get the godlam'd hell out of here."

"And one day when my allergy isn't a problem anymore, then I can help other people escape."

A smile played at the edges of his lips. "You wanna join the Rez?"

"Of course! What else would I do once we escaped? I want to help Molla. And I want to stop the . . . the . . ." I threw my hands up in the air. "I don't even have a word bad enough for the Uppers who've done this to us."

"Godlam'd shunting bastards is my name of choice."

I laughed a little. "Okay." My gaze switched to the aluminum case still by his side. "So where does this injection go?"

His eyebrows rose. "Yeah? You sure?"

"I'm sure," I said, getting caught for a moment in the bright aquamarine of his eyes. We had so little color in our world, his eyes seemed doubly extraordinary against the gray of the walls and his uniform. Then there was how, when I looked at them, something inside my chest seemed to loosen, like a melting ice cube in a hothouse.

"Great." He grinned. "Roll up your sleeve." He clicked open the case and pulled out a small tube, about the size of a marker, and took a cap off the end of it. Two tiny needle tips pointed out the end.

"This is a cocktail of all seven allergens. But just tiny trace amounts to start immunizing you against them. We build up your tolerance bit by bit, then next time you're exposed to the real thing, hopefully it'll be harmless."

I held out my arm and he leaned close with the needles.

"Just a tiny prick." He bit his bottom lip as he concentrated. He took my upper arm in his cool hands to steady it, then inserted the needles. I winced but he quickly pulled back.

"All done. We'll do these for a while, then we'll test some skin and blood samples to see if it's working."

"You have contact with the Resistance while you're here?"

"Of course. There are the people posing as my parents. And there are more of us hidden in all the sectors. They'll help us coordinate an escape as soon as we're ready." He closed up the aluminum case and got to his knees, lifting it back up through the ceiling. "Okay, well, good night, Zoe." His face seemed to soften as he said it.

"Oh wait," I said, putting a hand on his leg to stop him. "What do we do about Molla? How do we get to her without arousing suspicion? We can't let them get her. We can't let her be . . . deactivated." I whispered the last word.

He nodded, suddenly serious. "It'd be too dangerous trying to bring her here. We saw what happened last time with your brother coming in. Though . . ." He paused, thinking. "I'm surprised they've allowed you and Max to study together so much—school officials are usually very wary of letting people congregate."

"Why?"

"Well think about it. All that's keeping them in control is a tiny, minuscule piece of hardware in people's heads." He reached over and tapped the side of my head with a finger. "When you imagine the sheer cracking number of people they've enslaved, and the number of glitchers that has been growing with every generation, there's something going on."

He shook his head and dropped his hand. I realized with surprise that I'd been holding my breath the whole time his fingertip had been against my skin. "It's why so many of you are forced to live underground. To control the environment as much as possible, and because something as simple as touch could potentially trigger a malfunction. It's even why they allow the space for separate bedrooms for families, even spouses. It would be more efficient if everyone slept in one room, but they know bonds can form when people are in close physical contact, bonds that might become stronger than the V-chip control."

"Really?" I smiled in wonder at the thought.

"Well, not the adult V-chip. Nothing can get past that. But otherwise, yes, it's our nature." He leaned in. "The V-chip really only works in part because people accept it. People'll give up almost anything to think that they're safe from pain and fear. I mean, I get it. I really do. It's so much crackin' easier to accept an easy solution—even if it means letting yourself be lied to. The hard thing is finding the strength in yourself to stand up against the tide and say *shunt no*, I refuse!" His eyes were alight with passion as he talked, but he pulled back and laughed a little at himself. "Sorry, I can get worked up about this stuff."

"It sounds so simple and yet so impossible." I felt a mix of sadness and joy.

He leaned in, his face close to mine. "I know."

He had such a nice face, with light brown skin and heavy eyebrows and, most of all, those eyes. I leaned in for a closer look. They looked green from far away but up close I could see they were a darker green around the edges that melted into a translucent blue in the middle, with a million little bright aquamarine flecks that seemed to sparkle. I thought that was a good word for Adrien himself—all of him sparkled and he lit me up until I sparkled inside, too. I suddenly felt so happy right now, so much more warm and contented maybe than I'd ever been.

I had a flash of memory—of his face, closer than it was now. Of his lips on mine, his hands cradling my head and the sensation like I was falling, like my stomach had dropped out and was replaced by a flickering, hot fire.

My breath hitched and I pulled back from him, lifting a hand to my lips in shock at the memory. "Adrien," I said, feeling out of breath at the intensity of the memory.

Adrien's face seemed almost for an instant to show a glimmer of response, but he covered it quickly and didn't answer my question. "See you at the Academy tomorrow, Zoe," he whispered, his eyes lingering on mine for a moment before his face became a mask again.

He got up and moved the ceiling tile, then pulled himself up into the darkness. I watched him go, my frozen fingers still touching my lips, till finally, he was gone.

My dreams that night were a long replay of the strange stirring lightness at seeing Adrien's animated face, his eyes glittering up when he looked at me. Happiness expanded inside of me the longer we sat together.

And then, on the brink of a wild soaring joy, the dream changed again back to the old nightmare. This time it began earlier. My brother and I were creeping through the forest. I could smell the leaves, feel the foreign breeze and all the countless noises surrounding us.

In the dream, Markan had turned back to me and I studied him. He was taller, older. His features were more sharp than round. *Shh, Zoe,* he had whispered. *Don't make a sound.*

But I was confused. We were on the Surface and I knew I wasn't supposed to be there. And Markan wasn't supposed to be acting like this. He was behaving anomalously. I was supposed to report anomalous behavior.

Shh, Zoe. Don't make a sound.

But I did. I did make a sound. I'd heard my voice, though it was like I was split in two—hearing myself scream to alert the Regulators in the clearing we were passing by—and watching it happen with horror at the same time.

The Regulators came running from all directions, crushing the green brush beneath their feet. I saw Markan's face go white with terror. He ran, but they were faster. From then on the dream was the same as always—his face crashing into the ground, them lifting him up, his face covered in blood. Screaming and thrashing.

All the next day I was so preoccupied, nauseated with the memory that I barely heard it when the Microhardware

Engineering instructor leaned his head out of a classroom and called my name as I passed his door between classes.

I dropped my hands to my side and stopped. "Yes?"

"I request your assistance arranging the equipment."

"Yes, sir," I said, inwardly frowning.

"Here, take these to the supply closet." He handed me a tray of microfusing tools. I looked at him, trying to cover my look of alarm. What if my instructor was actually a Monitor? The realization dawned on me with sudden dread. Of course. It made sense that Monitors didn't just pose as students. Instructors had the perfect excuse to stare at students all during class, watching us when we didn't think anyone was looking.

I took the tray and headed toward the small closet at the back of the room. I wasn't Linked, but I didn't want to whisper the words to Link me back in case he overheard me. I walked in the back equipment closet, scanning the floor-to-ceiling shelves for an empty space to set the tray down.

I didn't notice the instructor had followed me until he closed the closet door behind us. I took a sharp intake of breath, but managed to swallow my scream. I was trapped. He was holding me captive until the Regulators came to drag me away for deactivation.

I turned to face my captor just as his body shimmered and morphed into Max's. He had a very satisfied smirk on his face.

"Max!" I squeaked, the release of adrenaline flooding me in relief. I put down the tray and knocked him in the chest with both palms. "I can't believe you scared me like that!"

"I just needed to talk to you. I didn't mean to scare you."

"A little warning next time would help," I said, still trying to catch my breath from the shock. "I thought you were—" I couldn't even finish the sentence. I hugged my arms around myself.

"Hey, it's okay." His face was soft and he reached out for my hands. He smiled, dimples showing.

I breathed in and out slowly, the terror trickling away.

"I was going crazy thinking about you. And I decided I'll help with Molla. Whatever you want me to do.

"Ouch, my hand, Zoe." He laughed and I realized I was clutching his hand so hard my nails were digging in. He leaned in, his broad shoulders and strong jaw outlined in the dim light of the closet. "Glad to know you care."

"Of course I care," I said. "So you'll contact Molla? How?"

"Same way I'm doing here. Posing as an instructor. I'll try to catch her later today. I'll let her know I'm looking out for her and help her work on hiding her emotions so she doesn't get noticed by the Regulators."

I smiled as the last of my frustration ebbed away. "Max, that is such a good thing. Just think how much better she will feel. And here." I pulled a small drive out of my pocket that Adrien had given me in case I found a way to get Molla alone again. "Give her this upgrade, then she'll be able to click herself in and out of the Link like I can."

Max took the drive and nodded, then looked up at me. "All I want is to make you happy." The tenor of his voice deepened. "I know I've been pushing you. I just get so . . ." He paused, brow furrowing. "I don't know, frustrated. Upset. All the emotions get uncontrollable sometimes. But it's only because you mean so much to me."

"I understand." I suddenly thought about Adrien and the image I'd had at the end of our meeting last night—the one that was maybe a memory of kissing him. It made me feel guilty, being here with Max.

"You understand? You do?" Max sounded surprised.

"Sure. All this emotion," I said, "it's confusing. It makes

thoughts get all mixed up." I didn't know if I was talking more to Max or myself.

"Exactly." He smiled.

"I should get going before it's noticed I'm gone. I am so glad for your help with Molla." I squeezed his hand one last time.

"See you at lunch." His dimples caught the light. I put my hand on the door, but before I could step out, it was suddenly yanked open from the other side. I jerked back, my body instinctively turning rigid and blank. I was working to keep my heart rate within range when I saw it was Adrien.

"I just had a vision," he said, pulling the door closed behind him. When he turned back to us, his face was pale and pinched with worry. "Molla's about to get caught."

Chapter 16

"WHAT DO WE DO?" I whispered.

"Hold on, we have to think about this," Max said, glaring at Adrien. "Maybe we should stay out of it if they already suspect her. We'd be throwing ourselves in harm's way."

"Not an option. If she's caught, she'll talk. *You* might be safe," Adrien said through gritted teeth to Max before looking back to me. "But Zoe's cover'll be cracked. Do you care about *that*?"

Max pushed Adrien hard in the chest. "I cared about her before you ever—"

"Guys, stop!" I stepped between them. "We don't have time for this."

Max's nostrils flared, but he stepped back and raised his hands. "Fine, so what did you see, Future Boy?"

"Max, you gotta go get Molla out of class. There's going to be a graphic video in her Community History class about a historic mass-deactivation event—it's going to make her start crying. Crying *loud*. They've already been Monitoring her, and it'll be the last step to confirm their suspicions. Please, Max. Make up whatever excuse or disguise you need, but get her out of there and give her the upgrade so she can control when she glitches. Think you can handle it?"

"You questioning my abilities?" Max stepped forward, invading the small space between him and Adrien.

Adrien held his hands up. "'Course not. I know you can do it, that's why I'm asking."

"And what are you two going to be doing?" Max's voice was still a growl.

"Hopefully, hacking into Central Systems and altering her subject records so she drops off their radar."

Max was quiet a moment. "Fine. But I'm doing it to protect Zoe, not to help you." He pushed past Adrien to lean in and whisper to me, "I'd do anything to keep you safe."

Max's breath was hot on my neck, and I was uncomfortably aware of Adrien watching us only a few feet away.

"I'll see you soon," I said. "Be safe."

He nodded and was gone. When I looked back at Adrien, his face was all hard lines, a mask I couldn't read. He swallowed stiffly and I watched his throat bob up and down.

"Let's go," he said, his voice a bit distant. "We'll split up and walk normally when we leave. We need to look as non-anomalous as possible."

I nodded and before I could say another word, he was out the door. I followed, keeping my steps measured and controlled. *Order first, order always*, I repeated in my mind. Above all, I had to stay calm. I had to ignore the constant thoughts and images of what would happen to Molla if we failed.

We walked down familiar hallways and corridors. It was a passing period so the halls were packed with students. I stared straight ahead, stealing looks at Adrien whenever I could in order to make sure I was keeping up with him. I turned when he turned, paused when he paused, all with a perfect studied indifference.

We paused as we turned down a short hallway. A pale gray door blocked our path into the restricted block, where Adrien had told me we'd find one of the few access points for the Central Academy data mainframe. I watched anxiously down the hallway as Adrien inserted a chip in his wrist ID scanner. When it was all in place, he turned to smile at me, but not before I saw a flicker of anxiety cross his eyes. He wasn't sure this would work.

My heartbeat ratcheted up a few notches and I barely kept it in check as he held his wrist in front of the scanner. It let out a loud beep, and I released the breath I hadn't realized I'd been holding. I took another worried look up and down the hallway, but it was still empty. After a pause, the scanner light switched from red to green, and we heard the welcome sound of the door lock sliding out of place.

I breathed out a sigh of relief as we entered an empty hallway. Our footsteps echoed loudly off the narrow whitewashed walls. Sweat gathered at the nape of my neck. Adrien might be able to erase the video feed of us coming here afterward, but if a person discovered us, there would be no explanation for our presence here.

Adrien ducked into a doorway alcove. I stepped into the small space with him. It was so quiet I could hear his every breath. He pulled a small drive out of his bag and attached it to a small port in the wall.

"What's that?" I asked, my voice barely audible.

He smiled at me. "A distraction." He turned his attention back to the device. Embedded wall projectors lit up, creating an orange 3-D cube about a handspan in length. I watched in fascination as Adrien's fingers clicked through the interface at rapid-fire speed. He bit his lip in concentration, but he looked confident—like he'd done this hundreds of times before. Maybe he had. I watched him, wondering what he must have seen in his life to make him able to stay so unafraid and calm as he crouched here in a hallway with me.

"There," he finally whispered, pulling back. I heard a door open somewhere down the hall, and then voices. Adrien quickly pushed me farther into the shadow of the alcove corner, covering his body with mine. My eyes flicked up anxiously at him. He was so tall he had to crane his neck at an awkward angle to look down at me. We stood close with our chests pressed together, breathing at the same time. I watched a droplet of sweat trace its way down the side of his neck. Maybe he was more nervous than he let on.

The voices came closer and I instinctively leaned into his chest, wishing one of us had the power of invisibility. We didn't even dare to breathe as the footsteps came closer and closer. We were standing in a corner, hidden, but by no means completely out of sight. And there was nowhere to run if we were caught.

One set of footsteps seemed to falter near us. There was a clatter like some small device had been dropped. The steps paused. I could see the small black scanner on the ground, inches away from the shadow of our hiding spot. The systems tech walked over, bending slowly to retrieve the device.

I gripped a handful of Adrien's shirt tightly in my fist, willing myself to silence the high-pitched ring pounding in my ears and the hum vibrating down my forearms. *No.* This was not the time to lose control. I repeated the Community Creed over and over in my head, but I couldn't completely still the tremor in my hand. I looked into Adrien's eyes and could tell by his panicked expression that he felt my power was threatening to break loose.

The tech paused, as if sensing it, too. He had crouched down to retrieve the device, the scanner in his hand, but he remained still for a moment. Down the hallway, the other footsteps had stopped, and I heard a muffled voice call out. The tech straightened abruptly, placing the device in his belt and proceeding methodically down the hallway.

My hands continued to tremble, and I felt a stinging prick

behind my eyes as I fought to quiet the shaking all through my body. Adrien held me close for another few seconds. When my hands had finally stilled, he pulled gently away, holding a hand up to wait. He peeked around the alcove corner, then motioned me to follow behind him.

I looked both ways down the empty hallway. When I caught up to Adrien, he'd pulled out another small device and put it directly in front of the thumbprint scanner.

"Stay back till I call you," he whispered. The door hissed open and he slid inside. I waited for several anxious seconds outside.

"It's clear," he called quietly, and I came in. Stacks of two- and three-dimensional monitors filled the small room. There appeared to be three different work stations, but the chairs were empty.

"Where are all the systems engineers and techs?"

Adrien raised the thumbprint machine to close the door behind us, then sat at one of the consoles and started typing rapidly in the 3-D interface cube. "I caused a system malfunction in the Academy mainframe server hub on Sublevel Four. It's protocol for these three techs to cover Sublevels Three through Eight. If there's one thing you can count on Link drones for, it's to obey protocol. Plus"—he smiled—"I saw in my vision that we got in here without any problem."

"But did you see if we get *out* okay?"

"Don't worry." He waved a hand. He continued typing.

"Just a little bit further." His thick eyebrows bunched up in concentration as he went deeper into the directory object files. Lightning-fast code flashed across the interface as he hacked his way past security wall after security wall. He was *good*. All Academy students learned some advanced programming. I was one of the best in my class, but I could still barely follow Adrien's code.

"How do you know how to do that?" I whispered out in awe.

He grinned, his face illuminated in the orange light of the interface. "I've been hacking Community security tech since I could walk and talk. That's life in the Rez for you."

He bit his lip as he came to denser code. I quieted, not wanting to distract him, but I couldn't keep my legs from shaking nervously as I paced around the room. There was no telling how long we had until the techs came back.

"All right. The video files of this hallway have been deleted and replaced with a loop of empty hallway. No one scanning the camera feeds will know we were here." He zoomed in on an object file. Molla's profile spun along the side of the projection cube.

"How long have they been watching her?" I whispered, leaning in to look.

"A few weeks now. She's been cited for six anomalous incidents." He pointed to the screen to show me. "When a subject gets to eight reports, they get hauled in for a diagnostic. Or if there's a terminal event, like what was about to happen to Molla today, they skip straight to deactivation."

"I hope Max was able to get there in time."

"I don't see any flags in the system," he said. "That's a good sign."

I breathed out in relief.

"Okay, so let's just adjust this file," he paused, fingers moving rapidly. Then he smiled. "There, down to two anomaly citations."

I felt like jumping up and down with happiness. We'd done it. I felt a rush of good feelings swarming my chest. Molla was okay, and I had no doubt Max would be able to find a way to give her the upgrade so she wouldn't be in as much danger in the future. Everyone I cared about was safe.

Adrien was clicking on the interface again, backing out of the amended file, when he stopped and leaned in. "Wait, what's that?"

"What?" I asked, leaning in as well. I peered at the green column of stacked directories in the interface cube. Most of the files in the column were solid green, but a few glowed brighter. "You mean that directory collection there?"

Adrien clicked a few times, and both of our eyes widened. He slid the column sideways, and we saw several more student profiles come into view. Each of their anomaly citations were well beyond twenty.

"Six more?" I whispered. "What does that mean? Are they all glitchers?"

"This doesn't make sense," Adrien said, shaking his head. "There shouldn't be this many glitchers at the Academy. And why weren't they taken in for diagnostics and repairs ages ago?"

He bit his lip and clicked on the surrounding files. "I wonder . . ." His fingers moved at rapid speed and I saw several columns fill the cube.

"What are you looking at?" I whispered.

"The history of anomalous activity for this district. Hmm." He clicked and typed in more code. I watched as he worked. He came to a new directory. Only a few files glowed in these columns.

"What is that?"

"Anomalous activity to date. There hasn't been a lot of history of anomalous activity," he said. "But all of the sudden, the numbers have jumped."

I looked at him quizzically. "Could something be happening to trigger the glitches?"

"There have been more glitchers in this generation than ever before, it's true." Adrien's forehead was wrinkled with concern. "But this is more than just unusual." He paused, eyes widening.

"Shunting hell, Zoe, look at this." He'd been pulling up the glowing files and flipping through them, but he'd stopped on one in particular.

A profile rose up and spun in the cube in front of us. It was me. All the air in my lungs seemed to exit at once. But it wasn't me that had caught Adrien's attention. At the bottom of my profile there was a list of profiles linked to mine. Four of them. He opened up the one blinking yellow.

It was my little brother Markan. But at the same time, it wasn't quite him. This boy was older, leaner, wearing an outdated uniform. It was the boy from my dreams.

I read the data set in the sidebar.

Subject: Q-24, Daavd. DEACTIVATION 4/12/2274. Summary of Incident Report: After eleven anomalous incidents and attempted hardware rehabilitation, subject D. Q-24 attempted escape. Apprehended when accompanying sibling, Zoel, alerted Regulators at surface coordinates 9.103.23. Resolution: Prompt deactivation of D. Q-24 upon apprehension. Subject Z. Q-24 reintegrated into family unit after memory scrub.

"No," I whispered, reaching into the interface cube, searching for more information. I struggled to breathe. I felt like someone had punched me in the stomach. "No!"

I grabbed frantically at the screen, typing every tech code I could think of to open up more information in the profile, but all the other subheadings were blank and I hit a security wall the more I pressed. It had to be wrong. It was impossible. I shook my head back and forth frantically.

"Adrien, what else is in that file?" My voice was high-pitched, near hysteria. My heart monitor was buzzing, but I didn't care. This had to be wrong. "Show me what else is in that file!"

A high-pitched scream threatened to erupt from my throat. My arms shook with emotion and power, but this time I barely cared about maintaining control. For all I cared, my power could let loose and rip the data equipment from the walls, break down the doors and disable the entire Central System mainframe. It could bring the concrete maze of the Academy crashing down, crumbling it to dust. Anything to wipe away what I'd just seen.

The device Adrien had placed on the table beeped. "Shunt, Zoe, we have to get out of here. They've repaired the malfunction. They will be back any minute."

I barely heard him. I was staring at the green silhouette of the older brother I didn't remember having, my hands in fists so tight my fingernails broke my skin. My stomach twisted in pain.

The fragmented nightmares. The allergies. I *had* been on the Surface once before, exposing myself to the mold allergens. I'd been on the Surface and I'd betrayed my brother to the Regulators. Bile rose up into my throat. I had another brother. And I'd killed him.

Adrien had gathered up all his equipment and finally turned to look at me. His face was a mask of worry.

I felt a tremor of anger rip through me. It was sharp and electric, filling me to my fingertips and making my scalp tingle with energy.

"Zoe, you have to stop. Zoe!" Adrien grabbed my frantic hands, forcing me to look at him. "We have to go. Now."

I shook my head, my teeth gritted as streams of water poured down my cheeks. I wrenched my hands away from him. "He must have been trying to take me with him when he escaped.

He didn't want to be alone, so he took me with him. And then I got him killed!"

"You were only four years old!" Adrien pulled me away from the console. I fought to get back to the interface cube, but Adrien stepped in front of me, taking my face in both of his hands.

"Think of the others, Zoe," he said quietly, his eyes searching back and forth between both of mine until I stilled. "If we get caught here it will put Max and Molla in danger. We need to leave. Can you click yourself back into the Link?"

I stared at Adrien, seeing him and not seeing him. He grabbed my upper arms, forcing me to meet his eyes. For a moment I was grounded again, locking on to something real, something other than the uncontrollable emotions that were surging through my body, threatening to break free. I finally nodded and stepped back, feeling dizzy and light-headed.

I wanted it—I wanted the Link. I wanted to bury my crushing pain in the numbing stream of the Link's cold logic and order. But I didn't deserve comfort. I'd killed my brother. I deserved to feel every ounce of the empty and the cold. I deserved to fall into the pit of darkness that was ripping open like a jagged abyss in my chest.

Adrien shook me, bringing me back to the present. I finally lifted my heavy eyes to his face. "Beta Ten Gamma Link. Say it, Zoe."

I'd had an older brother. I'd gotten him deactivated. It was my fault. My fault, my fault, *my fault.* I clutched my stomach and sank to the ground. I was so heavy. I wanted to sink down right through the floor and disappear. I wanted to have never existed.

But I was a betraying coward, so I said it. I repeated after him dully, hating myself as I did: "Beta Ten Gamma Link."

"Let's go." He grabbed me by the hand and hauled me from

the room. We made it out through the long empty corridor, his hand in mine an anchor as he carefully maneuvered us back out of the doors of the restricted block. He pulled me down another hallway and into the alcove entrance to a classroom. The room was empty, but I heard footsteps in the next corridor beyond. It must be the end of the day. If we delayed too long, it would be noted that we were not following our strict schedules.

The Link News had filled my mind. The retina display readouts and subscript along the sides of my vision were bright and bracing and comfortingly familiar. I could forget everything in the numbness of the Link feed. If I let it, it could make me forget all the sudden sharp pain and guilt.

The alcove we were in seemed to dim, color leeching from my vision.

"Stay Linked until I come to your room tonight. Promise me," he demanded.

I nodded.

"I'll see you soon. Stay safe." He gave me a look I couldn't decipher, some sort of hesitation or fear, but then he shook himself and pressed his lips to my forehead. He gently pushed me out from the alcove into the hallway, and somehow I managed to make my feet move. Inside, there was a howling scream building up inside me, like a wild beast clawing to get out, but the graying chatter of the Link soon drowned it out.

Chapter 17

THAT NIGHT I LAY IN BED, staring at the ceiling, every deep breath searing a fresh wound in my chest. Adrien came to my room, but I didn't move or speak. He seemed to understand. He told me Max had disguised himself as a tech repair worker and disabled the video file before Molla had a chance to see it and become emotional in front of everyone. Then he'd given her the upgrade, so hopefully she'd be safe for the time being.

Adrien also told me he'd tried to find out more about the six glitchers that had come up in the database, but the information was locked behind a fortress of security that not even his hacking skills could breach. One more to add to a growing list of questions we couldn't answer.

I nodded as Adrien talked, but I was only half-listening. My mind was far away, as it had been all day. I'd almost lost it during dinner, watching my brother Markan and imagining another brother. Daavd.

Stupid! How stupid of him to take a four-year-old on an escape mission! Then I felt guilty for accusing him, when it was really all my fault.

My chest clenched with pain. I'd disconnected from the Link after dinner because I knew I deserved to feel every ounce of pain. I thought about all the feelings I had for Markan, or how much I'd wanted to be close to Max because I knew, intuitively, that family was important.

Maybe Daavd thought the same thing. He'd taken me because he was trying to save me. And I had betrayed him. The image from my dream rose up, of him crashing into the leaves. The blood. I couldn't stand myself. I couldn't stand being in this body, in this detestable, shunting skin.

"Zoe, what are you doing?" Adrien's voice broke into my thoughts.

I looked up in surprise. I'd forgotten he was here. He'd taken my hands in his gently and I looked down in surprise to see blood underneath my fingernails. I'd dug my nails into my upper arms deep enough to cut. I looked at Adrien in confusion, the horror of all my feelings too much a jumble to process all at once.

"I want to get away from myself," I whispered. I clutched my knees to my chest and rocked back and forth. "But I can't. I'm stuck here in my head with all these horrible memories and feelings and thoughts."

"Oh, Zoe," he said, his voice so soft. He pulled me against his chest and smoothed my hair in long, slow strokes. I closed my eyes, knowing I didn't deserve the comfort, but I couldn't manage to pull away either. I couldn't even cry anymore. It was like all the pain had clotted together into a sharp stone in my intestines, ripping its way through my insides.

"Zoe. I'm sorry, so sorry." His eyebrows were knit together. His face looked like I felt, like he was trying to share my sadness. I didn't understand why, but it did make me feel less alone. Then I felt a guilty pang for causing him to hurt.

I stared at the ceiling long after Adrien disappeared up through the tile for the night. He was another person who cared about me. Another person who could get hurt because of me.

All this time, all I'd wanted was to not be alone, but now I realized how much safer it was to have no one to hurt, no one to lose. If I got caught, if my pain showed or my powers re-leased on accident because I was wrapped up in guilt, all our lives would be at stake. I might deserve to hurt for what I'd done. I might even need it, but I didn't have the luxury. There was no more time for crying.

A couple of weeks later, Max and I rode the subway to his hous-ing unit. I hadn't wanted to come. I just wanted to stay con-nected to the Link. To remain numb and in control as I curled into a ball each night, making myself as small as possible. I felt like I could disappear if I just tried hard enough.

But I knew stopping my study sessions with Max might look anomalous. At school, I went through the motions, tried to immerse myself in life as a Link drone—an unthinking, un-feeling machine.

Max slid the door to his room shut behind us. He smiled, then pulled back and reached for his bag.

"Listen. I know you've been sad, so I got you something." He turned to me with his hands hidden behind his back. He grinned, dimples showing.

I was staring blankly at the wall, barely listening under the weight of the sadness that had come crashing back as soon as I disconnected from the Link. But I knew I should say some-thing. "What is it?"

"Something special, just for you."

I finally looked up at him and he stepped closer. "Close your eyes." He wiggled his eyebrows.

"Max," I said, managing half a nervous smile for the first time in a week. "What is it?"

"Close your eyes," he said insistently.

"Fine." I closed my eyes obediently and heard a click.

"Now, keep them shut," he whispered, his breath close to my face. I could hear the smile in his voice. "And *smell*."

Still confused, I inhaled deeply and my eyes popped open in spite of myself. It was the most incredible thing I'd ever smelled. I swore I could almost taste it, just from the aroma alone. I looked into the small box Max held toward me and saw a thick slice of something brown and moist-looking nestled in the box.

"What *is* it?" I asked incredulously, leaning in closer and taking another deep whiff.

"It's called chocolate cake." He was grinning, obviously enjoying my reaction. "Wait until you taste it." He pulled his other hand from behind his back, producing two forks.

I hesitated. "Really?"

He laughed. "Just take a bite already."

I didn't deserve anything so kind, and I almost said no. But Max looked so delighted, I took a small bite. It was so sweet, sweeter than anything I'd ever tasted before. And it seemed to melt in my mouth, smooth and creamy. I couldn't help the small moan that escaped my throat. I eagerly took another bite, a much bigger one this time.

Max laughed, his whole face lighting up as he watched me.

I gestured at the other fork. I knew I shouldn't be enjoying myself, but it was the first time I'd felt anything pleasant since I'd found out about Daavd. Daavd. His name still caught in my throat. I shook the thought away, smiling as hard as I possibly could for Max.

"I can't even think of a word for how good that tastes!" I said. "No words in my entire vocabulary are good enough to encapsulate the deliciousness of that— What was it called again?"

"Cake. Chocolate cake."

"Cake," I whispered reverently, then licked my fork again. "Where did you get it?"

He put the forks in the empty box and set it on the ground.

"I had some of this when I was pretending to be an official the other day. They had this event, where a bunch of the Uppers get together to talk and eat."

"What did they talk about?" I looked at him in confusion.

"Nothing!" Max laughed. "And everything! I mean, they were just talking about each other mostly, or other Uppers who weren't at the party." He laughed again, shrugging his shoulders.

"I'd gone hoping to figure out, you know, more of what's going on in the world. But none of them were talking about global corporations or anything like that. They were just talking about things like what clothes people were wearing, and they all laughed a lot, though mostly I didn't know what was supposed to be funny."

He shook his head, smiling in wonder. "Zoe, it was like nothing you've ever seen. And the food." He rolled his eyes. "You think this cake is good? They had meat, and I mean *actual* meat. And then this stuff called wine, which tasted really bitter at first, but then started making my head spin and I got really happy." He laughed as if the memory was so vivid he was experiencing it again. "I'll have to steal a bottle of it next time, you gotta try it."

"Max," I said, worry growing heavy in the pit of my stomach. He seemed to think it was all so great, but didn't he realize the danger he was putting himself in? All the feelings from the last week rushed back over me. They felt even heavier in contrast to the momentary lightness of forgetting myself with Max for a few minutes. I couldn't lose another person I cared about.

I put a hand on his arm. "I'm glad you enjoyed yourself, but you shouldn't go back. It's not worth it. Just one moment faltering, and they'd figure out what you are. What you can do. And they'd take you away from me. I'd lose you like I lost . . ." The words felt stuck in my throat. "Like my brother."

Max shook his head and waved his hand like he was sweeping all my concerns away. "Zoe, it's not like that. There's no danger. Don't you see? We don't have to escape. We can be safe right here. We can stay and eat cake every night and drink wine till it's coming out our ears!"

"What about the Regulators? The Monitors? The Chancellor? Every moment we stay here in the Community, we risk getting caught."

"That's for me to worry about. I've spent time around these Uppers, and the Chancellor. It will be a lot easier to work around them than you might think."

He took both my hands in his and the light shining out of his eyes was infectious. He was so confident, so sure of himself. His charisma was almost enough to sweep me away in spite of all my sadness and guilt.

"You and me, babe," he whispered, his glowing eyes searching mine. "We can make a life for ourselves. Just you and me. With the Rez, we'd be scraping by. On the run, fighting a battle we know we can't win. But with what I can do, this can be our *life*. We can have whatever we want. We can be happy."

I could almost believe him. Maybe I *did* believe him. Maybe there was some strange world that he could disappear into with his powers, and maybe there was even a way he could whisk me along with him to that world of chocolate cake and real meat and sparkling drinks that made you laugh all night. Wasn't that better than the suffocating worry and guilt? Wouldn't it be wonderful to lose myself like that, to let Max take care of everything? To pretend pain and sadness didn't exist?

"But what about all the other people?" I finally asked.

"Mmm?" he asked, still smiling and gazing into my eyes.

"All the other people who are left stuck being drones? How can we sit around eating cake when they're still in danger, still slaves?"

His brow furrowed. "There's nothing we can do about the drones." He shrugged. "We can only save ourselves. But the important thing is that we *can* save ourselves. We can be safe. Together. And happy." He took my hands again.

The cake in my stomach suddenly felt like a weight, sinking me further and further down. I pulled away from him.

"It sounds like a nice life, Max. Really. But I don't think I could live with myself, surrounded by people who have nothing while we have everything. I think the Rez can help us escape and be safe, and more important—we can help others. We need to have a real plan, for all of us. I'll talk to Adrien about it tonight and then maybe we could all meet." I picked up my tablet case and slung the strap over my shoulder.

"Adrien?" Max said with a voice so cold I looked up in alarm. He didn't sound right. He didn't look right, either. His face was mottled red, he had a pinched expression in his eyes, and his nostrils flared.

"Adrien?" he growled through gritted teeth. "You're meeting him tonight?"

"Yes." My voice trembled at the sudden change in him. "We need to all be together in this."

"Not with him," Max exploded. "Together is you and me. Not him!" He slammed the wall angrily, making me flinch.

"What is wrong with you lately?" I said, raising my voice too. "Stop *hitting* things. Stop yelling. Every time I see you we end up having a fight."

He breathed out hard and ran his hands through his hair roughly. "Everything was fine before that bastard showed up."

"You're the one taking useless risks for no reason, sneaking into officials' rooms and going to events and eating cake!" I felt bad as soon as I said it, but I kept barreling along.

"I don't understand who you are anymore. You're always going off in disguise and spending time with the Uppers. I feel like you're part of this whole other world now, one I don't know anything about. And you're not telling me everything, I can feel it." I searched his eyes. "You're keeping secrets from me, aren't you?"

He didn't say anything but his face softened. "Come on." He pulled me close and wrapped his arms gently around me. "No more fighting."

I felt suddenly exhausted. I wanted to go back to sleep now. Everything was so difficult—my relationship with Max, the buzzing electricity of my power threatening every moment to be released, the pain of knowing what I'd done to my older brother.

It did feel good to be held. When Max was like this, I could forget how twisted and painful everything was getting. He rubbed my back gently. He could be so kind when he wanted to be. I sank against him.

Max pulled me into him and put his lips against my neck.

I pushed him away. "Max, no."

"Why?" he said, a mixture of anger and hurt on his face. His moods were so mercurial, I could barely keep up. I sighed and rubbed my temple. Emotion was exhausting. Life had been so much simpler without it.

"You're always pushing me away. You know, maybe this new girl—Megan? Morgan?—will appreciate me more than you." Max's voice was acerbic.

I stepped back, stung. His mouth had twisted into a sneer. For a second, in spite of his handsomeness, he looked grotesque.

"Maybe I shouldn't come here anymore," I said in a whisper. I backed away, my whole body trembling.

"Stop." He grabbed my arm, his face softening in confusion. "Wait. I don't know why I say things like that." He let go of me and ran his hands through his hair.

"I just want to be with you so badly and then you come here and end up pushing me away at the last second. I think about you *all* the time. You're all I want." His voice was oddly high and close to breaking, and I could see the hurt on his face. "Why can't you want me, too?"

"Oh, Max." I put a hand to his face, wishing I could wipe the hurt away. "I didn't mean— I'm sorry—"

"Don't," he said sharply, his face hardening again. "Don't use his word. Not with me."

I didn't know how things had gotten so broken between us. I was poison. I hurt everything I touched. I didn't know what else to say, so I turned away. Max didn't try to stop me this time.

I stood after I'd closed the door to my room and let out the tears that had been threatening the entire subway ride home. I'd promised not to, but I let myself be weak just this once. The drops came in a flood, choking sobs that I only barely managed to keep quiet. I covered my mouth with my hands but I knew I was still being too loud. I grabbed my pillow from my bed and stuffed my face into it to muffle the noise. I sank to the ground beside my desk. I didn't know pain could last this long.

My ribs ached but I kept imagining Max's face. I didn't know why I couldn't care about him the way he wanted me to, and I hated hurting him. But then again, he hurt me, too. And then Daavd . . . oh *Daavd*. What was the point of *feeling* things when all I seemed to feel was pain?

"Zoe, are you okay?" Adrien's alarmed voice came from above me. He dropped down, landing with barely any noise on the bed and hurrying down the ladder to where I was sitting.

"I'm fine," I said, using another tissue and tossing it in the trash. "It's just . . . Max and I . . ."

"Did he hurt you?" Adrien's voice was furious.

"What?" I looked up. "No, of course not. We just—" I searched for the right word. "—keep misunderstanding each other."

"I'm sorry." He put an arm around me, trying to draw me in to his chest. I pulled away. I couldn't bear to see the same kind of hurt on another person's face that I cared about.

"Come on," Adrien whispered, tugging on my hand. I nodded and followed Adrien up the ladder to my bed so he'd be out of view if anyone came in, all the while taking deep breaths to try to start calming myself down. We were quiet for several minutes after we sat down.

"Everything hurts so much since I started glitching," I finally whispered, wiping my eyes with my forearm. "I feel like I'm full of all these pulsing pieces barely contained by my skin, like a rip might start in one place and then it would all fly apart." I broke off, staring up at the ceiling and shaking my head. "I just mess everything up. I can't do this right. I don't know how to be human. I'm doing it wrong. I just can't—"

"I'm sorry, Zoe." Adrien gently put one hand behind my head and tugged it forward until his forehead touched mine. "I'm so sorry. But hurt is *part* of being human."

"But is it worth it?" I looked into his green eyes, so close to mine. "What if the Community is right? Wouldn't it be better to never feel hurt or pain? Aren't we better off without it?"

His brows came together, his whole face softening. "Zoe, I know it hurts right now, but believe me, it's worth it. I know all you've seen is the bad side of emotion lately, but I promise you, you'll find the other side of it too."

I pulled away. "What, like pleasure?" My voice cracked. "That's all Max can think about."

"No, not just pleasure. There's other things, like, I mean—" He paused, looking away from me at the wall. "Like love." His voice was soft. "It's a word that has so many different meanings. Especially with family. No matter how much they hurt you." He leaned his head back against the wall, staring out into space.

"Love doesn't sound like a very good thing then," I said. "It seems highly illogical. My brother got killed because he loved me."

"No." His voice was adamant. "It wasn't love that killed him. It was this shunted-up system."

His eyelashes glinted in the dim light and his voice was intense. "Love between two people can make life worth living. Real love between two people . . ." He gulped suddenly and looked down at his hands. "It's like this amazing explosion of joy. It's way deeper than just normal happiness. It fills you to the very core, makes you whole." He coughed a little. "At least that's what, you know, what people say anyway. And friendship is a kind of love, too."

I thought back to my fight with Max. "Max doesn't seem to think friendship is enough."

"Well," Adrien said reluctantly, the warm openness of a few moments ago hardening. "I guess it's probably hard to deal with all the intense emotion and sensation, suddenly and all at once. He's never been taught how to cope with it. It's gotta be overwhelming for him."

"He doesn't seem overwhelmed. Just angry."

Adrien shrugged, smiling even though his eyebrows looked heavy and sad. "Anger's part of it too. It's a powerful emotion. All these emotions both of you guys are having—you were supposed to learn how to deal with them as you grew up, but you were robbed of that chance. What you feel for each other, I'm sure it's really powerful for both of you. And he's a teenage guy, so . . ."

He scratched his head and looked away from my gaze. "So you know, it's tough." He reddened suddenly.

"Why?"

Adrien let out a short, strangled laugh that sounded different from his normal laugh. "It's just a little different for boys. I mean, a lot of the time, even guys I know who've never been cracking chipped, all they can think about is . . ." His face turned red, "is, well, um. The passions."

I blinked. "Really? Do you?"

His mouth dropped open a little and he got even redder. "I mean, sure, yeah, you know, sometimes. Not all the time," he finished hurriedly.

I looked at him strangely, sniffling and wiping my nose one last time. "No, I *don't* know what you mean."

"Why is your face becoming discolored?" I asked, mystified. "Are you all right?"

"I'm fine," he said, his laugh high-pitched and odd-sounding again. His eyes widened and he made a little choking noise. He scratched the back of his head again and looked away.

"Really, why is your face that color?"

He laughed. "Just 'cause I'm embarrassed. I'm even embarrassed telling you I'm embarrassed!"

"Why?"

"This is a crackin' intimate topic, I guess." Adrien's face went a little rigid. "But listen to me, Zoe. Don't let that shunter Max pressure you to do anything."

"But you just said it's not wrong!"

"It's not." He stopped short, looking down. "If both people want it. You want to make sure it feels right."

"Feels right?" I threw my hands up in frustration. "I'm never going to get this."

"Sure you will," Adrien said, smiling. "I'll teach you."

Then his face went red again. "I mean, I just meant—I could teach you about emotions and help explain what emotion words mean."

I pointed. "Red face means embarrassed. I'm a quick learner."

He laughed, his face finally relaxing. His laughter sounded more normal again, and the rich sound of it made the heavy ache inside me hurt less.

"I like it when you laugh," I said. "And I'd like it if you kept teaching me."

"Okay." He smiled at me but with a different smile than the others he'd used. It felt like a private smile, just between the two of us. Something inside my chest seemed to warm at the sight. Max might have been my first friend, but now I felt like Adrien was my friend, too. Friendship felt really nice. Maybe Adrien was right. Maybe you could pile up enough good emotions to help outweigh the bad.

"Come on, let's get your injection, then we'll practice getting control of your telekinesis again. The more control you get over your gift, the more you'll be able to stand up against them, to stop what happened to you and Daavd from ever happening to anyone else."

I nodded, feeling a determination settle over me. I knew what he was offering me—a way out of my guilt, a way to funnel my pain. But even more than that, I kept saying I wanted to help others, to *do* something, but I hadn't been willing to develop my most powerful asset. I steeled myself. It was time for that to change.

Chapter 18

"HAVE YOU EXPERIENCED any anomalous events?" The Chancellor's hawk gaze pierced me, like she could see right through my brain to my glitching V-chip.

I breathed evenly, then answered, "No, Chancellor."

She leaned forward, the wrinkles around her eyes crinkling as she stared hard at me. There was something about her gaze, like her eyes were boring deep inside my head and tugging at something familiar at the back of my mind. The hair on my arms stood up.

"Tell me about the anomalies you experience." Her voice was gentle, but there was an intensity to her face, and an impatience beyond what I had ever seen in her before.

I stared back, suddenly nervous. I had clicked myself back into the Link, but I still felt like she could tell something was off about me. I willed myself to remain calm. "I have experienced no anomalous events."

Her eyes became slits and her nostrils flared.

"Tell me about other students who experience anomalies."

"I don't know of any students experiencing anomalies," I lied, smoothing the nervous hitch in my voice.

Her jaw clenched. She looked livid and got up to come around her desk. She leaned her face into mine. I could smell her sour breath, she was so close.

The high-pitched sound started as a quiet purr in my brain. It came more quickly since I'd been working on it. It sparked to life like an eager flame, but unfortunately, was still just as unmanageable. So far I was still unable to control or direct it. I felt the power build up under my skin, bursting down the sides of my arms and aching to come out through my fingertips. My eyes widened infinitesimally as I tried to slow its progression. Not here. Not now.

I made my gaze rest on the floor, soaking up the Link information playing at the edges of my vision, trying to swallow the power back down. I thought about anything other than the Chancellor only an inch away from my face. Or I tried at least. I managed to diminish the buzzing, but the fear was still too palpable. I could lose control any moment. With a sharp stab in my stomach, I realized she knew something. Somehow, she knew something about what was going on with me.

Think numb thoughts. Think numb thoughts.

I made my face a mask. Slightly disinterested, passive and compliant. The studied blankness I had perfected.

She pulled back all at once and went back to sit in her chair. A strange smile played at the corner of her lips.

"You are dismissed, Zoe," she said, waving her hand and looking away.

I stood up and turned slowly, methodically.

One foot in front of the other. Don't look back.

I walked through the door and it closed with a hiss behind me.

The Chancellor had never been so insistent before. What had changed? What did she know? It had been so many weeks since she'd even called me in, but I'd been foolish to think I was safe. The thought sent a slice of cold dread through me.

Then, suddenly, my breath caught in my throat. *Zoe.* The Chancellor had called me Zoe. My mind raced. How had she known to call me that name? I must have just misheard her. I was so paranoid all the time, I was imagining things to be anxious about.

That night I sat up against the wall of my quarters with my knees pulled up underneath my chin, waiting anxiously for Adrien to come. We'd been working on my gift every night, even though I still couldn't seem to control it. I'd managed to levitate a shoe and knock my pillow off the bed, but it was still erratic and imprecise. It was so frustrating. Adrien kept telling me we had to keep trying, but I just felt like a failure.

But I had to keep training. It was the only tangible thing I could do to combat the painful thoughts of Daavd—my determination to help others like him in the future. My daytime life at the Academy was just something I did robotically. All I could think about was getting home for my night training sessions with Adrien.

I stared at my blanket in the darkness while I waited, willing the ceiling tile to move. Nothing. The time seemed to pass with excruciating slowness. Finally, just when I was getting a crick in my neck from looking up for so long, I heard the distinctive metal scratching of the tile shifting.

Adrien's long legs came down onto the bed and immediately I felt a swell of relief. Adrien would make everything better. He always knew how to fix things.

"What took you so long?" I asked.

"Sorry," he said. "I had to sneak out and contact the Rez after school. I just got back."

"Why? What did you need to talk to them about?"

He sat down, not looking at me. "I needed them to check my hardware."

My stomach churned with worry at his strange mood. He was always so calm, so confident. This nervous Adrien scared me.

He grabbed my hand and smiled weakly. "Hey, it's nothing to worry about," he said quickly, finally meeting my eyes and holding my gaze. "Everything's fine. They checked me out and it's all normal."

"What made you think something was wrong in the first place?"

He looked away. "The Chancellor called me into her office today."

My monitor started buzzing. "She called me in, too."

He looked up at me in surprise.

"She knows something, doesn't she?" I tried to keep the panic out of my voice but didn't quite manage it.

"No." He let go of my hand and settled himself across the bed from me. "It doesn't mean anything. She's been calling you in for routine checkups and interviews since you got back. And from what I can tell, she's calling all of the student body in one by one to interview, looking for anomalous behavior."

"But why would she do that if she didn't know something?"

"I don't know." He shook his head. "I just don't know. Come on, it's time for your allergy therapy."

I nodded, but frowned as he took the familiar device out of the case.

"Did they get my results back from the blood sample yet?"

He shook his head. "Not yet, but we should know something soon."

I rolled up my sleeve. He gave me the injection and I watched him as he put the equipment away. He seemed distant, his eyes slightly unfocused.

"Something's just not right." I said. "The sooner my allergy results come in and we can organize our escape, the better. I don't think I'll be able to breathe until then." I paused, noticing Adrien's unusual stillness.

"There's something you're not telling me," I said quietly. "Is it about the Chancellor?"

For a second he closed his eyes, then he smiled softly at me.

"You're the one person I can't lie to. You know me too crackin' well."

Part of me wanted to ask him why that was. How could I know him so well when I'd only just met him? And why did I also know it was completely true? Instead, I asked, "So what's wrong?"

He shook his head uneasily. "That's just it. I don't know. I can't remember. I mean, I have this feeling that everything was fine but when I try to remember the specifics of my interview with the Chancellor, it gets all fuzzy. Was it like that for you?"

"No." I frowned. "I can remember everything. Do you think they installed some kind of memory disrupter in your head? One that even the Rez techs can't detect?"

"I don't know. It's possible. If we can trick their tech, surely they can trick ours." He let out a loud breath, sounding frustrated. "But they would have to know I was part of the Rez for them to even bother. And if they knew that, why wouldn't they just grab me and take me to a shunting interrogation facility?"

"But you still feel like something's wrong?"

He put his arms behind his head and leaned back into the wall, looking at the ceiling. "I just feel like there's something else, something that's hovering at the edge of my brain. It's like all the puzzle pieces are there but I can't quite put them together."

He shook his head like he was clearing his thoughts. "I had a vision right after I left the office, so maybe it was just some pre-vision cloudiness."

"Has that happened before? With the memory loss?"

"Maybe. Having the visions—how they manifest—it's been changing as I grow into the ability." He dropped his arms, seeming restless. "I just don't know. And I hate not knowing." He looked unsure, afraid almost.

223

"Hey." I moved closer to where he was sitting. "Don't worry about it, okay?"

I lifted my face, forcing him to look at me. "It's gonna be okay, all right? Whatever's going on, we'll figure it out. Isn't that what you always say?"

He leaned his head on one fist, squeezing his eyes shut.

"Right?" I said, more insistently.

He finally looked at me, a wan smile. "Right. There's just so much that could go wrong." He stopped himself, like he was biting back words. "I can't lose control on this mission," he said, his voice a little firmer. He didn't sound like himself all of the sudden. He sounded like he did when he was at the Academy, all traces of the fear and vulnerability I'd seen moments ago wiped away.

I frowned. "You don't have to pretend in front of me. You tell me it's okay to feel emotion. Why won't you let yourself?"

His face lost some of its hardness for a moment before regaining it a second later. He pulled gently away. "I can't afford to be weak right now. I used to be so confident and sure of myself, especially of my Gift. But lately . . . I've done dozens of missions before, but something about this one feels different. Like I can't rely on my visions like usual, and there's just too many people depending on me." His voice became vehement. "If anything happened to you because I couldn't see it in time—"

"Adrien—" I moved closer to him on the bed till we were sitting side by side. I interlaced my fingers in his.

In spite of the distant look on his face, his fingers tightened on mine. "Look, about the vision I had after I went to the Chancellor's office. There's another glitcher at the Academy. I guess that's been bothering me, too." He looked away.

"At *our* Academy? Another one?" I asked.

He nodded slowly and we both just looked at each other for

a silent moment. We both knew it was strange that so many glitchers would be grouped in one place.

"Was he one of the subjects you saw that day in the files?" I asked slowly.

"No. He's a recent transfer student. He's in Molla's year. I'm not used to having to coordinate so many glitchers at once. This is turning into a really cracked mission. I wish we could all meet together. We could see if they've been called into the Chancellor's office, see if they noticed anything off."

"Well," I said slowly. "Max found a safe place to meet if we needed it. If something's going on with the Chancellor, we need to work together to figure out what it is. Why don't I ask Max to set up the meeting place soon, then let you know where and when."

He looked uncertain for a moment but then slowly nodded his head. "But only if he's *sure* it's secure."

He turned to go, then stopped and looked back at me, his face soft again.

"Stay safe," he whispered, his voice intense in the quiet room. "Please, promise me you'll stay safe. No unnecessary risks. Don't try to contact the boy and don't talk to Molla or Max in classes or the hallways. It's clear they're watching us more closely than ever."

I didn't say anything.

"Please," he said, suddenly crouching back down and suddenly pulling me into a close hug. "Please," he whispered into my ear. "Stay safe, for me. Promise?"

I was shocked silent. For a stunned second, I let myself sink in against him. It felt so right to be here. So good to be held by him. Something else, some wild roaring thing seemed to erupt inside me.

"Promise?" he whispered again, his voice ragged, so far from the calm he projected the rest of the time. His arms tightened.

I held him back tightly. His closeness made the thing inside me take flight, like I was soaring, up, up, up.

"I'll try." I pulled back and looked in his eyes. Our faces were inches apart, and I noticed how long his black eyelashes were, how his strong eyebrows and deep-set eyes made my stomach feel strange inside. I let my eyes trace down his arrow nose to his thick lips.

And then I did what felt like the most natural thing in the world—like two magnets that had been pulled apart finally clicking together again. I leaned in and our lips met in the gentlest touch. I closed my eyes and my mouth melted into his. I didn't notice lips or teeth or tongues or anything else—I only felt a shining joy searing through my chest.

Adrien's eyes were open, watching me in what looked like shock. His body was completely rigid. I pulled back. Oh no, I'd done the wrong thing.

Then, so quickly I could barely register what he was doing, he cupped one hand gently behind my neck and pulled me in again. He kissed me, gently at first, but I could feel a desperate longing in him coming through the kiss, like he'd been waiting for this forever.

His other hand clutched my back, pulling me up onto my knees to meet him. I kissed him back and curled my fingers in his thick brown hair, pulling him in even harder. The kissing wasn't gentle now. It was raw with need, like I couldn't get him close enough, couldn't get enough of him at once.

His hands dropped to my waist, kneading my body with his fingers. The touch made sensations I'd never felt before rise up in me. A soft moan came from my mouth and his body shuddered in response. I clutched him tighter, wanting to cement every part of my body to his.

So this was what Max meant about pleasure. Max. The thought stopped me abruptly. I pulled away with a gasp.

Adrien looked at me a moment, a short silent moment. I had turned away, a wet droplet stinging my cheek. Adrien hesitated, then planted a whisper-soft kiss against my cheek: "Good night, Zoe." He pushed the tile aside and was gone.

I stared after him when he'd gone. I lay down, my face hot with the memory of what had just happened. I put my hands to my cheeks, to my lips, remembering.

Was it wrong? I felt guilty, like I was betraying Max. From the beginning, he'd been so worried about me wanting Adrien instead of him. I'd thought he was overreacting, but what if he'd noticed what I'd been too naïve to see—the electricity that was charged in the very air whenever Adrien and I were together.

I pulled my pillow underneath my head and closed my eyes tight. Sleep. I needed to sleep now. But I couldn't stop thinking about the feel of Adrien's lips on mine, of his arms curved around my back clutching me to him. Needing me, wanting me, and the pressure of his chest against mine . . .

I twisted in my bedsheets, wondering if I'd ever get to sleep.

I slipped down the hallway a few days later to the meeting place Max had told us about, making sure to follow his directions to stick close to the left-side wall, out of sight of the cameras. I looked at the door in the corner. I tentatively swiped the thin square card Max had given me in front of the glowing access panel. Max said he'd made copies of an administrator's card, explaining the non-drone admins didn't have implanted wrist chips like us. They used these external ones.

The door slid open easily and I stepped through.

"Zoe, good." Adrien ushered me in, then glanced both ways down the hallway before gently shutting the door behind me. My face suddenly flushed with heat. I put a hand to my cheek and hurried past him. Red cheeks meant embarrassed, I remembered, and flushed all over again.

I turned my attention to the room where Max and Molla were sitting. The room was full of crates and chairs and desks. Some were stacked up neatly and others were broken and in disrepair, all under a layer of dust. Max and Molla were sitting on metal chairs at one side of the room and Adrien was across the room along the other wall. Molla looked terrified and clutched Max's arm.

I looked back and forth between Molla and Max, surprised to see her holding on to him so tightly and even more surprised that he was letting her. He didn't look exactly thrilled to have her hanging on him, but still—he was making an effort. I smiled at Max, at the same time feeling awash with guilt. He was being so kind to Molla. The memory of last night with Adrien seared through me.

Max looked up at me and I quickly dropped my eyes. I was lying to him. After everything we'd been through, all he meant to me, I was hiding something from him. It was not a good feeling, but I couldn't bring myself to tell him. Not yet.

"Hi Molla." I walked over to her. "It's so good to see you."

She looked up at Max, trembling.

"It's okay," he said. "You can trust Zoe. She's the one who contacted you in the first place, remember?"

She nodded and smiled shyly at me. "Yes, I remember."

"I'm so glad we could all get here together," I said, taking one of her hands and squeezing it. "It's important to know we aren't alone, that there are people out there just like us who will help keep us safe."

"Just so we're clear," Max spoke up, "I'm here because Zoe and I are in this together. And if that means we have to escape with this Resistance, then so be it. But what I want to know is, what exactly will they want from us in return?"

Adrien brought two chairs out, taking one and gesturing for me to take the other. I didn't like the dynamics of how the room was parceling up, so I grabbed the chair and pulled it closer to the middle of the room. Neutral territory.

"The Resistance wants just what Zoe said—for you all to be safe."

Max smirked, then leaned toward Adrien, something menacing suddenly in his gaze. "Yeah right. They just want to use us for our powers."

Adrien inclined his head, staying calm. "I won't lie. They're interested our powers, too. But even if you didn't have Gifts and were glitching, we'd still want to help you."

Max rolled his eyes. "So how big is it? Exactly what kind of numbers are we talking about?"

"I don't know the details of all the cells. Only cell leaders are entrusted with that information."

"Well isn't that convenient," Max scoffed. "What *do* you know?"

"Max," I said sharply. "Adrien's trying to help us."

"Really?" Max stood up. "I'm not so sure. Think about it, Zoe. Your problems started right after he got here—that official calling you in for the diagnostic, the new Chancellor showing up—no one had noticed you before."

"The way my glitches and powers were behaving, it was bound to happen sooner or later. And to you too," I said. "To any of us, or all of us. That's why we need to work together—"

Max cut me off. "He shows up out of nowhere, but he knows all about you. Then he makes all these perfect promises about a place we can live free and help others. Doesn't that all seem a little too perfect? Like he's just telling you what you *want* to hear so you'll go along with him? Why can't you see—"

"Stop it, Max." My voice was sharper than I intended, but he was speaking such nonsense!

"And what about your powers?" Max said, turning to Adrien, who was still calmly seated. "Visions of the future? Tell me, Future Boy—what do you see? What's my future?"

"I don't know," Adrien said calmly. "I don't choose what visions I get and I haven't seen you in them."

"But you see Zoe," Max said. "What's her future?"

Adrien's eyes flickered over to me briefly. "Her future is whatever she wants it to be."

"What the hell does that mean? Either you've seen it, or you haven't. You're so full of your own lies you can't even keep your story straight."

"Max, stop it." I pushed in between the two of them. This wasn't how I'd hoped this would go at all. "We can only afford to meet once like this, so we have to make the most of it. He knows about another glitcher. That's why we're here."

"He's a boy in your grade, Molla." Adrien was visibly making an effort to stay calm. I could tell he was trying to salvage the situation, but was barely containing himself. He looked at Molla as he addressed her but she wouldn't look up to meet his gaze. Her tiny frame was quivering nervously.

"What's his power?" Max asked.

"His *name* is Juan," Adrien said, finally sounding annoyed at Max. "And his Gift is with music. I've seen visions of him playing the cello. He's phenomenal, a genius, and he can affect people's mood with it."

"So he can play some kind of a device called a cello. Why the hell would we risk our lives to rescue him? How does he help us at all?"

"Music *is* extremely important," Adrian said. "It's part of being human. Our ability to express beauty is exactly what this generation is gonna need to sustain ourselves, to feel hope. Creativity, artistic expression, it's the *best* of what humans are capable of. Besides, if he can affect moods, he might be able to keep crowds calm, distract others—"

Max didn't look impressed. "It's tactically useless."

"Max!" I said, not even knowing why I was surprised by his insensitive comments anymore. I'd been trying to stay calm, but the tension between the two boys was starting to rile me.

"I'm just stating the obvious."

Adrien's teeth seemed to grind together. "The Rez wants to provide a safe haven for any glitcher."

Max rolled his eyes. "Don't tell me you weren't thinking it, too. If this Resistance of yours has any hope of surviving, someone better be thinking like this—of the bottom line. Of only taking calculated risks. Why should we risk ourselves for him?"

"Because it's the godlam'd right thing to do," Adrien shot back.

Max yawned exaggeratedly.

I stood up. I couldn't help it. I was furious at him. "So going to parties and learning curse words is worth the risk, but a boy's life isn't?"

He stood up, too, facing me, his jaw working. "I do what I have to do to survive. And what's the point of having all these emotions and powers if I can't do what I want with them? Why should I risk everything I've worked for to help a stranger? I don't even know this drone."

"Because it's a *person* we're talking about. A person, like us." *Like my brother.* I didn't say it, but Max seemed to figure out what I meant.

"Zoe, get it through your head," he said heatedly. "You can't save everyone."

"Why not?"

"Because! It's going to get you deactivated!" He took my shoulders roughly in his hands, making me look him in the eye. "You have to start playing by their rules."

"That's enough," Adrien said, knocking Max's hands off me.

Max looked furious. "Don't you dare touch me, you bastard!" He pushed Adrien hard in the chest.

Adrien stumbled backward and fell. His head was inches from bashing into the corner of a stack of metal containers when I shouted, "Stop!"

My hand reached out as if I could catch him. Without thinking, the high-pitched buzzing roared to life in my ears and Adrien's body froze in midfall.

"You're doing it!" Adrien said, sounding excited, even though his body hung suspended in the air, the sharp corner still close to his skull.

"Keep me up," he said, "just like you practiced. Try to think about how you feel right now, what you're doing."

I blinked, the buzzing dimming now that I was consciously trying to hold on to it. I squeezed my eyes shut in concentration. The more I tried to focus on it, the weaker my powers became. I faltered for a moment and Adrien dropped a millimeter.

I let the panic overwhelm me again, losing control in order to gain control. It was a difficult balance, like going and stopping, pushing and pulling at the same time, but in that moment I felt myself connect to the perfect equilibrium. Even with my eyes closed, I could still see Adrien, but not like with normal sight—it was like I could *feel* his body broken into a hundred little geometric shapes, each plane curving and butting up against the next.

Everything around him was in sharp detail, too. Somehow I could feel all the corners and edges—like I was surrounding them somehow, like I'd brought them all inside my mind. The humming got louder in my ears as I felt out the contours of Adrien's entire body.

I lifted my arm to direct my energy. I felt his body lift up and away from the stack of boxes.

"Keep going," he said, still excited.

I moved him up higher until he was flush with the ceiling. He wasn't heavy—I couldn't feel his weight at all in fact. Gravity didn't matter here. There was only a three-dimensional space and objects filling that space.

I opened my eyes, a rush of power coursing through my veins, ready to burst out of my eyes with a blinding light. That's when I saw the look on Max's and Molla's faces. Max was smiling in a strange way I couldn't quite decipher and Molla was clutching his arm in terror and wonder. They were both standing up now.

I glanced up and saw Adrien bobbing against the ceiling. I blinked a few times. My strength was fading in and out. I was starting to doubt myself.

I tugged Adrien down but lost control before he got all the way to the ground. The buzzing stopped and Adrien dropped the last few feet and landed on the concrete floor with a grunt.

"I'm so sorry," I said, running over to him to help him up, but he was on his feet in an instant.

"That was cracking great, Zoe!" Adrien said, hugging me. I stiffened, casting an uncomfortable glance in Max's direction before shrugging out of his arms. Adrien took it in stride, seeming too excited to take offense.

"You were controlling it!" His eyes were shining with energy and it made my breath hitch in my chest, reminding me of last night.

Max pulled away from Molla and hugged me, swinging me around in an arc before putting me back on the ground again.

I laughed, feeling giddy. I hadn't been able to control the power in so long. I'd been secretly afraid it wasn't working anymore. Just being able to access it again made me feel centered, more in control of everything.

"Now if I could just do it all the time."

"You will, with practice," Adrien said.

"For once," Max said, "I agree with him. We can practice together, at my place."

I nodded, trying not to look at Adrien, the complexities of the situation settling back in again. I had to talk to Max about my feelings for Adrien, but I didn't even know exactly what they were. Like friends, but different from Max. More.

"I'll try to contact Juan," Adrien said. "I'd initially wanted to wait a little longer before getting us all out of here—" He glanced at me, then back at Max. I knew what he was thinking. He wanted to wait longer to give the allergy injections a better chance of working. "But I think maybe we should bring this last glitcher up to speed and get out as soon as we can. I feel the Chancellor circling closer and closer, ready to make her move. I don't like it."

He looked uneasy. His meeting with the Chancellor must have really put him on edge.

"How?" Max asked.

"I'm working with my contacts in the Rez. They're coordinating our escape, plotting out the maps and codes required to hack the system and give us enough room to get out undetected. They'll map out our route and the multiple safe houses we'll have to stop through to make sure we lose anyone who might be tracking us. When it's all in place, we will contact each of you individually. But be prepared to move soon, and quickly."

"And Markan? How will we get him out?" I asked.

"That's one of the things we're working on. We'll have to

stick an external drive in his neck port with a program that will make him follow without trouble till we're all safe."

I lifted my hand to rub my own neck uncomfortably.

"I'm sorry," he said, seeing me. "I know you hate that, but I think it's still the safest way."

I nodded. "Of course."

Molla suddenly let out a squeak. I startled and looked over at her. I had momentarily forgotten she was there, she was usually so shrinking and quiet.

"Someone's coming!" she hissed frantically.

My heart leapt into my throat. *No.* Max dropped to the ground out of sight behind one of the small overturned tables just as the door opened.

I hurried to the wall where some furniture was stacked but Molla was still just standing frozen in the middle of the room. Before I could hiss at her to get down, a brown-uniformed man stepped in. He was of medium height and build and his brown clothing identified him as a service worker. He looked at Molla dispassionately and followed her horrified gaze to me.

"You shouldn't be here. You do not have authorized access. This is anomalous." He moved to touch his arm panel.

Chapter 19

I SAW ADRIEN tense in the shadows, getting ready to launch himself at the man, but before he could, the Chancellor rose from behind an overturned table.

"Stop," she said calmly, ostensibly to the brown-uniformed man but I knew it was also meant for Adrien. Adrien froze and looked at Max's disguise in disbelief. He'd never seen Max's power in action before.

"Chancellor Bright," the man said, his hand paused in midair.

She tilted her head and trained her hawklike gaze on him. "What are *you* doing here?"

"I'm on a Resource Redispersal task. I was working down the hall when I heard voices. It was anomalous, so I came to look."

"Is anyone else here with you? Did you tell anyone you were leaving your post to investigate something which is none of your concern?"

"Anomalous events are the concern of every conscientious subject," he said robotically. "And, no. No one knows I'm here."

"Good," said Adrien, who had crept up behind the man while he talked to Max. Adrien raised a heavy-looking metal brace and slammed it into the man's head.

I gasped as the man crumpled to the ground. I clapped my hand over my mouth to keep back a scream.

Adrien looked over at me, then down at the brace in his hand. He dropped it to the ground with a clatter and took a step back from it like it was toxic.

Max morphed back into himself, a look of pure fury reddening his features. "I thought your visions always warned you of danger. How did you not see this, Future Boy?"

"I don't know!" Adrien said, sounding just as upset. He ran his hands through his hair. "It shouldn't be possible. It shouldn't be . . ." For a moment he looked lost and helpless and desperate.

I wanted to go hold his hand, but I myself was frozen in terror.

"What do we do now?" I tried to keep the hysteria out of my voice. I needed to stay calm. I went over to the man on the ground. I could see his chest rising and falling with each breath. Okay. We just needed to keep calm. Think logically.

"A blow to the head won't erase his memory, and he's seen all our faces," I said, trying to figure out a plan as I talked. I turned to Adrien. "Do you have some equipment that can erase memory?"

"No." Adrien looked at me, both hands still on his head. "I don't carry that kind of equipment with me most of the time, in case I ever get searched."

"You shouldn't have disabled him," Max said, advancing angrily on Adrien. "I had everything under control. I could have just told him not to mention he'd seen me."

"It wouldn't have mattered what you said," Adrien said. "Protocol is to make note of all details of anything anomalous, no matter what. If it's an incident involving an Upper, they just ignore it, but if the Chancellor saw this man's report, we'd have been cracked for sure. I couldn't take that chance."

"So how do we make sure he keeps silent? Do we deactivate him? Can we remove his memory chip?" Max asked.

"Max! How can you say that?" I hissed.

"Look, he's seen us. The way I see it, it's him or us, and that is an easy one for me," said Max. "Besides, he's got an adult V-chip. The guy is a drone for life. What difference does it make?"

I glared at him. We both turned to Adrien, but he hadn't even heard us.

Adrien was still staring at the fallen worker, a look of shock on his face. "I don't know how I didn't see this coming." His voice was high-pitched and frustrated. "It's never happened before. I've *always* been able to count on my visions."

"We'll worry about that later." I put a hand on Adrien's shoulder for a moment to calm him down, and then I crouched down beside the man. Logic. Order. "First we figure out what to do with him."

"What did the Resistance do before you developed all your advanced tech?"

"Unfortunately, the Rez did sometimes deactivate people," Adrien said grimly. "But a deactivation would still trigger an investigation, and I'd never do something so barbaric. But maybe . . ." He looked at the wall, his brows knit in thought.

"What?" Max said.

"Well." Adrien looked down at the man and frowned. "I did see a Rez fighter do a manual memory wipe once." His eyes flicked up to mine. "But it isn't pretty."

"Would he—" I looked down at the unconscious man and a shiver ran down my spine. "Would he be okay afterwards?"

Adrien bit his lip. "If I do it right, then yeah, he'd be fine. His recent memory will be fuzzy, but otherwise he'll be fine."

"And if we don't do it right?" I asked.

Adrien looked away and didn't say anything. He closed his eyes and swallowed hard. When he opened them again, his jaw was set firmly and he was all business.

"Zoe, bring me my tablet. Max, remove his shirt and then we'll turn him on his stomach so I can get to work."

My hands were trembling as I brought Adrien his tablet case. He clicked it open as Max rolled the man over.

"Make sure his head is to the side and that his breathing remains even," Adrien said to Max as he pulled out his tablet. To my surprise, he didn't turn it on but instead tipped it sideways and then cracked it gently against the concrete floor. Adrien pried the two halves of the case apart, revealing the inner electronics.

Adrien paused, looking up at me. "Do you have a spare hairpin?"

I slid a slim metal pin out of my hair and handed it to him without asking any questions.

"Molla, keep watch to make sure no one else comes this way." He pulled the two thin metal prongs of the hairpin apart until it was one long slim piece. "Max, see that fan in the corner over there?"

Max nodded.

"Strip its power cord and bring it over here."

Max moved to do what he said as Adrien worked to flatten the metal hairpin out. "Zoe, grab me one of the broken chairs over there."

I came back with the chair and Max brought the frayed power cable. Adrien was busy carefully prying out one of the hair-thin wires in the tablet.

"What are you doing?" Max asked.

Adrien didn't answer, just bit his lip. "Can I have another hairpin?"

I pulled out another and handed it to him. He used it like a pair of tweezers and slid the tiny wire under another cluster of thin cables. Finally he breathed out. "There. That should do it."

"Do what?" Max asked.

"I rerouted the power coupling in the tablet to regulate the amperage it can output."

I gasped as I looked at all the components gathered in front of Adrien and realized what he was going to do. "You're going to electrocute him!"

"I'm not going to electrocute *him*," Adrien said quickly. "Just his memory chip."

" 'Kay, Molla," Adrien turned to her. "I'm gonna need you to use your Gift—you can see through objects, right? I have to get this piece of metal," he lifted my hairpin, "into his head, but this won't work unless it makes contact with the memory chip. I need you to be my X-ray unit and tell me when I'm in. I know you can do it."

My mouth gaped open in surprise. I'd wondered if Molla had an ability and if it manifested yet. They must have talked about it before I'd arrived.

Molla's frightened eyes flickered to Max. He nodded. "Show them what you can do, Molls."

She came and knelt close to the man's head. I moved back to give her room. I felt helpless, but I knew the only thing I could do was stay out of the way.

"So why'd we take off his shirt?" Max asked.

Adrien wiped away some beading sweat on his forehead with his arm and swallowed hard. "To use as a rag for the blood."

My stomach lurched. Adrien swallowed again, then slid the pin into the tissue right beside the existing access port.

"Max," he said, "hold the chair. We're gonna have to use the leg like a hammer to get this thing in deep enough."

I forced myself to watch, even though I winced every time they tapped the slim hairpin further into the man's skull.

"Careful!" Max hissed. "It's gonna bend if you don't hit at the right angle."

A line of blood seeped down the back of the man's neck. I wiped it gently away with the shirt.

"Okay, Molla, am I close?" Adrien asked, his voice sounding strained.

"Another half-inch," she whispered, "and you need to angle more down, to the left." She pointed on the outside of the man's head and Adrien nodded. After several more gentle *thunks* of the chair leg on the hairpin, Molla held up her hand. "There! You got it. It's touching now."

Adrien gave one more gentle knock. "I want it a little embedded in the chip but not too far. How is it now?"

"Good," she said, and Adrien sat back on his heels, letting out a low breath.

"And now for the electricity." He grimaced.

Max handed him the cord, and Adrien touched the metal contact from the frayed end of the fan cord to one side of the tablet. Then he lifted the tablet so that the other side was touching the metal sliver sticking out of the man's head. "Zoe, will you go plug in the cord now?"

I nodded and swallowed. I took the cord, my hand hovering over the plug in the wall for a second. What if this didn't work? What if when I plugged this cord into the outlet, I killed the man? My stomach twisted at the thought.

"Zoe?" Adrien said. "Do you need me to do it?"

"No," I said, forcing my voice to be calm. "I've got it." I plugged in the cord.

There was a slight pop and spark from the tablet board and the service worker's head twitched once. Adrien pulled the tablet case away from the pin. "Okay," he said, finally smiling. "I think we did it."

"And he's okay?" I hurried back over to the man, putting my hand on his chest. It kept rising and falling. He was still breathing. I grinned up at Adrien, who nodded.

"He should be fine." Adrien breathed a huge sigh of relief, then let out a shaky laugh as he gathered up the equipment. "Okay, we need to get out of here. Max—"

"Already ahead of you," Max said, and the next second he looked exactly like the service worker lying on the ground. "He probably had a small trolley if he was moving furniture. I'll get it, then we can cover him up and I'll move him somewhere far away from this part of the Academy."

Adrien nodded. "Hurry up, though. When he wakes up, his heart monitor will start going off from the pain and someone will come check it. But you should have time to be long gone. Zoe and Molla, you should get out of here, but be careful. Stay in the camera blind spots."

I nodded, and Molla and I slipped out the door behind Service Worker Max.

A week later, we still didn't know what had happened to the service worker. Max tried impersonating an official to look at the service logs but didn't find anything, and Adrien hadn't wanted to risk hacking into the mainframe again. All we were left with was questions. Did the manual wipe work? If it didn't, had Monitors been assigned to observe us? But if so, why had they waited to bring us in? All we could do was hope that the decision to let the worker live wouldn't cost us our lives.

My nights were restless, filled with repeating nightmares. Instead of Daavd's face in the chase nightmare, it was Max's. He'd been chased down by Regulators and I hadn't saved him. I'd let him down, let him get hurt.

Just like I was doing in real life.

I had to tell Max. Before I spent any more time with Adrien, before I kissed him again. . . . The thought of kissing

Adrien sent a shiver of excitement down my spine. Which was then followed by another wave of guilt. There were too many other lies in my life. I couldn't stand to have one between me and Max. In spite of what I couldn't give him, he was still my best friend. He was still family.

I peeked inside Markan's room but he wasn't home yet. It felt nice having the apartment all to myself. I was so rarely alone and unwatched.

I slid the door open to my room and then jolted in alarm and almost dropped my tablet case.

"Adrien!"

"Sorry." He grinned and dropped down the last few steps from the ladder. "Didn't mean to scare you."

"What are you doing here?" I glanced back through my bedroom door to make sure Markan wasn't about to come through the front door. "My brother will be home any minute."

"Sorry, I just had to see you," he said, coming closer.

I stopped looking back out the door and smiled at him. Just being near him made all the tension seep out of my muscles, replaced by a tingling excitement.

His expression seemed to darken.

"What's wrong?" I asked.

"Nothing." His face cleared as he smiled, his green eyes sparkling. He came closer and took my hand gently. I felt my stomach swoop at his touch.

He lifted his other hand to my face and I trembled. Then he kissed me, gently and slowly. Like it was a question he was waiting for me to answer. I had asked myself so many questions of my own about our kiss the other night, but the instant his lips touched mine, all of my doubts and fears washed away.

I sank against him, all my emotions breaking loose in our kiss. He responded, pulling me against him roughly, and it only made my heart beat faster. My heart monitor started buzzing between us but I didn't care. It hadn't beeped in ages. A little now was worth it. I pulled him closer, pressing against him, but just as I reached up to tangle my hands in his hair, he pushed me away.

"Wha—" I started dreamily, but suddenly it wasn't Adrien standing in front of me anymore.

It was Max.

All the relief I'd felt a moment ago vanished instantly. A heavy pain hit the bottom of my stomach like a rock, taking my breath away.

"I knew it!" he yelled, slamming his fist into my bedroom wall. His face was red with fury.

I felt my mouth drop open and my throat choke with thick guilt. "Max, I'm so sorry. I was going to tell you." I tried to reach out to him but he yanked his arm away.

"Tell me what?" I looked away from him, hot water burning at the back of my eyes.

"Tell me what?" he said, angrier this time. He was seething, but I could see and hear the hurt behind it. For once, he wasn't masking himself. "That your heart monitor buzzes when *he* kisses you but not when I do?"

"You know you are important to me, right?" My eyes swam as I said it.

"But?" He spit out the word.

"But I also feel for Adrien . . . like . . ." I stumbled over my words, seeing the flare of Max's nostrils. I had to get it all out now. "Like togetherness feelings for him."

"Don't say that." His voice was hard, angry. "You don't mean it."

"I do. I'm sorry. It just happened. I didn't ask for it to happen, but it did. I never meant to hurt you, Max. And I was going to tell you—"

He came toward me now and he gripped my upper arms, his fingers like a vise.

"Ow, Max, you're hurting me."

"You don't understand. He's a liar. He's tricking you. The whole Rez isn't who he says they are." Max's voice dropped. "He's not one of *us*. He's using you."

"He's not." I tried to pull away from his grip. "He makes me feel—"

"What?" he yelled, letting me go and thrusting me away. "Tell me about what he makes you feel? I'll kill the bastard!"

"Stop it, Max. Someone will hear." I went over to him, trying to touch his arm, but he shrugged me off, staring at me with a look that made me shrivel up inside. "I'm so sorry," I whispered.

He turned away and punched the wall so hard it made a dent. He let out a shout of pure rage and I flinched.

"I won't let him have you!"

"Max," I whispered, putting a hand on my aching chest. Adrien had once told me that hearts could break if something hurt enough. I hadn't understood what he meant at the time, but I did now. My heart was breaking, but I couldn't turn back now. He deserved to know everything.

"I think I was already his, before you and I even . . . I mean, I think I started to feel things during the time I was away. I don't remember it all but I think that's when it first happened. It was before we even became friends," I whispered. I was trying to find anything to make it hurt less now.

"It should have been me who rescued you that day you disappeared. I was coming for you, too. Before he got in the way," he spat.

"Stop it—"

"Zoe, listen to me!" he cut me off sharply. "You don't know anything about him. Think about it. He knows all about you from his visions. He knows all the right things to say to you. Isn't that a little bit suspicious? And then there's his Resistance. I've looked into it, and they do all kinds of experiments in chemical warfare and coercion. They're as bad as the Community. And Adrien's helping them get to you. To make you *think* you like him so you'd work for them. They need your Gift. But I'm not like that," he said, his voice intense as leaned in. "I want *you*. Just you."

He came at me and put his mouth on mine and pushed me up against the wall, crushing me under his weight.

"Stop it." I tried to push him away but he was stronger.

He stopped kissing my protesting mouth, but he still trapped me there, hands on both sides of my head against the wall.

"You'll want me," he said in a growl, keeping me captured against the wall. "One day. I'll make you want me."

"Let me go," I whispered, all patience gone, and something worse, something I'd never expected to feel around Max—fear.

"Move back," I said firmly, so furious at him for making me afraid. The anger started a buzzing in my ears. "Before I *make* you."

He laughed darkly, pulling back and holding his hands up to show he wasn't trapping me anymore. "Don't you see? That's why you're perfect for me. You have the darkness underneath, too."

His words were like a punch to my stomach. So he saw it too—the guilt that hung like a weight around my neck. He knew that, at my core, I was a betrayer. What I'd done to my brother would mark me for life.

"Maybe," I finally managed to whisper. "But it's still Adrien I want."

He took another step back. He stood still for a long moment and I could see his throat bobbing up and down as he swallowed repeatedly. It was a terrifying silence. Finally, he lifted his forearm to swipe at his eyes and hurried out of the room.

I felt like my stomach had been hollowed out, scraped clean of any goodness inside me.

I'd hurt Max. I'd betrayed yet another person I cared about. I wanted to call him back, to somehow make things better, to help close the deep wound I'd made, but I didn't know what to say.

The front door slid shut behind him.

Chapter 20

IT HAD BEEN TWO WEEKS, and Max still wasn't talking to me. I walked with him to the cafeteria like always. We were trapped in our routine, forced together to avoid suspicion. He couldn't avoid me, but I could sense from the furious heat pulsing from his body that it was taking every ounce of effort to be near me.

What he *could* do was ignore me. Which he did. I picked at my food, feeling him like a silent fuming boulder beside me. I tried over and over to catch his eye but he never gave any indication he even knew I existed. I finally gave up trying.

Then, as I was about to stand up and collect my dishes, I heard a low scream from the other side of the room.

My eyes widened as I craned my neck to see what was going on.

A boy screamed and thrashed, trying to get away from the two Regulators who'd just grabbed him. It was Juan, the boy Adrien had pointed out to me earlier, the one who was a glitcher.

"Help me!" he screamed. "Someone, please help me!"

I looked in panic at all the staid faces around me in the cafeteria. Everyone watching dispassionately. I looked back at Juan.

He managed to wrench away from one of the Regulators, but the other one still had a firm grip. I scanned the room as calmly as possible. There were more Regulators everywhere. The ones not holding Juan were surveying the rest of us as if they were looking for a reaction.

With a sudden wave of dizziness, I recognized what was happening in this moment. It was exactly the same as my nightmares of Daavd. The anger burned in me, and I felt my power respond, bursting instantly to life at my fingertips.

One Regulator pulled out a syringe.

I couldn't stand here and watch this happen. I couldn't do nothing. Not this time.

The buzzing was at a fever pitch inside me. I started to rise, but Max's fingers gripped my arm like a vise under the table. I looked at him, knowing the panic must be showing in my eyes. He blinked in surprise, as if he saw something in my face he'd never seen before. He quietly shifted his legs, locking them around mine and ever so slightly shaking his head in warning. I looked helplessly back at the boy.

But my power was not as easily quieted. I felt myself losing control, but I had nowhere to direct it. A fork on a nearby table fell to the ground, unnoticed in the commotion. A tray of food in front of me shifted first to the left, then the right. Max gripped me harder.

Juan sank to the ground, unconscious. The Regulators dragged him from the room. He was limp in their arms, his feet skimming the ground behind him. I felt sick. Everyone around me began gathering up their things calmly, as if nothing had just happened.

They're monsters. We're all monsters.

I stood up, barely remembering to take my case with me as I hurried out of the room. I was a monster. I could have stopped it all somehow, but I didn't want to risk Max's safety. To risk my own. The power had been right at my fingertips. I could have saved him. But I didn't.

I hurried into the bathroom so I could let out my feelings in the privacy of a bathroom stall. I had to stuff my fist in my mouth so I wouldn't scream. All my power raced through me, begging for release. I let out just a fraction of the energy as gently as I could, allowing it to shake my body in tremors that knocked me into the stall doors. I slid to the floor of the stall and wrapped my arms around myself as if I could physically hold it all in.

Max was waiting for me when I came out. He took my arm hard and steered me to the wall, out of the way of the students filing by on the way to their next class period. He was rougher with me than usual. Harder and colder than he had ever been before last night. But I deserved it.

"Promise me you aren't going to do anything *stupid*," he hissed in my ear.

I shook my head, feeling nauseous as I pictured Daavd, then Juan, dragged away. "We have to help him. That could have been any of us!" *It should have been me,* I added silently.

"Stop it," Max said shortly. "Do you trust me?" he asked, his voice still hard.

I swallowed, feeling my throat clog up again. I didn't know why he cared so much after how I'd hurt him, but I nodded anyway.

"Then trust me when I say I'll look into it," he said, pulling us back into the crowd of walking students.

I looked at him uncertainly.

"I promise. Just don't do anything dangerous in the meantime," he hissed.

The rest of the day went by in a haze. I clicked back into the Link, unable to trust myself. I'd been so sure that the next time something like this happened in real life, I wouldn't stand idly by—that I'd act. I wouldn't allow someone else to be taken like I'd let them take Daavd. But I'd just stood there, again. Letting it happen.

I closed my eyes hard, but over and over the scene replayed. Daavd's face replaced Juan's as it spooled out again in my mind, until I thought I wasn't going to be able to hold back the water that had been threatening to pour out of my eyes all day.

That night, I didn't look up when I heard the ceiling tile shift. I curled up in a ball, hiding my face in my pillow.

"Zoe," Adrien said, his voice full of emotion. "Are you okay?"

I didn't say anything. He touched my shoulder but I jerked it away.

"Zo, look at me. The Rez is handling it. If they can do anything for Juan, they will."

I sat up, hope blooming for the first time all day. "Do you think they can get him out?"

Adrien didn't say anything for a second. "You need to be ready for the fact that sometimes there's nothing we can do. After they've transported a glitcher to a secondary location, it's usually impossible to get them back before they're reprogrammed or . . . or they do other things to them."

"Like deactivate them, you mean." A fresh pain burned in my chest. Adrien tried to hug me but I pushed him away.

"No, I don't deserve comforting. I'm a monster. Just standing there, watching it happen."

I dropped my head, sobbing quietly.

"I thought I was different now," I managed to say between sobs. "At least before, I was numbed by the V-chip. What's my excuse now?"

"Zoe, stop it," Adrien said heatedly. "There was nothing you could do that wouldn't have gotten us all taken away with him. Max and I just stood there, too. Do you think we're monsters?"

"No!" I said automatically.

"Then why do you get all the blame? Why are you cracking taking this all on yourself? It's not your fault. It's the

Chancellor's fault and all of the Uppers who've done this to us."

But I shook my head when Adrien tried to pull me close. "It could have been you, or Max, or . . ." My voice broke. "Or Markan."

"You can't think like that."

"Would it have been any different?" I stared at the wall, feeling sick. "I have this horrible feeling that it wouldn't be. That I betray everyone who comes near me. What I did to my own brother. And then Max, too. All he wanted was for me to want him."

I turned and crumpled into Adrien's chest, crying harder all of the sudden. He held me tight. "What else is wrong? Zoe, you're scaring me." His voice was tense.

I heard the muffled thud of Markan's door sliding open.

"Hide, hide," I whispered urgently to Adrien, pushing him back up the ladder. "Close the ceiling tile and hide up on the bed against the wall."

He hurried as quietly as he could back up the ladder. I went to listen at the door. I heard footsteps, but they walked past my door and on toward the bathroom. I sighed out and leaned my head against the wall. Adrien stayed silent.

I climbed lightly up the ladder. Adrien was lying down, his long body taking up the entire length of the bed so he'd be out of sight. I lay down, facing him, far enough apart that only our bent knees touched. I curled my hands up under my pillow.

"Tell me about hate," I whispered quietly.

"Zo." He curled up one arm under his head like a pillow. We were close enough together that I could smell the cool mint of his breath.

"Tell me," I repeated stubbornly.

He sighed out, rubbing his temple with his other hand. "Hate is a strong emotion. One of the strongest humans have."

"But what *is* it?"

He frowned, thinking. "I don't know how to describe it. How to define it. It's like when anger against someone or something becomes so strong it consumes you. Life is so hard and people are so shunting cruel to each another, sometimes I think hate is what comes most naturally to humans."

"And it makes people want to deactiv—to kill each other?"

He nodded.

"Have you ever hated anyone?"

"Of course. I hate the Uppers and this shunting Link system that has put us all in this position. . . ." He leaned in, his head slightly sideways. "I hate the people who put *you* in danger."

His green eyes flashed in the dim light of the night luminescence panel. Our faces were six inches apart now. "But the thing is, the opposite of hate is love. . . ." He looked away from me and ran a hand through his hair. Then he looked back at me with an intensity I'd never seen in him before.

He moved closer.

Three inches.

Two.

The electricity I'd felt from him the other night was tenfold, burning out from his eyes. I lifted a hand to my chest monitor and tried to breathe to calm myself down.

"Then tell me about love again," I whispered.

He scooted closer still, taking my hand from my chest monitor and entwining his fingers with mine.

"Hate's a strong emotion, but . . ." He paused, looking down at our hands. His thumb rubbed mine, sending little popping sparks through me. "I like to think that love is stronger. Even though love makes no sense to me sometimes—that it even still exists seems like a miracle."

He closed his eyes, drawing back a bit. "I've seen so much.

Hate and death and brokenness and pain. People trying to survive and failing." His face looked haunted by the memories.

"People hungry for power and willing to do anything to get it. But love?" He looked back up at me again. "A love that makes people sacrifice for one another—give up everything, even their lives? I never understood it."

"Adrien," I said, squeezing his hand tighter.

He leaned his forehead toward mine. "Love shouldn't exist but it does. It's the biggest anomaly, some might say the biggest defect, of the whole human race. But it's the most beautiful anomaly. I understand that now. And I would give up anything for you, even if you don't feel the same way." He swallowed hard. "Because I love you."

He breathed out heavily and sat up. He put his elbows on his knees and rubbed his temple with both hands so that I could barely make out his face.

I could hear my heart pounding in my ears. I was still, too much in shock to fully understand what he was saying.

He looked at me, uncertain of my reaction. His voice became distant suddenly. Detached. "I saw in a vision right before you returned to the Academy—I saw you and Max kissing. That's why I haven't said anything about how I feel. But the more time I spend with you, and after we kissed the other night, I just couldn't *not* tell you."

"I do feel strongly for Max," I said slowly. Adrien winced, so I hurried on. "But not in the way you think." I sat up. "He was the first one who was there for me when I came back and was so scared and alone. But he always wanted something from me." I paused. "More than I could give him. I didn't know why. I only realized recently, and that's why he and I got in a fight."

"You don't have to explain to me," he said quickly, shifting to get up and leave.

"Adrien." I grabbed his arm to stop him. "The fight was about *you*. Because I told him of what I feel for you. Of what I think I've been feeling for a long time now but didn't know how to put into words. I . . ." My voice trembled as I finally said it. "As much as Max means to me, I have stronger feelings for you. I don't really even understand them, they're so intense."

His face froze and he sank slowly back down to sit on the bed. "You do?" His voice was barely audible.

I nodded and watched the uncertainty in his face slowly turn to hope like an unfurling bloom.

"I think—" I started in a whisper, then took a confused breath. I looked away and felt a rush of memories. The confusion I'd felt at how Adrien's touch made me feel, the electricity between us. But it was more than that. It was the times we'd spent talking. The connection I felt to him that was unlike anything I felt for anyone else in the world—the way he seemed to put all my feelings into words, the way he felt about life, his hopes and dreams, the way he'd opened up a new world for me. Being with him made me want to make my own dreams, discover my own path. I was my best self when I was with him. I looked back up, the realization flooding me like the brightest silver of happiness.

"The way you describe it—it's just how I feel. It's *love*," I said with awe, laughing with the joy of the discovery. I couldn't believe one day could hold such wildly opposite emotions from one moment to the next. "I *love you*, Adrien."

He blinked rapidly, stunned. "Say it again," he whispered.

I laughed and pulled him close. "I love you," I whispered in his ear. Then he grabbed me in his arms, squeezing me in a tight hug one second and then kissing me like he could never get enough the next.

I laughed at his genuine, complete joy and kissed him back.

We kissed for a long time, clutching each other clumsily at first, blinded by euphoria.

Tomorrow, I'd think about all our problems tomorrow. Right now there was only this, only him.

The flying sensation came again but it was like we were soaring together—like I couldn't tell where my body ended and his began. He finally pulled back, still cupping my face in his hands.

He laughed. "Zo, look up."

I did and saw my pillow levitating and spinning above our heads. I gasped in wonder and it fell, plopping on my head. Adrien just laughed and kissed me again.

"I can barely cracking believe this is happening," he said. "I mean, I'd seen you in my visions. I knew you were important to the Rez, but I hadn't seen how important you'd become to me. My life's been so hard for so long—and the world is too cracked to ever believe I'd get to be this happy." He laughed, his eyes shining.

His words made my insides light up.

He pulled back a moment, staring at me as if convincing himself that I was actually there, in his arms. "I had that vision of you and Max and I thought I'd lost you." His words came out in a rush. "And then you looked at me like I was no one, or worse, someone to fear. Just when I thought I'd made peace with the fact that you'd forgotten me forever, I'd spot some glimmer of recognition, some little hint that maybe . . ." There was water brimming at the edges of his eyes, and the pain he'd felt poured over into me. I wanted to take it away. I never wanted him to feel that way again.

I cut him off with a soft kiss.

"This is real," I finally said. "We found each other again, and you're never going to lose me," I said.

He smiled, leaning down to kiss me back, a deep kiss that

let loose all the passion and fear and hurt and hope that must have built up inside him.

Eventually he pulled away. It was getting late, but I didn't want him to go.

"Soon we'll be away from here," he whispered, one hand stroking the hair around my face. "You'll be safe."

"Why are we suddenly leaving so soon?" I asked after a few quiet minutes. "What about my allergies?"

He paused, his hand midstroke through my hair. His body tensed under my hands. "I just have a bad feeling," he finally whispered. "Like I'm not seeing things right. I don't know why I didn't see what happened today coming." His eyebrows cinched up in worry. "Something is off with my Gift. If I can't trust my visions, we're completely in the dark. It's too risky."

I wrapped my arms around his chest and squeezed. "I'm sure your visions will sort themselves out."

I closed my eyes, wishing guiltily that I could stay like this forever. Suddenly I felt his body stiffen in my arms.

My eyes flew open, thinking Markan or my parents had opened the door to my room, but it was firmly shut. I looked at Adrien. His face was frozen, his eyes vacant.

"Adrien!" I whispered, shaking him. His body was rigid. He didn't respond. My heart monitor was about to start vibrating, but then he blinked and looked like himself again.

"Adrien, are you okay?"

His face was pale and there was a sheen of sweat across his forehead. I'd seen that look before. He'd had a vision.

"Was it Juan?" I asked worriedly.

"No." He looked at me, eyes wide. "We have to escape. Now. Tomorrow."

"What?" I sat up, matching his alarm. "Why, what did you see?"

"Molla's pregnant."

Chapter 21

"WAIT, WHAT?" I ASKED, completely confused. "That's not possible. She's too young. They wouldn't have let her into the fertility clinic."

"There are other ways." He slammed his fist into his open palm. "Max! Godlam'd shunting fool," he said, his face furious. He looked away. "I'm sorry. I shouldn't have just dropped it on you like that. I mean . . ." He swallowed. "I understand if you're . . . jealous."

"I don't understand," I said quickly, "I thought he felt very intensely about *me*."

"Um, well . . ." He trailed off, looking up like he was trying to figure out the words. "Not everyone has strong feelings for just one person at a time."

He ran a hand through his hair. "Anyway, the point is we have to get her out. *Now*. Molla's never been the best at hiding her emotions. She won't know what to do, and she's going to know something's wrong. Someone's bound to find out. And if that happens, we're *all* cracked."

I frowned. "Well, wait. It was a vision of the future, right? So maybe eventually they will, what did you call it? Fall in love. That's good," I said, smiling as I thought about it. "He should be happy with someone who can love him back."

"Zoe, it didn't feel like something far off in the future. It seemed like she's pregnant now. Present time. We have to get out immediately."

———

I felt the tugging guilt when I looked at Markan at breakfast the next morning, but the feeling was followed by one of determination. I might have failed Daavd, but I would save Markan. We'd get him out. He'd be safe with me, and even if he didn't turn out to be a glitcher, he'd be safe and free. The thought brought a flush of happiness.

In spite of all the worries about Juan and Molla, I had to work hard not to break into a giant grin every time my thoughts wandered back to Adrien. *My* Adrien. I wished I could let out shouts of happiness that echoed down all the monotone tunnels. I wanted to dance on the gray subway platform and grin until my face cracked in half. I caught myself before I actually broke into a smile and, instead, sat down at the table to eat my protein patty.

I noticed my father watching me, his gaze uncomfortably observant. I took a big bite of bread even though it felt thick in my throat. Just a little while longer, I thought. Just a little while longer and I'd be free from the stalking eye of the Community. Adrien said he'd arrange our escape and that it might even happen today. Then I could be myself. I could openly say, do, and feel as I pleased.

Finally, what might be my last breakfast in the Community was done and I slipped through the front door. I walked the hallway of the housing unit, trying hard not to look like I was hurrying. There were a few people in the tunnel with me and I slowed my pace to match my impatient footsteps to their calm ones.

One woman with short-cropped red hair broke out of the usual formation to walk very close beside me. I glanced over, but her face was neutral. We kept walking. She remained blank, but she stayed close to me. My mind raced. Was she a Monitor, or maybe a Rez agent? Was I caught, or was I rescued?

I started cautiously scanning the tunnel in my peripheral vision, looking for an opening to turn down in case I needed to escape.

The woman leaned over and whispered, "Turn in to the next service door."

My eyes widened but I kept my pace steady. Trying to look as non-anomalous as possible, I pulled open the next service door on my left as if it was something I did every day. The woman followed right behind me. The doors in the tunnels were the old manual kind, so at least I didn't have to swipe my arm panel to open it. I looked around warily at the old equipment and pipes in the room until the woman shut the door quickly behind us.

The woman's image shimmered and then it was Max standing in front of me. I breathed out, unaware I'd been holding my breath in terror.

"Zoe, you aren't safe. We've got to escape, just you and me. Right now."

"Did Adrien send you?" I asked excitedly. "Is the plan ready."

"Zoe, listen to me!" he said, grabbing my arms. "I know you won't want to believe it, but Adrien isn't who you thought he was. He's a Monitor. He's been working for the Chancellor the whole time! He even reported Juan."

"Stop it!" I pulled away with a flash of anger. "I have had *enough* of your ridiculous suspicions. Now your feelings about him are actually becoming dangerous and right when he's about to get us all safely out of here."

"I knew you wouldn't believe me." He shook his head, looking suddenly weary. "Maybe you'll believe it when you hear it from his own mouth." He dropped down and started setting up a tablet projection on the floor.

"We don't have time for this! We should be finding the Rez agents and getting Juan, Molla, and Markan out of here."

"That's what I was doing when I found this," he said, sounding furious. "I hid after school and impersonated a Regulator. I went to find out about the boy but they just looked at me strangely and said the boy had already been transported."

"Oh, no." I sank down to sit beside him. We'd failed Juan. My stomach cramped up painfully at the thought. We missed our chance.

"So then I snuck into the Chancellor's office, thinking maybe she'd have a record of where he was being sent."

I looked up at Max in surprise. He noticed and laughed darkly. "Is it so surprising that I would try to help him, Zoe? Is that what you think of me?"

"I'm sorry." I put a hand on his arm. He'd taken so many risks.

"When I was in her office, looking through her files, I found this. It's dated two days ago." His voice had turned grim.

He clicked a fingernail-size drive into the tablet and the video began. It was a stable image of the Chancellor's room. She was sitting at her desk and looked up. Another figure entered the room. My heart seemed to stop in my chest. Adrien.

"Sit down," the Chancellor said, and he sat in the chair directly across from the desk. "Have you had any visions recently?"

"Yes," Adrien said.

"Tell me about them."

"There's another boy who is glitching. Subject Juan T-73."

"It's a fake," I whispered my eyes glued to the image. "It's not real. They could have altered this easily, after they'd caught Juan."

"Just keep watching," Max said.

On the video, the Chancellor paused and clicked open a 3-D directory. She tapped on a name and the face appeared in the cube of light. "Is this him?"

Adrien leaned in. "Yes."

The Chancellor smiled, patting his hand. "Very good, Adrien. That is very helpful. Now, tell me more about the girl. Zoe."

Adrien shifted in his seat and didn't say anything for a moment.

"Tell me, Adrien."

"I have seen visions of her as the leader of the Resistance." Adrien's voice sounded oddly stilted.

"You are helping her learn to control her powers?"

"Yes."

"Does she suspect that you have been talking to me?"

"No."

"She trusts you, then?"

"Yes. She tells me things she tells no one else."

"Such as?"

"She's afraid for her brother, Markan. She fears he will be captured just like her other brother and that it will be her fault again."

The Chancellor nodded. "Good. If the visions of her are true . . . We will bide our time. It will be difficult, so stay near her. Keep her trust by whatever means necessary."

"Yes, Chancellor."

"And you administered the switched tube I gave you for her last allergy injection, correct?"

"Yes, Chancellor."

"Excellent." The Chancellor's thin lips twisted into a smile. "Thank you. You are dismissed."

The video feed stopped and the screen went blank.

My legs felt frozen.

"It's not true," I whispered. "It's not real. They just digitized Adrien's image and voice and then manipulated it. It would be so easy for them to do."

"What about the things he was telling her?" Max said. "Did you know he was giving you injections, or did he disable you to do it?"

I looked at Max in disbelief at what I'd just seen. "Yes, I knew about them," I said. "They were for my allergy. So that I could survive on the Surface when we escaped. But this is all wrong. Fake. Adrien wouldn't do that to me. He wouldn't hurt me."

"Don't you get it?" Max said angrily. "He's the Chancellor's tool. She's using his visions to learn all about us. He's a Monitor. Maybe they caught him out at his last Academy and made a bargain with him. Maybe he joined her voluntarily. Either way, we've got to get the hell out of here."

"No!" I said. "If you knew Adrien, you'd know this couldn't be real."

"What about the other things he told her?" Max asked, looking angry but also pained, as if he knew he was hurting me but had to do it anyway. "The things you've told only him? About your allergies, your dreams, and about your brother? No one else knew that, Zoe. Not even me."

I shook my head, violently. "Then they must have cameras or audio devices in my room."

He pulled away from me angrily. "Why are you refusing to see what's right in front of your face! He tricked you. He used you. He played on the fact that you're naïve, that you've never felt those kinds of emotions before. That you're so damned trusting!

"It's all a lie, he just told you what you wanted to hear. And if we don't make a break for it right now before they know we've figured them out, they'll deactivate us or turn us back into drones. They've already got Molla, and I only barely managed to escape to come find you. Come with me, Zoe. Let's get the hell out of here before it's too late!"

"No . . ." My voice broke and tears brimmed over. No, no, *no*. I paused, torn. I trusted Adrien without question, absolutely. I *loved* him.

But what if I couldn't trust my feelings? What if Max was right and Adrien *had* been manipulating me? There was still so much I didn't know about him, so much I didn't know about this world, let alone the world that might or might not exist outside it. What could I trust?

"What about when I went missing?" I asked, still trying to work things out. "He helped me escape."

"You can't even remember that time clearly, Zoe," Max said. "They probably took you away to run some tests and experiments on you. They could've implanted false memories so you'd trust him. You know they can do that."

His eyes opened wide as if he just thought of something. "Zoe, he must have had a vision of me trying to get you and Molla out. That's why all this is happening now."

My resolve began to crack. Liquid hot fire rose inside of me, a tide of hurt and pain and confusion. I didn't know what to believe, but I knew everything was wrong. My power buzzed in my chest, but I held it still. This was a pain I had to keep inside.

Max tossed the projection pyramid in his tablet case and swung it over his shoulder. He stood up, dragging me with him. I followed mutely, letting him direct me. I felt disconnected from the situation, disconnected from my own body even. A freight train of thoughts and memories and feeling were tumbling one over another in my mind. I couldn't sift through them quickly enough. I couldn't make sense of anything. None of this made sense.

"We can get on the subway and go to this place I found in

the Central City. I can hide us, impersonate officials as we go so we can travel and get as far away from here as we can. We'll go to the other side of the sector, or even go to other sectors if we have to. We can reintegrate and stay under their radar, switch out our wrist chips and become other people. If Adrien has visions of us and they come for us, we'll run away again. Whatever it takes, so long as you're safe."

Max transformed back into the redheaded woman and opened the door. He stuck his head out, looking carefully each way before pulling me out with him.

My mind was a storm again. It seemed there was no other explanation. What if Max was right, and Adrien was helping the officials. One thing was sure, we were all in danger now.

I wasn't sure we could help the others, but Max was right here in front of me. For once in my life, I might be able to help someone I cared about.

But at the same time, my whole chest ached. *Adrien.*

Max pulled me sharply sideways so that we were moving along the wall of the busy tunnel, whispering at me to keep my head down so the cameras wouldn't catch our faces. When the tunnel opened up to the subway platform, he maneuvered us into the flood of people. The redheaded woman's thin hand grabbed my wrist in a pinching grasp and pulled me to a corner along the side of the tunnel.

"Regulators," Max whispered in the woman's soft voice, nodding to the platform.

A group of Regulators stood where the tunnel narrowed before opening onto the subway platform. There were twice as many of them as usual, scanning faces and checking wrist IDs at random. I tried to quiet the fear that had gripped my chest. Our only way out was through that narrow passage. There was no way we'd make it through without getting caught.

"What do we do?"

"They're probably looking for us. Adrien must have had a vision. *Damn.* Cover me while I change."

He dropped down, ostensibly to retie his shoe. I leaned over him, terrified and trying not to look anomalous while I blocked him from sight. When he stood up again, he looked exactly like Chancellor Bright. He grabbed my arm roughly and pulled me out onto the platform. He strode right up to the Regulators.

"I've got the girl," he said in the clipped tones of the Chancellor's voice. "But the boy eluded me. Spread out and keep looking. I'll take her directly to the holding facility."

The two Regulators nodded once and motioned to the others across the room. They left, fanning out and grabbing people roughly every so often, turning them around to check their faces, then shoving them back in line to continue their placid progression down the tunnel. I breathed out when I heard the low rumble of the train approaching. I didn't know what we'd do next, or how I could work out a way to keep Max safe and still find Adrien. But I knew we had to get off this platform.

The train slowed to a stop. Max, still disguised as the Chancellor, pulled me authoritatively to the front. Everyone parted to make way until we were at the front of the line.

My chest was tight with tension but I felt better when I saw that all the Regulators were at the opposite side of the platform. In a few seconds, we'd be on the train and hurtling away from them.

But then the train doors slid open with a hiss, and the real Chancellor stepped out with Adrien, a half-dozen Regulators, and a wicked grin on her face.

"Adrien!" I heard myself cry out in disbelief before I could even think. The sight of him with the Chancellor sliced like a jagged knife into my stomach. It took everything I had not to fall to my knees with the shock and pain of it.

Max shifted again, shoving me to the side and shouting, "Run, Zoe!"

The real Chancellor snapped her fingers. Regulators surged forward off the train as Max turned to run, dragging me along behind him. I looked over my shoulder. Adrien was watching everything calmly, not even looking at me. I felt sick. Max tripped as one of the Regulators caught up and grabbed his coat.

Max.

I instinctively spun around and thrust my hand out. Time seemed to slow, then stop. The high-pitched buzzing in my head consumed all other thought. The Regulator who held Max was thrown backward into a column, his head cracking against the concrete with a sickening thump.

Max transformed again, this time into a short man. He ran to me and pulled my hand, but I didn't move. Instead, I lifted my arm, and all the other Regulators who'd come running after us were yanked backward as if an invisible explosion had sent them flying.

The drone subjects on the platform stood silently, watching with indifference, typing their anomaly reports on their arm panels.

My power pounded in my head, taking my fear and rage and pain and channeling them down my arms in electric currents to my fingertips.

Adrien walked straight toward me.

"Zoe!" Max screamed in the man's low voice. "Let's go."

"Run, Max. Go!" I said, calling to him over my shoulder. "I will hold them off for you. But I have to stay. I have to know!"

I turned away, my focus all on Adrien. I zeroed in on him, sensing the planes and curves of his body with my mind. There had to be something, some explanation.

And then I felt it with my mind.

A tiny hard drive stuck in the back of his neck port. *I knew it.*

This wasn't him—he was under the control of some hardware. A joyous relief washed over me, but it was quickly replaced by determination. I tried to yank the drive out with my mind, but in all the chaos, I couldn't focus long enough to get it out. The Regulators had been such big targets. But this felt like searching for a pebble in a pile of boulders.

Max transformed again and looked back and forth between me and the exit tunnel that led back the way we'd come. His eyes pleaded with me. But I had already made my choice. I turned back to Adrien.

"Subdue her!" The Chancellor's voice rang out across the silent platform.

I was tense, walking on the balls of my feet. I knew what I had to do. Just a little closer and I'd be able to pull out the port drive manually.

"Adrien," I said, "I know this isn't you."

He was a step away now, far enough away from the Chancellor that she wouldn't be able to stop us when we ran. With Max's help and my power, we'd be able to escape. I was sure of it. I reached out again with the humming energy, my blood pounding in my temples at the effort. I reached with every fiber of my being, my mind trained solely on the port on Adrien's neck where the tiny port drive had been inserted.

Adrien reached out for me, and in one final burst of energy, I was finally able to grasp the shape of the small drive with my mind. I yanked it out, sending it shattering against the concrete wall.

Adrien blinked once. I sighed in relief, nearly collapsing to the ground in exhaustion.

"Subdue her!" the Chancellor screamed.

Adrien hesitated only a moment and then reached for me. He jammed a syringe into the side of my neck before I could even scream in disbelief. I felt the needle's pinch and saw the ground rushing up. As the world went black, I looked up and saw a pair of aquamarine eyes gazing coldly down into my own.

Chapter 22

I WOKE WITH A START, but when I felt the pillow underneath my head, I breathed out slowly. My neck was sore and my throat felt dry, like I hadn't had water for days.

I slowly tried to sit up, but my head felt full of rocks.

"Where is Max?" a voice asked anxiously. "Is he safe?"

I blinked and saw Molla sitting across from me on a small cot in a tiny gray room. It was little bigger than my bedroom, just big enough for two cots and a small square space in the corner for a toilet. Molla jumped over to my cot and beside me.

"Where's Max?" she repeated.

With a forceful blow, it all came back to me. It was all real. It had really happened.

Adrien was a Monitor and he'd betrayed me. I'd been so worried about hurting others, I'd never thought about being betrayed myself. The pain cut so deep that I felt it in my bones, in my toes, in my fingers, and most of all, in my heart. How was my heart still beating? It should have stopped, should have broken, should have split into pieces from the ripping pain.

"I don't know," I said to Molla, trying to keep my voice even. I hugged her hard. "I don't know if Max got away—they got me first."

She clutched me back just as desperately.

"Max told me they'd caught you," I said. "I'm so sorry we got you involved in all this."

She pulled back, face pale. "It was horrible. The Regulators grabbed me right after I got to school."

She blinked rapidly. She put a hand to her mouth. "Not again," she moaned, grabbing her stomach. She ran over to the toilet and threw up.

"What's wrong?"

She wiped her mouth and then crawled back to lie down on her cot.

"It's been like this for a couple days." Her face was wet with tears. "Something must be wrong, but I didn't want to go to a diagnostic doctor. I didn't want them to find out I was glitching."

She sobbed into a thin gray sheet, and I smoothed back the hair from her face.

"Everything's going to be okay," I told her. I hoped she couldn't hear the tremor in my voice.

She turned over on her side, clutching her pillow. I sat down on the edge of her cot, rubbing her back gently. Eventually her breathing calmed down. After a while she was so still, I hoped she was sleeping.

My chest clenched with the sudden memory of Adrien calmly sticking the needle into my neck. Adrien telling the Chancellor about me on the video. I slid from the edge of the cot to the cold floor. The pain was so heavy. I curled up in a ball and put my palms against my eyes like I could scrub out all the memories.

Max had been right all along about Adrien. He'd known from the beginning that Adrien wasn't someone to be trusted. He'd even tried to warn me, but I wouldn't listen. I'd believed what I wanted to believe.

I'd just taken Adrien at his word. Taken *everything* at his word. And my trust in him had led us to this. There was certainly no way we were going to be able to escape deactivation this time. But even if we didn't get deactivated, even if by some miracle we managed to escape, where would we go? Without Max's help we wouldn't be able to go undetected for long in the Central City, and I couldn't survive on the Surface.

I closed my eyes as a wave of dizziness and fear swept over me. Every step along the way Adrien manipulated me so perfectly. To make me follow him, to trust him, and then to fall in love with him. And I'd lost everything.

I'd even believed him when he told me that one of the Rez workers had implanted subroutines in my head to fool the diagnostics. Now I was sure they had done something to my hardware, but whatever it was hadn't been for my protection. And I had just let it all happen.

The emotion I'd been able to hold back for Molla's sake finally broke free and tears poured down my face. Adrien had turned every pure and wonderful thing I'd felt into a dirty lie. Into a mockery. I squeezed my legs in tighter to my chest, wishing I could disappear.

As the minutes passed with me crumpled on the floor, another realization hit me with a shudder. Markan. There was no way I'd ever be able to save him. He would grow up in the Link system without me. They'd wipe me from his memory chip. And one day he would receive his adult V-chip and forever lose the ability to think, to feel, to be himself. Another devastating failure.

It was too much pain to bear. But slowly the burning ache of hurt in my chest morphed into a fiery anger. For the first time since I'd glitched, I understood feeling angry to the point of violence. Adrien had done this to us. Adrien had brought us to the attention of the authorities. He had led us right into the Chancellor's clutches.

My teeth clenched with rage. I wanted to hurt him. I wanted to take from him what he had already taken away from me.

I barely noticed the buzzing in my head, not until the cot opposite Molla flew into the wall with a loud crash, crumpling with the force of my anger. Molla jerked up, eyes terrified and heart monitor buzzing.

"Oh, Molla. I'm so sorry." I reached out to her, but she shrank away from me, clumsily stumbling off the cot and backing away from me against the far wall. Her eyes locked on me in terror. She was afraid of me.

I turned away from her, my anger giving way to shame.

Maybe Molla had good reason to be afraid. I was overcome with emotion, and I couldn't control it. Without that control, there was no predicting what my power was capable of. My head buzzed with the pressure and the power of it, begging to be released.

I squeezed my eyes shut, trying to control myself. I breathed deeply and repeated the Community Creed over and over in my mind, even though every word of it made my skin crawl. But I had to keep myself under control. Molla was the only one left I could protect, and at all costs, I had to keep my head clear. I would have to fight to save her from whatever lay in store for us, and I couldn't risk harming her accidentally with my power.

Right as I wiped the tears from my face in my new resolve, the door opened and the Chancellor entered. Adrien followed behind her.

My eyes must have flashed my hatred for the woman, because she smiled as she surveyed what I'd done to the cot. The buzzing in my head grew instantly louder with my alarm. The power was prickling to get out.

"Don't even think about it," she said sweetly. She turned her shoulders toward Adrien, her smile still fixed on me. "Please, follow me."

Molla had jerked up when she saw the Chancellor, her body quivering all over in fear as she huddled into a corner.

The Chancellor turned on her heel and left the room without another glance back. I looked over at Molla's terrified face. Then my gaze shifted to Adrien, standing coolly behind her, nudging her to her feet. My hot rage toward him roared back to life. My nostrils flared as I tried to rein in my fury.

"I understand hate now," I whispered to him in an icy voice before following the Chancellor. It took every ounce of control not to lash out at him. I wanted to hit him until I saw blood.

But I stopped myself, because no matter what, I had to keep Molla safe. Holding on to that thought kept me sane and focused. I kept calm, my hands barely trembling with the effort to keep my power at bay.

I took stock of the situation, glancing around me. With luck, I could direct my power accurately, but I still had no idea where we were being held. I had no idea what forces stood outside these walls. And I still struggled to call on my power voluntarily. I couldn't risk it. Not yet. One mistake could get Molla killed.

My eyes flicked around the narrow rectangle hallway as the Chancellor led the way. It looked like the hallways in the Academy, but the secure metal doors we passed looked doubly reinforced. This must be a holding facility where they brought subjects who behaved anomalously. But were we at the Academy? Or had they taken us somewhere else?

I scanned everything as thoroughly as I could as we passed, trying to determine our location. We went by a window to a research facility room, and I saw several technicians interfacing with computer screens. For a flash, I saw an image of myself on one of the screens. Then I saw an image of one of my drawings—the one I had done of Markan smiling.

I gasped. They knew about the drawings. How was that possible?

I knew that their records on me included some anomalous reports. I knew that my recent attempted escape and the demonstration of my power meant that they had enough information to deactivate me immediately. But the drawings. It just didn't fit. When had they discovered those? I remembered thinking the drawings had been out of place when I'd returned from the Surface. How long had they known about me? And why had they taken so long to bring me in?

My head spun, trying to put all the pieces together. This didn't make any sense. *What was going on?*

The Chancellor finally stopped and swiped her wrist in front of an access panel. A door slid open and I followed her into a larger room. The room was square and gray and it looked just like an empty classroom. A few chairs were scattered against the wall. It looked so benign, so absurdly normal.

"Nothing is what it seems, child." The Chancellor smiled and dismissed the Regulators. I took note of their number, in case they would be standing outside the door. I might be able to overpower the Chancellor and Adrien, but it would be difficult to fight so many Regulators with a panicked Molla in tow.

"Please, sit." She gestured toward one of the few chairs lining the wall.

"I'm fine standing," I said, grinding out each word. She had all the power. *For now.*

"Stubborn. Max warned me."

I blinked, startled. I narrowed my eyes at her. "What?"

The Chancellor waved her hand dismissively. "Don't be misled by what you think you know. I am here to help you."

I barely held in a scoff, but the Chancellor only nodded.

"I've been watching you for a long time, protecting you from detection and deactivation. I was hoping that through our meetings you might eventually begin to understand and trust me, but the supervision of the Uppers made it difficult. And then with your attempted escape, I'm afraid you left me no alternative. The timing is not ideal, but I trust in time you will understand."

"Understand what?" My voice was hard. "That you took me and my friends? That Adrien's been spying for you?"

She shook her head. "I am not the enemy you believe me to be. I am not part of the system that oppresses you and your friends. The only thing the Community managed to get right," she said, her eyes suddenly glistening, "was that the age of humanity as it was has indeed passed. But it is we who are the real future of humanity, not them. Don't you see?" She leaned in close to me. "I'm one of you. I'm a glitcher."

My eyes went wide in disbelief. "What?" I managed to choke out.

She laughed. "I'm like you and your friends." She looked me in the eye and I studied her silently. The Chancellor? A glitcher, too? It was impossible.

"I was fourteen, and just another girl on the labor farm, a place worse than any of you can imagine. On the farms, we were stripped of our basic humanity." She pursed her lips and stood up straight. "Take enough away from a person and they start to seem like an animal, a tool, a nothing. That's what I was to them. But *I* woke up." The Chancellor's voice became suddenly hard and firm.

In spite of my determination to stay cold, a trickle of pity welled up inside me. Maybe she was lying, but I knew the kinds of horrors that had happened to countless subjects all across the sector. Or rather, I knew what Adrien had told me. So many lies, I didn't know how much to believe.

"Where's Max?" I asked. "And Juan?"

"They are safe." She smiled. "You'll see Max soon. Listen, I understand your anger, Zoe," she continued. "I *understand* your need to save others. Believe me. In the wrong hands the Link gives the power to do the unthinkable, and they must be stopped. But you're going about it all wrong. You don't have to leave. You don't have to join the helpless Resistance. This world should be *ours*, and I'm working from the inside to change it. To make it the Community we were promised."

"But," I started, my mind whirring to make sense of everything she was saying. "How? The Resistance has been around for years trying to take down the Uppers."

The Chancellor smiled. "My Gift is very . . . subtle, very persuasive. I can compel anyone close enough to me to do what I want. It's how I've been able to survive undetected." Her smile turned cold. "The Uppers give me the information I need to know. Then I make them forget. For the worst of them, I've encouraged them to administer their own punishments. I've developed my Gift slowly, but eventually I managed to simply take up the part of an Upper. I've been moving up the ranks ever since."

"If that's true," I said slowly, still trying to figure out if she was lying or not, "then why become Chancellor of an Academy? Why not just install yourself as Chancellor Supreme of the sector?"

She'd been pacing but she stopped and turned to me. "I'm not strong enough to take down the entire Upper system on my own. I realized early on that there must be others like me. And I was right. There's a veritable explosion of Gifted subjects in your generation. Installing myself at an Academy was the best way for me to discover and collect glitchers old enough to fight, before they get the final adult V-chip installed and lose their powers forever. When I heard about your anomalous incident and then disappearance, I was intrigued. I decided this would be the next place for me to recruit. I need your help, Zoe."

She took another step toward me. "I've been transferring in other anomalous students to see if they would develop glitcher abilities as well. We've kept it quiet, of course. The systems databases have been regularly scrubbed so that the high number of anomalies don't go reported. We've had to maintain appearances, perform regular diagnostics and so forth, but it has all been a show for the Uppers. They have no idea the work I've been doing here."

I blinked. This was too much to take in at once. Could it be true that she was really on our side? She was powerful, there was no denying that. If what she said was true, then we wouldn't have to run or leave our home, we wouldn't have to face the adult V-chip or worry about deactivation ever again. But what about Adrien? He'd lied to me to help her. And there was something not quite right about the Chancellor's promises. Something hovering at the edge of my mind that I just couldn't quite grasp.

"No glitcher ever needs to be afraid again once we're in power," the Chancellor continued, oblivious to the turmoil that was going on inside me. "You can stop what happened to your brother from ever happening again."

"What?" I felt my eyes widen as I looked at her. What could she know about Daavd?

"It's such a shame. He would have been so useful to us. He would have escaped, if you hadn't started screaming as you passed by a checkpoint."

She paused, studying my face. Memories, the ones I tried to bury, rose up. The look on my brother's face right after I'd called out to the Regulators—shock, betrayal, and forgiveness, all in the single breath before he'd taken off running and been chased down.

"Interesting," she said, studying me. "They wiped your memory, but you seem unusually able to cling to bits and pieces of things you shouldn't. Zoe, I *understand* you. Together we have a real chance to overthrow the Uppers. Just think of it. The oppressive Community gone forever. Any glitcher would be free to think and feel and demonstrate their powers. Complete freedom."

Her eyes glistened with triumph at her own words, and I felt myself almost swept up by them. If she was right, we didn't have to run away to fight the Community system. We could infiltrate it from the inside. With enough glitchers, it would be possible.

I kept watching the Chancellor. She was confident, passionate, and powerful. She smiled sweetly at me and it almost reached her small eyes. Almost. There was a strain on her face, and it sparked the twinge of warning in my stomach again. Everything sounded so perfect, but it felt like there was something she wasn't telling me.

And then I grasped it. The question that had been in the back of my mind, just out of reach. The Chancellor was going on and on about rescuing glitchers, about saving them from being repaired or deactivated. But what about everyone else?

"What happens after we overthrow the Uppers?" I asked. "Are you going to upend the entire system of V-chip control?"

She looked at me, a sad expression on her face as she shook her head.

"It is unfortunate, but the V-chip is necessary. Getting rid of it would mean there would be no more glitchers. But it was never the V-chip that was corrupt, it was the officials who controlled it. The V-chip makes it possible, for the first time in the history of our species, to truly have world peace."

Her soothing voice washed over me. "None of the drones will ever have to experience pain or sadness or destructive passions. We will cleanse the ruling class of corruption and everyone in our society will fulfill their roles in a perfect, orderly manner. We'll take better care of the subjects than the Uppers. No more labor farms. We can create a true Humanity Sublime. Logical. Orderly. *Perfect*."

I stared at her openmouthed. I didn't want to admit it, but some part of me agreed with her. I hadn't seen the world. Adrien had told me about how horrible it was. I remembered his face when he'd talked about the horrific things he'd seen in his life on the run with the Rez. I myself had even wondered if people weren't better off without emotion. What little I'd seen of hate and anger and jealousy had shown me that. A world without pain or hurt. There would be a heavy cost, but what if what the Chancellor was offering me, imperfect as it was, was still the best solution for a world too broken to fix?

But then I thought about my brother and the smile I'd always wanted to see on his face. If the Chancellor had her way and he never glitched, he'd stay a drone forever. Sure, with the Link system, no one would know pain or war, but they'd also never feel happiness, see beauty, or be loved. Didn't everyone deserve at least a chance at joy? Not just glitchers, but every single living person? Who were we to decide who got a chance at that life? Who were we to decide who was worth saving?

Suddenly I could see clearly. No. I was not like her, and she did not understand me. "You talk about ideals—" I paused, shaking my head in disgust, "But really, underneath, this is just a way for you to gain all the power. You're no different than the Uppers."

The strained, saccharine smile on the Chancellor's face disappeared instantly. She gritted her teeth and her cheeks turned splotchy red with instant rage.

"Don't use that tone with me!" Her voice turned hard. "I've had enough. I thought you would see reason, but it is clear that you are incapable."

She realized her mistake, quickly calming herself. Her expression quickly stilled, turning back into the sweet placid smile. But it was too late. I had already seen the real face of the Chancellor.

The buzzing suddenly burned through me at her change in tone. I had to get Molla away from this woman. My teeth clenched, and my fists began to shake with the effort. Everything inside me was screaming to unleash my power and get Molla and me out of here.

The Chancellor frowned as if in sympathy.

"Oh, dear. You are still having difficulty controlling your powers. I was afraid that might make this challenging." She gestured toward Adrien.

"Believe me, Zoe, I am so sorry to do this to you. I was hoping to avoid this, but I know there is only one reliable method to control your power. And it is going to upset you."

Adrien moved to stand behind Molla, a knife pressed against her throat.

"Stop it!" I yelled, starting forward.

I saw a thin line of blood from where he'd pushed too hard. I froze, not daring to take another step in case he kept pushing. Rage burned in my chest. My power begged to tear him apart. But I held it in. I had to protect Molla.

The Chancellor observed me, smiling as my arms began to still.

"Much better. But I'm afraid it's just not quite enough. It's a pity. If only you weren't immune to my Gift, none of this would be necessary." She turned to speak into her wrist communicator.

"Bring in the other subject." She turned her hawk gaze back on me and smiled.

The door opened and two Regulators dragged in someone so beaten and bloody, at first I didn't recognize him. But then

I saw the blond hair, the angular jaw. It was Max. My heart seized up in my chest at the sight of him. They flung him to the ground like a bag of flour.

Molla went wild when she saw him. She let out an agonized scream that sounded more animal than human. It echoed throughout the room despite Adrien's hand clamped over her mouth. She began to furiously jerk about in Adrien's arms, struggling to break free and run to Max's broken body.

"Max!" I started forward but the Chancellor just clicked her tongue at me.

"I don't think so, Zoe. Remember Molla."

I looked over at her. She was still struggling. Adrien twisted one arm behind her back, the knife edge still dangerously close to her throat.

"Molla, stop it!" I shouted, my voice ringing in the empty room. "You have to stay calm. For Max."

She slowly stopped struggling, but she still looked wild and lost. The screams died down to a constant, painful whimper, and her eyes streamed a steady flush of water. Her wide gaze was trained on Max's broken body, crumpled at the Chancellor's feet.

As calmly as I could, I looked at Max, surveying the damage. My chest ached just looking at him. His beautiful golden hair was matted with dirt and blood. One eye was swollen shut, purple with bruising around his cheekbones and jaw. His lip was split open. All of the skin I could see was red and tender. He lay on the ground with a studied stillness, as if any movement at all would be too painful to bear. I watched his back carefully, relieved every time I saw the subtle rise and fall. He was breathing.

I looked at the Chancellor, keeping myself perfectly still as I scanned the exits and calculated the exact position of Adrien and his knife. If I had the right opportunity, I could overpower them and take Molla. If I could disarm one of the Regulators outside the door, we could be armed enough to have a fighting chance. The Chancellor looked at me as if she was reluctant to carry on.

"I know this is painful for you, but you do understand this is the only way for us all to be safe around your volatile powers. And as for Max, I assure you that his current unfortunate condition was his own doing, and I take no pleasure in it. He understood the terms of our agreement. When I offered him a position as Monitor, he seemed to truly grasp the importance and scope of my mission. But it seems he has suddenly changed his mind."

"No!" I said immediately. "That's not possible." Max a Monitor, spying and reporting on glitching students? All my confusion suddenly wiped clear. She was lying. Max was trying to save me from *her*, and she was a fool to think her twisted lies would trick me. But she kept talking, oblivious to my growing disgust, and the buzzing that had started to ring in my ears.

"Poor thing. Maximin is such a good little liar. A veritable chameleon. He'd helped me keep an eye on the Uppers, and he was quite skilled at it, too." The Chancellor frowned. "Max had access to everything he ever wanted. But he was willing to throw it all away. All that power, everything he could ever want—simply for the possibility of escaping with you.

"If Adrien hadn't had a lucky vision, Max might have gotten away with it, too. And why did you want to escape, Max?" She laughed, turning to Max and putting a rough hand on his shoulder. He cried out in pain.

"Stand up."

Molla strained against Adrien's grip again as Max started to move. She started twisting in Adrien's arms, her sobs filling the tense silence.

Max hobbled to his feet, even though it looked like it hurt

him to do it. Dried blood was caked on his forehead and his lip was cut and bleeding. I hurt just watching him. I looked back at the Chancellor, wanting to hurt her for hurting him. For lying about him.

The Chancellor put a hand underneath his chin to make him look her in the eyes. "Tell them, Max. Tell them all about your scheming."

"Stop it!" Molla shouted, her mouth breaking away from Adrien's hand for just one moment. She started sobbing louder.

"Don't you get it, you sniveling idiot?" She turned to Molla, addressing her for the first time. "He doesn't love you. He will never love you, not even after he put a baby in you. He was going to abandon you so he could run away with her." She pointed at me, then turned back to Max.

Molla's eyes widened and she stilled, stunned.

"Max," said the Chancellor, quietly. Her eyes stared into Max's face intensely. All the pain showing on his face seemed to disappear instantly, and his eyes glazed over. His body tilted toward the Chancellor.

"Tell them," she said. "You thought you'd found a way to escape my powers on the train platform, didn't you? That I couldn't latch on to you to control you when your image kept shifting. And it worked, for a while. But I'm much faster than you can imagine." She leaned into Max's face, her blazing eyes an inch away from his. "Now, tell them!"

"It's true," Max said, his voice rough, and raspy. He stared straight ahead as he spoke, looking completely empty of all that was Max. "The Chancellor approached me months ago. She caught me shifting on a surveillance camera. She offered for me to join her voluntarily and be a Monitor. She told me I could have everything I ever wanted. I'd be able to live like an Upper, with Zoe. We'd be allowed to live here together and never have to give up glitching or get the adult V-chip. I thought I could keep us safe. Keep Zoe safe. All I had to do was watch and tell the Chancellor about what I saw. I accepted her offer."

My heart sank, but I held back the water that stung behind my eyes and willed myself to keep listening.

"She told me to get close to Molla, so I did. But all I really wanted was for Zoe to want me back. I asked the Chancellor to make her want me and she got angry. Because she can't. She can't control Zoe," he said quickly, words stumbling over themselves. "She doesn't know why. She tried over and over again to control Zoe after she returned from the Surface, but it never worked." He finally looked at me. "I had to run. She was never going to give me what I wanted, so I was going to have to take it for myself."

"That's enough about that," the Chancellor cut in, her voice sharp and angry. She looked at me and smiled.

"No," I whispered to myself. I was stung by doubt, questioning everything I thought I'd known. I'd been so wrong about everything else, obviously I couldn't trust my feelings. After everything we'd been through together, Max and Adrien had *both* been spies? They had both betrayed me, giving information to the Chancellor and helping her capture and control other glitchers?

This had to be a trick. The Chancellor had admitted she could control people. She could be making him say these things.

Molla whimpered again and I looked over at her. She looked ill and weak, and her knees buckled under her, the knife pricking the side of her neck. She bolted back upright, screaming in panic and yanking harder to get away from Adrien. Another bright spot of blood appeared.

"Molla, stop struggling," I yelled at her. "Please stay still. Stay calm."

"Enough," the Chancellor said irritably, and Molla became

perfectly still. It wasn't natural. She was under the Chancellor's control.

Max had dropped back to the ground. His face was dripping blood.

"Oh Max," I said, tears brimming.

I still didn't know whether I could believe he'd been lying to me all this time. But memories flashed through my head— all the times I'd gotten the sense that Max wasn't telling me everything, even outright lying to me sometimes. The look on his face when I'd gotten back from the hospital and he told me he was "taking care of things." His certainty that he'd never get caught in spite of all the risks he took. I'd attributed it to his overconfidence, but what if there was another reason? What if he knew he'd never be in any real danger because the entire time he'd been working *for* the Chancellor?

"Listen. I am on Max's side. I am on your side." The Chancellor's voice softened and turned smooth. "I know you want to save your friends, and not just them. You want to make a difference, to save lives, don't you? Adrien has had so many visions of you, of all your pain and how desperately you want to be useful. If he could remember, he would tell you all about it."

I felt like the air had been knocked out of my chest. I looked over at Adrien, a tumble of confusion in my mind. Of course. For the first time since the incident at the train platform, I looked, *really looked*, at Adrien. My anger and hatred must have blinded me. His body was rigid, his face carrying the same blank expression that I had just seen on Molla's. The Chancellor was controlling Adrien, too.

The realization tore through me. It was possible, just possible, that the Chancellor could have made Adrien share his visions with her and then forget. Could it mean— My heart seemed to expand outward as a rush of emotion washed over me. Had he not betrayed me after all? Could Adrien really love me?

So many emotions struck me at once, I could barely sort them out. Joy that he could still be the boy I had fallen in love with, that the past few months hadn't been a lie. Pain and guilt at ever having doubted him. And terror. I was terrified for him, now that I knew he was a prisoner in his own body, unable to control himself as the Chancellor made him hurt Molla.

"This is your last chance," the Chancellor said. "Will you join me voluntarily?"

I turned to her, letting the anger I felt inside of me begin to rise up and grow. She was lying about everything. She never really wanted to help glitchers be free, she just wanted to use them. She was building an army of glitchers, controlled and manipulated completely by herself. But she couldn't control me. For whatever reason, her compulsion power didn't work on me.

"This is the difference you want to make in the world? This is how you want to save glitchers?" I gestured at my friends in the room. "We'd never be free with you. We'd just be trading one form of mind control for another."

The Chancellor smiled, only thinly veiling her anger. "The ends always justify my means."

She sighed. "It is clear to me that you have made your choice. But unfortunately, you have made the wrong one. Now I will be forced to take other measures. Would you like me to demonstrate my Gift?"

She looked at the others. "Hurt yourselves."

Max began beating his head savagely with a fist. Adrien had dropped the knife from Molla's neck and stabbed himself hard in the leg while Molla threw herself into the wall, headfirst.

"Stop it!" I screamed, running over to stop Molla from hurling herself at the wall again.

"Cease," the Chancellor said calmly. They all froze where they stood. Blood seeped through the leg of Adrien's pants. A thin line of blood dripped from Molla's forehead.

"You're a monster!" I screamed at the Chancellor, going to Molla and tearing some cloth from her shirt to wipe her head.

"Am I?" the Chancellor said calmly. "I can make them do much worse. Molla," she said, tossing a small device at her. Molla caught it and stared at it in confusion.

"Deactivate yourself with this weapon if Zoe attempts to harm me." The Chancellor turned back to me. "I can order them to kill themselves and they'd do it."

My eyes widened in horror.

"Don't worry. I won't, at least not Adrien. He's much too valuable. Molla on the other hand," she said, waving a hand as if swatting a fly. "She's entirely expendable. Seeing through walls is useful enough, but we have cameras for that."

A cruel expression settled on the Chancellor's face. "Zoe, there really are no other options for you. I compelled Adrien to inject you with a whole host of new Surface allergens. The outside world is completely deadly to you, even if you think you could somehow escape me. No amount of immunotherapy can change that now."

She frowned, appearing sad but not quite apologetic. "I know I must seem harsh, but I'm unused to having to find ways to persuade people to do as I ask. I haven't had to do so in so long, I've almost forgotten how."

She put her hand on my shoulder. "You will stay here with me. There's nowhere else to go."

She held out her hand to me, waiting. I stared at it. If I didn't go along with her, everyone in this room would be lost. She'd kill Molla and enslave Max and Adrien. And what about my brother?

I glared at the Chancellor. Every option in front of me was

horrible in its own way. She was the one putting me in this corner with her cloying mixture of threats and promises. I could join her and protect all the people I loved, but everyone else was still doomed to live and die without ever knowing what it ever truly felt to feel alive.

All the moments since I'd begun glitching began parading in my mind—that first glimpse of color, the fear of my night-mares, the wild joy of drawing and capturing beauty on paper, the exquisite taste of strawberries, the unimaginable blue-green of Adrien's eyes, the horrible depression I'd felt after I found out about Daavd. All the things I could do and feel by choice.

If we didn't fight, if we just stayed here and built on what the Community had created, the drones might have a peaceful life, but it wouldn't be a life they'd chosen for themselves. How could I not fight with every last fiber of my being, even if I knew it was hopeless, for the chance at something better? Sud-denly I knew I had my answer. Really I'd known all along.

Anger bubbled up inside me, itching in my balled fists. My eyes flashed between the Chancellor and the hair-trigger weapon Molla was holding to her own temple. On the peri-phery, I could see Adrien, still bleeding, with the knife poised to slash his skin. My anger burned into a searing rage.

The high-pitched hum raised to a scream in my ears. It flooded through me like a burst dam. The entire room sharp-ened in detail—the overwhelming rush of rage at the Chancel-lor and love for Adrien brought a focus I'd never had before. It was without effort. It was instinct. I had been trying so hard to control my power, to rein it in and hide it inside of me, but I'd finally learned to let myself go completely. The power was part of me, and I could use it as instinctively as walking. The realiza-tion flooded in as every part of me sizzled with power: Control over my power only came when I abandoned control.

With a burst of invisible energy, I hurled my mind outward

until it encompassed the entire space. I could feel the sloping contours of each of the other four bodies in the room, the rustle of their clothes against their skin, every micromillimeter of space in between them, and lastly, the hard lines of the weapons.

Again, I had the sensation that the room was inside me, like it was a 3-D image held captive in my mind. I could zoom in on any part of it, passing easily beyond the inconsequential barriers of metal and skin. I zeroed in on the Chancellor's chest and suddenly I was inside—I could see the blood vessels and feel the four chambers of her pumping heart.

My hatred rose up inside me. It would be so easy to deactivate her. I saw the Chancellor's eyes widen as if she could feel the intrusion. I felt the single beat of her pulse as she made the decision to make Molla pull the trigger.

My rage seared red, burning away all doubt and fear.

No.

I felt Molla's finger shift infinitesimally and I surrounded the metal in her hand and ripped it away from her just as it fired. The laser shot across the room in a flash. It sliced into the wall with a sizzle as it fell.

I turned and time seemed to slow. Adrien jumped to his feet. He ran straight toward me, knife raised.

I looked at him but reached out through my web of energy to where the Chancellor stood. No matter what, I had to save them from her. I closed my eyes and located the main blood vessel leading to her brain. But could I kill her? Could I take that final step and risk becoming a monster myself? Just as Adrien jumped toward me with the knife, I closed my eyes and squeezed the vessel shut.

I turned in time to see awareness come back into Adrien's face, but his momentum was already set, the knife coming right at my chest. He swerved to the side at the last second, and the knife crashed so hard into the concrete floor that the blade broke from the handle.

The Chancellor's body crumpled to the ground.

Molla shook her head, eyes widening in terror as she looked around her. Her whole body was shaking. "I was there inside, watching but I couldn't stop myself. I couldn't stop it!" Her cries edged on screams.

I ran over to Molla and smoothed down her hair, tugging her trembling body into my arms.

"Get Max up if you can," I yelled to Adrien. "We have to get out of here now."

"After what he did?" Adrien said incredulously.

"Is she dead?" Max's voice was oddly calm. I spared a glance for him, still curled up on the floor. He was looking at the Chancellor's ashen face.

"No," I said, looking away. "I just couldn't do it. I couldn't be like her. I stopped the flow of blood to her brain for a few seconds to make her pass out. So we have to get out of here now. *All* of us," I said pointedly to Adrien, gesturing to Max.

Adrien's nostrils flared but he nodded in one sharp motion and hauled Max up to his feet. Arm still around her back, I led Molla out the door. Max could barely stand but Adrien dragged him along behind us. Adrien's leg was bloody and I knew it must be hurting, but he walked forward steadily.

We hurried down the hallway with the metal holding cells. "Which cell is Juan in?" I asked Molla, slowing down.

"We don't have time!" Adrien yelled.

"Which cell, Molla?" I said, just as loud. She looked up at me, her eyes glazed with terror.

"Molla, focus." I grabbed her face so she was only looking in my eyes and not everywhere around us. "Are there any people in these rooms we've gone by?"

"There was a boy," she finally said, voice trembling.

"Where?"

"Two doors back on the left."

I ran back, not caring that Adrien was cursing loudly. I heard him drop Max and come after me.

"This one?" I pointed at a door. Molla nodded. I let the rage swirl back up again until the humming was singing through my mind. I thrust a web around the door and forced it sideways in its track. It made a grating noise as cables snapped. The boy on the other side jumped up in surprise.

"Juan?" I asked.

He nodded, looking terrified.

"Come with us," I yelled, grabbing him by the shirt and pulling him out of the room before he could ask any questions. "Keep up."

I ran back to Molla while Adrien grabbed Max around the chest to haul him back up again. Juan came up behind us and we made our way to the end of the hallway.

"Help with Max," I commanded him, pointing. Juan hurried to shoulder Max's sagging body and Adrien ran to the access panel in front of the door blocking our path. I heard him say the manual-override commands and tapped my foot impatiently.

"They aren't working!" Frustration rang out clear in his voice.

His face suddenly paled. "I must have told the Chancellor about the manual-override codes I'd learned to access. Oh God, Zoe, what else did I tell her?" The horror widened on his face as he realized all the possible ramifications.

I took his face in my hands. "Hey, look at me," I said gently. "We can't think about that right now. We have to focus on getting out. Okay?"

He closed his eyes for a short moment, then opened them and nodded a quick sharp nod.

"Good." I stepped up beside him. "Now, move out of the way."

"Wait, Zoe," he said, grabbing my arm, "this gate is a quarter ton of steel, there's no way—"

I thrust my power outward again in a way that was becoming comfortably familiar. It was flowing all through me, sizzling with electricity on my scalp and in my fingertips. Adrien didn't understand, but I didn't have time to try to put it into words for him. It wasn't about how big or heavy something was. It was about shifting objects to occupy a different space. I thrust both doors backward into their tracks. The screeching sound was deafening.

I smiled at Adrien. "You were saying?"

He shook his head, staring wide-eyed at the opened doors. He looked at me and grinned. "I am way crackin' out of my league being with you!"

I laughed, feeling half-delirious with adrenaline, and raced through the door. "Where to now?" I asked Adrien. "How do we get out of here? Tell me you memorized the blueprints of the holding cells."

"Of course. Follow me," he said. He took Max's other arm to help Juan carry him.

"Why are we dragging him with us again?" Adrian asked.

"He was just like me, Adrien," I said, looking at him over Molla's head. She was following mutely, eyes only on Max.

"We were both scared and alone," I said. "The Chancellor made him promises of things he thought he wanted. I'm sure she told him everything he ever wanted to hear. He couldn't have known it was all a lie."

"But he figured it out eventually," Adrien said, all the

lightheartedness gone from his voice. "And he put all of us in danger. He put *you* in danger."

"So did I. With Daavd," I said as we came to the end of the hallway.

"But you didn't know what you were doing!"

Molla stiffened beside me. "Regulators," she whispered, terror making her body start shaking again. She grabbed Max's arm, I wasn't sure if it was to steady herself or shield him.

"Where?" Adrien said, looking around in confusion.

"Twelve of them on the other side of the door up there," she said. "They're waiting for us."

"*Cracking hell*," Adrien and I said at the same time.

Chapter 23

ADRIEN SHOT ME a grave look.

"Are their guns laser or bullet rounds?" I asked Molla.

"I don't know." Molla's voice was shaking. "How do you tell?"

"Can you see through the guns with your vision?" Max asked Molla, his voice still horse, but he was standing more on his own now. "To see if there are clips filled with bullets?"

Molla leaned in closer to the wall, squinting. "Yes, bullets. I see them."

I nodded. Adrien glared at Max, then looked back at me. "Zoe, what are you thinking?"

"Is there another way out?" I asked Adrien.

"No," he whispered.

Max managed to whisper, "I'm too weak to shift and become the Chancellor. Besides, she'd have warned them about me."

"That decides it, then," I said. I called up my power and it responded, crackling and eager. It sang to me again, the immense sense of energy pulsing throughout my body. "We'll have to go through." I focused all my power on the door. "Stay back, all of you."

"Wait, Zoe," Adrien said, "you can't!"

I let out a feral yell and poured the momentum of my mind forward. The door ripped outward with a roar of crumbling concrete and twisting metal. I sent it crashing forward into the Regulators who waited on the other side.

The door was only big enough to knock half of them down. The others pulled their triggers, pumping bullets toward us. I felt the bullets whizzing through the air, and I dropped to my knees with my hands to my forehead.

The hum in my mind was taking over. It felt like a giant wedge splitting open my skull. My shout became a scream, but before it overwhelmed me, I wrapped webs of air around the hundred and twenty-three bullets in midair. Only then did I see that Adrien had taken the same fraction of a second to throw his body in front of me. He knocked me down and spread his arms over my head, face clenched, ready for the bullets to hit him.

Instead, the bullets fell harmlessly from the air like metal raindrops as they all clattered to the concrete floor. Molla, Max, and Juan huddled in the corner by the wall, looking stunned.

I threw Adrien off of me. "Stay behind me," I yelled furiously at him, then turned my attention back to the Regulators. If they were surprised, their blank faces didn't show it. They probably weren't capable of surprise. They set new clips in place in the silence and raised their reinforced arms to release another volley of bullets.

I dropped the bullets again before they got to us, but I didn't know how long I could keep this up. It was exhausting to focus hard enough to catch each of the speeding bullets in time. Most of the Regulators knocked down by the wall had managed to free themselves from the rubble. I couldn't keep an eye on everything else that was happening.

I felt the consuming energy bubbling up in my chest and let it seep out of my pores, my eyes, my fingertips. I focused it on the twenty-four lightweight alloy guns, pushing through the outer casings. I felt out the inner contours of each weapon, almost tasting the metallic oil on my tongue.

And then I ripped them apart from the inside out. The guns

exploded in the Regulators' hands. Flying shrapnel from the weapons wounded a few, but most of them shook it off and stood up, ignoring their bleeding hands and faces.

Without a word, they arranged themselves into a block formation and ran at us, mindless of the pain under the control of their V-chips. My vision flooded with rage at both the violence these men intended and the fact that they themselves weren't to blame. They were all so young—the same Regs-in-training that were everywhere in the Academy. It wasn't their fault they'd been chosen for Regulator duty. But I still had to stop them. I had to end this.

Adrien's shouted warning behind me, Molla's screams, and the sound of the Regulators' feet pounding the floor all twisted together into a crazed cacophony. I closed my eyes and sent the energy out one last time, flowing over the block of the twelve Regulators coming at us.

I screamed as the hum became a burning pain in my head— this might finally be too much for me. I felt myself start to fracture, to rip into pieces in the attempt. I pushed onward anyway, through their skin, through the hard metal plating around their skulls, then deep into their brains. I located the sliver-thin outline of the V-chip architecture in one body, then the next and the next, straining with my hands pressing against my own head as if I could somehow keep myself from coming apart.

I felt my body being hauled backward—Adrien must be trying to pull me to safety but I didn't let myself even spare a backward glance. Almost there . . . *Almost there*, three more, two, one . . .

"Zoe!"

All as one, I crushed the twelve tiny fingernail-sized embedded V-chips and all the minuscule alloy webs attached. Adrien pulled me out of the way just as the Regulators, carried forward by their momentum even as their eyes widened suddenly with self-awareness, toppled over one another like dominoes into a pile of muscle and metal right in front of us.

We stood, torn and bleeding, amazed at the rubble before us. I looked down at my own hands in shock.

"What did you do?" Adrien whispered over my head and only now I realized his arms were wrapped around me, again trying to shield me with his body.

I looked up weakly. "I freed them," I said. "Come on, help me walk. Let's get out of here."

"Zoe." Adrien's jaw was dropped open. "How did you— What did you—"

"Help me up," I said again, and he must have heard the pained note in my voice.

He helped me stand, and my legs felt like jelly. It felt so strange to be back in my body after encompassing the whole room. The hum was gone completely, and I felt like it would be a while before I'd be able to call on it again. Adrien started leading us around the mountain of confused Regulators but I stopped him and turned. They were young enough, they should survive the destruction of their internal hardware. I could only hope that with their V-chips completely destroyed they would be stable, not like the young glitching Regulator on the train months ago. I watched them warily, but they were all calm, if a bit dumbfounded.

I was exhausted, but I tried to put as much force as I could in my voice. I looked at them, one with blood dripping down the side of his bionic head implant, another missing at least half his left hand. I thought about apologizing, but I knew the word *sorry* wouldn't have any meaning to them.

Instead, I said, "You are free from the Community now. Come with us if you want to stay free." Then I turned back to Adrien, so tired I barely cared if they took my offer or not.

"Get us out of here," I said. He nodded and led us up through more hallways. Most of the Regulators followed too, offering their wrist chips to gain access to the entire facility. The hulking young men were silent, but when I gave orders, they followed them. I guessed they were used to being ordered around and I was the closest thing to an authority they had now.

As we waited for the elevator tube that Adrien said would lead us out, he suddenly went rigid beside me. I'd been leaning on him for support so heavily, I almost fell down, taking him with me. A young Regulator caught both of us and steadied us.

"What's wrong with him?" Molla shrieked. I hadn't looked at her in a while but I guessed she wasn't taking all the terror and near-death experiences very well.

"He's having a vision," I said, slumping against the wall for support. Adrien's body relaxed after a few moments.

"What is it?" I asked, closing my eyes and hoping it wasn't something else horrible. The Chancellor had said she'd made my allergies worse. What if he saw me get to the Surface and go into an allergy attack that would kill me? But when I opened my eyes, I saw him grinning.

"It's my mom. She's tracked down some of the Rez and they're coming. But we can't go up that way." He nodded at the elevator as the door pinged and slid open. "The Chancellor will have set off the alarm by now. I saw a safe way out, though, and the Rez will meet us there."

"But how could your mom know where we'll be?"

He took my arm and helped me stand. "She must have had a vision, too."

"Good." I was breathing hard from the exertion of staying upright. "Because I don't think I'm going to be taking on any more Regulators any time soon."

He laughed and kissed my temple, then we led our unusual group down several perpendicular tunnels, the Regulators' wrist access chips still opening up every door in our path. The Chancellor must not have figured out what I'd done. How could she have? I barely believed I'd been able to do it. They opened the last door and there was only darkness beyond.

"It's the service stairwell," Adrien said. "We can get one of the Regulators to carry you up the stairs—it's three stories up. But I want you to stay here until I come back with the biosuit for you so you don't have an allergy attack." He saw my confusion. "I saw my mom carrying one in my vision."

"But the biosuits only have enough oxygen for a few hours. What will happen then?"

Adrien swallowed, his eyes uncertain for a moment. "I don't know yet. But right now we don't have any other choice."

We looked at each other wordlessly, and then I nodded.

"Take Molla and Juan with you," I said, grabbing his arm as he turned to go. I leaned in and whispered, "They'll probably be hysterical about going to the Surface like I was the first time. This will give them a few extra minutes to get used to the idea."

He nodded.

I went over to take Molla's hands. She seemed almost catatonic, staring blankly off into space.

"Adrien's going to take you up now, okay, Molla?"

She didn't respond.

"Max," I said, turning to him, though I couldn't quite bear to look him in the eye now that I'd learned the truth of all he'd done. "Can you help?"

"Molla," Max said, his voice stronger than it had been.

"Molla, find all the extra trackers they embedded in Zoe," he said. He was looking at the floor

At the sound of Max's voice, Molla's eyes seemed to clear a

little. She looked at Max and he nodded, so she reluctantly turned to me. Her gaze narrowed as she scanned me head to toe. "Here." She pointed behind my left ear. "Here and here and here." She pointed at my right shoulder, right hip, and left ankle.

"Is that all?" Max asked.

She nodded.

"Go with Adrien now," he said. "Do whatever he says and don't worry about being on the Surface. I promise you it's safe."

"But I want to stay with you, Max."

"Go," Max ordered, somewhat harshly, but then his voice softened. "I'll be right behind you."

She nodded again, looking slightly less skittish.

Adrien took Molla's arm and led her through the doorway up into the darkness. Juan followed behind.

After they were out of sight, Max's gaze shifted to me. We stood, surrounded by five of the tall, silent Regulators. I looked away uncomfortably, my arms crossed. I might not have wanted to leave Max at the mercy of the Chancellor, but that didn't mean I could forget what he'd done.

"Molla seems to forgive you," I finally said, my voice sharp.

He shook his head. "She just doesn't believe it yet. She doesn't believe I never loved her, or that I was willing to throw her to the Chancellor without a second thought—just for the chance of getting to run away with you." The pitch of his voice raised. "I'd do it all again."

"But she's *pregnant*," I said, turning to him face-to-face, the pain and anger at his betrayal bubbling up now that I really had the time to think about it. "How could you leave her?"

"I didn't know she was pregnant," he said, looking down.

"Would it have changed your mind if you had?"

"No." He met my gaze steadily. "I still would have left her because all I ever wanted was you. You were the first person I felt anything for after glitching. I loved you before I even knew the name for it. Everyday I'd sit beside you, inhaling your scent, looking at your beautiful face. Every night, dreaming about you. You eclipsed everything else. It was you. Always you."

"All you wanted was the power the Chancellor promised you," I said, angry and sad.

"If that were true," he said with a dark laugh, "I would never have left her, never tried to save us. She promised me the world, all the power, all the pleasures I could ever want, and I was willing to give it all up."

He took a step closer to me and I flinched. Two Regulators moved silently in front of me, blocking Max.

"But at what price, Max?" I said, my eyes filling with tears. "You were willing to sacrifice Molla and Adrien, to leave them behind to the Chancellor's monstrous plans. If you thought I could have lived with that, you never really knew me at all."

"You were never going to know," he whispered softly. "I was going to protect you from it all. We were going to live a life beyond your best dreams, you and me together forever. It would have been perfect. But then Adrien came and he was all you could see." His voice turned bitter. "You were supposed to be mine."

I shook my head at him incredulously. I'd been so reluctant to believe the truth when the Chancellor told me, but it had all been true. Every single horrible detail. And *still*, he wasn't repentant. He didn't even think he'd done anything wrong.

"Maybe you've told these lies to yourself so many times you believe them," I hissed, suddenly furious with him. "But I was never going to love you in the way you wanted me to. And the fact that you would have lied and manipulated me, allowing us to be free and happy at the expense of others, trying to force me into feeling something for you—you're no better than the Chancellor. And now . . ."

My voice broke but I kept his gaze, even as the tears spilled over. Max had been working with the Chancellor for months, spying on all of us, lying to us, willing to leave everyone behind— Oh god, Markan— My stomach dropped out from under me. I felt like sinking to the ground. We might make it out of the city, but the Chancellor would have Regulators right on our heels. We wouldn't be able to get to my brother.

I shook my head at Max. He'd ruined all our plans. Without him my brother could have been safe. "I might be able to forgive you," I said, my voice still trembling with anger, "maybe even someday trust you again, but you'll *never* get what you want. I will never love you, Maximin."

Max opened his mouth, taking a step backward as if I'd hit him. All his masks were gone and I could see the real Max, the hurt and shock and confusion on his face—like a little boy learning what pain felt like for the first time.

I instantly felt sorry, but before I could say anything, I heard rapid steps on the stairs behind us. I turned to see Adrien, bio-suit in hand, and my body melted in relief and tiredness. It was almost over. Max and I could work out all this later when things had calmed down and we'd both had some rest.

I stepped into the biosuit and Adrien helped me secure the helmet.

"Come on," Adrien yelled. "Let's get out of here. You and you." He pointed at two Regulators. "Carry her up."

A burly brown-haired Regulator swept me up into his arms. His blue jumpsuit was in tatters, so my face was pressed up against the hard alloy of his metal-reinforced chest. He nodded to another one of the Regulators, who came up beside him.

"Come on, Max." My voice was muted through the helmet, but still loud enough to be heard. I was so exhausted I could barely keep my eyes open any longer, but I managed to wave weakly at him to follow.

His jaw tensed and I saw him swallow hard. His fists were clenched at his sides. "No, actually, I think I'll stay," he said calmly.

"Max," I said impatiently, looking awkwardly over the shoulder of the man carrying me. "Don't be a fool. She'll deactivate you."

He stood up and backed away from the Regulators, a bitter smile on his face. "No, I don't think she will," he said.

"Wait!" I said, suddenly realizing Max was being serious. I was angry with him, sure, but I couldn't bear the thought of losing my best friend. I was already forced to leave Markan behind, I couldn't leave Max too. "No, you have to come! Max!"

Max gave a slight, hard smile. "And do what? Join your little band of Resistance fighters? Spend every day watching someone else live the life I always wanted with you? Don't think so." He half-turned, then paused.

"But, watch out for yourself, okay?" His voice had softened ever so slightly. "You have no idea what you're getting yourself into. The Chancellor's going to crush the Uppers, and then the Resistance. They're nothing compared to the power she's gathering."

He stared at me a moment longer, all the pain and anger and betrayal reflected in the pool of water floating in his eyes.

It felt like I was losing a part of myself. *Max.*

"Come on," Adrien yelled down to the Regulator holding me. "We have to go *now* or we'll never get out."

The man nodded once and then we were moving, my body jarring with every step, before I realized what had just happened.

"Wait, I—" I yelled, struggling to be let down. But the Regulator holding me just kept going.

"Max!" I screamed again, straining in the Regulator's arms, my heart sinking with every step we took away from him. "Max!"

I tried to look back, reaching out in the direction of Max's retreating back, but soon all I could see was the solid darkness in the stairwell. The sound of heavy feet on the stairs surrounded me, and then, before I would have thought possible, the door at the top was opened and moonlight filled the night sky. It was the first time I'd ever seen the moon but all I could think about was the stubborn boy we'd left behind at the bottom of the stairs.

Chapter 24

THE BUMP OF THE ROUGH ROAD jolted me against the door. Adrien reached over to steady me. I stayed by the window, staring numbly out at the slowly lightening earth. It was almost morning. The group had split up at a hastily arranged transfer spot, and Adrien, his mom, several of the ex-Regulators, and I were all in the back of a supply van heading south.

We were safe for now, but in the quiet van, everything that had happened that night kept whirling around and around in my mind like a fan blade: After all my promises to myself, there'd been no way to escape with Markan. How long would it be before we could reinfiltrate the city to get him out? And Max. What would become of him? Would he go back to the Chancellor? Was she hurting him even now as we drove away to safety? Or had she instantly put him under her compulsion, making him do whatever she told him to without question?

"Hey." Adrien's voice broke into my thoughts. "You've got that look on your face again—the one that says you're worrying about all the things you can't control."

"I just can't believe he didn't come," I whispered, still staring out the window. My voice sounded strange coming through the face mask.

"Max made his own decisions," Adrien said, "and he's the one who has to live with them."

I shook my head, wanting to argue, but Adrien put his hands

on both sides of my face mask and turned my head gently away from the window to face him.

"We're out. We're safe." His voice was rough and earnest and suddenly I could see that the past few days had taken their toll on him as well. "Can't that be miracle enough for today?"

The blue-green of his eyes caught the first rays of the morning sun, shining brilliant like a beacon. The radiance of color and life in his eyes made my breath catch in my chest. I suddenly thought of all the things he'd taught me about the world, and about love, joy, and pain—about what it meant to be fully alive, for better and for worse.

I nodded. "Yes," I said, my voice high and almost breaking. "It's more than enough."

I managed a wan smile, then settled my head down against his chest, snuggling underneath the crook of his arm as well as I could in the bulky suit. He put his arm over me, rubbing my back occasionally.

"Look." He pointed out the window at the sun. "Your first dawn. In the Old World, they used to think dawn was a symbol of hope."

I entwined my gloved hand with his, looking out at the rolling hills as the rays of sunlight splashed outward, slowly erasing all the night's dark shadows.

I didn't know what kind of future we could possibly have in such a dangerous world. I didn't know if I'd be able to survive on the Surface, if we'd be able to find a safe place for me to live free of allergens and the Chancellor's detection. I was told the Rez had spent weeks preparing a temporary space for me to live, but everyone's faces go blank and tight whenever I ask if we'll make it there in time. If we do, I still didn't know if we would be able to save Markan, or Max. I didn't know what to expect from the Resistance, or its band of glitching misfits. I didn't know if it would ever be possible to stop the Chancellor or upend the Link system so people in the Community could be free forever.

For the moment I felt safe, but the battle was only just beginning, and not even Adrien could tell me how it would end. I turned from the window, choosing to focus on the things I did know. I loved Adrien, he loved me, and for now, that was enough.

"Hope, huh?" I thought about it, then slowly nodded. "I think they were right."

Zoe might be free, but she is far from safe.

The next book in this action-packed series
will keep you guessing at every turn.

OVERRIDE

Zoe thinks she's escaped, but she's about to face a greater danger than she'd ever imagined. Joined by new team of powerful teen glitchers, Zoe should be stronger than ever, but her powers are failing her. And as the Chancellor's greatest enemy, there's a target on her back, and not everyone on her team can be trusted.

"A taut, irresistible novel, *Glitch* delivers a pitch-perfect blend of action, romance, and twists that take your breath away."— Andrea Cremer, *New York Times* bestselling author of the Nightshade series, on *Glitch*

Available February 2013

St. Martin's Griffin
www.stmartins.com
www.heatheranastasiu.com

Chapter 1

MY HEART POUNDED in my ears. The low humming sound, muffled by the wall, was just loud enough to hear over my shallow, panicked breaths. I sat up on my loft bed and paused to listen before carefully easing myself down the ladder. The pads of my bare feet landed on the cold floor. There was barely enough space for me to stand up in the eight-by-six-foot room, but in order to reach the far wall I had to squeeze between the treadmill that pulled down from the wall and the shower/toilet combo at the foot of my bed.

I moved silently. Only two people at the lab knew I hid right behind their walls, and today couldn't be the day the rest of them found out. My life depended on it. The Resistance had been careful enough to erase the tiny alcove from the schematics. Officially, the room, just like me, didn't exist.

I paused with my ear inches from the wall. In the three months I'd spent hidden in this confined space, I had come to know every sound. Learning them was a matter of habit almost as much as it was a matter of survival. I paused, focusing intently on the rhythmic *click-click-click*. I leaned my forehead against the wall, letting out the breath I held. Just an ordinary sound, a normal shift in the perfectly regulated air systems. I should have known. I was in one of the few places with the kind of heavy air-filtration systems I needed to survive. It worked like clockwork, and without it, almost any Surface allergen would kill me quickly, thanks to the Chancellor.

I closed my eyes and my heart rate slowed. It was remarkable how quickly I could move from alarm to complete relaxation and back again. Another matter of habit.

I climbed slowly back up to my bed, feeling anxious. This alcove might be my safe haven, but sometimes it felt like a prison. The bed was too short to stretch out and the ceiling too low to sit up completely. The confinement was strangling. Sometimes I'd look at the walls and they seemed nearer than before, like the room was closing in on me, inch by inch.

I slept during the day, for as many hours as I could, but time still stretched out endlessly. Lately I'd begun parsing the days into manageable thirty-minute pieces to make the long and painful monotony less overwhelming—half an hour drawing, jogging on the treadmill, unfolding and then refolding my clothes, pacing back and forth across the narrow floor, counting the objects in my room, studying the Resistance's history texts—the real histories, not the lies we learned in the Community. And training, endless training.

In the early mornings I'd spend countless more half-hours staring at the cool slab of ceiling above me, watching as the thin string hanging from the air duct blew back and forth in the allergen-free air. In my mind I replayed the past over and over and wondered how it could have turned out differently.

I closed my eyes and swallowed. I just had to make it long enough to get there.

It was maddening to sit here knowing Adrien and the Rez were out there fighting the Chancellor and the Community while I was stuck caged in this tiny room. My fingers itched to unleash the power locked inside me and fight to protect the people I loved. I was tired of being the helpless prisoner. I wanted to feel like I had some control again. But I couldn't even control my power anymore. When we escaped the Community, I had reached into people's bodies and crumpled the miniscule hardware in their brains. I had ripped heavy lock-down doors off their tracks. But now . . .

Every day I trained. I sat in the tiny space and worked and strained until I wanted to cry out in pain. But it was no use. I'd stare at my tablet for ten minutes straight, willing it to move just an inch, but it wouldn't budge. Not because the power wasn't there. Exactly the opposite—there was too much of it. I could feel it building up inside of me even now, pressing against the backs of my eyes and making my hands twitch.

I was having one of those restless early mornings. I propped myself up on my elbow and looked at the drawings papering the wall by my bed. Mom, Dad, my younger brother Markan. The people I'd left behind. And the people I'd lost. Max.

I reached out and touched the picture of Max's face. I'd tried to capture how he looked when I first knew him, when everything had been simpler and we'd been friends. We'd been drones together, subjects in the Community where we were tightly controlled by emotion-suppressing hardware. It was a dangerous place for anyone who managed to break free, but somehow we'd found each other. We'd protected each other as we explored the new unnatural powers that developed as a side effect of the hardware glitches. I'd trusted him, before I even fully understood what that word meant.

But that was all a long time ago now. That was before I'd known that someone you think you know can look you in the face and tell you lies.

I thought about the last time I'd seen Max, right after I'd learned he'd been working for the Chancellor as a Monitor the whole time. He was an informant, reporting on people who were glitchers like us, getting them captured and "repaired," or worse, deactivated. And he hadn't felt remorse for any of it.

"I was going to protect you from it all. We were going to live a life beyond your best dreams, you and me together forever. It would have

been perfect." His voice had turned bitter. "You were supposed to be mine."

My face burned hot at the memory, and I shook my head. I remembered the disgust on his face when I told him to escape with us.

"And do what? Join your little band of Resistance fighters? Spend every day watching someone else live the life I always wanted with you? Don't think so."

It was a wound I opened and salted over and over again. It tortured me to remember, and the anger felt fresh and hot every time I repeated his words. But the truth was, I needed the anger and the pain. I held on to it deep in my chest like an anchor holding me in place. It reminded me that I was here, that I was alive, and that one day I'd be able to fight the Chancellor. I needed to stay strong for that day.

If it ever came.

I turned my eyes away from Max to the other face that was featured most often in my drawings. Adrien, with that smile he saved for me when no one else was looking. I sighed. His was the only face on my wall that didn't fill me with regret.

The last time I'd seen him had been ages ago, while he was passing through on his way to spend time working at the Foundation. It was going to be a school for glitchers, and best of all, it would have an air-filtration system equal to the research lab here. I'd be able to join him there without fear of the air I breathed, or that any sound I made might get me caught and killed. But I couldn't picture it. Being able to live without constant fear, to meet more glitchers like me, and to see Adrien every day—it seemed like an impossible dream.

Tears threatened. I reached up to trace Adrien's face, and a tremor ran through my hand. A flash of fear washed over me. The gentle quaking had been plaguing me all day, first in my thighs, now my hand.

Not again. It shouldn't be happening again so soon.

I flexed my hand, then made a fist, and the shaking stopped. I swallowed hard, trying to quiet my rising alarm. I hadn't gotten my telekinesis to function properly in weeks, and the power raged like a wild beast clawing underneath my skin. Adrien always called our glitcher powers Gifts, but I was beginning to suspect that he was wrong. Our minds may have evolved to develop our superhuman powers, but the human body hadn't. Maybe we were too fragile to contain that kind of power.

I looked at my hands, marveling at what pulsed just underneath the surface, threatening to break free. I laid facedown on the bed with my arms underneath my stomach in the vain hope I could hold them in place. I knew what was coming next, and it was going to hurt. I clenched my teeth in the darkness, willing my body to stay still and quiet. Above all, I had to stay quiet.

In the darkness, I worried for the hundredth time whether we really understood the nature of our powers. I wondered if our Gifts weren't actually a curse.

I'd only been asleep for a few minutes when I woke to my knuckles banging repeatedly into my cheek. I sat up abruptly and watched my tremoring hand like it belonged to someone else's body.

"Shunt," I murmured, suddenly fully awake. My arm kept at it, but now the shaking had moved up to my shoulder. The normal telltale buzz of my power grew louder in my ears until it was a high-pitched screech.

"No, no, no," I whispered, climbing awkwardly down from my bed as well as I could. I glanced at the clock on the wall above my head. It was an hour into the workday. Somehow I had to stop from going into full tornado-mode, or I'd be caught for sure.

The first time my power had gotten uncontrollable like this I'd been lucky, it was nighttime when no one was around. Milton, one of the people at the research lab who knew I was hiding here, had been slack-jawed after he finally pushed his way into my trashed room the next morning. The metal of the bed had been twisted in on itself like a figure eight and the toilet had come loose and made a dent in the concrete of the opposite wall. All my drawings and clothes had been shredded, and I'd sat huddled in the far corner with my arms over my head, bruised and bleeding.

But Milton was kind. He said I reminded him a little of his sister, a drone he had to leave behind in the Community's control. He told me stories about her while he helped me clean up.

Later, when Adrien visited, he said maybe it was because I was boxed in here and not able to use my power. But he didn't understand. It was more than that. The power was changing, and I was changing with it. I couldn't control it anymore. I didn't know how I ever had. It was getting bigger, consuming me from the inside like a slowly fattening parasite.

I reached up and managed to grab my pillow and blanket right before my legs buckled and I landed on the ground. There was barely enough space to lay flat, but the floor was safer than the bed. With what little muscle control I had left, I wedged myself between the shelf and the toilet to keep myself as secure as possible. I squeezed my eyes shut.

Both of my arms shook uncontrollably now. I flipped myself onto my side to get the pillow under my head and put part of the twisted up blanket between my teeth. The tremors moved to my torso and down to my legs. My whole body jerked up and down. My elbows, shoulder blades, and heels slammed painfully into the cold floor. I wanted to scream, but I was afraid if I opened my mouth even the tiniest bit, all my power might accidentally burst out.

The screech inside my head became a long howl. The beast wanted release. I ground my teeth further into the blanket and tried to brace myself for each time my body smacked into the ground. Again and again and again. I winced with each hit, aching from the impact on bruises that had never fully healed from last time.

I just had to get through this and then I could rest.

The shaking became wilder, and as it reached an apex my foot banged against the wall, making a loud *tap, tap, tap* noise every time it hit. I focused all of my energy on my legs, trying to hold them still, but my body was out of my control. A whimper of fear escaped my lips. If the wrong person heard me, it was over.

I thought I was going to pass out from the pain, the panic, and the fear. I prepared for the worst, knowing I couldn't hold on much longer. The power built up like expanding gas in an enclosed space, begging for release. I couldn't keep it in. It was going to come out. I clamped my mouth shut tighter but it felt like I was ripping apart from the inside.

Just when I thought I was about to burst wide open, the seizing began to quiet down. The shakes slowed to trembles, then just a shiver, and then I lay still. Sweat dripped down my temple and slid into my eyes with a salty sting. I wanted to wipe it away, but I was so tired, my arm felt leaden. I rolled over onto my side and breathed slowly as I gathered my strength. Then I eased my way to my knees, pausing with each step, and eventually rose to my feet.

I felt as if I'd been running on the treadmill for a day and a half. I had nothing left. But at least I'd be able to sleep now. I climbed tiredly up the ladder to my bed. My arms shook again, this time not from excess power, but from exhaustion.

But right when my head finally rested on the thin mattress, a scratching sounded from the wall, right at the hidden entrance to my room. I froze. Milton shouldn't be bringing me food yet. Someone must have heard my foot banging into the wall. They could have easily followed the sound back to the wall panel that doubled as the secret entrance to the alcove.

Fat tears squeezed out of my eyes. I wasn't strong enough to fight. I rolled my tired body over toward the wall. Whoever came in wouldn't see me right away, but I knew it wouldn't help much. I was a muddle of fear and exhaustion. After so much effort, so much sacrifice and patience, I couldn't lose it all like this, facing my enemies while weak and afraid—

"Zoe, it's me," came the whisper from below. My heart leapt at the sound of Adrien's voice. All the tension went out of my body like a wave. I half-climbed, half-fell down the ladder and launched myself into his outstretched arms. He wasn't supposed to be here until next week. Did it mean I could finally get away from this horrible place? I parted my lips to ask, but couldn't find the strength to care about anything but his warm arms around me.

My hair had come undone from its braid during the shaking episode, and Adrien curled his fingers into it. I sank against him, breathing him in. My exhaustion lightened in his embrace. It was always like that when I was with him. I tipped my head back and he kissed me. His lips were gentle, and for a moment I forgot all the loneliness and fear of the past few months. All I could think about was the soft texture of his lips and the way love for him bloomed inside me like a light cell blinking to life in a pitch black room.

But all too soon he pulled away. His eyes were cloudy. "There's not much time. We've gotta move. Now."

He turned and let go of me, and my weakened legs gave out from under me.

"Zoe!" Adrien caught me around the waist, pulling me back up. "What's going on, are you okay?" He set me down on the closed toilet lid, the only place to sit other than up on my bed.

"I'm fine," I lied, blinking and trying to get a breath. "I just gotta get some rest. Can we leave in the morning?"

But when I looked back over at Adrien, he was already pulling out the biosuit box and opening it up.

"We've got to leave *now,* Zoe, not tomorrow morning. Fit your feet into the rubber boots first, then we'll pull the rest of the suit up."

"Why now?" I asked, blinking and trying to make sense of everything that was happening. I stepped into the boots.

"I had a vision. There's gonna be a raid on this facility soon."

It took a few more moments for what he'd said to sink in. "Wait, you mean . . . No! They know I'm here?"

"Not yet," Adrien said, managing to sound halfway calm. "The Chancellor was just named Under-Chancellor of Defense. Right off, she ordered inspections of any place with the kind of air-filtration system she knows you need to survive. I thought we'd have more time. I mean, there's about fifty facilities like this in the sector and there's no way she'd know this is the only one the Resistance had access to." He shook his head. "But I saw it. This lab's gonna get hit."

"When?"

"I don't know." He ran a hand roughly through his hair. "It felt like a short-term vision, like it might happen in the next few days." He looked back up at me. "Maybe today even."

I felt a dizzying wave of panic. They were coming for me. The horrifying reality of the situation settled in, clearing away some of my remaining cloudiness and exhaustion.

"I was gonna send a com," Adrien said, "but I was afraid any communications would get intercepted and decrypted. I didn't wanna accidentally be the *cause* of the inspection."

Another cold realization swept through my chest.

"But wait. Where are we going?" I asked. "If the Foundation isn't ready yet, this lab's the only place we have access to with air safe enough for me to breathe. What happens in twelve hours when my biosuit runs out of oxygen?"

"We're going to a Beta site nearby. They have a few spare oxy tanks there. It'll buy us some time to figure out the rest."

He held out an arm to help me stand up enough so he could pull the heavy padded suit up to my waist. There were three separate layers to it, and it smelled strongly of plastic and stale air.

"It's dangerous, I know," he continued. "But we don't have a choice. If we move fast enough, maybe we can get out of here safely. Maybe we can change the vision." His jaw tensed for a moment. "Otherwise what's the point of seeing the future?" I wasn't sure if he was talking to me or to himself.

"Have you ever done it? Changed something you've seen?"

He didn't answer me, just lifted up the top half of the suit. "Here, fit your arms in."

I shrugged my arms into the heavy sleeves of the suit and sat down again to rest while Adrien clipped one of the compressed oxygen packs onto the belt at my hip and hooked it up.

He fit the thick helmet with its see-through faceplate over my head, adjusting it so the edges were firmly aligned with the body of the suit. The whir of precious air circulating through the mask filled my ears. He reached for the suit's fore-arm panel to run a quick diagnostic that would check for tears or leaks, and that's when I saw it: the red alarm light began flashing silently in the corner.

I gasped and looked over at Adrian. We both knew what it meant.

The Inspector was already here.